# CRASH...OR COVER-UP?

"A SUSPENSEFUL TECHNO-THRILLER...
WHITE HOUSE—STYLE."
—*The Florida Times-Union*

"*THE PASSENGER* PACKS A PUNCH."
—*The Orange County Register*

*Praise for*
# THE GENERAL
### by Patrick A. Davis

*It began with a torture-style execution not seen since the Vietnam War. It ended with a conspiracy that reached the highest levels of the U.S. government. . . .*

"One of the most exciting first novels I've read in a long time." —W.E.B. Griffin

"A hard-hitting, no-holds-barred novel of mystery, suspense, and betrayal . . . One of those inside–Washington, D.C., stories that seem more fact than fiction. Patrick Davis creates the kind of sharp, crackling dialogue that keeps the reader nodding in recognition while turning the pages furiously." —Nelson Demille

"A tense, gung-ho military thriller . . . lots of action." —*Kirkus Reviews*

"The characterization is fine, the twists and turns plenty, and the thrills fast-paced." —*The Virginian-Pilot*

"Everything you could want in a thriller. The mystery is puzzling, the action is intense, and I could not stop turning the pages." —Phillip Margolin

"A sure winner." —Dale Brown

*Also by Patrick A. Davis*

# The General

THE

# PASSENGER

## Patrick A. Davis

BERKLEY BOOKS, NEW YORK

THE PASSENGER

A Berkley Book / published by arrangement with the author

PRINTING HISTORY
G. P. Putnam's Sons hardcover edition / August 1999
Berkley mass-market edition / December 2000

The Penguin Putnam Inc. World Wide Web site address is
http://www.penguinputnam.com

ISBN: 0-425-17769-6

BERKLEY®
Berkley Books are published by The Berkley Publishing Group,
a division of Penguin Putnam Inc.,
375 Hudson Street, New York, New York 10014.
BERKLEY and the "B" design
are trademarks belonging to Penguin Putnam Inc.

PRINTED IN THE UNITED STATES OF AMERICA

10  9  8  7  6  5  4  3  2  1

*To my father- and mother-in-law, Jim and Jeanne Roche,*
*for the gift of their daughter, Helen*

# Acknowledgments

So many people contributed to making this novel a reality that I'm not sure I can adequately express my gratitude, but I'd like to try.

My deepest appreciation to my U-2 brethren, current and former, who helped me keep the technical facts straight. To Nathan Green, my Learjet advisor, who put up with all my inane questions and deciphered the complex electrical wiring diagrams into something understandable, and to Major Roger Mostar and Major Forest Green, for their guidance on the intricacies of a military crash investigation. Thanks also to my ex-commanders, Colonel Butch Hinkle and Colonel Richard Graham, for their inputs that kept the story line credible. Rich actually flew the SR-71, which is sort of like a U-2 but a helluva lot faster.

As always, I owe an enormous debt to my talented and enthusiastic circle of readers who praise and criticize with equal passion: Doug and Bonnie McInnes; Verle and Lucille Miner; Cecil and Barb Fuqua; Bob and Katie Sessler; Doug and Ann Anderson; Linda Green; Pat Graham; Karel Hinkle; Maria Wildman; Dr. Bill Burke, who kept me straight on the medical technicalities; Marie Trichka, who runs the Book Trader, the best little bookstore in Texas; and, of course, to the best parents in the world, Bill and Betty Davis.

A tremendous amount of the credit for the book also goes to my teacher, friend, and agent, Howard Pelham, who gave me my start and has helped me more than he'll ever know, and to Christine Pepe, Putnam's editing whiz, who displayed the patience of Job when I was mired in the murk of my first draft.

I'd also like to thank Tom McFall, the American Airlines safety guru, for allowing me to pick his brain on accident investigations, and the staff of American's Dallas flight office, for their continued support.

Finally, to the readers, I ask their understanding for any omissions I made in this novel. As with any work of fiction, I used literary license to streamline certain procedures to avoid confusion and keep the story flowing.

# THE
# PASSENGER

*Duty then is the sublimest word in the English language. You should do your duty in all things. You can never do more. You should never wish to do less.*

—GENERAL ROBERT E. LEE

## Thursday, March 3, 1994

It was a little after six-thirty P.M. and I was still in my Pentagon office, pecking out a monthly summary of Air Force plane crashes for my boss, Major General Maxwell Cramer. A Gordon Lightfoot cassette played softly on the small tape deck on my desk. I peered into the computer screen and grimaced. General Cramer, Chief of Air Force Safety, was not going to be pleased at the February results; three planes had gone down with a total of nine fatalities. Cramer would tear into me the moment I handed him the report.

I sat back, feeling more than a little disgusted. I'd been on Cramer's staff for only a couple of months and was still having a tough time adjusting to his outbursts. I kept trying to convince myself there wasn't anything personal behind them, but I was beginning to wonder. Cramer seemed to enjoy riding me, needling me incessantly, mostly about little things. He seemed to love giving me projects with un-

realistic deadlines or publicly criticizing my reports, which were perfectly fine.

When someone gets on a general's hit list, the Pentagon grapevine kicks into overdrive. I was constantly being asked what I had done to piss Cramer off. Answer: I didn't know. I'd never even met the guy until I began working for him. Go figure, huh?

The music began mellowing me a little and I pushed back from my desk, my eyes going to a row of framed pictures on the far wall. Most showed me in a flight suit, wearing a cocky grin as I stood next to an F-15 Strike Eagle fighter. One was taken after my first mission over Iraq, my dark hair matted with sweat, the exhilaration of combat evident on my face.

I still hadn't completely accepted that I'd never fly again. The Chief Flight Surgeon of the Air Force had denied my request to be reinstated to flight status, a decision that didn't take me by surprise. The Air Force didn't have much use for a fighter pilot with a back that resembled a Tinkertoy. Something about how another ejection would probably kill me.

That's what busted me up in the first place, during the Gulf War, when a missile had practically blown my fighter in two. I'd ejected too low to get a full chute and fractured my back on landing. Three surgeries in two years and a gallon of superglue had made me functional, but not good enough to fly.

Now I would spend the rest of my career in boring staff jobs, pushing paper while my buddies got plum assignments as operations officers of fighter wings.

Still, my career was going well. I'd made full colonel a couple of years early and knew if I kept my shoes shined and my nose clean, I had a shot at a star. Cramer notwithstanding, the only major hurdle I faced was the fact that I was single. The Air Force was big into generals having a

spouse so there'd be someone to handle the wives' teas and bake sales, that sort of thing. An antiquated notion that might be considered more than a little sexist, but hey, that's reality. The way the military looked at it, if I really wanted to make a star, I should get a wife. Anyway, I'm not overly concerned about joining the constellation club. I was happy to still be breathing.

Not like Cole Rison.

The cassette player hissed and then clicked off. In the ensuing silence, my eyes drifted to the desktop. Under the Plexiglas, a small, tattered photo showed two tanned men in flight suits, arms around each other, grinning at the camera. The lean, dark-haired major with the mustache was me, John Quinn; the sandy-haired captain was Cole Rison, my electronic warfare officer. The picture had been taken just before our final mission over Baghdad. I stared at Cole for a few moments before turning away.

Almost four years had passed, and I still felt the guilt. I had to be the hero. My hand dropped to the lower desk drawer, where I kept my emergency bottle of Scotch. I'd long since come to define an emergency as anytime after official duty hours.

"Colonel Quinn?"

My hand hovered by the drawer as I glanced at the attractive brunette who had pushed in my door. She stood there expectantly, a jacket draped over her arm.

"Yes, Josie?" I said, my hand climbing up to the desk.

Even as head of the Safety Liaison Office, I no longer rated Josie Brent as my personal secretary. She now supported everyone in the five-man office since the Air Force, citing budget constraints, hadn't replaced Mrs. Stout when she'd retired last month.

"I'm leaving, Colonel Quinn," Josie said. "Anything you need before I go?"

I shook my head. "Everyone else gone?"

Josie nodded.

"Fine. I'll lock up."

Josie started to leave, then stopped. "Major Billings says you're doing the accident summary."

I shrugged. "His kid had a school play."

She gave me one of her shiny-eyed looks. "That's real nice, boss."

"Yeah, yeah, I'm a big softie." I winked. "Now, beat it."

She grinned and closed the door.

My hanging around to finish up the report so Billings could get home for the game was no big deal. I was divorced, no kids. Nothing waited at home for me except a microwave pizza, a stiff drink, and maybe a few minutes of a Bullets game.

In a way, I envied Major Jeff Billings. When my ex-wife Jennifer and I got married, kids were never really an option. I wanted them; she didn't. End of discussion. Maybe that was for the best, considering we split up. They say divorce is hardest on the kids, and that may very well be true.

But it was damn tough on me.

I thought about the Scotch in the drawer again, but resumed my pecking on the keyboard, only to be interrupted by the phone.

"Safety Liaison. Colonel Quinn," I mumbled somewhat distractedly into the receiver.

"John, it's Tim Sweeney. The general wants to see you ASAP."

Lieutenant Colonel Tim Sweeney was the no-necked ex-football All-American who served as one of General Cramer's executive officers. Tim's no genius, but he's a scratch golfer and his father-in-law is a two-star, so he'll go far.

"Christ, Tim. You said the old man was gone for the day. Look, can you stall him? I need a few more minutes to finish this report."

"Forget the report, John." There was a click. "John, there's been another goddamn crash," Cramer's high-pitched voice cut in. "Get your butt over here! Now! And bring me a list of personnel for a safety investigation board."

"Yessir. When did it—"

But Cramer had hung up.

Visitors often wander around the Pentagon's hub-and-spoke system of interlocking corridors and hallways like rats in a B. F. Skinner maze, though the design is quite efficient once you get the hang of it. There are five concentric hallways, or rings, that expand outwardly from the center, labeled A to E. They intersect ten numbered corridors or spokes. An office number is like points on a grid map, telling you its precise location in the building. For example, General Cramer hung out in room 5E161, which was on the fifth floor, E-ring, between corridors one and two.

After grabbing the Crash Response file, I hurried out of my third-floor office, popped up two flights of stairs, and hustled down corridor 2 until I got to the E-ring. With their outside view, E-ring offices were the location of choice for most of the Pentagon's heavy hitters. The rule was you had to have at least two stars to be guaranteed a window seat.

I took a left down a gray-tiled hallway. The Office for the Air Force Chief of Safety was the fifth door on the right. As I turned the knob, I heard General Cramer's voice. He sounded pissed.

There were three desks in the large, plush anteroom. The two belonging to the execs were empty. At her corner desk, Martha Chan, Cramer's secretary, glanced up, a phone to her ear. Her pretty face spread into a sympathetic smile. *Go in,* she mouthed, motioning to her left.

The door to Cramer's office was open, and I could hear

him shouting something about a Learjet crash. Lears were part of the Air Force fleet that hauled senators, congressmen, and other assorted D.C. bigwigs around. I stuck my head through the doorway.

". . . don't give a damn, Major!" Cramer snarled into the phone. "You call me the moment they confirm word on survivors!" He slammed down the receiver and shoved back from his desk, his face tense. Lieutenant Colonel Sweeney stood poised before him, one hand holding a pen over a notepad.

The first thing most people noticed about General Cramer was that his appearance didn't match his voice. He was a husky man with thick black hair and rugged good looks. A major general at just forty-four, his rise had been phenomenal, due in no small part to his pedigree. Cramer's father and grandfather had been four-star generals, and Cramer was on everybody's shortlist to become the chief of staff someday. Cramer's elevation was particularly notable because he was a bachelor with a reputation as a ladies' man, a double whammy for most senior officers. Now, I wasn't under any illusions that since Cramer could get two stars with a couple strikes against him, I could get one. Unless I was willing to change my name to Cramer, of course.

"Tim," Cramer barked. "Call General Ware's office. Tell them there's no news yet on survivors. And notify the Andrews command post I want updates every ten minutes."

My eyebrows crawled up at the mention of General Ware. Since when did the chairman of the Joint Chiefs become personally interested in the crash of a jet?

"Yessir," Lieutenant Colonel Sweeney said. He gave me a quick nod and shot past.

"John, get in here!" Cramer motioned me to a chair. "And close the goddamn door!"

Cramer impatiently checked his watch as I took a seat.

"We have to make this fast. A Lear from Andrews just crashed shortly after takeoff. I'm putting you in charge of the accident investigation. You've got a 1930 briefing at the Andrews command post with General Stinson before catching a helo out to the crash site. I also— Something wrong, John?"

Cramer's comments had caught me off guard, and I was struggling to regain my composure. "Uh, no, sir. I'm just a little confused. Air Force regs say Air Mobility Command is supposed to appoint the safety investigation team."

"Screw that. There's no time to get someone sent out from AMC Headquarters in St. Louis."

"Sir, I'll at least need time to organize the safety investigation board members."

Cramer waved a hand. "Forget it. Just get out to the site and begin the preliminary investigation. Now, where's that list?"

I removed a sheet from the file and slid it over, feeling a sense of trepidation. There was no way Cramer would be jumping through hoops if the Lear had just been carrying military personnel or low-ranking government types. Someone important had been on the crashed jet.

Cramer donned black eyeglasses that made him appear professorial and began reading.

Air Force regulations were clear about who could comprise the safety investigation board. The members' qualifications were what one would expect: pilots, maintenance personnel, an air traffic controller, a flight doctor, maybe a human factors expert, even a meteorologist if weather was thought to be a factor. But to ensure objectivity, no board member could be from the base from which the downed plane was stationed.

"Looks good," Cramer said, glancing up. He tossed his glasses on the desk. "I'll handle the team's notification.

You get me answers. The White House is breathing down General Ware's neck and he's breathing down mine."

*White House. Christ.*

"Yeah, John," Cramer said. "This thing is big. The Lear was carrying a passenger." He paused. "Mr. Joshua Thurston."

The name was familiar. . . .

"President Halloran's half brother."

"Shit—"

"A bucketful and then some," Cramer said. "General Ware has already called President Halloran over in Russia and told him the news."

I twisted in my chair, recalling that the President had departed the day before for a summit with the Russian president. I tossed out a little cough.

"Now what, John?" Cramer asked irritably.

I hesitated. "Frankly, sir, I'm wondering why you're putting me in charge. I'd have thought a crash investigation with this kind of interest would be assigned to a general officer."

Cramer sat back, his brow knitted. "That struck me funny, too. But Ware insisted he wanted an 0-6 in charge."

For an instant, I was tempted to ask why Cramer had selected me for a high-visibility investigation over one of his fair-haired boys. But that would be pushing it. Instead, I said, "Didn't Mr. Thurston work here in the building?"

Cramer nodded. "The Army's assistant deputy secretary for manpower."

"What was the plane's destination?"

"Fort Bragg, North Carolina. He was on his way to attend a retention conference."

"Who were the Lear's pilots?"

Cramer glanced down at a paper on his desk. "Lieutenant Colonel Rick French. Captain Judd Wilson was his copilot."

I shot forward. Though I knew Judd Wilson only casually, Rick French was a good friend. We'd met two years earlier when I was the wing safety officer at Andrews and he was the Lear squadrons operations officer.

Cramer's face softened. "I'd forgotten you spent a few years at Andrews."

I nodded. "You mentioned survivors. . . ."

Cramer shook his head. "We had an unconfirmed report. Doesn't look good."

His intercom buzzed. "Sir, General Ware is on line two," Lieutenant Colonel Sweeney said.

While Cramer talked on the phone, I watched the wall, my mind on Rick's wife, Janet, and their two teenage daughters, Mindy and Sara. I wondered if they'd been told. I hoped not. I didn't want them to worry until verification of survivors could be made.

"Dammit!" Cramer said, hanging up. "Looks like you're going to get some help on this crash investigation whether you want it or not, John."

"Sir?"

He eyed me. "The White House notified General Ware that they've requested the NTSB send someone to assist on the investigation."

"Sir, they've got no jurisdiction in military accidents unless a civilian aircraft is involved."

Cramer snorted. "Like that matters. Don't you watch the news? These days the NTSB are the goddamn glamour boys of crash investigations."

My jaw tightened. "Sir, the White House is saying they don't think we can handle—"

"Save it, John. Just make damn sure you cover all the bases on this thing. We can't afford to have anyone second-guessing our conclusions."

I nodded, tight-lipped. "Who is going to be in charge of this investigation, General?"

Cramer responded with a thin smile. "Why, you are, John. The NTSB's role will be strictly advisory."

"Who are they sending out?"

Cramer shrugged. "General Ware didn't have a name. Someone will meet you at Andrews."

I checked my watch and glanced at the paper I'd handed him. "I want to add a name to that list, sir."

"Who do you have in niind?"

I braced myself for his response. "Lieutenant Colonel Chen."

Cramer looked incredulous. "That insolent bastard! Out of the question. Besides, I thought he'd retired."

"He's on terminal leave, sir. His retirement isn't official for another month." Terminal leave was the military's term for someone burning up accrued leave prior to separation from the service.

"No, John. This thing is way too sensitive politically—"

"Sir, you said the White House wants answers. No one works faster than Ted."

Cramer gave me a hard look. "Wasn't Chen your deputy when you worked safety at Andrews?"

I nodded, surprised Cramer would know about my relationship with Ted Chen, since I'd never told him. But this wasn't the first time I'd been puzzled by the general's familiarity with my past.

"You think you can make him toe the line, keep that smart mouth of his in check?" Cramer asked.

"Yes, sir." That was a lie. No one controlled Ted Chen.

Cramer gave me a curt nod. "He screws up, it's your funeral."

"Fine, sir. One more thing. Ted might be more receptive if you called to tell him his terminal leave is canceled."

For a second, I thought Cramer might tell me to go to hell. Instead, he growled, "What's the number?"

I recited it from memory. "It's a bar in Oxen Hill," I explained, and rose to my feet.

Cramer did a double take.

"The Happy Hawaiian Lounge," I said. "Ted bought the place when he worked at Andrews. He lives upstairs. Tell him to meet me at the Andrews command post."

"A goddamn bar?" General Cramer said, and shook his head.

He was punching numbers as I left.

I crossed the Woodrow Wilson bridge in my blue Camaro with the crumpled fender I keep meaning to get fixed and headed east on I-495 toward Andrews Air Force Base. With rush hour dying down, I'd make the trip in thirty minutes.

Simultaneously cracking the driver's window and fishing into the glove compartment for a cigarette, I wondered again why Cramer had chosen me to handle the investigation. For starters, I was a very junior colonel without a lot of pull, and I certainly wasn't the most experienced investigator on the staff. Not that understanding Cramer's rationale really mattered; orders were orders.

As I lit up, my thoughts drifted to Lieutenant Colonel Rick French. We weren't exactly close, but then I didn't have many close friends. I'd been to his house for dinner and we'd fished the Chesapeake a few times. We'd also meet at the Happy Hawaiian Lounge occasionally to toss back a few with Ted.

Rick was the last guy in the world I'd expect to crash a jet. He was steady, meticulous, not the type to make a stupid flying mistake. Even when we went fishing, he'd drive me nuts because he always insisted on donning bulky leather gloves before unhooking the fish, just to make sure he didn't poke himself. No, a guy that careful wouldn't screw up enough to kill himself. That meant something catastrophic must have happened to the plane.

Possible scenarios flashed through my mind, all of them horrifying. I saw the plane pitch over, maybe catch fire as Rick pulled desperately on the controls. The ground continued to scream toward him. Time compresses, slows, heightening the fear and panic. But in the end, there is only acceptance . . . and regret.

Maybe that's not exactly what had happened to Rick, but it had to be close. Despite the preliminary report, I'd been kidding myself. I'd seen enough catastrophic crashes of passenger aircraft to know there wouldn't be any survivors. There never were. All I could do for Rick now was to find the cause, but I would need time.

A frayed wire, a loose bolt, a pinhole leak—a thousand things can make a plane go down. A couple years back, a cargo jet caught fire and crashed, killing all seventeen people on board and six more on the ground. We chased our tails on that one for three months before a chemical analysis on residue found on a single charred wire gave us the answer. It turned out someone had spilled a can of Coke on an electrical panel, creating an electrical short and starting the fire. The point was that ascertaining the cause of a crash is a complex, exhausting procedure. For that reason, pressure from the White House for quick answers worried me. Rushing leads to things being overlooked. If the cause isn't found to be mechanical, invariably the pilot is blamed, especially if he's conveniently dead and unable to defend himself. I didn't want any part of an investigation

that would even hint that Rick was responsible until all the facts were in. But with pressure from the White House and some civilian peering over my shoulder I might have my hands full.

Which is precisely why I insisted on bringing in Ted Chen.

General Cramer's characterization of Ted as an insolent bastard was an overstatement. Cramer was angry because of a crash investigation Ted had been involved in the year before. Captain Kyle Mathison, the son of a popular three-star general, had lost control of his fighter during a rejoin and slammed into the lead jet. Captain Mathison had managed to eject, but the lead pilot was killed. Pressure had been applied on the board to cite the dead pilot as the cause. Ted had refused to go along and brought out evidence that proved the general's son had caused the accident.

I smiled, crushing out my cigarette. Now, don't get me wrong. Ted has his faults. He could be obnoxious and a pain in the ass. But he had the kind of courage of his convictions I could only dream about.

The road sign ahead said Oxen Hill in two miles. My town house was just over the next rise to the right, a couple of blocks away from the Happy Hawaiian Lounge. I was tempted to stop by and pick up Ted. But Ted had a temper, and he would still be angry from General Cramer's call. I made the easy choice and drove past.

Ten minutes later, I pulled up to the Andrews main gate. A female security cop lazily glanced at my colonel's decal, then snapped to attention, saluting me through. I tried not to smile and failed. I still wasn't accustomed to people's reactions to a full colonel; I'd been wearing my eagles for only three weeks.

As usual, Andrews AFB was lit up like a Christmas tree. The base is beautiful, with wide streets, neatly manicured

lawns, and redbrick buildings that always seemed to look freshly scrubbed. Even the military personnel strolling around looked like recruitment posters with their crisp uniforms and perfect haircuts. But that was to be expected; Andrews was the Air Force's show base and the home of *Air Force One*.

The command post was in the large three-story Wing Headquarters building down Command Drive. The parking lot was jammed, but I managed to find a spot near the front that said "Colonels Only," which struck me as a bit funny. Another little perk that would take some getting used to. Removing my cell phone from the charger on the console, I hustled up the front steps three at a time.

It was a long walk down the second-floor hallway to the red security phone. Facing the one-way mirror on the steel door, I identified myself to the voice on the other end. As I waited, I stared at the gaunt, lined face in the mirror. I was thirty-nine but looked at least forty-five. The work grind was taking its toll on me, and the more-salt-than-pepper hair sure didn't help. I sighed. I was aging . . . fast.

The door buzzed.

Nodding to the sergeant by the door, I walked into a large dark room filled with glowing screens, silhouetted faces hunkered over them. The first thing I noticed was the noise: jumbled voices, ringing phones, and the incessant clacking of printers. Darkened figures scurried about seemingly helter-skelter. I looked around as my eyes adjusted to the darkness.

"John, good, you're here! General Stinson is waiting."

A figure quickly approached. I squinted. "Hi, Rita."

"Christ, what a zoo!" Major Rita Sollar exclaimed. As the Wing Public Affairs officer, she was the Andrews media guru, which was a pretty big job with all the press

sniffing around the President. "Everybody and their brother has been calling. Mostly the press. CNN, the wire services, local TV, you name it. I don't know how they found out so fast." She let out an exasperated breath.

At six feet, Rita was almost my height. With her short blond hair, lightly freckled face, and blue eyes, she had a wholesome girl-next-door look. We'd known each other six years, ever since she married a flying buddy of mine, Marty Rich. They divorced four years and two kids later, when Rita caught Marty sleeping around. Rita and I dated a few times after her marriage ended, but quickly determined there wasn't any romantic chemistry between us. As Rita explained it, we were too much alike personality-wise, and it seemed like we were dating ourselves. Still, we've remained close. On occasion, when she's in a pinch for a sitter, she'll corral me into watching her two girls. For the past few months she'd been seeing a stockbroker in Baltimore. Rita was getting serious about the guy, and I hoped it worked out.

"You know it's hard to keep a lid on a plane crash, Rita," I said.

"But the response has never been this overwhelming—" She blinked, her eyes going to the eagles on my jacket. "Hey, I guess I better call you sir, huh?"

I made a face. "Give me a break. Any confirmation on survivors yet?"

Her voice softened. "General Stinson just returned from the site. No one made it."

I closed my eyes for a moment. "Anyone notify the families?"

Rita nodded. "Chaplain Staley is with Linda French. Judd Wilson was single, and his folks live in Ohio. A casualty notification team out of Wright-Patterson is en route."

"When did the Lear go down?"

She checked her watch. "Around 1750 or so. Dropped from radar about ten minutes after takeoff. A little west of Quantico. It went down on a farm near the town of Somerville in Fauquier County. C'mon, everyone's in the briefing room." She turned and led me toward the back.

"Anyone from the NTSB show yet?" I asked, sliding up next to her.

A head shake. "Word we got is Dr. Johnson won't arrive for another thirty minutes."

The name meant nothing to me. "A medical doctor?"

"Ph.D., I think." She paused, then casually added, "By the way, General Stinson thought it'd be a good idea if I was part of your team. Maybe as the board secretary. . . ."

I suppressed a smile. "This was Stinson's idea, huh?"

"Well . . . maybe I suggested it. But you're not the most dynamic guy, John. Someone's got to help you with the press—"

"You're hired," I said. "And thanks."

She grinned as we made a right down a short hallway.

When we reached the door to the briefing room, Rita turned to me, concern on her face. "You be careful, John. The visibility this thing is generating is unbelievable. General Stinson has been on the horn to the White House twice in the past thirty minutes. I've never seen anything like it."

"And your point is?"

"Visibility kills, John," she said softly.

She was right, of course. The publicity in this case meant my investigation would be second-guessed by the brass every step of the way. If I made a mistake, my career would be over. That was when it hit me.

"What is it, John?" Rita said.

But I was thinking maybe I understood why Cramer had picked me after all.

"John . . ."

I patted her arm. "Relax. I'll be okay. Let's go in. Sounds like the briefing has started. What's this?" Rita had pressed something into my hand as she reached for the door.

"Mints, John. You smell like a damn chimney."

A dozen somber-faced officers in military uniforms were packed around the briefing table, staring at a grid map. Most were maintenance and flight operations supervisors, with a couple of security police thrown in. Brigadier General Chuck Stinson, the portly Andrews Air Force Base Wing Commander, was bent over the map, pointing as he talked.

Rita and I slipped inside quietly, listening for about ten minutes as General Stinson gave an overview of the crash. An overweight man in his early fifties sporting Mr. Magoo black glasses, Stinson looked more like a computer geek than a military leader. But he was as tough and competent as they come. He spent most of his career as an *Air Force One* pilot and had been a real favorite of President Reagan.

"... confirm the wreckage is relatively contained," Stinson was saying. "Apparently, the cockpit sheared off

from the fuselage on impact." He jabbed a finger on the map. "The wreckage landed on a horse farm here, approximately three hundred yards from the tree line. Fortunately, there was no fire." He stepped back. "Any questions?"

"Sir," I said, moving forward.

Stinson turned and gave me a tired simile. "Hello, John. I heard you got tagged for this. My condolences. Should I send flowers?"

"Good evening, sir," I said, smiling back.

"Anything you need, just ask."

"I appreciate it, sir." Removing a notepad from my jacket, I looked down at the map.

"You catch the brief?"

"Most of it," I said. "Rita mentioned you just returned from the crash site."

"Yeah. I flew out with Doc Bently and Colonel Ogden. Only had a chance for a quick look."

"Ogden the on-scene commander?"

A nod.

"Who are the rescue personnel on site?"

"Doc Bently and his medical team. Quantico trucked in additional emergency personnel and equipment." Stinson nodded to two officers. "We'll be sending security and maintenance personnel out shortly to take over recovery operations. Frank, Ken, your guys ready to roll?"

"Soon as we're done here, sir," a thick-necked lieutenant colonel said. A major wearing a security cop's beret nodded his agreement.

I made a few notations. "How about the pilots' radio transmissions to air traffic control?"

"We've talked to the FAA," Stinson said. "The crew made a Mayday call and asked for an emergency return. Apparently the call was garbled, but mentioned something about intense heat."

"But the plane never caught fire," I said, continuing to write.

"No." Stinson shrugged. "Which makes me think maybe they had an erroneous fire indication. And ATC says the radar track gave no indication the plane was experiencing any significant flight control problems."

My head popped up. "None?"

Stinson shook his head, his eyes darting to a young captain. "ATC ever fax out the NTAP printout they promised?"

"Yes, sir." The captain stepped forward and removed a computer printout from a folder, which he placed on the table before us.

I leaned over the printout. NTAP stood for the National Tracking Analysis Program, which was a fancy name for a graph depicting the plane's radar track over the ground. The plane's flight path was depicted by a series of X marks with corresponding ground speed, altitude, and heading information annotated to the side. My eyes locked in on the numbers.

The Lear's departure to the west looked normal until 9,000 feet. Then the plane had abruptly turned back eastbound. I studied the ground speed and altitude readouts, trying to see if there were abrupt deviations. That would indicate the plane was experiencing severe flight control problems, maybe lost an engine or—

Stinson abruptly began talking, a finger tracing the jet's return flight path. "Heading is steady, airspeed steady, descent rate under a thousand feet per minute . . . no change . . . no change . . ." His finger stopped at the last X mark.

I stepped back, confused. I'd been expecting to see indications of a loss of control that would have caused the aircraft to plunge to the ground.

"I don't get it," Rita murmured behind me.

"Doesn't make sense," Stinson said.

Everyone else stared, offering no comment.

But it was right there on the table in black and white. For some reason, Rick French and Judd Wilson seemed to have flown straight into the ground.

General Stinson tapped the NTAP printout thoughtfully. "What's your take, John?"

I hesitated. "Same as yours, sir. Something obviously malfunctioned at nine thousand feet. Rick and Judd tried to bring the jet back, and they couldn't."

Stinson continued to look at the printout. "Two hundred and fifty knots. Plenty of airspeed to pull up." He gave me a searching look. "But they didn't."

I knew what he was thinking. Pilots, preoccupied with a malfunction, sometimes lost their situational awareness and flew into the ground. In one recent case, the pilots had been changing a burned-out bulb on the instrument panel. The weather had been bad and they neglected to monitor their descent, and ended up slamming into a hillside. What was left of them barely filled a Baggie.

"Rick was a damn good pilot, sir," I said. "Besides, it's a clear night. He would have seen the ground corming up."

"Yeah." Stinson shrugged, turning to Rita. "The helo ready?"

"Yes, sir. Pad two. We're still waiting for Dr. Johnson from the NTSB."

"Aw, hell—" Stinson ran a meaty hand over his face. "Get the NTSB on the horn. Find out what the holdup is."

"Yes, sir." Rita bolted out.

Stinson cleared his throat sharply and looked around the room. "Briefing's over. Move out. Any problems, I want to know ASAP!"

The crowd disbursed, heading for the door, but Stinson and I hung back.

"You know anything about Dr. Johnson, sir?" I asked.

Stinson shook his head. "Not much. Got plenty of horse-power, I understand. Assistant director or some such shit. General Cramer says you're bringing Chen in on this?"

I nodded.

"Smart move." He grinned. "Ted's going to be damned upset, though." Unlike most of the brass, Stinson liked Ted. The two of them went back to the days when Stinson had been an *Air Force One* pilot and Ted had been the maintenance officer. Ted had saved Stinson on a number of occasions by making last-minute repairs on the big jet in time for a presidential trip.

I gave him a rueful smile. "I'm hoping Ted cools off by the time he gets here."

"Fat chance." Stinson checked his watch. "Two more minutes. Dr. Johnson doesn't show, go ahead and take off. I'll send Ted out, too. Who else is on the board?"

"Lieutenant Colonel Cal Brice will be my deputy. He's flying in from Scott in St. Louis. Tom Blaney is coming out from Wright-Patterson to oversee the maintenance—"

"Good man," Stinson grunted.

"And Major Mattie Parker will be the FAA liaison. She's sharp and a whiz with computers. I also asked for Dr.

Harmon Masters out of Brooks in San Antonio to look at human factors."

Stinson nodded his approval. "Good group." He paused, his face somber. "You'll need all the help you can get on this one, John."

"Tell me about it," I said with a wry smile. "So you got a place for us to work out of, sir?"

Stinson waved an arm around the briefing room. "Here. Civil engineering is coming over to wire up a phone bank and install a couple of computers and fax machines. Anything else you need?"

I looked around. "A couple of file cabinets and a copy machine. Maybe a couple of desks, too. The big metal ones. That's about it."

"No problem."

"How about the hangar? Know which one we'll be using?"

"We'll be taking the wreckage to number six."

I glanced down at my notebook. "You check the Lear's maintenance history, sir? Anything to suggest a faulty fire indicator?"

"No. The plane went through a major maintenance overhaul a few months back. It's flown two hundred hours since then with no problems."

I frowned. During a major overhaul, a jet is stripped and reassembled with new or refurbished parts. Someone could have screwed up, left out a critical component, or rewired something wrong. Then I remembered that damn NTAP profile. A plane just doesn't fly that smoothly with a significant mechanical malfunction.

Behind me I heard the door open, then Rita's voice: "Gentlemen, Dr. Johnson."

Stinson looked past me, his face opening into a smile. "Good evening, Dr. Johnson."

"Good evening, gentlemen," a woman's voice said. She sounded slightly out of breath.

Maybe I was tired, or maybe the title of doctor threw me. But after almost seven years the name hadn't rung a bell. Neither did the voice.

I turned around casually and found myself jolted back into the past.

**S**he had to be as surprised as I was, but she appeared completely cool as she looked me over. Her red hair was pulled back to reveal her lovely oval face, and there was only a hint that her smile had a plastic quality. I caught the familiar scent of her perfume.

"Hello, Colonel Quinn," she said formally. "Dr. Jennifer Johnson."

I felt the stares of General Stinson and Rita as I came back to life.

Jennifer held out a hand, and we shook. She seemed to flinch at my touch, but maybe I was imagining it. I stood awkwardly by as she introduced herself to Stinson.

Even in her bulky sweater and jacket, I could tell she had kept her figure. Jennifer would have; appearance had always been extremely important to her. I was thinking how young she looked, and recalled myself in the mirror.

Johnson? Jennifer was using her maiden name.

I glanced down to her ring finger for confirmation. Nothing.

Stinson coughed, giving me a sideways glance. "We're a little pressed for time, Dr. Johnson. Colonel Quinn will brief you on the situation during the flight."

"That will be fine, General." Jennifer glanced at me, looking amused.

"Rita," Stinson said, "Drive Dr. Johnson to pad two."

I started to follow them out, but Stinson tapped me on the arm. Taking the hint, I hung back as Jennifer and Rita left.

Stinson folded his arms, his eyes boring into me. "What the hell was all that about?"

I shrugged. "I know her, sir."

"Is that a fact? This thing is too goddamn important, John. Now, if you've got something going with Dr. Johnson, I want to know."

"Sir, it's personal."

"Dammit, John! Don't give me that crap."

I took a deep breath and told him.

He got a sick look. "Aw, Christ—"

I spun and walked out fast, half expecting to hear Stinson order me to stop. When he didn't, I hustled out of the command post before he could change his mind. As I stepped outside of the building, a staff car was heading down Command Drive—Rita and Jennifer on their way to base operations.

I watched for a moment, then went to my car, trying to ignore the tightness in my chest.

Andrews Base Operations was located in the long, red-brick air terminal building on the south side of the flight line and to the left of the control tower. I parked up front in another colonel slot. I was almost to the automatic doors at the entrance when a sharp voice called out my name. I

turned and spotted a diminutive figure hurrying toward me across the asphalt.

"Glad you could make it, Ted," I said.

"You son of a bitch," Ted Chen said.

Trim and dapper in his Air Force blues, with his black hair combed straight back and sporting a pencil-thin mustache, fifty-year-old Lieutenant Colonel Ted Chen reminded me of Errol Flynn, only shorter. A third-generation Hawaiian, Ted had been the youngest homicide detective on the Honolulu P.D. when he was shot trying to apprehend a suspect. His wife, Tiki, pregnant with their second child, had insisted he quit police work, so Ted had joined the Air Force, planning only to stay long enough until something better came along. But Ted discovered he liked working on airplanes and was good at it. Economics also played a part in his decision to stay: he had five kids by the time his initial commitment was up. He couldn't afford to leave.

Ted's experience as an ex-cop was what made him such a talented accident investigator. He studied crash sites the same way a detective looks at a crime scene, picking up subtleties and nuances most of us never noticed. He was the best. That fact alone should have assured him promotion to full colonel, maybe even general.

But over the years, Ted's abrasive personality tagged him as a troublemaker among the military elite. When he came to work for me, I tried to get him to tone down his rhetoric, particularly when dealing with senior officers. My efforts proved futile; Ted couldn't stop being Ted. He relished the role as the maverick who bucked the system and continued to butt heads with superiors who disagreed with him, adding to his already impressive list of influential enemies. I wasn't surprised when Ted was passed over for colonel. Neither was he.

When I gave him the bad news, Ted didn't seem to give

a damn. For most people, the casual indifference over not making a promotion was an act to save face. In Ted's case, I didn't think so. He had his bar, he had his family. He had a life outside the military. I was always a little envious of the freedom that gave him.

The reason Ted and I worked together well was that I'd figured out early on he was a whole lot smarter than me. So I stayed out of his way and let him do his thing.

Ted stalked up to me. "What the hell is this, John? I'm supposed to be retired."

"Sorry, Ted. But I need—"

"The bar was packed. One of the waitresses didn't show. Now Tiki's stuck practically trying to run everything by herself. General Cramer says bringing me in was your bright idea." He glowered at me, hands on hips.

"Rick French was the pilot," I said quietly.

Ted blinked, stunned. "Christ, John, I didn't know." He continued to stare up at me, his smooth face now a mixture of guilt and sadness. "Any chance he made it?"

I shook my head. "So how'd you know I was here?"

"I was coming in the West gate when I spotted you heading out from Command Drive."

"What do you know so far?"

Ted shrugged. "Not much. Called the Command Post to get a brief from Major Sanchez, but the phones were ringing off the hook. Asked for you, but Sanchez said you were in some meeting. General Cramer mentioned the passenger was the President's half brother."

I nodded. "This is big, Ted."

"Yeah, I'm beginning to see that," he said dryly.

I filled him in as we went through the doors into base operations and down a long corridor that opened into a large room with pale-green walls. We passed a sign that pointed out the pressroom, where correspondents cooled their heels waiting for *Air Force One*. To our immediate

right was the operations counter, where pilots filed their flight plans. We headed toward the double glass doors near the back. Once outside, we followed the redpainted walkway to the tarmac, where *Air Force One* picked up the President. A Blackhawk helicopter was parked on a pad fifty yards beyond the short mesh fence. The blue staff car slowly pulled away from the chopper and came toward us.

Ted had been nodding occasionally as he listened. When he spotted the helo, he stopped dead.

I grinned. Ted hated to fly. The .45-caliber bullet he'd taken in Honolulu had torn a hole through his stomach and left it sensitive to just about everything, but especially air travel. A couple of times he'd had the dubious honor of tossing his cookies while flying on *Air Force One*.

Rita honked the horn of the staff car as she passed. We waved.

"Major Sanchez said there's a convoy leaving," Ted said hopefully. "Maybe I can catch a ride."

A high-pitched whine touched our ears. The helo's blades began to turn.

"Sorry, Ted," I said, expecting an argument.

Instead, Ted surprised me with a resigned shrug.

We started walking. "By the way, there's something about Dr. Jennifer Johnson you should know," I said.

"What's that?"

"She's my ex-wife."

The Blackhawk helicopter climbed slowly into the night sky, banking slightly as it made a southwesterly turn toward Virginia. The three of us were strapped onto web seats in the cramped cargo bay, Jennifer and me on the right, Ted on the left.

Our faces were visible under the soft glow of red lights emanating from the ceiling. I had taken the seat next to Jennifer because I didn't want to appear juvenile by seem-

ing to avoid her. She never said a word to me, even when I introduced Ted.

As we leveled off, the baby-faced sergeant on the jumpseat to my left leaned down, shouting to make himself heard over the chattering blades. "Should only take twenty minutes, sir."

"Thanks," I hollered back. "You've been to the site?"

The sergeant nodded vigorously. "Wreckage don't look too bad."

"What do you mean?"

"Still looks like a plane, sir. Nothing like that airliner we worked last year. The one out of Dulles, remember?" He shook his head. "That was a mess. The plane went in nose first. We hauled nothing but body parts for two days." The helo dipped suddenly. "Better tighten up the belt, sir, could get a mite bumpy." The sergeant flashed a cocky grin and turned away.

Past him, I could see the glow of the cockpit lights and the shadowed faces of the pilots. I tugged on my lap belt and looked out the rectangular window. The night was clear with a full moon, and we were maybe a thousand feet up. To the north, I could make out the Woodrow Wilson Bridge and the dark outline of the Potomac River running beneath. In the distance, Washington, D.C., glowed brightly. We'd be crossing into Virginia soon. I settled back and tried to relax, but I was becoming wired. I wasn't sure if I was feeling this way because of Jennifer or the upcoming investigation.

Jennifer was staring straight ahead. After a moment, she looked to me. I waited for her to say something, but she turned away.

Across from us, Ted had his eyes closed, a hand on his stomach.

I folded my arms and closed my eyes and became aware of Jennifer's perfume. I risked a glance. She was still re-

markably beautiful. Her skin was taut, her complexion flawless. Her red hair was longer, perhaps, and she seemed thinner.

We'd met in flight training when I was an instructor pilot and Jennifer was my student. Women pilots were still a big deal back then, and Jennifer had this fantasy that she was going to become the first female fighter pilot, maybe even an astronaut. But learning to fly for her was hard. Twice she almost washed out. Like many trainees, she was too mechanical in her flying, thinking too much instead of reacting. I spent long hours working with her, and we grew close. I never planned the next step, but the time was stressful and we were together so much, and the next thing I knew, we were sleeping together. By the time she graduated, we were madly in love. With Jennifer coming up for assignment, we hurriedly got married without really thinking things through.

It was a mistake.

Jennifer saw herself as a female aviation pioneer. I wasn't important, starting a family wasn't important. Only her dreams and career mattered. She was always at work or on the road, anyplace but at home or with me. When we were together, we argued constantly.

While I didn't like it, I understood what drove her. As she tells it, her father, a senior Boeing VP, had been controlling and domineering. Her childhood had been one big competition for his approval. Yet nothing Jennifer ever did seemed good enough. Still she pushed and worked and achieved. She graduated near the top of her Air Force Academy class and went on to earn a master's in aeronautical engineering at Columbia. Next came pilot training and a career. All along, Jennifer was sure that if she worked hard she'd be a star in the military. I had to agree. The Air Force was pushing women pilots. Smart, beautiful, and ambitious, Jennifer couldn't fail.

But she did.

Her troubles began when a congresswoman undertook a push to get women into combat. To make her point, the congresswoman convinced half a dozen female military pilots to speak out in the media against the military's policy, and one was Jennifer. I tried to talk her out of doing it, telling her she would be committing professional suicide, but she refused to listen. For a couple of weeks, she ran around Capitol Hill giving interviews and hobnobbing with the politicos, all the while basking in the attention. When the bill the congresswoman was pushing failed, the reporters and politicians left, leaving Jennifer to pay the price. Overnight, she became a pariah on base. No one did anything overt, but her superiors made it clear her career was over. Without even consulting me, she arranged a transfer to another base, hoping for a resurrection. When that didn't work out, she made the decision to resign. She wanted me to quit, too, but I'd had enough. By then, other than an occasional visit, we'd been living separately for almost a year. I found I could live without her, and so I told her I wanted a divorce.

Faced with life on her own, she really lost it, accusing me of abandoning her. She couldn't have been more wrong. For three years, I'd tried to make the marriage work. I put up with her striving, her desire to make a name. I allowed myself to get put last on her list and I always tried to be there for her when she needed me. Now I was tired. Then Jennifer brought up children, claiming she'd changed her mind. She really pushed the point, saying what she really wanted was to settle down and start a family.

Though I knew better, I was tempted. Frankly, I still loved her. But I knew Jennifer wouldn't change.

Anyway, that was our marriage. Once the divorce was final, she disappeared from my life.

PATRICK A. DAVIS

Jennifer coughed and looked at me. "I'd like that briefing now," she said into my ear.

"Fine."

"First, I'd like to set a few things straight. The situation is awkward, and I want to know if you can handle it."

"I can."

"Good. I also want you to know that my feelings toward you won't affect our professional relationship."

I wasn't sure what she meant by that, so I just told her what I knew.

Ten minutes later the sergeant pumped a thumb downward. "Site's coming up! Make sure you're strapped in!"

I pressed my face against the window. We were well south of the Northern Virginia suburban sprawl, following a roadway into the heavily wooded countryside southwest of the Quantico Marine base. Interspersed among trees and darkened fields, I saw an occasional winking light from a house or a trailer. The sparseness of the population surprised me, since the area couldn't be more than an hour's drive from D.C. Then I saw the crash site against a line of trees, a well-lit clearing glowing in the night courtesy of the Marines, who had set up portable light generators.

The helicopter banked sharply, then rolled out. That's when I spotted the winking red and green lights circling above us, a mile away. Moonlight glinted off the side of the aircraft as it turned toward us. The silhouette told me it was too small to be a military helicopter.

I pointed out the window. "Press is here."

Jennifer acted as if she hadn't heard me, and Ted sat with his eyes closed.

I returned to the window as we descended rapidly toward the lights.

We landed on an enormous field of scrub grass maybe six inches high. A small two-lane road paralleled the plot to the east, while thick woods made up the northern and western boundaries. A ramshackle farmhouse was barely visible at the far end. To the right were two long buildings that I took to be stables or barns. As we climbed out of the helicopter, I saw a couple of helos already parked, along with a half-dozen military Humvees and an assortment of trucks. Spotlights set up around the perimeter had the entire area bathed in light. Maybe thirty people, all in uniform, strolled around with little colored flags, pausing occasionally to mark a piece of debris. The colors were used to delineate the types of debris: red for body parts, white for pieces from the aircraft, green for electrical wiring, yellow for fuel contamination. The fact that there were very few flags visible confirmed that the plane had come down relatively intact. Had the jet come apart in the

air—say, from an explosion—there would be hundreds or even thousands of little flags everywhere.

More soldiers were stationed along the road where a number of vehicles had pulled up. A small crowd of onlookers had gathered in front of the soldiers. The flashing of cameras told me most were probably press.

Thirty seconds after dropping us off, the helicopter lifted off. To the north, the news helicopter was still circling, careful to stay far enough away not to be cited by the FAA for violating the airspace over the site.

After the prop blast from the departing helo subsided, we looked around, trying to get our bearings. Except for Ted. He was rocking side to side, eyes closed, taking deep breaths. In response to Jennifer's concerned query, he just nodded bleakly.

"Over there," Jennifer said. Ted and I looked to where she was pointing. Our view was partially blocked by one of the choppers. In the distance we could see the tail of a plane, and we started toward it.

"John!"

A stoop-shouldered, sandy-haired Air Force colonel hurried toward us. Many people considered General Stinson's deputy, Colonel Nathan Ogden, to be overly pushy and demanding—a military throwback who still adhered to the antiquated notion that everything had to be done by the book. In the nineties feel-good military, I found Ogden's hard-charging style refreshing; he got things done. As the on-scene commander, his task would be to organize the recovery of the wreckage and transport it to a hangar at Andrews for analysis once we finished with our preliminary on-site investigation.

Ted threw up a shaky salute as Ogden approached.

Ogden returned it. "General Stinson said you were on the way, John." He gave Ted a sympathetic smile. "How was the flight, Ted?"

"I'll live, sir," Ted said.

I introduced Ogden to Jennifer.

"Looks like you've got the situation pretty much under control, Colonel," Jennifer told him, watching the Marines traipsing over the field.

Ogden nodded. "We were fortunate Quantico was close by. Marines did a good job getting the site sealed."

I pointed to the crowd along the road. Lightbulbs continued to flash. "How long has the press been here?"

"Arrived about thirty minutes ago, with more on the way," Ogden said. "They're squawking to be allowed in. I called Andrews to have Public Affairs sent out to assist. Major Rita Sollars will arrive in about an hour."

I checked my watch. "Have her set up a briefing for around 2200 hours. Make sure she checks with the White House and finds out what we can release on the passenger, Thurston."

Ogden nodded.

Jennifer pointed toward the farmhouse. "Anyone there see the crash?"

"It's been abandoned for years," Ogden said. "The farm is owned by some guy in Florida, who bought it from a woman when her husband passed away."

"So you've found no witnesses?" Jennifer asked him.

"Not yet. Can't be more than a dozen families living around here. Most of those live east of Somerville, maybe five miles away. With all the trees around, not much chance anyone would have seen the plane coming down unless it came right over them. Another problem is the traffic on that road, which is practically nonexistent. It dead-ends a couple of miles to the west and only provides access to this area. We've got men checking the few neighboring residences, but we're not holding our breath. Except for the place on the other side of the tree line, the nearest neighbor is a mile away."

"Did you recover the bodies yet, Nate?" I asked.

"Only the passenger."

"What about Rick and Judd?"

Ogden shook his head, his face grim. "Not much hope of getting them anytime soon. Don't think there'll be much left to recover anyway. Cockpit got pretty much destroyed."

I thought of Rick's wife. "I'd like to take a look."

"Let's go."

Ogden led the way, Jennifer at his side. Ted and I brought up the rear.

Since the Lear was only a six-passenger corporate jet, the wreckage wasn't particularly large. The aft portion of the fuselage lay at an angle and appeared surprisingly undamaged. Even the engines, which normally separate on impact, were still attached. The front portion, where the cockpit had been, was now a gaping hole. The left wing had snapped off and lay crumpled and bent thirty yards away. Portions of the right wing were still connected to the fuselage with about five feet of the end missing.

As we approached I scanned the area, wondering what had happened to the cockpit. A path of scarred dirt led from the wreckage back a few hundred yards to the initial impact point. No pieces of the cockpit were visible. Then I noticed the fuselage was sitting a couple feet above the earth. Mangled metal gleamed beneath it. The cockpit had separated shortly after impact and the fuselage had rolled over and crushed it. Ogden was right. There wouldn't be much of Rick and Judd to recover.

Red cones had been placed in a wide perimeter around the wreckage. We stopped as we approached them. The air was heavy with the smell of fuel.

"Not too close," Ogden said. "Still a lot of fuel around. Don't want anyone digging around until we get more fire

equipment. I'm surprised the plane didn't ignite on impact."

"That's not unusual, Colonel," Jennifer said, looking around. "The plane hit almost parallel to the ground, so there wasn't much of an initial impact angle. The engines remained attached, which means there was no heat source to ignite the fuel in the wings."

I pointed back to the broken and splintered tops of the trees. "The plane clipped those coming in. The flat trajectory verifies the NTAP printout from the FAA. The pilots must have had at least some control."

"Have you found the voice and cockpit recorders?" Jennifer asked Ogden.

Ogden shook his head. "Once we confirmed there were no survivors, I kept everyone away from the wreckage until the recovery personnel are in place."

"Why is that?" Jennifer asked.

Ogden blinked as if he couldn't believe Jennifer had asked the question. Nor could I. Ted gave Jennifer a curious look.

A critical tenet of crash investigations was that absolutely nothing from the aircraft was removed from a site until a team was in place to photograph and record the exact location of every item. That way the items could be relocated in the hangar in their precise relative positions so the wreckage pattern could be studied. When a plane disintegrated in the air, this process could take weeks or months. In this case, with everything pretty much intact, the team would be finished in a few days.

"We can't," Ogden said to Jennifer, and explained the procedure.

"Oh," Jennifer said, and gave an embarrassed smile.

"Where'd you find the passenger's body, sir?" Ted asked.

Ogden pointed. "See the marker off to the left?"

Everyone looked. I saw a handful of markers but couldn't distinguished their colors. Ogden was pointing to one marker almost a hundred yards away from the initial impact point. A long way for a body to be thrown, I thought.

Ted walked in the direction Ogden pointed.

"Where's the body now?" Jennifer asked.

Colonel Ogden gestured to a Humvee across the field. "Over there. Dr. Bently will take him back to Quantico later for transport to Dover."

"Dover?" Jennifer said. "I would have thought the Armed Forces Institute of Pathology at Walter Reed would handle the autopsy."

"They provide the medical examiners," Ogden said. "But the autopsy is usually performed at Dover Air Force Base. I know. Doesn't seem logical when the autopsy could be done at Walter Reed, but that's the military for you." He glanced at me. "You need anything, let me know. I've got to find out what's keeping the heavy equipment."

"Thanks, Nate."

Something on the tail section of the jet caught my eye. As Ogden left, I walked past the red cones toward the wreckage.

"John!"

I looked back.

"And what do you think you're doing?" Jennifer demanded.

"My job." I started to turn away.

"Without waiting for the fire crews?" Her voice was low, but there was no mistaking the contempt.

I faced her, forcing back a smile. I pointed to the horizontal stabilizer—the big fin that ran perpendicular to the tail and helped control the plane's pitch. "Notice anything unusual?"

Her rancor evaporated as she studied the tail. "The sta-

bilizer appears to be set for level flight, but . . . it's hard to be sure from here."

I nodded. "I just wanted to be certain."

We stared at each other. After a three-count, she started toward the wreckage. I followed.

Up close, we could see little black marks running up the tail next to the stabilizer. They were indices, telling us the precise angle at which the stabilizer was set. Since the plane had crashed with the gear up, we could also easily look into engines, attached just in front of the tail. Using a small flashlight, Jennifer peered into the left engine.

"Looks clean," I murmured over her shoulder.

She didn't reply.

I went around to the right engine and inspected it. Jennifer was walking back to the cones when I finished. When I strolled up she wasn't smiling, but she wasn't looking at me as though I were scum, either.

"Clean?" she asked.

"As a whistle, and we were right about the stab. The pilots had it trimmed for a shallow descent. Matches what I saw in the radar profile."

She shook her head. "Doesn't make sense. They obviously knew they were descending. Why fly it into the ground?"

I shrugged. "Not because they had an engine fire."

We stood in awkward silence for a moment.

"Think I'll take a look at the body," she said, and walked away.

I watched her and wondered if we could work together after all. I also made a mental note to check the regulations. Maybe there was something in there that said you couldn't work a crash investigation with an ex-wife.

If there wasn't, there should be.

To my left Ted was hunched down by the red marker, studying something on the ground with the aid of his flash-

light. He bent almost flat and then abruptly stood, splaying the beam around. He slowly began walking away, head down, obviously following something of interest on the ground.

"Sir!"

An overweight master sergeant and two airmen carrying video and camera equipment trudged toward me.

The photo team arguably had one of the most demanding tasks. Tonight they, along with a couple of recorders, would handle the photographing and documenting of every piece of wreckage.

"Hello, Sergeant Matthews." I nodded to the airmen.

"You want us to set up now, sir?" Matthews asked. He was puffing, his heavy face dripping sweat.

"You have enough light?"

"Piece of cake, the way they've got this thing lit up," Matthews said.

"Fine. Get what you can from the perimeter for now."

The men set down their equipment.

"You get a chance to photograph the dead guy yet?" I asked.

Matthews looked around. "Sergeant Colby did that before they moved the body. He's with Captain Brisby and Lieutenant Morales. They're around someplace."

"Brisby and Morales the recorders?"

Matthews nodded. "Sir, you know when we can move in for the close-ups of the fuselage?"

"When maintenance shows and removes the fuel. Maybe a couple of hours." Matthews groaned, but my attention was on Jennifer as she walked toward the Humvee. I decided to look at the body too.

**A** young corpsman in creased whites emerged from the Humvee as I approached. He was maybe eighteen, blond, sporting a mustache that was visible if you really looked.

"Help you, ma'am?" he said to Jennifer. He saw me coming and saluted.

Jennifer turned, noticed me, and her jaw tightened slightly.

I sighed, returning the salute. I couldn't win.

"I'd like to see the body," she said.

The corpsman popped the rear latch of the Humvee and rolled out a gurney with a black body bag.

"I'll take care of it," I said, sliding past him. I started to reach for the zipper.

Jennifer's hand snaked out, grabbing it. She gave me a cold look, and I stepped back. She pulled the zipper about halfway down.

Mr. Joshua Thurston appeared to be sleeping. He was

wearing a dark suit and looked about fifty, with thinning brown hair. Bits of grass clung to his jacket, shirt, and hair. There were also marks on his clothes that resembled grass stains. His portly face was covered with red splotches, as if he'd been a drinker.

"He must have been lying facedown when you found him," I said to the corpsman.

"Yes, sir."

"Died from trauma to his chest," a voice called out.

A rotund Air Force lieutenant colonel in an ill-fitting uniform and greasy-looking hair sauntered up, munching on a Snickers. He squinted through wire-framed glasses. "Hiya, John. They tagged you too, eh? Hey, those eagles look sharp."

I never cared much for Dr. Chip Bently. He was pompous, overbearing, and, even by my lax standards, a slob. Patients complained about him regularly, but the Air Force, critically short of doctors, ignored the complaints and continued to promote him.

"Hi, Chip."

Wolfing down his candy bar, Bently stared at Jennifer with more than passing interest. I coughed sharply to get his attention and made the introduction.

The grin Bently flashed was just this side of a leer. "Pleasure, Dr. Johnson."

Jennifer nodded vaguely and looked uncomfortable.

"The body doesn't appear too damaged," I said.

"That's because most of the damage was internal," Bently replied. "Chest was crushed, ribs broken. Probably bled to death internally."

Jennifer was peering at the corpse's face. "What are these marks?"

Bently stepped to her side as I looked down.

Jennifer pointed out two deep reddish marks along the ridge of Thurston's nose.

Bently shrugged. "Just some bruises."

"That's obvious," Jennifer said. "I'm wondering how they got there. Most of the trauma is to the body, and the rest of his face is unmarked."

"Who knows?" Bently said. "Maybe he sustained those before the crash."

I was watching Jennifer. She still had her eyes on the corpse. She frowned and reached down, gingerly touching the upper chest. She recoiled. "Christ, he's soaking wet."

"Yeah," Bently said. "Funny, eh? Clothes are completely soaked through."

I felt the corpse's shirt. Moisture coated my fingers.

"It's definitely not fuel," Jennifer said, stating the obvious. "I don't recall any water around. . . ."

I held my fingers up to my nose. The pungent scent was familiar.

"It's sweat," Bently said.

Jennifer and I looked up. "You're sure?" I asked.

"Damn straight. This ole boy sweated like he was in a sauna before the crash."

My eyes went to Jennifer. For once she was looking at me.

"Cabin fire," she said.

I nodded.

Jennifer turned, heading back toward the wreckage.

Bently grabbed my arm as I started to follow. He gave me a wink, and his fat face spread into a wolfish grin. "Some looker, eh, John?"

"Fuck you, Chip," I said.

The corpsman was laughing as I left.

The airmen were slowly walking around perimeter, clicking away at the fuselage with their cameras. Sergeant Matthews followed with a video camera.

Ted now stood near the broken wing some thirty yards away. He seemed to be scrutinizing the jagged edge that had separated from the fuselage. He looked up when I called and came over. Jennifer did the talking, telling him what we'd learned. Ted listened without comment, his face thoughtful. He shrugged and guardedly replied, "A cabin fire is possible, though we've seen no evidence of fire on the wings or engines."

"That has to be it," Jennifer said, her voice excited. "The cabin's the only thing we haven't checked."

Ted stroked his mustache and said nothing.

"I wonder how it started," Jennifer said. "Electrical short—"

Ted cut her short. "Was there any soot on his clothes?"

Jennifer glared, irritated at being interrupted.

Ted was referring to the passenger, Thurston. I tried to recall.

"No,"Jennifer said. "Just bits of grass."

"You're certain?" Ted asked.

"Yes."

"He didn't appear burned at all. Maybe his skin?"

"No,"Jennifer said. "His face was a little red."

Ted shook his head. "Then there couldn't have been a fire in the cabin. In that enclosed space, Thurston would have sustained some type of burns. At the very least, he would have been covered with soot and ash."

Jennifer opened and closed her mouth. I couldn't tell if she was bugged by Ted's logic or the absolute certainty in his voice.

"Something generated heat in the cabin, Ted," I said. "If not a fire, then what?"

Ted seemed to smile. "I think I know."

"You want to share that tidbit with us, Colonel Chen?" Jennifer said dryly.

"I'll need to check the cabin first," Ted replied.

THE PASSENGER                                        47

Jennifer's jaw tensed. She started to reply.

"Let's take a look," I said quickly. I led the way, expecting Jennifer to follow.

But when I glanced back, Jennifer was glaring at us, arms folded across her chest.

"I don't think your ex-wife likes me," Ted remarked as we approached the fuselage.

"That's okay. She doesn't like me much either."

Ted chuckled. "Yeah, I noticed. Careful." He pointed out a puddle of fuel. I skirted around it.

Walking around aviation fuel isn't really that dangerous; in liquid form the stuff has a high flash point. The real danger is the fumes that build up in a confined space.

We entered the cabin through the jagged opening toward the front where the cockpit had been torn from the fuselage. The ceiling was low, so I had to crouch. Ted just ducked his head a little.

The first thing I did was take a couple of deep breaths. No excessive concentration of fuel vapor, and I felt a breeze coming through the opening. I turned to Ted.

"Ventilation in here is good. We'll be fine." He flipped on the flashlight in his hand. I pulled mine out, trusting his

word we wouldn't turn into Roman candles. Our beams darted around the tiny cabin. Within seconds I knew Ted's earlier conclusion was right. Seats were torn off their mounts, the ceiling was cracked, windows were shattered, and there was crap everywhere. But there was no evidence of soot or ash or burning of any kind.

"No fire," I said.

Ted didn't reply. His beam was pointing at the plastic molding along a window. "What is it?" I asked.

He stepped back. "Take a look."

I leaned over. The plastic was melted, fused to the liner of the wall.

"Here, too," Ted said.

I followed his light. More plastic molding. Melted.

I smiled at him. "So there was heat in here."

"Yeah, but no fire. That's significant."

I knew what he was getting at now. There was only one heat source on an airplane hot enough to melt plastic but not enough to cause a fire. "A bleed air leak."

"Not necessarily a leak."

I frowned. "What are you saying?"

Ted's face became troubled. "I'll explain outside."

Ted took fifteen minutes before he was ready. He removed panels on the engines and poked around for a while. He unlatched a couple more along the fuselage, giving occasional grunts when he saw something. Then he returned to the cabin, rummaged around, and came back out.

I hung back, figuring I'd just be in his way. Peering up into the inner workings of a plane meant little to me. I flew jets, I didn't build them.

"Okay," Ted said when he came over.

We walked over to the cones, where Jennifer was waiting.

She had her back to us, staring toward the road where a

minor commotion was going on. A line of large vehicles had stopped, and some of the Marines were scurrying around, waving and shouting. I could see a number of trucks and flatbed trailers with construction equipment. The lead vehicle appeared to be a fire truck. It turned off the road onto the field, and the rest began to follow.

"They made good time," I said as we approached Jennifer.

Jennifer turned. "Well?"

Ted talked as Jennifer listened without interruption. I took her response to be a grudging acknowledgment that Ted knew what he was talking about.

I chastised myself for not considering bleed air as an option. Bleed air is a euphemism for the hot air bled from the engines that is used for cabin pressurization and, after being cooled, airconditioning.

". . . unique to the Lear," Ted was saying. "There's an emergency pressurization system that, when actuated, pours hot air off the engines directly into the cabin. It's supposed to be used only in an emergency depressurization situation at high altitudes, and for a very short time. At low altitudes with relatively high ambient air temps, the heat can get over three hundred degrees. At those temps, the crew would have been incapacitated in minutes."

"Let me get this straight," Jennifer said. "The Lear has a switch—"

"Two switches on the instrument panel in front of the co-pilot," Ted corrected. "One for each engine."

"Okay, two switches. And if they're placed in the emergency position, hot bleed air is dumped directly into the cabin. That sounds crazy."

"Remember," Ted said, "the system is only used in emergencies, to provide an immediate air source to reestablish cabin pressure. The design is for high-altitude use, where the outside temp is fifty to sixty below. At am-

bient temperatures that low, the air coming off the engine into the cabin will be much lower than the three hundred degrees."

"And the pilots have to manually flip a switch to activate this system?" Jennifer asked.

Ted nodded.

"There is no automatic activation?"

"Sure, but only when the cabin altitude exceeds nine thousand, five hundred feet. We know that couldn't have been the case, since the plane never climbed above nine thousand feet."

"What about the automatic system malfunctioning?" Jennifer asked.

"Virtually impossible. It's pressure activated off an aneroid switch and extremely reliable."

Jennifer had nothing to say. I shook my head. I didn't like where this was going.

I looked right at Ted. "Do you think Rick or Judd inadvertently flipped the switches?"

Ted didn't look happy. "John, I'm not crazy about the possibility, but we have to consider it."

"Wait a minute," I said. "Couldn't a bleed air duct have ruptured?"

"Sure," Ted said. "But I looked. I saw some ducting that had separated during impact, but none that showed evidence of a blowout. Most of the ducting runs below the flooring of the cabin. Again, no evidence of a rupture."

"But you couldn't have checked them all, Ted."

"No, but from what we saw in the cabin, that wouldn't make sense."

He'd lost me. Jennifer seemed equally puzzled.

"I don't follow you," I said.

"Only the plastic was melted, remember, John? None of the fabric on the seats was heat damaged, or the carpeting, or the cabin walls."

I was catching on. "A relatively low temperature heat source."

"Absolutely," Ted said. "Bleed air from the high-pressure ducts runs in excess of six hundred degrees."

Jennifer said, "Then if one of those had blown—"

"Damn," I said. "The cabin would have shown much more damage, maybe even caught fire."

Ted shrugged. "We'll know for sure when maintenance checks the valves for the emergency system to see if they are working properly. They can also tell us if any ducts are blown."

Jennifer said, "And if the valves are open and no ducts were ruptured . . ."

We were both watching Ted.

He paused. I knew what was bothering him; he didn't want to be the one to hang Rick. Finally, he said, "Actually, the key point is whether any ducts are ruptured since the position of the valves won't tell us much. When the airplane isn't powered, like now, the valves are spring-loaded to the open position. When electrical power is applied, a magnet energizes the valves closed."

"Hang on," I said. "That means a loss of electrics in flight would open the valves."

"Only if it's a total electrical loss, including the battery. But we know that didn't happen. Remember, you said the crew made a radio call to air traffic control."

I gave a reluctant nod. "So if there was power for the radio . . ." I swore under my breath as my voice trailed off.

Jennifer cleared her throat. "You're saying that if there are no ruptured bleed ducts, then by process of elimination the pilots must have hit at least one of the switches to open a valve in flight."

Ted nodded. "It's the only other bleed air source. But that leaves us with a tougher question—" He stopped abruptly, looking over my shoulder.

Shouts continued to erupt from behind, and we heard the rumble of truck engines. We turned to watch the line of vehicles lumbering over the field toward us.

"Colonel!" a voice yelled down from the fire truck. "Where do you want it!"

I stepped forward, thinking they were talking to me. Then I spotted Ogden a few yards away, pointing and gesturing.

With a screech, the fire truck slowed to a stop by the cones. Other trucks laden with maintenance equipment began parking beside it. Figures emerged and went over to Ogden. He began barking orders, and people scurried to obey. Ted sauntered over to him, leaving me alone with Jennifer. She hugged herself and ran her hands over her shoulders.

"Cold?" I asked.

She looked surprised. "A little."

"Congratulations on getting your doctorate."

A thin smile. "Thanks."

"In aero?"

A nod.

"You still doing some flying?"

"No."

I gave up. She was responding with all the enthusiasm of a prisoner of war under interrogation.

We watched the scene unfolding around us for a few moments.

"So what are these men going to do?" she asked.

I frowned. Like her earlier question to Ogden, she was again indicating a lack of experience with crash investigation procedures. "They'll probably first extract any fuel remaining in the wing tanks. Then they'll try to find the cockpit and voice recorders. After that, they'll log the exact location of each piece of wreckage before hauling it back to a hangar at Andrews. Everything will also be

rechecked at Andrews to ensure there is no break in the chain of custody. We'll also try to recover as much of the remains of the pilots as possible and send that off to Walter Reed so they can run the tissue sample tests. You know, check for alcohol, drugs . . . usual crap."

She nodded.

"That basically how your people handle it?"

A pause, then another nod.

Silence again.

The big lieutenant colonel from the briefing had joined Ogden and Ted. Ted was doing the talking.

"For what it's worth, I apologize," I said quietly.

Jennifer showed no reaction. I wasn't sure if she heard me.

"Jennifer—"

"Don't, John." She sounded tired. "It's over."

"Is it? You're obviously still angry at me, which isn't exactly conducive to working together."

Her face turned hard. "Don't flatter yourself, John. I got over my bitterness toward you years ago."

"Be serious, Jennifer. The way you're acting, it's still pretty clear you resent—"

"Guilty," she interrupted. "I *do* harbor some resentment, which is natural. You walked out on me when I needed you. But I'm not angry, John. There is a difference." She smiled coldly. "Now, if you can't handle the situation, I'm sure you could notify your superiors and ask to be replaced."

I was silent, fighting off the temptation to respond. A few maintenance men nearby were staring at us, and the last thing I wanted was to create a scene.

Without another word, Jennifer walked away.

Ted approached a few moments later. If he'd caught my discussion with Jennifer, he gave no sign. "Not much we

can do around here. It'll take maintenance an hour to finish defueling."

"The point you were going to bring up earlier. You were wondering why Rick and Judd didn't manually close the switches again before the heat incapacitated them."

"The million-dollar question," Ted said. He hesitated. "Look, I'm not trying to nail Rick, John. Hell, I liked the guy."

"I know." I started to leave to smoke a cigarette and think.

"I'm going to take a look at Thurston's body, John," Ted called.

I kept going. "Fine."

"I want to look at his fingernails."

*Fingernails?*

I walked toward the road where the Marines had set up the barricade. The size of the crowd and the number of cars had grown dramatically. I counted three of those large satellite trucks used by TV crews. Cameras flashed continually now, and I could make out a number of people carrying TV cameras. Just over the tree line, a second press helicopter circled. The scene made me wonder what the hell I'd gotten into.

About fifty yards from the road I lit up and considered the possibility that Rick had made a mistake. But no matter what Ted implied, I would never be convinced. Sure, there had been pilots who screwed around in the cockpit and ended up killing themselves. But not Rick.

I took a drag, and my thoughts turned to Jennifer. During most of our marriage, Jennifer had been outgoing, pleasant, basking in the attention she received from being a beautiful woman in a man's world. Now she was cold, hard, and bitter, and I wondered if my presence was responsible. I really didn't think so. There was a toughness

to her now that hadn't been there before. I could see it in her eyes and the way she handled herself.

"You have another one?" Ted called out, jogging toward me.

I frowned as he approached. "I thought you quit."

He grinned. "Tiki thinks I did, but it's damn difficult when you run a bar. Now I'm acting like a kid, sneaking smokes when she's not around."

I smiled and tossed him the pack and the matches. At work, Ted always acted cocky and confident, the guy in charge. At home, Tiki ran the show.

"So what's so important about Thurston's fingernails?" I asked as he fished out a cigarette.

Ted flared a match, took a couple of quick puffs, and tossed back the pack. "Just wanted to confirm a little theory."

"Which is . . ."

Ted almost smiled. "That Mr. Joshua Thurston survived the crash."

My eyes popped wide. "You're certain?"

"Pretty sure." Ted exhaled slowly. "I thought it was a possibility from what I saw in the area where his body was found. His fingernails confirmed it."

My mind tried to make a connection. "I'll bite. How?"

"You saw the spot where his body was recovered, right?"

"Yeah." I dropped my cigarette and stepped on it.

"Pretty far from the impact point, wasn't it? A body doesn't get tossed that far, especially considering how flat the plane came down."

"I wondered about that."

"Anyway, when I went over to the marker I noticed a path flattened in the grass leading away, like something fairly heavy had been dragged along."

I understood then. "You think Thurston pulled himself along the ground?"

Ted nodded. "There were tiny bits of grass and dirt beneath his nails, and his hands were filthy. He also had grass stains on the front of his clothes."

I thought it over. "Not that it really means much. Thurston obviously succumbed to his injuries."

Ted gave me a curious look but remained silent.

"You got something else?" I asked.

Ted puffed quietly. He shrugged. "It's probably nothing."

I could have pushed it, but I knew Ted. He'd tell me when he was ready, if he still thought it was important.

From the road we heard angry reporters shouting at the Marines. The natives were getting restless.

"So how long you think the crew had until they passed out?" I asked. "Five minutes?"

"Maybe a little longer. Assuming the plane's outflow valve was open, the temp would have been lower than three hundred degrees. Plenty hot, though."

The outflow valve was the point at which air exited the cabin. When open, it cooled the cabin a little by enhancing airflow. Still, the heat would be excessive. I recalled what a sauna felt like at a hundred degrees.

I said, "We have to assume that if Rick had accidentally flipped one of the switches and the hot air rushed in, he would have closed it. Be crazy not to."

Ted dropped his cigarette and ground it out carefully. "If he knew what was causing the problem."

"He knew."

"Maybe the copilot hit the switches. Rick could have thought he had a blown duct. The emergency pressurization system is not something often used."

"C'mon, Ted. Rick knew the Lear like the back of his hand. The switches would be the first thing he'd check."

Ted became quiet. "Okay, John. I'll dig through the

maintenance records, talk to the crew chiefs. Maybe something was installed wrong. Maybe—"

He broke off, and we looked to the sky.

Low on the horizon, a helicopter was chattering noisily toward us. Landing lights winked down from the darkened silhouette.

It was bigger than a Blackhawk. Much bigger.

The helo slowed as it came over the field, descending into the light. Soon I could see Marine markings and a white roof. The craft touched down in a swirl of dust and debris, and the giant blades slowed as the engines whined down.

"*Marine One*," Ted said. "The President's helicopter."

"But it can't be the President," I murmured.

The passenger door near the front slowly opened.

We saw Ogden sprint toward the helicopter, Jennifer trailing quickly. We followed, cutting across the grass.

By the time we reached *Marine One,* four figures had emerged and were being greeted by Ogden. A short, stocky man was in the lead, followed by a rail-thin Air Force four-star general whom I recognized as General Thomas Ware, the chairman of the Joint Chiefs. Two other men in dark suits stayed a few paces back—aides or Secret Service.

We stopped a few feet from a small crowd that stood in a semicircle maybe twenty yards away. Jennifer moved toward the front. I didn't bother trying to join her.

A female sergeant nearby asked, "Anybody know why they're here?"

No response.

"So who's the short dude?" someone else asked.

"McKenzie," a voice answered. Not that it took a genius to know who the stocky man was. All one needed was to

see a picture of the President of the United States and look to his right. Riley "Mac" McKenzie, the White House chief of staff, was always there.

In his early forties, "Mac" McKenzie was the youngest and most powerful of President Roland Halloran's advisers. McKenzie had first gained prominence as a political pollster with an uncanny knack for deciphering the whims of a fickle electorate. Press reports and political pundits called him everything from pompous and arrogant to savvy and brilliant. On one point agreement was universal: Mac was a modern-day Rasputin with unprecedented influence over the President.

President Halloran's reliance on his young chief of staff was understandable. An ex-governor of Virginia with little name recognition, Halloran had been given little chance to win his party's nomination, much less the presidency. Then McKenzie took over the campaign and engineered what many considered the most astonishing presidential victory in recent memory. By following McKenzie's philosophy to always "go with the polls," Halloran had sailed through his first term. Now two years into his second term, Halloran held a 70 percent approval rating——a phenomenally high number considering that Halloran's reelection campaign was under investigation by an independent counsel for financing violations.

Riley McKenzie looked over, his face searching the crowd. He waved. "Jennifer!"

Jennifer strode confidently toward the group.

Ted and I shifted over a little to get an unrestricted view.

"Interesting," Ted murmured. "McKenzie knows her name."

Jennifer smiled and shook hands with McKenzie and General Ware as though they were old friends. She was doing all the talking. McKenzie and General Ware responded with an

occasional nod. Colonel Ogden drifted off to the side, his face grim.

"Solves one mystery," Ted said.

"Which is . . ."

"Your ex. Apparently she can smile without her face cracking."

I nodded. Jennifer was practically beaming now.

"Ogden's looking a mite put out," Ted said.

Watching Ogden, I wondered what Jennifer was saying that was bothering him.

"I've met McKenzie a few times," Ted grunted. "When I was working on *Air Force One*. He's an asshole."

Jennifer was still smiling, eyes riveted on McKenzie. She obviously didn't share Ted's sentiments.

"We should go on over, John," Ted said.

I shook my head. While I didn't like being excluded, I knew you didn't barge in on a four-star and a White House power broker without being invited.

"Meeting's breaking up," Ted said a few moments later.

Jennifer was leading the group away, gesturing like a tour guide. They walked in the direction of the wreckage, the two men in suits trailing behind. Colonel Ogden suddenly broke away. No one from the group appeared to notice his departure.

Ted turned to me, his face grim. "I thought you were in charge, John."

"So did I."

Ogden was striding toward us, looking angrier than I'd ever seen him.

"Uh-oh," Ted said.

"We need to talk," Ogden growled at Ted and me. He spun and led us toward a Humvee.

The crowd surrounding us had seen Ogden coming and dispersed fast. "Jeez, the old man looks pissed," someone said as they ran off.

Ogden leaned against the Humvee, his face pinched in a scowl. "Goddammit, John, what are you guys trying to do!"

I blinked, confused. "I'm not sure—"

"Christ!" Ogden pressed his face inches from mine, spitting all over the place. "You're supposed to maintain objectivity. You're not supposed to make up your fucking minds until you look at all the facts."

I stepped back. "Nate, if you would—"

"And you call yourself a friend of Rick's." Ogden shook his head in disgust.

Now I was angry. "You want to tell me what this is about?" I snapped.

"Railroading Rick. Calling the crash pilot error—"

"What! That's absurd! Did Jennifer—" I clammed up, trying to curb my rage.

Ogden's eyes went to Ted, then back to me. "You guys didn't know?"

"Sir," Ted said calmly, "we haven't a clue what the hell you're talking about."

Ogden let out a deep breath. "Dr. Johnson was spouting crap that the cause of the accident is likely to be pilot error. Some bullshit about the pilots activating the emergency pressurization system. Made it sound like it was a consensus."

I was shaking my head. "That's just a possibility, but . . ." I looked at Ted. "Tell him."

When Ted finished, Ogden still didn't look happy. "Rick would never make a bonehead mistake like that."

"No," I agreed.

"What really pisses me off is Dr. Johnson's blatant disregard for procedure," Ogden said. "She should damn well know you don't make preemptive, unverified judgments in an accident investigation."

"Maybe she has her reasons," Ted said softly.

"Like what?" I asked.

Ted shrugged. "Big investigation, lots of visibility. Maybe she thinks she'll look good by wrapping this thing up fast."

I wanted to say Jennifer would never sacrifice ethics for ambition. But that had been the old Jennifer. Now I wasn't sure.

Ogden grunted. "All I know is you better keep your eye on her, John."

"Okay—"

"Tell her not to shoot her mouth off. Hell, I'm not sure she even knows what she's doing."

"What do you mean?"

Ogden waved a hand at nothing in particular. "She was pumping me about recovery ops. She sounded like she didn't know what the hell was going on."

I didn't have a response.

Ogden jabbed a finger in my chest. "You damn well better find out what really happened."

"I will."

Another jab. "And don't let that bitch hang the pilots until you're sure Rick and Judd fucked up. I mean goddamn positive."

"I won't." But at the back of my mind, I was bothered by Jennifer's apparent influence with McKenzie. If she convinced him that pilot error was the cause, it might not matter what I or the Air Force decided.

"Nate, maybe we should bring up our concerns to General Ware," I said. As soon as the words were out of my mouth, I knew I'd made a mistake.

Ogden snorted and gave me a look of disgust.

I should have guessed his reaction. To many in the military, General Ware was considered a sellout, a yes-man who'd received his appointment only because he'd agreed to go along with the administration's extensive defense

cuts. This sentiment was not without merit. General Ware's promotion three years earlier had been a complete surprise, elevating him over a number of more senior officers. Since he'd become the chairman of the Joint Chiefs, he'd quietly supported a downsizing of the military that now approached 30 percent.

Ted saved me from a response. "By the way, sir, why are they here?" he asked Ogden. He was looking toward the wreckage, where Jennifer was giving an animated show-and-tell to McKenzie and General Ware.

That question had been bugging me, too. A White House chief of staff flying out to a crash site didn't make sense.

"They came to retrieve Thurston's body," Ogden said.

"You're kidding," I said.

Ogden pointed toward the Humvee in which Thurston's body had been placed. Two corpsmen were lifting a stretcher carrying a body bag. Doc Bently was standing nearby, conferring with the two men who had arrived with McKenzie. Bently looked our way, gesturing toward us. The two men watched us for a few moments. One was tall, with a blond flattop haircut, the other heavy and balding. The blond man wrote something down on a notepad.

"Who are those guys?" I asked, feeling a sense of unease.

"Secret Service," Ogden said.

The men shook hands with Bently, then followed the corpsmen as they carried the body toward the helicopter. After a few steps, the blond man abruptly turned and walked quickly back across the field toward the wreckage.

"Where are they taking Thurston?" Ted asked.

Ogden shrugged. "I'm assuming to Dover for the autopsy." He glowered toward Jennifer's group. "I'd better find out what other bullshit she's feeding them." He left in a hurry.

I focused on Jennifer, who was hovering by McKenzie's shoulder, closer than I thought was necessary.

"John," Ted said. "Wasn't Doc Bently going to arrange for the body to be flown to Dover in a couple hours?"

"Yeah."

"So why couldn't they wait?"

"He's the President's brother."

"He's dead. What does it matter?"

I shook my head.

The blond Secret Service man approached the group. He immediately went to McKenzie and said something. McKenzie and the agent stepped away and huddled together. Moments later, McKenzie glanced at Ted and me. He looked away quickly when he saw us watching him.

"Wonder what Doc Bently told them," Ted said.

**D**oc Bently was leaning back in the Humvee's passenger seat, eyes closed. I reached in through the open window and shook him.

"Hey—" Bently sat up and squinted through his glasses. "What the hell, John." He ran a hand over his fleshy face.

"What did you tell them, Chip?" I asked.

"What? Who—"

"Those two Secret Service types."

"Oh, right. . . ." Bently rummaged under the seat and produced an open soft-drink can. He took a drink and then belched loudly.

"What'd they want, Chip?" I asked again.

"They wanted to know where we found the body, the extent of the trauma, cause of death. You know, the usual crap."

"Nothing about us?"

Bently frowned. "Oh, sure. They wanted to know the name of the lead investigator."

"Anything else?"

"Nope. Except I did mention the little fact about Thurston perspiring profusely. I also mentioned those red marks you brought up. Remember? I said I didn't think they were any big deal, but the autopsy should be able to tell if they're significant. I think I mentioned you had a few questions about them. You and Dr. Johnson." He started to grin, caught my glare, and quickly cleared his face to neutral.

"That it?"

Bently drained the can and tossed it in the back. "Pretty much. What do you care, anyway?"

"Just curious." I stepped away from the window.

"John . . ." Ted said softly.

Bently said, " 'Course, if there's something I should know, John—"

"There isn't," I snapped at him.

"Jeez, John, you don't have to get sore—"

"McKenzie's coming over here," Ted cut in.

I looked.

The honorable Riley "Mac" McKenzie was strolling toward us, and so was the rest of his entourage.

Ted and I went out to meet them.

McKenzie stepped forward wearing a big smile, the tall Secret Service agent by one elbow, General Ware by the other. Jennifer stood off to the side. Ogden had remained at the wreckage.

McKenzie stuck out his hand. "Colonel Quinn, I'm Riley McKenzie." Up close, McKenzie seemed even shorter and heavier, and his round face was even more pockmarked than his pictures indicated. His eyes were very blue and, combined with the grin he was wearing, projected a feeling of open sincerity that almost made you want to check to see if you still had your wallet.

But I gave him my best smile anyway. "Good evening, sir. It's an honor," I said as we shook hands.

McKenzie stared at Ted for a moment. "Haven't we met, Colonel Chen?"

"Yes, sir," Ted said. "I handled maintenance on *Air Force One.*"

"That's right." McKenzie seemed pleased with himself for remembering, while Ted looked like he couldn't care less.

Then General Ware introduced himself. He was a rangy man, a couple of inches taller than my six-two and a good twenty pounds lighter. He had close-cropped graying hair and a cleft chin a quarter could fit into. I'd met him after the Gulf War, when his hair had been brown and there had been more of it. I knew he'd remember me.

"Hello, John," Ware said. His voice sounded like it came out of a barrel. "It's been a while."

"Yes, sir."

"How's the back?"

"Fine, sir."

To McKenzie, Ware said, "John is one of our heroes from the Gulf, sir."

McKenzie frowned. "Don't tell me. The kamikaze guy who took out the tanks. . . ."

I felt my face redden. I noticed Jennifer was actually looking at me with interest.

"Sure, I remember," McKenzie said. "Wasn't there some problem with the medal . . . ?" He drifted off, his eyes seeking out Ware.

The debacle had caused an uproar among the Air Force hierarchy. In the postwar euphoria, the Air Force PR types decided the public needed a hero to rally around. They were going to have a medal-pinning ceremony at the White House, with all the requisite hoopla. They never figured I

wouldn't play along. To avoid embarrassment, the Air Force canceled the ceremony and hushed up the incident.

I was thinking hard, trying to come up with something that would get me out of explaining everything to McKenzie.

"John turned it down," Ware said quietly.

McKenzie looked stunned. "Is that right? Why?"

"John didn't think he'd earned it," Ware said. "We awarded it to him anyway, but he won't wear it."

McKenzie was staring at me now; so was Ware; so was everyone else. I didn't know what to say, so I just nodded like an idiot and kept my mouth shut.

McKenzie looked like he wanted to pursue the matter, but the Secret Service agent stepped forward. "Sir, we have less than thirty minutes."

"Thanks, Kroft," McKenzie said.

I breathed a sigh of relief, my eyes on Kroft. He was a monster, at least six-five and two-thirty, with a buzz haircut and a nose that looked like it had been broken more than once. I wondered if the robot act was something they taught in Secret Service school or he'd been born blessed with a winning personality.

McKenzie checked his watch. "I'll make this quick, John. I've briefed Jennifer . . ." He smiled at her. "She can fill you in. The President and Mr. Thurston were extremely close. This accident has hit him hard. The President is very interested in what went wrong. As a courtesy, we'd like to be kept informed on all facets of the investigation."

I nodded, curious why he was telling me. Ware certainly had already given his approval, and up to now, McKenzie acted as if Jennifer were running the investigation.

"Agent Kroft will be your liaison. Kroft!"

The big man stepped forward, and we shook hands. "Look forward to working with you, Colonel."

"Thanks."

I put Kroft at forty. He could have been older, though his physique made him appear youthful.

McKenzie said to me, "Keep Agent Kroft posted. The President has made it clear he plans to be very involved in the investigation. He's even considering cutting his trip short for this." He paused. "I'm sure he'll want a briefing from you upon his return."

I tried to sound calm. "Fine, sir."

"Agent Kroft will contact you when we get it set up. Thank you, gentlemen." As McKenzie walked away, Jennifer tucked in close by his side.

General Ware called out, "Be with you in a moment, sir."

McKenzie didn't look back.

Ware stepped over to Ted and me, his face tense. "How long until you come up with something definitive, John?"

I hesitated. "Sir, that's hard to say. A couple of weeks if—" I clammed up when Ware scowled.

"Not good enough, John. When you brief the President, he's going to want answers. I expect you to provide them. Understood?"

"Sir, that may not be possible—"

"Dr. Johnson says you're already close to calling this thing pilot error."

I shifted my feet. "There still may be mechanical—"

"But at this stage, the most likely cause appears to be pilot error, right?"

"Sir, it's too early to tell."

"You agree, Ted?" Ware snapped.

"Colonel Quinn is correct, sir. It's too premature to make a judgment now." Ted spoke slowly, as if addressing a child. I tried not to smile.

Ware locked him with a stony stare. He puffed up, shifting his glare to me. "You do understand the military can't be seen as covering for the pilots."

I nodded.

"Fine. You will concentrate on the pilot-error angle first, understand. Rule them in or out first."

I was tempted to tell Ware to go to hell. But he was a general, and I didn't feel like ending my career. "Yes, sir."

Without another word, Ware turned and walked rapidly toward the helo.

"Prick," Ted muttered.

I nodded. My eyes were on Jennifer, who was huddled with McKenzie by the steps leading into the helicopter. They seemed to have a lot to say to each other. I mentioned that point to Ted.

"No mystery there, John," he said. "It's pretty clear now McKenzie brought her into the investigation."

"Oh? Why?"

Ted shrugged. "McKenzie's a control freak. He probably wanted someone he could trust keeping an eye on the investigation." He paused. "She could be a problem."

McKenzie was climbing up the steps of *Marine One* now, stopping to wave to Jennifer before disappearing inside. She beamed back.

"She already is," I murmured.

The engines on *Marine One* suddenly roared to life. Ware hustled up the steps, and the passenger door folded closed behind him. Moments later, the blades began turning, picking up speed. The big helicopter rocked gently and rose awkwardly into the night.

As the sound of the chattering blades faded, Ted faced me. "So are we going to pursue the pilot-error angle, John?"

"What do you think?" I growled.

Ted nodded, approval in his eyes. We heard a shout and turned.

"We're almost ready for the press briefing, John," Major Rita Sollars called out.

**R**ita came over quickly, carrying a clipboard. She was breathing hard, her forehead glistening. But as Rita had told me more than once: women don't perspire, they glow.

"Hi, Ted," she said. "Enjoying retirement?"

"Funny girl," Ted said. But he was smiling.

"When'd you arrive?" I asked her.

"Mmm, maybe twenty minutes. We had to hustle to get everything set up in time." She pointed across the field to two men in Air Force uniforms who were setting up a portable PA system. A third walked around them, placing red cones to mark off the briefing area. Beyond, a throng of press trailed Ogden and an escort of Marines from the road to the site.

"It's definitely a rush job," Rita said. "I'm not sure how long the PA batteries are good for, but, hey, what do they expect? Is it true? That was McKenzie on *Marine One?*"

"Yeah," Ted said. "The boy wonder personally flew out to pick up Thurston's body."

I checked my watch. Less than five minutes to brief time. We began walking. "Rita, did you contact the White House about what we can release on Thurston?"

Rita nodded. "I spoke with Fred Nissen, the communications director. He doesn't want you to say anything about Mr. Thurston other than what's in the press release." She slipped a page from the clipboard and held it out.

I motioned for her to keep it. "Just give me the highlights."

"It confirms that Mr. Thurston was killed in the crash," Rita said. "Lists his age as fifty-two, widowed, with no children. It emphasizes the close relationship between President Halloran and Mr. Thurston, and that the death of his brother has hit the President very hard. It also gives some background on Thurston. You want that?"

"Uh-uh. You told the press this is going to be short and sweet and I won't be taking questions?"

"Yeah. They weren't very happy about that, and they're pretty upset you won't allow them closer to the wreckage. You done many of these press conferences?"

"A couple. Nothing this big."

"Sometimes they can get brutal, John, especially if they think they're being kept in the dark. Get in and get out fast."

"Yes, ma'am."

A sigh of exasperation. "I'm serious, John. Some of these jokers are in an ugly mood. You tell him, Ted."

"She's right, John," he said quietly. "Don't hang around too long."

"I'll be fine," I said.

We walked in silence. Ahead, Jennifer, talking on a cell phone, slowly made her way to the briefing area.

"She's very pretty, John," Rita said. "Jennifer. Your ex-wife."

I glanced over, startled. "Uh, thanks."

Ted looked at Rita. For a second I thought he was going to make a derisive comment, but he remained silent.

A minute later, we reached the circle of cones. Rita's men made a few adjustments to the PA microphone on a stand in the center and quickly stepped off to the side. Wires ran from the mike to two small speakers placed out front. One of the spotlights had been shifted, brightly illuminating the area. A handful of Marines were beyond the cones, restraining a crowd of at least a hundred reporters and cameramen. Ogden and Jennifer stood in the middle of the circle, trying to ignore the deluge of questions from the crowd.

TV cameras and long boom mikes were everywhere. The logos on the cameras told me all the big names were there—CNN, the major networks, the local affiliates, plus a few foreign networks.

Rita gave my arm an encouraging squeeze as we stepped into the light. Ogden looked relieved to see me, while Jennifer gazed at me with casual indifference.

I nodded to Ogden, who stepped up to the microphone, palms extended toward the crowd. "Quiet, please! Colonel John Quinn is in charge of the crash investigation and will be giving the briefing."

"About time!" someone shouted.

"Quinn? Is that with two *n*s?" another voice asked.

"Yes," Ogden said. He stepped aside, and I moved forward.

A murmur of anticipation rose from the crowd as people jostled for position, many holding up small cassette recorders. I stared calmly into the sea of lenses, waiting for the noise to die off. Flashbulbs went off continually. I focused lower, trying to avoid being blinded.

When the noise finally died to a buzz, I introduced myself as the Air Force's chief accident investigator. In my best Joe Friday imitation, I covered the highlights in the clipped monotone characteristic of military briefings. I told them a jet had gone down with three fatalities and that Mr. Joshua Thurston, the President's brother, had been the lone passenger. I mentioned that weather wasn't a factor and that we still hadn't recovered the voice and flight-data recorders, and we had no theories as to the cause of the accident. I went over the recovery and investigation process, emphasizing that these things take time, and that all possible causes would be thoroughly studied. I finished by saying the Air Force was deeply saddened by the tragedy and that our thoughts were with the family of the victims. The whole thing took ten minutes, tops. Immediately, the barrage of questions began:

"Why was Mr. McKenzie here?"

"Who were the pilots?"

"Were they experienced?"

"When will you recover the black boxes—"

"Sorry," I shouted. "No questions." I stepped back.

Rita gave me a wink.

"That's it, ladies and gentlemen," Ogden said. "No questions. Please, if you would just move back—"

"But you haven't told us anything!" a voice bellowed.

Rita came forward. "There will be a briefing scheduled at 1500 hours tomorrow afternoon at Andrews—"

A deluge of angry comments cut her off.

*To hell with this.* I began walking away.

"What about pilot error, Colonel Quinn?" a deep voice sang out.

I kept walking.

"I heard it was pilot error," the voice said.

I slowed.

"No denial, Colonel Quinn? Is that because it's true?"

I turned around fast. Ogden was staring at a short, heavy man standing near the front. He was in his fifties, and had a graying beard.

I walked right up to the man. "Where did you hear the pilots were responsible?" I demanded.

The crowd suddenly quieted. The man gave me an arrogant smile. "A source, Colonel." He paused. "A reliable source."

"That's incorrect," I said.

"Is it? Then you're willing to go on record as officially denying that pilot error is the cause, Colonel Quinn?"

"Of course I can't—" I blinked. The man sounded confident, almost cocky. A warning bell went off in my head.

Rita slipped behind me and whispered, "John, just leave."

I took a few deep breaths, trying to figure the guy's angle.

"John . . ." Rita said. I felt her hand on my back.

I shrugged her off, my eyes locked on the man. "Of course, I can't deny pilot responsibility—"

"Then you're admitting the pilots could be the cause, Colonel," the man interrupted.

"That's strictly conjecture at this point."

"Is it? My source says the focus of your investigation is the pilots. Do you deny it?"

"Sir, your source is misinformed," I snapped. As soon as the words were out of my mouth, I knew I'd made a mistake. The man's eyes lit up, his beard spreading into a broad grin.

"My source is from the White House," the man announced.

He had me. He'd baited me, hooked me, and reeled me in. And everyone there knew it. I became aware of all the cameras staring me in the face.

*Christ.*

"Now, Colonel," the man said, "do you still deny the focus of your investigation is the pilots?"

My mouth felt dry. "No comment."

"Is the Air Force trying to cover up responsibility—"

"Pilot error is indeed a consideration," a voice called out behind me.

I spun around.

Jennifer didn't even glance my way as she pushed past me to the mike."We won't know for certain until we do more analysis, but pilot error is something we're looking into."

For an instant there was silence. Then the questions came seemingly all at once.

"Please," Jennifer said firmly. "One at a time." She pointed to a reporter up front and deftly began fielding questions, answering each in rapid succession:

". . . I am Dr. Jennifer Johnson of the NTSB. I was brought in to assist the Air Force."

". . . No, I can't comment on the specifics of why I think pilot error might be the cause."

". . . Yes, it's unusual for the NTSB to be involved in a military investigation."

I barely listened. I was staring at Jennifer, my teeth clenched. I couldn't believe what she was doing. I was so mad, I could spit.

Then came a question from the man with the beard. He was looking right at me when he said it. "Dr. Johnson, are you saying you contradict the statement of Colonel Quinn?"

Jennifer hesitated, glancing at me. Her face was completely blank. "We all have our opinions," she said.

The man grinned, "Good enough for me."

I wanted to rip the mike from Jennifer's face, shake her, ask her what the hell she thought she was doing. Instead, I walked away.

Commotion erupted behind me as reporters scattered to call in their stories or rush their video footage to the studio. I heard Ogden shouting, trying to establish control. I was already thinking of tomorrow's headlines and wondering if I'd still be running the investigation by then. Not that it really mattered.

I wasn't running it now.

I took refuge in the shadows fifty yards away, watching as reporters hopped in their cars and vans and peeled out like they were at Le Mans. The walk had helped cool my anger down below the homicidal level, and I was trying to rein in the rest. Giving in to my emotions was the last thing I could afford, and I knew it.

As I lit up a cigarette, my hands were shaking. I listened to the shrill chirping of crickets, which I hadn't noticed before. I kept waiting for the feeling that I'd been kicked in the stomach to go away.

Rita and Ted approached slowly, coming to a stop a few feet away. I expected Ted to tell me I blew it, but he just shook his head unhappily.

"You okay, John?" Rita asked.

"I'm fine," I said, struggling to sound calm.

"What are you going to do about her?" she asked.

I slowly let out a breath. "Nothing."

"Nothing?" she said, incredulous. "Dr. Johnson over-stepped her authority big time. You're the boss, and she cut you off at the knees. She should be tossed from the investigation."

"How?" I asked.

"Huh?"

"How do you want me to get her removed?"

"Talk to General Cramer—"

"Can't," I said. "She was brought in by the White House."

Rita looked dumbfounded.

"John's right," Ted said. "Jennifer was handpicked by McKenzie. She pulled that stunt because she knew she'd get away with it."

Rita gave a slow head shake. "How do you know?"

"We know," Ted said.

I rubbed my eyes. "It was my fault anyway. When I finished the briefing, I should have walked away. But, Jesus, that guy pissed me off."

"Don't be too hard on yourself," Rita said. "Fritz Walling can be pretty rough."

My eyebrows went up. "*That's* who that was?"

"Hell, I thought you knew," Ted said.

"The beard probably threw you," Rita said. "Fritz hasn't had it long."

I let out a harsh laugh.

No, I hadn't recognized him, but I knew the name well enough. Fritz Walling was the Pulitzer Prize-winning investigative reporter at *The Washington Post*. For twenty years he'd been exposing the seamy side of Washington politics—congressmen, senators, city politicians, bureaucrats, Fritz went after them all. Fritz had uncovered kick-back schemes, sex scandals, drug rings, you name it. Tenacious and competent, Fritz was also known to be petty and vindictive, often using his column to go after politi-

cians to settle what many considered personal vendettas. The fact that he often targeted opponents of President Halloran wasn't lost on his critics, who blasted him as being the administration's hatchet man in the media. But like him or not, everyone acknowledged his power. Fritz could make or destroy political careers.

"Damn, he's good," I said.

"Walling?" Rita asked.

"No. McKenzie."

A glance at Ted told me I'd lost him too. I explained.

When I finished, Ted was slowly running a finger over his mustache. Rita had her arms folded, a skeptical look on her face.

"It's a possibility, John," Ted said. "After all, somebody must have tipped Walling off."

"And you think it's McKenzie," Rita said to me.

"Absolutely."

Rita said, "You think McKenzie leaked the fact that General Ware ordered you to pursue pilot error to Walling."

"Yes."

"So Walling could set you up."

"Right."

"But you have no idea why. I dunno, John . . ."

Her condescending tone annoyed me. "Dammit, Rita, McKenzie had to have leaked it. Hell, Ware orders Ted and me to focus on pilot error, and twenty minutes later, Walling throws it in my face. How could he know that so fast unless he was tipped off? McKenzie was probably calling him from *Marine One* as he flew out of here."

"Okay, but—"

"Why else do you think Walling was baiting me, egging me on? He knew the focus of the investigation is to be the pilots. He just wanted me to deny it so he could accuse me of lying, covering up, make me look like an ass." I ran a

hand over my face. "Which, if you noticed, is just what happened."

"Why couldn't Jennifer have leaked it?" Ted asked.

"Jennifer?" The question caught me off guard. "She wouldn't have had time, Ted. Walling was already here—"

I stopped when I recalled having seen Jennifer on the phone. "You think she was talking to Walling on her cell phone?" I asked.

He shrugged. "It's possible."

"Uh, guys . . ." Rita said.

Ted and I followed her eyes and saw a Marine jogging toward us. He stopped two paces away and snapped a salute that appeared spring-loaded.

"Sir, we've got a minor situation. Colonel Ogden thought you should know."

I saluted back. "What is it, Corporal?"

"We found a woman wandering around. She's extremely upset, so we took her over to Colonel Ogden in the briefing area."

"What's her problem?" I asked.

"Her daughter is missing, sir."

The only people remaining in the briefing area when we walked up were Ogden, Jennifer, the Air Force technicians dismantling the PA system, and a tall, silver-haired woman wearing a dark jacket and slacks. A gaggle of reporters were again camped out on the road.

Jennifer and the woman were huddled together, talking quietly. Ogden, arms folded, watched from a few paces away. He noticed us and came over.

Removing his baseball cap, Ogden ran a hand over his thinning scalp. "Sorry to bother you, John. I don't think it's anything, but that bitch, Dr. Johnson—"

Ted coughed sharply. "She's Colonel Quinn's ex-wife, sir."

Ogden looked stunned.

"We've been divorced for years, Nate," I said quickly.

"I see." Ogden gave me an odd look. "No offense—"

I waved a hand.

A look of relief crossed his face. "Anyway, Dr. Johnson insisted we check out the lady's story. As if we haven't got enough to do."

"What is her story, Nate?" I asked.

Ogden sounded tired. "Mrs. Gibson lives on another farm on the other side of the trees. She came home maybe an hour ago, expecting to find her daughter. Her daughter's a junior at George Mason and was going to drive home after her last class. Mrs. Gibson arrived home to find her daughter's car parked out front, but the girl was gone."

"She could be out with friends, sir,'" Ted said.

"Mrs. Gibson says her daughter wouldn't go off without telling her or leaving a note."

"Maybe she's out taking a walk, sir," Rita said.

"Mrs. Gibson was adamant the girl wouldn't go out this late."

"She call the cops?" I asked.

"Yeah," Ogden said. "They told her they don't consider someone missing until they've been gone for twenty-four hours. They took the girl's description and said they'd keep an eye out. The daughter would be hard to miss. She's tall, six-three. She plays basketball for George Mason."

Jennifer had her arm around Mrs. Gibson now, comforting her. I wondered why Mrs. Gibson could possibly think her daughter was here. I asked Ogden about that.

"Because of the camera, John."

I frowned.

"Her daughter's camera is missing," Ogden said. "The mother says the camera is an expensive, professional

model. The girl is apparently majoring in photojournalism. Mrs. Gibson heard about the crash on the radio, driving home. When she couldn't find her daughter and noticed the camera missing, Mrs. Gibson put two and two together and figured Allison—the daughter—must have seen the plane go down and run over to take pictures. According to Mrs. Gibson, her daughter has done some freelance work, local-paper stuff, nothing big."

"Explains the girl's car still being at home," Ted said, eyeing me.

I shrugged. Frankly, I thought the girl must be out partying with friends.

"Sir," Rita said to Ogden, "who were the first units to arrive?"

"The county cops," Ogden said. "They arrived about twenty minutes after the crash. The Marines showed maybe an hour later." Ogden pointed. "The cops are manning a checkpoint up the road. We haven't run the girl's description by them yet. Sergeant Ralston, the head of the Marine detail, is passing around the girl's description among his men. Nothing."

"Then the girl wasn't here," I said. "No one forgets a girl who is six-three."

"That's what I tried to tell Mrs. Gibson," Ogden said. "Look, John, you mind handling this thing? I want to be around when they raise the fuselage. The crane operator's kinda new. Be hell to pay if he drops the damn thing."

I looked toward the wreckage, where a motorized crane was moving into position near the fuselage. Once the fuselage was out of the way, the cockpit would be accessible and we could finally recover Rick French and Judd Wilson.

"I'd better run too," Rita said as Ogden hustled off. "General Stinson wanted me at Andrews ASAP." She gave

me a reassuring smile. "Don't take the press conference too hard, John."

"I won't," I lied.

As she hurried away, Ted said quietly, "I'll be able to tell if Mrs. Gibson's got anything to worry about, John."

"Fine," I said, and we walked over to the two women.

Jennifer calmly watched Ted and me approach. "Colonel Ogden filled you in, John? " she asked.

I nodded, tight-lipped. I was having a hard time keeping my anger in check.

After Jennifer made the introductions, Mrs. Gibson gave me a tentative smile. She was in her mid-fifties, sharply featured, with stylishly cut gray hair that fell just below her ears. Her jacket was leather and looked expensive. Her slacks appeared to be silk, and she wore a diamond on her finger the size of a marble. But it was her eyes I really noticed, big and round, filled with worry.

"My daughter was here, Colonel," Mrs. Gibson said. She spoke softly, with a northeast accent, more New England than New York.

I said, "Mrs. Gibson, are you certain your daughter couldn't be out with some friends? Maybe someone called at the last minute, picked her up."

Mrs. Gibson responded with an emphatic head shake. "No. She has no friends nearby. We just purchased the farm last year. Allison usually stays in town, in her apartment by the school. She came to keep me company while my husband is away. If Allison had gone out for the evening, she would have left a note. She's . . . she's good about that." Her mouth trembled slightly. "Allison is our only child. She knows I worry."

Ted stepped forward. "Where is your husband, ma'am?"

"At a medical conference in Denver. He's a cardiologist. I . . . I need to call him . . ."

Ted nodded sympathetically. "What about your daughter's purse, ma'am? Did you notice if she took it with her?"

She seemed surprised by the question. "It's still on the kitchen table."

"When she goes out for the evening, I assume she takes the purse with her."

A nod. "Always."

"Was the house locked when you came home?"

She thought. "Unlocked. I didn't use my key."

"And your daughter's keys?"

"They were lying by her purse. On . . . on the kitchen table."

Ted smiled. "Thank you." He stepped back. I tried to read what he was thinking, but his face was blank.

I said gently, "Mrs. Gibson, none of my men remember seeing her. I'm afraid there's nothing we can—"

"She was here, Colonel," she said, her voice cracking slightly. "I know it. Allison—" She broke off, looking lost. "She . . . she couldn't be anywhere else."

Jennifer gave Mrs. Gibson a reassuring pat on her shoulder.

"Mrs. Gibson, do you have a picture of your daughter?" Ted asked.

"In my purse. In the car. . . ." She gestured vaguely toward the road.

Ted said to me, "I can scrounge up a Humvee, run the picture over to the cops at the checkpoint?"

"Okay."

"I'd like to go," Mrs. Gibson said, looking to Jennifer. "Please."

Ted hesitated.

"Of course," Jennifer replied.

For an instant, Ted's eyes flashed in irritation. He shrugged. "Sure. Why not? We can take your car, Mrs. Gibson. Be quicker."

Mrs. Gibson took Jennifer's hand. "Thank you for your concern. I must sound like a silly old woman."

"Your daughter will turn up," Jennifer said softly.

As Ted led Mrs. Gibson away, a cool breeze brushed my face. Rita and her techs passed by a few yards away, carrying their equipment. Rita waved, and I waved back, while Jennifer watched us in silence.

I grew increasingly irritated with the way she stood there, so cold and aloof. The stunt she had pulled at the briefing still gnawed at me. I hadn't deserved that. Rita was right. I should say something, have it out with her. I reached out to tap her on the shoulder—

"He's awfully good," Jennifer said quietly.

I dropped my hand.

Jennifer faced me, surprising me with a hint of a smile. She looked tired and drawn, but still lovely. "Ted asked those questions like a pro."

"He was a cop," I said. "A Honolulu hormicide detective. 'Book 'em, Danno' and all that."

"Really? He doesn't look like a cop."

I resisted the urge to ask her what a cop does look like. "He was a good one. But Ted's good at everything he does." I hesitated, gazing at her. "He can be a little difficult

at times, but if you work with him, you'll find out he really knows what he's doing."

Jennifer smiled again, a nice smile. "I'm starting to see that."

"Who knows? Maybe you'd even like him, if you gave him a chance."

"I suppose . . ." She turned away, leaving me still off balance wondering about her sudden change in attitude.

I watched her profile, the light framing the lines of a face I knew so intimately. She began chewing on her lower lip.

"You know," I said. "I'm not bad either, when you give me a chance."

She stiffened visibly, and I knew I'd made a mistake. I wasn't even sure why I'd said it. The words just came out, and I suddenly felt embarrassed. I wondered if I should just walk away.

Instead I stayed, watching the way the wind caught her hair, whipping it over her face. She didn't move.

A minute went by before she turned to me. "I'm sorry, John," she whispered.

I could feel my heart pounding.

She brushed hair from her eyes. "I shouldn't have done it. But . . ." Her voice drifted off.

"Why, then?"

"I . . . can't. I don't want to talk about it."

"I deserve an explanation. You humiliated me."

"Please. I said I'm sorry. Let's leave it at that." She sounded sincere, and I could see regret in her eyes.

I was tempted to press the point, but knew it wouldn't get me anywhere. And she had apologized, which was something that didn't come easy to her. "Okay. No questions." I gave her a little smile.

We gazed silently toward the road where Ted was helping Mrs. Gibson into a white Cadillac.

As they drove away, Jennifer asked, "You think the girl came here, John?"

"No. Even with all the commotion, someone would have noticed her. Mrs. Gibson is overreacting. Her daughter's only been gone a few hours."

A pause. "She's just being a mother."

When I didn't reply, she said, "You don't know what it's like having a child, do you, John?"

The question startled me. "Uh, no."

"Too bad," she said quietly. "Maybe then you'd understand." She walked away.

I watched her, shaking my head in amazement. She couldn't have been more obvious if she'd come right out and said it. No wonder Jennifer seemed to bond with Mrs. Gibson, share her concerns and anxiety.

Jennifer had a kid of her own.

I don't know why I was surprised. She'd been considering having children when we split. At the time, I thought she was just trying to entice me to stick around with all the talk about starting a family. She must have gotten remarried, had a child. But she wore no ring. Divorced? If she was a mother, why didn't she just say so?

I heard the sudden roar of a diesel engine and looked to the wreckage. The crane's long metal arm was rising slowly above the fuselage, pulling the cables taut. Dozens of people were circled around, watching. The crane's engine groaned in protest, smoke pouring from the exhaust.

A moment later, the fuselage slowly staggered into the air.

It was time to recover the bodies.

"Hold it, Danny! Hold it!" the ruddy-faced sergeant by the truck shouted to the young airman in the cab of the crane. The crane's arm pivoted another foot and jerked to a stop, causing the fuselage to sway precariously on steel cables ten feet above a flatbed truck. The sergeant glowered at the airman, then peered intently at the distance between the bottom of the fuselage and the truck bed. He motioned downward.

"Okay, slow! Easy!"

The crane's engine whined sharply, and the fuselage rapidly dropped three feet.

"Goddammit, Dan! I said slow!" the sergeant roared. "Get your head out of your ass!"

The descent stopped. The man in the cab appeared flustered. A moment later, the fuselage began inching downward.

"Better. Fine. To the right— Easy!" The sergeant jabbed a thumb. The crane's arm swung a few inches.

"Perfect!" The sergeant crossed his fists. He began motioning downward again as the fuselage descended. A moment later, the torn cockpit of the Lear touched down gently on the truck bed.

The sergeant glanced up at the cab and grinned. The airman beamed.

"Now I know why you were worried," I said, giving Ogden a sideways glance.

Ogden smiled. "The kid makes it exciting."

"Did Ted mention we'd like to inspect those emergency depressurization valves?"

"Yeah. We'll remove them at the hangar. May take a while, since we'll have to jack up the fuselage to get into the hellhole panel to pull 'em."

We were standing maybe ten yards from the truck, watching with twenty other maintenance troops and another dozen Marines. The loading operation had taken almost fifteen minutes, which was fine with me. I'd been dreading the next step.

"Ready, John?" Ogden asked me.

I nodded. "Someone getting Doc Bently?"

Ogden rolled his eyes. He didn't like Bently any more than I did. Spotting a female airman, he sent her after Bently, then we slowly walked over to what was left of the cockpit.

Even though I'd investigated more than a dozen aircraft crashes, I still wasn't used to the carnage. Some years earlier, when I was a student at the Air Force Mishap Investigation Course, a seasoned instructor told me the job is easier when you think of the victims not as people but as evidence to be processed and collected. It was good advice, but damned hard to follow, especially when the unrecognizable remains you're looking at were once a friend.

The Learjet's cockpit, once large enough to seat two

men, was essentially flattened, all mangled metal and wires and no more than a few feet thick. The top of the crushed cockpit was visible just above a shallow trench that was roughly the width of the plane and maybe four feet long, the approximate length of the cockpit.

Four grim-faced maintenance men wearing surgical masks were crouched beside the trench, inspecting the wreckage with flashlights. A captain stood over them, a clipboard in his hands, ready to record each item as it was removed. Next to him stood a staff sergeant with a camera.

One of the maintenance men, a thin, black sergeant, reached over with a gloved hand and removed a small object. His back was to us, and we couldn't see what he'd found. The captain made a notation on the clipboard. The staff sergeant aimed his camera and the flash went off.

"What's that, Sergeant Fuller?" Ogden asked.

Fuller turned and held out his hand.

"Jesus," Ogden murmured.

I blinked rapidly, my stomach tightening.

The sergeant's gloved hand held part of a finger. Light reflected off a gold wedding band still attached.

"Okay, Fuller," Ogden said.

Sergeant Fuller carefully placed the finger in a large vinyl bag.

I took a couple of deep breaths.

"You okay, John?"

I nodded. "Have them hold the ring for me, Nate."

Ogden gave me a questioning look.

"That's Rick's. I'd like to give it to his wife."

"Sure, John," Ogden said softly.

A moment later, I asked, "When will you be able to remove the flight-data and voice recorders?"

"Hard to say," Ogden replied. "We're going to have to go slow. Maybe by morning. I'll call Chad Owen and give

him a heads-up. Tell him we want a rush job. No more than forty-eight hours."

"Thanks, Nate."

Chad Owen ran the NTSB's Office of Research and Engineering, which analyzed all black-box data for military and civilian accidents. Chad was a retired Air Force pilot and an acquaintance of Ogden's.

I watched for another five minutes. The men pulled off various pieces of twisted metal, occasionally removing a few more grisly remains. As they worked their way down, the body parts they found were a little larger than the finger, but not much. Rick and Judd had essentially been melded into the metal, their bodies literally exploding from the force of the fuselage that had rolled over them.

"So what do we got?" a voice called.

We turned.

Bently's face was flushed with excitement. He nodded to Ogden. "Hi ya, sir." He winked at me. "You in a better mood, John?"

I gave him a curt nod. "I'm fine, Chip."

"Good, good." Bently hurried past us to the trench, blinking furiously through his thick glasses. "Hoo boy, I'd say death was definitely instantaneous." He produced a flashlight and knelt down, splaying the beam around. "Christ, it'll take a week to sort out who's who, not that it matters, I suppose. Hope the family doesn't plan on having a burial soon. Hell, at least they won't have to fork out a lot of dough for a big coffin. We might get lucky if their boots survived, make IDs off the toe prints . . ."

"Bently talks too goddamn much," Ogden said under his breath.

I turned away in disgust, not trusting myself to respond.

Jennifer and Ted stood together maybe thirty feet away. They were talking to Master Sergeant Matthews, the guy in charge of the photographers.

Ted and Jennifer together? Maybe she was giving him a chance after all. Ted looked my way and motioned for me to join them. His face told me he was onto something important.

"Excuse me, Nate," I said.

Sergeant Matthews was leaving as I walked up.

Ted took one look at me and his face became grim. "That bad?"

"That bad," I said. Jennifer gave me a halfhearted smile.

"So what's up?" I asked Ted.

Ted hesitated. "Frankly, I'm not sure, John. One of the Marines found something in the field that seems to back up what Mrs. Gibson said about her daughter coming here."

I sighed. "Ted, we haven't got time to waste—"

"Hear him out, John," Jennifer said.

I studied her. "Okay."

Ted said, "Corporal Branson was in charge of the detail searching for parts from the plane. Anyway, he approached Jennifer and me after Mrs. Gibson and I returned from talking to the cops—"

"How'd that go?" I asked. "Anyone remember the daughter?"

"Dead end," Ted said. "They were certain she wasn't around."

"That settles it," I said.

"Not quite, John," Ted said. "Branson gave me something interesting that one of his men found. At first I thought Matthews or one of his men dropped it. But Jennifer reminded me what Mrs. Gibson said about her daughter having a camera." He looked to Jennifer. "So we asked Matthews. He says it's not one of his."

I was getting impatient. "Just tell me what Branson gave you, Ted."

Ted reached into his jacket and drew out a small plastic cylinder. "A roll of film," he said.

"So what?"

"It's a diffierent brand of film from what Matthews and his men are using," Ted said.

I was trying to make the connection. "So what if it's different—"

"No one else has been taking pictures here," Ted said. "Not the press, not any of us except Matthews and his crew." He paused, giving me a meaningful look. "No one."

"It had to have been the daughter," Jennifer said.

I considered the possibility. "Ted, you honestly believe the girl was here?"

Ted nodded. "I don't think there's much doubt, considering what Mrs. Gibson told us. The girl wouldn't leave her purse and keys if she had gone somewhere for the evening. She almost certainly wouldn't have left the house unlocked. That tells me she went somewhere in a hurry. We know she didn't drive anywhere, so that means she walked. Throw in the missing camera . . ."

"But the cops never saw her," I said.

"She could have left before they arrived," Jennifer said.

I ran a hand over my face. This was the last thing I needed. "The cops showed about twenty minutes after the

crash. Why would the girl leave so quickly? You'd think she'd hang around, snap up photos of the emergency crews responding, get pictures of the recovery." I shook my head. "It doesn't make sense."

"There's something else, John," Ted said quietly. He held out the film cannister. "The ASA. It's a thousand."

I didn't know anything about photography. "Okay . . ."

"It's made for taking pictures in low illumination," Ted said.

"Like on nights with a full moon," Jennifer added.

I slowly eased out a breath. "Where did the Marine find it?"

Ted led us to a point roughly fifty yards past the marker where Thurston's body had been recovered. We were beyond the spotlights, but we could easily make out each other's faces in the moonlight.

We carefully scanned the ground with flashlights. The grass spread out before us like a mottled green carpet.

"Sergeant Branson sent the Marine back out to mark the location," Ted said. "Anybody see a marker?"

"Here," Jennifer said. Her light was trained on a small white flag that fluttered gently in the slight breeze.

Ted and I joined her.

"The grass has been walked on some," Ted observed.

"Must have been the Marines," Jennifer said.

Ted leaned down, eyes focused on the ground. He straightened, making a slow circle with his flashlight. The beam stopped, highlighting an area a few yards away. "The grass is really trampled down over there." He walked over and crouched down, then picked up a few handfuls of grass. He studied them carefully before tossing them aside, moved over a few feet, and squatted again. He looked up and motioned to me.

"Shine your light here." Ted pointed with his flashlight.

What I saw was a rough, firmly packed circular outline in the grass maybe three or four feet wide. Here and there were clumps of uprooted grass. I still had no idea why Ted was so interested in that particular spot.

He pocketed his flashlight, leaned close to the ground, and intently studied the grass, one small section at a time. He occasionally paused to push the grass aside to reveal the dirt. I followed him with my light.

"What's he doing?" Jennifer whispered in my ear.

"Don't know," I said.

Ted suddenly paused, then reached down and picked something up.

"What is it?" Jennifer asked.

Ted held out his hand. I trained my flashlight on the object, which gleamed back.

Jennifer give a little gasp while I stared, stunned.

In Ted's palm was a woman's silver barrette. "This girl's in trouble," he said.

"Why?" Jennifer asked, her voice sounding loud in the quiet. "Why is she in trouble?"

But Ted didn't reply. He just kept turning the barrette, studying it.

"Ted . . ." Jennifer said.

Finally Ted's eyes flickered and he gestured toward the circular pattern in the grass. "A hunch more than anything. But some of the marks suggest there was a struggle here. Notice the way the grass is torn in places—"

"Wait a sec, Ted," I said. "You can tell there was a struggle here just from that?"

"Not conclusively. But if you look carefully, you can see clumps that were twisted free from the ground. That's significant. That couldn't happen if someone—say, one of the Marines—had just walked over it a few times. The twisting is consistent with someone who is shifting his feet with force, as if trying to gain leverage. Look . . ."

Ted produced his flashlight and pointed the beam on the ground. He made a hard, twisting motion with his foot. When he stepped aside, his light revealed a clump of uprooted grass.

"Okay," I said. Jennifer's worried look indicated she thought Ted was making sense too.

"I also think it's particularly suggestive that we found two objects dropped by the girl. The film and this." He held up the barrette. "One she maybe drops accidentally. But both in nearly the same location, no way. Not accidentally. Something happened here."

"You think she was fighting with someone," Jennifer said, stating the obvious.

Ted didn't reply. He was staring intently across the field toward the tree line.

Jennifer reached for his arm. I gave her a head shake and she frowned, but withdrew her hand.

After a few moments, Ted began talking in a soft monotone. "She would have come from her parents' farm through those trees. With the full moon she would have been able to see the crash site clearly. She hurried toward the downed plane, maybe stopping to take pictures. She reached this spot and there was a struggle. . . ." He kicked at the grass, shaking his head.

I said, "This girl was big and an athlete. She would have been hard for one man to control—"

"That's pretty evident, John. From the way the grass is torn up, I don't think there's much question that there was more than one man. I also think the girl must have put up a struggle."

Jennifer shivered at the image. "She must have been terrified."

"The question is, who were they?" Ted said.

"And why didn't anyone see them?" I added.

"It must have happened during those twenty minutes," Ted said.

Jennifer said, "Twenty minutes?"

"The time between the crash and when the cops arrived," I told her. "That would explain why there are no witnesses."

Jennifer looked stricken. To Ted she said, "You don't know any of this for certain?"

Ted hesitated. "No."

"She could be all right, couldn't she?"

"It's . . . possible."

Jennifer gazed at him. "I hope you're wrong," she said softly.

I reached into my pocket and removed my cell phone.

"Who are you calling?" Jennifer asked.

**T**en minutes later, we returned to the site where we'd found the barrette, accompanied by Sergeant Jimmy Ray Nesbitt of the Fauquier County Sheriff's Department. Jimmy Ray was fortyish, short, jowly, with a belly that hung a full two inches over his belt. He spoke with one of those exasperating slow drawls that made you want to finish his sentences. As we walked, Ted gave Jimmy Ray the film cannister and barrette, explaining their implications.

Jimmy Ray obviously wasn't buying Ted's suppositions. It was also obvious that Ted was getting frustrated.

"So, lemme get this straight," Jimmy Ray said, adjusting the brim of his hat. "Y'all figure this girl was hanging out at this spot and someone jumped her, maybe made off with her?"

"Something like that," Ted said irritably.

Jimmy Ray looked around. "Well, I dunno, Colonel.

That don't seem to make no sense. We don't even know if that silver doohickey is hers."

"No," Ted said. "That's why you need to check with Mrs. Gibson. Immediately."

"And we will, yes, sir. But even if it is the girl's, that don't prove nuthin' bad happened. Kids that age are apt to take off now and then. Happens all the time."

Ted's eyes turned into slits. "So you're not going to do anything?" His voice was barely above a whisper.

"Now, Colonel," Jimmy Ray drawled, casually scratching his ear. "I'm not saying I'm not believin' you. It's just a mite early. But we'll look into it, I promise. In the morning most likely. We're kinda short tonight on account of the crash and all."

Ted's jaw muscles tightened. His fists clenched and unclenched. I recognized the signs and hurried forward—

"Goddammit, Sergeant!" Ted exploded. "This girl is in trouble. Something happened here. Now, if you don't get off your fat ass—"

"Ted!"

But Ted paid me no attention. He was seething, his face inches from Jimmy Ray's. "If you don't check this thing out now, you better hope the girl turns up unhurt, or I—"

"Dammit, Ted!" I grabbed at his arm.

He shrugged me off. "I'll personally kick your ass!" He poked Jimmy Ray in the gut. "You got me!"

"Shut the hell up, Ted!" This time I grabbed his arm and hung on.

Ted spun toward me, blinking in sudden recognition. He slowly relaxed.

Jimmy Ray's mouth hung open in shock.

I let go of Ted's arm. "Damn you, Ted—"

Ted abruptly stalked away.

Jimmy Ray swallowed repeatedly, looking more rattled

than angry. "Now, there was no call for that. No call at all. I'm just doin' my job."

I said, "I'm sure you are, Sergeant—"

"Mind if I handle this, John?" When I looked back, Jennifer was smiling at Jimmy Ray.

I drew Ted aside as Jennifer went about soothing Jimmy Ray's ruffled feathers. She stood close to him now, her hand on his arm, her face attentive and sympathetic.

"You were way out of line, Ted," I said. "I'm in enough hot water. What the hell got into you—"

I stopped. Ted was grinning cheerfully at me. I couldn't believe it.

"You think this is funny?" I snapped.

"Ease up, John," Ted said. "I was just trying to make a point."

*"What?"*

"Guess I must have been pretty good. Convinced you." He looked pleased with himself.

I stared at him in astonishment. "You mean that was an act?"

Ted chuckled. "Sure. I wanted to light a fire under Sheriff Bubba. Get him to take this seriously."

I sighed, shaking my head. Sometimes Ted could be so exasperating. "For chrissakes, Ted. If that guy files a complaint—"

"Relax, John. There's not going to be a complaint." Ted nodded toward Jennifer and Jimmy Ray.

A moment later I understood. Jimmy Ray and Jennifer were laughing now. Jimmy Ray's hat was off, and he was running a hand over his dark hair. He also appeared to be sucking in his gut.

"She's good," Ted said.

I nodded.

"Now the question is how do we get the film back," Ted said. "I never should have turned it over."

I glared at him. I was still annoyed. "Forget it."

Ted gazed at me evenly. "That film could be important, John."

"It's not our job, Ted. We're crash investigators." I braced myself, expecting him to argue the point.

A shrug. "Whatever you say, John."

"That's it?"

"That's what?" He gave me a blank look.

"Nothing." I checked my watch. "It's almost eleven. You need to hang around for anything else?"

"Can't think of anything."

"I'll arrange for a helicopter and let Nate know we're leaving. Tell Jennifer."

"Sure, John. And I'll even apologize to Jimmy Ray."

I was immediately wary. "Be nice to him, Ted."

Ted smiled. "You know me, John."

I'd gone maybe thirty paces when my phone rang. "Colonel Quinn—"

"What the hell is going on with the investigation, John!" an incensed voice demanded. "By God, I ought to fire you right now."

I stopped, my mouth suddenly dry. "General Cramer, if you let me explain—"

But Cramer started up again, shouting in my ear. "CNN is running your press conference every thirty minutes! You hear me? Every thirty goddamn minutes you're on the screen practically telling the world the Air Force is covering this thing up! I just got off the phone with General Ware. He wants your ass. Jesus!"

The phone hissed. In the background, I heard rapid-fire breathing. Cramer seemed on the verge of a coronary.

I was getting angry, but fought to remain composed. "Sir, the press conference was nothing but—"

Cramer abruptly came back on. "John, I gotta tell you, I'm disappointed. You let me down. You let the Air Force down. You embarrassed us—"

That did it. "Goddammit, sir, I was set up! Someone leaked Ware's order to me to Walling! Someone from the White House! Walling was there to make me look bad. The whole thing was a damn charade—" I stopped, my pulse racing. I was gripping the phone so hard, I thought I might break it.

A long silence. Then: "You through, John?"

"Yes."

"Want to tell me about it?"

When I finished, Cramer asked, "General Ware actually ordered you to concentrate on the pilots?"

"Absolutely, sir. Ted was there."

"And you think McKenzie leaked that to Walling?"

I chose my words carefully. "I think it's highly likely. If not McKenzie, then someone on his staff."

"Why?"

"I don't know, sir. I don't think it's to discredit me personally. That wouldn't make sense."

"No." Another pause. "But what if someone wanted to discredit the investigation? The Air Force? Make us look bad."

"Why, sir?"

"Hell, I don't know, John. But I'm certain of one thing. That investigator from the NTSB made you look foolish for a reason. I tried to get her removed, you know. But she's apparently a fucking untouchable. I told General Ware I wanted Dr. Johnson out. Ware told me to forget it. He said McKenzie had personally requested her."

No surprise there.

"John, General Stinson said Dr. Johnson is your ex-wife.

Is that true?" This time there was an edge in Cramer's voice.

*Christ.* "Yes, sir."

Cramer swore. "Then her reaction. Could that be personal?"

I thought. "It's possible, but I don't think so."

"This is straight? No bullshit?"

"Yes, sir." I waited to be relieved, knowing Cramer couldn't risk having me continue.

I couldn't believe it when he said, "Fine. For now, you're still running the investigation. I'll run interference, keep people off your back as long as I can. But I have to tell you, that press conference hurt, John. Dr. Johnson pulls something like that again, we're not going to be able to stand the heat. You understand what I'm saying?"

"Yes, sir. What about General Ware? If he's insisting I be removed—"

"Screw him," Cramer said. "As the chairman, he isn't technically in the Air Force chain of command. I'll talk to General Railing. He'll probably go along just to yank Ware's chain."

General Railing's animosity toward General Ware was legendary. As the Air Force chief of staff, General Railing had been one of the front-runners to become chairman of the Joint Chiefs when Ware had been selected.

"I appreciate this, sir."

"Forget it." Cramer's voice softened. "Besides, how would it look if the Air Force fired one of our war heroes? Just be careful, John. You only get one fuckup."

The phone went dead, and I stared at it, knowing I'd been lucky. But I wasn't naive. If I didn't finish this thing soon, I would be gone. Cramer's and Railing's stars would mean little if the big boys at the White House began pushing.

I felt exhausted, not physically so much as emotionally. I had the sense of being overwhelmed by forces I didn't

understand. As I slipped the phone into my jacket, I wondered who would gain if I or the Air Force was discredited. One name came to mind.

I looked back to Jennifer.

I found Ogden sitting in the driver's seat of his Jeep Cherokee, door open, speaking into a cell phone. He gave me a wave and continued talking. I waited a few paces away.

Ogden mentioned the name Chad a few times, so I figured he must be talking to Chad Owen, his NTSB buddy. Ogden climbed from the Jeep, his face apologetic, and held out the phone to me. "Chad Owen wants to talk to you, John. And it's not about processing the cockpit or voice recorders."

"Oh?"

"About Jennifer," he said in a tone that told me the news wasn't good.

I didn't know Chad well, but on the few occasions we'd met, he'd struck me as low-key and professional, certainly not the type who would disparage someone without a good reason.

We spoke for less than five minutes. Actually, Chad talked, I listened. He started off by telling me that Ogden had mentioned Jennifer was my ex-wife and he hoped I wasn't going to be offended. But he'd seen the press conference on the news and figured he'd better tell me what he knew.

According to Chad, Jennifer's appointment to the deputy directorship of the NTSB had caused considerable resentment. The problem wasn't that she'd come from outside the agency; the position often went to political appointees. What bothered people was her complete lack of experience in aircraft accident investigations—she'd been a professor at the University of Virginia at the time of her selection. To bring herself up to speed, Jennifer had

worked a few accidents, mostly those involving small civil aircraft. True, she was a quick study and had picked up the rudiments of running an investigation. But an accident of this magnitude was out of her league. Chad thought her involvement in this investigation bordered on the criminal.

I asked him if he knew how Jennifer received her appointment to the NTSB.

"Actually, I'm not certain about that, John. I'd only be speculating."

"Speculate away."

A pause. "Well, a few years back she was a White House fellow—"

"She was?"

"You didn't know?"

"No."

"Well, anyway, there's a rumor she's connected to someone very high up in the White House."

"Who?"

"Don't know. All I can tell you for sure is she gets invited for a number of functions."

That was good enough for me. "Thanks, Chad."

Once the Command Post confirmed the chopper was en route, I went to round up Jennifer and Ted. After maybe a hundred yards, I heard someone call my name. Then I spotted two military policemen angling toward me, escorting a tall, slender woman wearing dark slacks and a turtlenecked sweater. For an instant, I thought they had found the Gibson girl.

But as the group walked into the light, I could see the woman was black. She was also one of the most beautiful women I'd ever seen.

"Hey, Colonel Quinn! Sir!" One of the cops waved.

*Now what?* I thought.

The military cop on the left, a staff sergeant's emblem on his blue beret, came forward while the second cop and the woman hung back about ten paces. The woman looked at me, her face completely calm, as if she didn't have a care in the world.

"Know who she is, Sergeant Green?" I asked, reading his name tag.

"Miss Kendra Banks, sir. We spotted her inside the perimeter." Green handed me a pocketbook.

"You check out her IDs?"

A head shake. "She started to raise a fuss, and we thought maybe it would be better, you know, to have you handle it, sir."

"You don't have a right to look through that, Colonel," Miss Banks called out. "Or haven't you heard of illegal search and seizure? Now, if you ask nicely . . ." She sounded amused.

I looked to her, making no move to open the pocketbook. "She a reporter?" I asked Sergeant Green under my breath.

"I'm not sure, sir. She has a press pass, but . . ." He paused, then with a note of caution, added, "She said she works for the Richter Institute."

I understood his concern. The Richter Institute was one of the most well-known and respected public watchdog organizations in the country. Richter specialized in ferreting out examples of government abuse and corruption and giving the details to newspapers. They'd generated a lot of headlines over the years and possessed an enormous amount of political clout. Maybe not as much as Ralph Nader or Common Cause, but they weren't far behind. If Miss Banks worked for Richter, I had to be careful. After pissing off most of the press corps, the last thing I needed was to get on their hit list.

"Guess we'd better find out her story, Sergeant," I said.

"Relax, Colonel," Miss Kendra Banks said to me. "I wasn't trying to sneak in to take any pictures or compromise your investigation. You can ask your men. I'm not even carrying a camera." She indicated the handbag slung over her shoulder, the amused smile still on her face.

"It's true," Sergeant Green said. The other cop, a young kid, bobbed his agreement.

As I studied Kendra Banks, I was thinking she could easily be a fashion model. She had it all—the large, expressive eyes, high cheekbones, flawless skin. Sure, I was being a little sexist, but she didn't fit my image of people who were drawn to work for dogood outfits like Richter. It's kinda like running into someone who looks like Julia Roberts and being told she's an accountant.

"May I?" I said, holding out the pocketbook.

"Be my guest. I've got nothing to hide." She gave me a

sympathetic look. "The press conference was a little rough, huh, Colonel?"

I tried to think of a witty response but came up blank. I produced a flashlight and ran it over her IDs.

Richter's was just below her driver's license. I caught her age. Thirty-seven, but she looked younger.

Handing back her pocketbook, I said, "You want to explain why you broke into a restricted zone, Miss Banks?"

She shrugged. "Your guards wouldn't let me through, and I wanted to talk to you, Colonel."

"Oh? About what?"

"That," she said, "is confidential." She looked to the cops.

I hesitated. "Take a break, guys. Stay close."

The cops drifted about twenty yards away.

I folded my arms. "Well, Miss Banks . . ."

"Call me Kendra, Colonel."

I gazed at her evenly. "What is it you want to talk to me about . . . Miss Banks?"

"I think I might be able to provide some information about your investigation."

"Such as . . ."

"Such as why the plane crashed."

I did a double take that came close to snapping my neck.

She grinned. "Yeah. I thought that would grab your interest."

"What is it you know?"

"Now, now. Not so fast, Colonel. First, I need your assurance you will keep everything in the strictest confidence."

Staring into her beautiful eyes, I felt a wave of annoyance. Who the hell did she think she was, making a demand? "I don't make deals. Now, if you have information, you're obligated to—"

"Colonel," she interrupted, "I don't *have* to do anything.

You have no idea what you're dealing with, and I do. You want my cooperation, we work out an arrangement under my terms."

"I can have you taken in for questioning."

"Don't be silly, Colonel. I'll just deny we had this conversation. Besides, you're in enough trouble. You try to haul me in and I'll have you tagged with a lawsuit so fast it'll make your head spin."

Odds were she was just blowing smoke, but somehow I didn't think so. She was projecting a confidence bordering on cockiness.

I said, "Miss Banks, may I remind you that this is an official investigation. I am not authorized to make any arrangements until I confer with my superiors—"

"No. No conferring with anyone. I'm taking a risk coming here as it is."

I squinted at her. "Risk? What risk?"

"Do we have an agreement?"

"Of course not. I can't— What's this for?"

Kendra Banks abruptly extended a card to me, her face locked in a flat smile. "Call me when you change your mind, Colonel."

I hesitated, then took the card.

"You need me, Colonel," she said softly. "You just don't know it yet."

I thought to hell with it. I should take her in and put up with the grief. Then I read the card.

"You're an attorney?" I asked.

The smile turned cool. "I run Richter's legal department."

"I see."

She let the revelation soak in for a moment, then asked, "May I leave, Colonel?"

I looked away. Off in the distance, I saw Ted's compact frame coming toward us.

"Colonel?"

We both knew I had no choice. I nodded, motioning to the two cops. "You can go."

As she was escorted away, she shot me a tight smile that seemed more like a smirk. I turned my attention to Ted, noticing he kept glancing at Kendra Banks as he came over.

"What's Kendra Banks doing here, John?" he asked.

"You know her?"

A curt nod. "What did she want?"

After I told him, Ted went quiet. Finally, he said, "You might want to reconsider calling her, John."

"Why?"

Ted slowly mouthed the words: "Kendra Banks . . . Ken Banks . . ."

I stared back dumbly. "You're certain?"

"Positive."

"Jesus."

Now I knew why Ted was interested in Kendra Banks.

Fifteen years earlier, her father, the Honorable Kenneth Banks, had been the first black governor of Virginia and a rising political star. Many thought he would someday be a serious contender for the presidency or at least someone's top pick for the veep slot.

And maybe he would have, except one night he came home, made himself a drink, and sat down in his favorite chair. When he'd finished the drink, he put a pistol in his mouth and pulled the trigger on his life and his political career.

was twenty-four at the time, and my world was flying and little else until I met Jennifer. I wasn't much of a news hound, but the story was big and I still remembered most of it. Governor Ken Banks was up for reelection and considered a shoo-in. Shortly before the election, a white girl on his campaign staff went on TV and announced she was having an affair with him. That the girl had no evidence to back up her story didn't seem to matter. Virginia was still the South, and the possibility the story could be true was enough. Banks lost the election in a landslide. His career never recovered. A couple years later he blew his brains out. The connection that made this particularly interesting was the identity of the man who won the election.

Everybody's favorite president, Halloran.

"So tell me," I said, focusing on Ted. "How'd you recognize her?"

Ted shrugged. "When the scandal broke, Kendra Banks

was in the papers and on the evening news a number of times. A woman who looks like her, you don't forget."

"What happened to her father doesn't mean she knows anything about the crash."

He gave me a long look. "Then again, she might."

A good point. "We might be able to still catch her if we—"

"Uh-uh. Not here. Too many press around. Someone might wonder why we're so interested in Governor Banks's daughter. Better to call her and arrange a meeting."

I eyed him. "We should probably clear it with General Cramer."

Ted snorted. "Cramer's a worthless prick."

I sighed. Ted's animosity toward Cramer stemmed from the accident investigation involving General Mathison's son. Cramer had pushed Ted hard to get him to back off. "We should still let him know."

"After, okay, John? Let's see if Kendra Banks has anything useful first."

Not exactly the letter of the regs, but I didn't feel like arguing. For obvious reasons, having Kendra come to Andrews for a meeting was out. "My place tomorrow morning?"

"Fine. And when you talk to her, don't mention we know who she is."

"Why?"

A shrug. "I'm curious to see if she brings it up."

I still wasn't sure I understood. Kendra Banks's card had a cell-phone number. I waited a few minutes to ensure the two cops had finished depositing her outside the secured area. She answered on the second ring.

"What took you so long, Colonel?" she said. She still sounded amused.

The Blackhawk helicopter touched down gently on the brightly lit landing pad behind the base operations building at Andrews Air Force Base. Moments later, the engines died and the blades began winding to a stop. The young sergeant hopped from his jumpseat and popped the latch on the cargo door, sliding it open. He was the same man we'd flown with earlier. He flashed a toothy grin. "Good night, sir."

I smiled at him as I unstrapped. "Thanks for the lift, Sergeant."

Jennifer crawled out, and Ted and I followed. As usual, Ted looked like he was going to be sick.

"Have you tried airsickness medication?" Jennifer asked him. "Maybe some Dramamine?"

"Just makes it worse," Ted said. He had both hands over his stomach and looked positively gray. "Christ—" He bent over and began running across the concrete ramp toward base operations.

Jennifer looked at me, concerned. "You think we should see if he needs any help?"

"Help is the last thing he wants."

Ted was running surprisingly fast. He reached the fence, shot through the opening, and raced up the walkway. As Jennifer and I began walking across the concrete, Ted disappeared into the building.

"You've been awfully quiet," Jennifer said. "You've barely said two words since we left."

I was surprised she'd noticed. "I'm just tired."

"I'm worried, John."

I knew she was referring to the missing girl, so I said, "Did you convince Jimmy Ray to investigate?"

"I think so. He said he was going to call it in as a missing person. He said if she doesn't return by tomorrow, they'll probably assign some detectives."

"You did all you could."

She sighed. "I just hope it's not too late."

"We don't even know if she's really disappeared, Jennifer. Maybe there's some other explanation."

"You believe that?"

I hesitated. "I suppose not."

"Maybe the pictures will tell us something," Jennifer said.

"When is Jimmy Ray going to have them developed?"

Jennifer looked over. "Not Jimmy Ray. Ted."

"*Ted* has the film?"

"You didn't know? Ted had me ask Jimmy Ray for it. Jimmy Ray was reluctant, but I told him there might be some pictures related to the crash. We have to send over some prints to the sheriff's office."

I shook my head. I should have guessed.

We went through the fence and up the red walkway into operations. Passing through the glass doors, we stopped in the main operations room. It was empty except for a petite

black female airman sitting at the ops counter reading a copy of *People* magazine with Cher on the cover. She glanced up. "Colonel, the staff car and driver are waiting outside."

"Thanks." To Jennifer I said, "I'll wait here for Ted. The car will take you to Command Post." I handed her my card. "In case you need to contact me. Let's plan on meeting in hangar six around ten. That's just a block north of here."

Jennifer nodded, slipping the card into her jacket.

I waited, my hand extended to take her card.

"Good night, John," she said quietly.

I awkwardly withdrew my hand. "Good night. Know your way out?"

She shook her head.

I pointed. "Just follow that hallway to the exit. You should see the car."

"Thank you." Her eyes lingered on me for a moment, then she walked away.

I just watched.

"Something I can help you with, sir," the airman called out.

"Uh, no." I went over to the small lounge area and slumped into a chair.

She'd always been enamored by power and those who had it.

In a way, that probably explained why she was attracted to me. As her instructor pilot, I determined whether she would succeed or fail. We got together when it looked like she might not make it. At the time, I think I knew she was probably using me. Not that I cared. A gorgeous woman wanted me, and that was enough.

While in the Air Force, she had a pattern of seeking out jobs working for generals. The association made her stand out from the crowd; she wasn't just another faceless lieu-

tenant or captain. She knew currying their favor would help her get ahead. That's one of the things that got in the way of our marriage. She was always volunteering for additional duties, projects, anything to impress the bosses.

So her attraction to McKenzie didn't surprise me. What I didn't understand was why she and McKenzie seemed clandestine about their relationship. He was single as far as I knew, and apparently so was she. Knowing Jennifer, I would have thought she'd want to be seen parading around on McKenzie's arm.

At least Chad had cleared up a question that had been bothering me. Now I understood Jennifer's confusion over investigation procedures. But her inexperience posed an even more troubling concern: Why in the world would McKenzie have placed someone unqualified in such a politically sensitive investigation? Unless . . . unless what?

A cover-up?

Crazy. If that were the case, the last thing McKenzie would want in charge would be an inexperienced person. To pull off a cover-up, he'd need someone who knew the ropes, knew how to manipulate an investigation.

Besides, Jennifer would never let herself become involved in something illegal. It wasn't in her nature. A little manipulating and ass-kissing to get ahead, sure, but not something like this.

Yet seven years was a long time. People change—

Footsteps.

"Hi, John. Jennifer gone?"

I glanced over and struggled to my feet as Ted approached, wiping his face with a wet paper towel.

"Feel better?" I asked.

"Yeah." He made a face. "That was close. I barely made it to—"

I waved him off. "You can skip the play-by-play."

Ted continued to towel his face as we went down the hallway toward the exit.

I looked right at him. "Jennifer told me."

Ted blinked innocently.

"The film," I said.

"Oh, *that*—"

"Dammit, Ted, you should have told me."

"Would you have agreed?"

We'd reached the door. I faced him. "That's not the point."

"Maybe I'd better explain—"

"Forget it. I already know. You obviously think the girl's disappearance and the crash are connected." Then I pushed through the door into the night.

We walked slowly as Ted explained his theory. While I didn't disagree with him, I still thought it physically impossible for the two events to be connected. For starters, there was no way whoever abducted the girl could know the plane was going to crash on that abandoned farm. Even the pilots had no idea where they were going to come down. Truthfully, I was glad Ted had managed to retrieve the film from Sheriff Jimmy Ray, since it was the only thing we had that might possibly shed some light on what had taken place. But no way I'd give him the satisfaction of hearing me say it. The last thing Ted's ego needed was more stroking.

We came to my car first. I leaned against the driver's door and offered Ted a cigarette. We lit up, and I squinted at him through the smoke. "You know what you're saying sounds crazy."

Ted took a drag, exhaling slowly. "A plane crashes and a girl disappears. That's a helluva coincidence. I don't like coincidences."

"When can you get the film developed?"

"The audiovisual lab is going to be running round-the-

clock to process the crash film. I'll drop the roll off on the way home and have them rush it. They should have us the prints by morning."

"Tell them to keep this quiet," I said. "I don't want word getting out we're running off on some wild-goose chase. I'm in enough trouble."

"Sure, John," Ted said, eyebrows knitted. "Something happen you want to confess to Father Ted about?"

I hesitated, then told him about the calls from General Cramer and Chad Owen.

When I finished, Ted was staring across the flight line. His face was oddly calm. "So McKenzie is romantically linked to Jennifer," he said.

"I think so."

He turned and studied me. "That doesn't bother you?"

"I'm fine."

Ted considered me for a few more moments, like he wasn't sure whether to believe me.

I sighed. "Anything between us ended long ago."

He seemed to smile. "Damn curious that McKenzie would put someone so inexperienced on this case."

I didn't reply. I didn't want to go there again.

Ted picked up on my reluctance and didn't push the issue. His cigarette glowed bright. "I'm getting bad vibes, John."

"I know."

"Reminds me of the crash I worked on last year. The one involving General Mathison's kid . . ."

"I remember."

"The same bullshit is happening now," Ted said. "Sure, I know there's always some politics involved in a crash investigation. 'Course, that's usually after the board findings are released, when the maintenance and pilot generals bicker among each other, trying to deflect blame. First Cramer tried to stick his nose into the thing. Then General

Mathison piled on, trying to get us to wrap up the investigation. The only difference now is the pressure is not as subtle." He let out a harsh laugh. "I get the feeling we're only going through the motions. Someone else has already decided the damn outcome."

"To hang this on Rick and Judd," I said.

Ted nodded. "Which begs the question—what is it they are afraid we'll find?"

We puffed in silence for a few moments.

"You really want to see this thing through, John?"

"More than ever now."

He flicked his cigarette away. "Better ask yourself one question first?"

"What do you mean?"

"Your career. You're the boy colonel on your way to being the boy general. The truth can be expensive. Gotta be sure if you're willing to pay the price."

"I am."

"Don't decide too quick. Think about it." He stared at me, his voice becoming distant. "I never told you General Mathison tried to get me to back off with a bribe. Of course, he wasn't talking money. He said I had a choice. If I continued pushing the case against his kid, he would see my career was finished. But if I played ball, he'd pull strings, make sure I got promoted." Ted paused. "You know, I was tempted. I mean, really tempted. Making colonel is a big deal. You're somebody. And the extra dough would've helped. I still got two kids in college."

"You obviously turned him down," I said.

"Sure, but I'm trying to tell you I almost said yes. Never in a million years did I think I could be bought. But I could. Anybody can. And you know what got me through it? This is going to sound crazy, but it's true."

"What?"

"Being shot. I almost died on the operating table. God-

damn bullet had turned my guts into chopped liver, and the docs couldn't stop the bleeding. It was touch and go for a couple days. That kind of thing centers you, keeps you focused on what's important."

"You always seem to know what's important," I said, stepping on my cigarette.

A faint smile. "Lucky me. Got myself cashiered out of the service, but at least I can look my kids in the eye. Think about what I said, huh?" He gave me a wave and shuffled away.

I climbed into my car and drove home.

It was almost midnight when I pulled into my numbered carport in front of my town house. Climbing from my car, I heard a soft purr. Mrs. Dickey's Siamese cat, Jasper, suddenly appeared at my feet. I picked him up and slung him under an arm. Mrs. Dickey was my next-door neighbor. She was seventy, slightly senile, and frequently forgot to bring Jasper in for the night.

The house was immaculate when I walked inside, which told me my housekeeper, Doris, had been there. Doris and I had a relaxed arrangement: she gave me two mornings a week, but I never knew which ones. Doris was a widow with a couple of young kids and had trouble sticking to a set schedule.

I dropped Jasper on the kitchen floor, went over to the pantry, and poured him a scoop of dried cat food. He nibbled a bit, then followed me into the living room. Like the rest of the house, the living room was furnished function-

ally in early bachelor: a sofa, recliner, and most important of all, a liquor cabinet. A plain oak entertainment center containing my TV and stereo sat in the corner. Jennifer got almost all the furniture in the divorce. I didn't mind; I felt I owed it to her since I was the one who'd filed. Not that she needed my charity, since her family would help her out financially.

Next to Jennifer's long absences from home, money concerns had been the greatest strain on our marriage. With Jennifer's dad a big man at Boeing in Seattle, she'd grown up with money. The problem was after we got married, she continued to spend like she still had it—designer clothes, new cars, the big house we couldn't afford. Early on, we had some blowups over her spending. Eventually, I gave in. I loved her and wanted her to be happy. But the financial pressures were always there, and the more we made, the more she seemed to spend.

After we split, I was looking at thirty thousand dollars of debt, which was my half in the settlement. While I struggled to pay everything off, I'd learned to get by with just the essentials. Now, even though I could afford more, I'd gotten used to the uncluttered lifestyle. Crap-free living I called it.

Jasper hopped on the sofa as I went over to the liquor cabinet and poured out two fingers of Jack Daniel's.

I took a large swallow, relishing the sensation as the liquor burned its way down my throat. I plopped down on the sofa and Jasper nuzzled up close. I petted him and drank, eyeing the blinking light on the answering machine sitting on the end table. Finally, I leaned over and punched the message button.

"John, Mother. Just thought you might like to know Colleen Simpson has moved back into town. You remember Colleen? You went out a few times. She's moved back to Sequim from Seattle. She's working for Century

Twenty-one here in town. She was asking about you. I mentioned you'll be visiting this summer. Here's her number. Give her a call. . . ."

I smiled. Mom was always trying to set me up. I think she still held the fantasy that I was going to give her grandkids. I dated occasionally, but my last serious relationship had ended almost six months before. Sheila was a military dentist who got transferred to Germany. We made all the requisite promises to stay in touch, but I hadn't heard from her in two months.

". . . Oh, big news, John. Weyerhaeuser made an offer on the mill and your father is actually considering selling. I know, I'm shocked, too. But he's not a young man anymore. And lately . . ." She paused. "To tell you the truth, honey, I'm not sure your father's pride will allow him to take the offer. You know him. He'd rather die than see the Weyerhaeuser name over the mill. Maybe if you could talk to him, convince him it's for the best." She gave a soft sigh. "Love you. Call Colleen when you get a minute. She'll be so excited."

As I waited for the next message, a twinge of sadness tugged at me. Never in a million years did I think my father would give up the family lumber mill, which, fifty years ago, had been one of the largest in northwest Washington. But that was before the big lumber companies moved in, making it tough on the independent mills. My dad was one of the few operators who managed to survive.

I guess I shouldn't have been surprised Dad was selling out. After all, he was seventy-two and he'd had some heart problems. Did I think he was going to run it forever?

My younger brother Brad and I always knew Dad wanted one of us to take over. But like many kids, the thought of spending our lives in Sequim, a small dairy town of four thousand, including the cows, was stifling. So we left home at the first opportunity. I got an ROTC schol-

arship to the University of Washington. Brad's an advertising executive in New York and the ultimate yuppie. He's got the summer house in the Hamptons, drives a Porsche, and is engaged to an ex-Revlon model. No way he was going to give that up.

So that left me.

A click. A man's voice: "Colonel Quinn, Hal Mobley from *The Washington Times*—"

"Bye, Hal," I said. I punched delete.

Five seconds later: "Colonel Quinn, Herb Rosser. I work for *Newsweek*—"

I deleted it and the seven other messages from reporters that followed. Funny how popular you become when you make an ass of yourself on TV.

Leaning back against the sofa, I closed my eyes. My mind felt tired, slow.

I tried to keep my mind blank, but the questions kept coming. What did McKenzie hope to achieve by discrediting the investigation? Was he trying to hide something? If so, what? How deeply was Jennifer involved? What about Kendra Banks? Did she know anything we could use? I tried explanation after explanation, but nothing made sense.

As the events of the day slowly played through my mind, I kept returning to the possibility that the crash and missing girl were connected.

I visualized the crash site. The girl sees the plane go down. She runs toward it through the woods. She has the camera. She takes pictures of the plane. She moves closer. She sees someone—a man or men—who don't want to be seen. There's a struggle. . . .

I opened my eyes, shaking my head.

What possible reason could there have been for someone to attack her? There was certainly nothing of signifi-

cance about the wreckage. And who else could have been there? Hell, the farm was in the middle of nowhere—

The clock in the hallway chimed two A.M.

The story was certain to be the lead on CNN. I picked up the TV remote and punched a button. The screen flickered, and I forced myself to watch.

Barry Garner, the dark-haired, leading-man-handsome CNN commentator, sat at the anchor desk, his face knotted in appropriate concern, saying, ". . . have confirmed a military jet crashed shortly after takeoff from Andrews Air Force Base near Washington, D.C., killing Mr. Joshua Thurston, President Halloran's half brother. Details of the accident are sketchy, but CNN has learned . . ."

Garner droned on, providing a general overview of the accident and background on Thurston. As he spoke, various images flashed over his shoulder: Thurston, President Halloran, the White House, the crash site, a shot of the torn fuselage . . .

Suddenly there I was, standing at the microphone, my face stern.

I sat up fast, and Jasper's head shot up in annoyance.

Garner's voice abruptly quieted, becoming conspiratorial. "Questions about the Air Force's ability to objectively investigate the crash were raised during a news conference earlier this evening. Colonel John Quinn, the Air Force chief crash investigator, seemed to suggest he might be less than forthcoming as to the true nature of the crash, particularly concerning the extent to which the pilots might be responsible. . . ."

I swore.

". . . Marcia Sorenson attended the press conference and filed this report earlier."

A plain-looking brunette in a dark suit appeared, a microphone in her hand, the glow from the lights surround-

ing the wreckage visible in the background. She looked directly into the camera, her face troubled.

"A routine press conference meant to answer questions over the tragic crash that took the life of Mr. Joshua Thurston has raised concerns about the Air Force's ability to launch a thorough and objective investigation. Colonel John Quinn, the lead Air Force crash investigator, clearly became agitated when Mr. Fritz Walling, the noted *Washington Post* columnist, confronted him with information that a reliable source, later revealed to be from the White House, had confirmed Air Force pilots were the focus of the investigation. After a testy exchange, Colonel Quinn seemingly issued a denial of the allegation, only to be apparently contradicted moments later by Dr. Jennifer Johnson, the deputy director of the NTSB, who is assisting in the investigation. Dr. Johnson indicated the investigation was focusing on pilot error as the cause."

The picture changed to a wide-angle shot of Jennifer and me. Then Walling's voice, out of the picture, asked Jennifer if she was contradicting me. The camera zoomed in on Jennifer. Her face was confident, assured. "We all have our opinions," she replied.

The camera quickly panned over, catching my reaction in close-up. I looked enraged, out of control. I spun and stalked off. The camera stayed on me.

I sagged back against the sofa, completely numb. I drained my glass in two swallows.

Jasper cocked his head, watching me.

Marcia continued: "The obvious question is, whom do we believe? Are the pilots the focus of the investigation, as Dr. Johnson and Mr. Walling profess? If so, is Colonel Quinn's denial the result of his desire to keep that aspect of the investigation from the public?" She paused. "Or is his response an indication of something more troubling. Will the Air Force be willing to admit pilot error caused the

death of the brother of the President of the United States?" A suggestive silence, then: "Marcia Sorenson, CNN, near Somerville, Virginia. . . ."

I clicked off the TV and stared vacantly at the screen. Then I grabbed the bottle from the bar.

For almost an hour I sat there drinking in the silence, trying to understand why it was suddenly open season on me. When I finally stumbled upstairs to bed, the only answer I could come up with is that someone was afraid that I'd find something.

But what?

## Friday

**T**he cold shower stream struck me full in the face. I remained under it for a full minute, shivering, trying to jolt my foggy brain awake. When I turned the water off, I still felt sluggish. Too little sleep and too much booze. What the hell did I expect?

Twenty minutes and three extra-strength Tylenols later I was dressed, at the breakfast table, sipping coffee and eating a bagel. I tried not to wince at the sunlight streaming through the kitchen window. Copies of *The Washington Post* and *The Washington Times* sat unopened by my elbow. Jasper, at my feet, ate the food I'd placed out last night. The radio in the living room was set to a morning show. An annoyingly cheerful voice was saying, ". . . almost seven-thirty on a beautiful Friday morning. The forecast is calling for mid-fifties, clear skies most of the day, with a chance of clouds later. Jamie is standing by in helicopter four with the latest traffic report. It's a madhouse out there, right, Jamie—"

I reached over and unfolded the *Post*.

The front-page headline read:

PRESIDENT'S BROTHER KILLED IN JET CRASH

Below, in smaller letters: "Air Force Pilots May Have Made Mistake."

I scanned the article, which was at least as damning as the CNN report. I was mentioned in the second paragraph, just after a statement implying pilot error might be behind the crash. I was described as evasive, contradictory, arrogant. The press conference was criticized as confusing, a debacle.

The third paragraph went into some detail about my confrontation with Fritz Walling. He came off as reasonable—just a reporter doing his job. No surprise there; the *Post* was his damned newspaper. The next paragraph covered Jennifer's remarks, explaining how she seemed to contradict my earlier denial. My objectivity was questioned.

I skipped down to a quote from Walling: "From Colonel Quinn's statements, clearly he is not the right man to run an unbiased investigation. Considering the political sensitivities, it is an open question that the Air Force can be relied upon to investigate itself. In my judgment, the Air Force should give serious consideration to turning over the entire matter to the NTSB, or at the very least removing Colonel Quinn—"

I angrily tossed the paper aside. Jasper looked up, startled. He resumed eating as I picked up the *Times*.

PLANE CRASH KILLS PRESIDENT'S BROTHER, the headline read. There were two articles. I finished them in five minutes. I felt like kissing the *Times* reporters, even if they were both guys.

The *Times* write-ups were matter-of-fact and straightforward, essentially providing information on the crash and Thurston. While one article had described the news con-

ference as testy, it had refrained from hyperbole, and had even implied that Walling had been the instigator of our confrontation. The article also suggested that the Air Force had a right to refrain from commenting on specifics until more facts had been gathered.

There was something else that had noticeably been absent from the *Post*. I picked up the *Post* again to be sure. I scanned the rest of the front page and a second related article. Then I forced myself to read Walling's column in the op-ed section, which was an expansion of his earlier statement that the Air Force should excuse itself from the investigation or replace me.

I set the paper aside.

No mention anywhere that I could find. But I understood. The *Post*'s purpose was to destroy my credibility, so, of course, they wouldn't mention the medal—

The phone rang.

"You read the morning papers?" General Cramer asked, fatigue evident in his voice.

"I read them, sir. The *Times* write-up was fair. But the *Post*—"

"Was a crock of shit. Yeah. We expected that, considering Walling is on the staff. The way I figure it, the *Times* and the *Post* cancel each other out. And the local morning news shows were pretty even-handed. You catch any of those?"

"No."

"Should have. Sure, you took some hits for losing your temper. But they played more of the press conference, so people could see Walling was the instigator. He came off like an ass. So far that's what's saving your butt."

"Sir?"

"I just got out of a meeting with General Railing. I gotta tell you it was tough convincing him, but once he saw the local newscasts, he okayed keeping you on. Between you

and me, I think he's worried if we yank you off the case the spin doctors are going to treat it like an admission of guilt. But you better be a damn choirboy from here on out. You got me?"

"Yes, sir—"

"That means you keep your mouth shut. Have that Public Affairs major from Andrews . . ."

"Major Sollars."

"Right. She runs the press conferences. You don't go anywhere near reporters. You just worry about getting the goddamn investigation done."

"Yes, sir." I expected Cramer to hang up.

"Ah, John, General Mort Dixon called. The President will be flying back from Russia tonight. General Dixon says you're tentatively on the President's schedule to brief him sometime tomorrow morning." Dixon was the DOD liaison to the White House.

*Lucky me.* "I see."

"Now, I was talking with General Railing. He agreed. Enhancing your credibility is critical. We think it's important that the President realizes you're an MOH winner. You catch my drift? . . ."

I sighed. "I'll wear it, sir."

"Atta boy," Cramer said, and hung up.

I went upstairs to the small bedroom that served as my study and rummaged through the bottom drawer of my desk. The blue felt box lay under a stack of old sports magazines. I placed the box on the desk and opened the top. The medal glinted bright against the sunlight streaming through the blinds. I stared at the thirteen white stars on the blue ribbon.

MOH. The Medal of Honor.

Cole Rison and I were roaring across the Iraqi desert in our F-15 Strike Eagle fighter, returning to our base in Saudi

Arabia after a bombing run. I'd just told Cole in the backseat to take us home when we got a call from AWACS asking us to respond to a Special Forces platoon about to be overrun by Iraqi tanks.

I acknowledged, saying we were out of missiles. AWACS ordered us to go anyway, so we turned toward the coordinates.

Five minutes later, we spotted the three-tank column and the platoon of Army grunts dug in less than three hundred yards away.

We went in gunning the tanks. The bullets bounced off harmlessly. As I rolled in for a second pass, the missile warning system screamed and there was a deafening roar. The jet pitched up violently, and smoke filled the cockpit.

I heard Cole shouting, telling me to eject. But at that instant I saw the tanks off the nose. "No, Cole!" I yelled. Even now, I'm not really sure why. I think I was just reacting, desperate to do something to help the grunts. I shoved the nose over, pointing the jet at the tanks.

Tracers from the tanks' machine guns screamed by our canopy. At five hundred feet, I gave the order to eject and pulled the handle. The next thing I remember was being shot up the rails. My vision grayed for an instant from the G forces, then cleared. A split second later, I felt a tug and looked up. The chute started to billow open. Off my shoulder, I glimpsed Cole, tumbling, falling.

Then I realized the ground below me was closing fast. I looked down.

Too low—

I blacked out when I hit. When I came to, I was lying facedown, my legs partially covered by my parachute, the hot sand burning my face. I tried to rise, screamed, and fell forward as pain shot through my back. I lay there, moaning. To the left I saw the shattered and burning remnants of the two lead tanks. Pieces of the jet were scattered around

them. The third tank had been spared the brunt of the impact, but was on fire from jet fuel.

Fighting off the pain, I searched for Cole. Just over a slight rise, I saw a still shape on the sand. I blinked in horror as the grim realization sank in.

Cole never got a chute.

I returned to the present when I heard the phone.

"Colonel Quinn," I answered, wondering if it might be Jennifer or a nosy reporter.

Instead, a familiar male voice said, "Morning, Colonel. Agent Kroft. Hope I'm not calling too early."

The big Secret Service agent with McKenzie. He sounded friendly enough, but I knew he wasn't just calling to say hello. "I'm having coffee, Kroft. What's up?"

"I wanted to relay that you and Dr. Johnson will probably be briefing the President tomorrow—"

"I already got the word."

"Oh," Kroft said, sounding surprised. "I can arrange a car—"

"I'll drive."

"Fine. Just give your name to the White House police at the southwest gate."

My call waiting began beeping. "That it?"

A long pause. "Uh, Dr. Johnson asked me to look into the disappearance of a young woman, a Miss Gibson."

"It's possible that the Gibson girl has returned home."

Another beep, then silence as the caller hung up.

"She's still missing," Kroft said. "I just spoke with the Fauquier County sheriff's office. Dr. Johnson mentioned something about a roll of film you found, possibly belonging to the girl."

A warning bell went off in my head. "What about it?"

"I was wondering where it was. I thought I might take a look, see if there's anything of interest."

"I don't have it, Kroft."

The phone started beeping again.

"Odd," Kroft said. "Colonel Chen mentioned he thought you had taken it."

*Damn Ted.* "He's mistaken."

Another beep.

When Kroft spoke, there was an edge in his voice. "May I remind you that you are to give me your full cooperation. Now, if you want me to bring this up with my superiors, I will."

He had me trumped with his my-boss-is-bigger-than-yours playing card. "Look, it's being processed at the base audiovisual lab. How about I have them run you a set of prints?"

"That'll be fine."

I told him he could pick them up from me later at the hangar. I was about to hang up when he said, "Uh, Colonel . . ."

"Yes?"

Kroft spoke slowly, as if considering each word. "You will come across aspects in this investigation you won't understand. Do yourself a favor. Don't try. Do your job and nothing else."

"The hell is this, Kroft. Some kind of—"

But the dial tone told me I was talking to myself. I glared into the phone, then switched over to the other call.

Another dial tone.

A moment later, I heard the squeal of tires. A car door slammed. I looked out the study window.

I went downstairs to open the front door for Ted.

Three minutes later, Ted sat at the kitchen table as I poured out two mugs of coffee from the pot on the counter. As usual, he looked perfectly groomed, every hair in place. Even his shoes were shined to a high gloss.

"Sorry to put you on the spot, John," Ted said. "But that film is none of Kroft's business. His interest made me suspicious as hell."

I passed him a mug. "You could be right." I explained about the call.

"Sounds like a threat to me," Ted said.

"That's what I thought at first—"

"At first?" Ted said. "You don't think it was?"

"Hell, I don't know. If he was trying to intimidate me, he certainly didn't seem to be trying very hard."

He looked at me doubtfully. "So we still have to hand over copies of the pictures?"

"Can't see any way around it."

Ted sipped his coffee. Jasper was sitting on his haunches, staring intently at him. Ted reached down and scratched his head.

My voice softened. "Kroft mention to you the Gibson girl is still missing?"

Ted nodded and sat back slowly, ignoring Jasper, who continued to rub against his leg. "You never saw a picture of the girl, did you?"

I shook my head.

"Christ, John, she looked young. Pretty thing. Just a kid. . . ." He fell silent.

I sipped, not bothering to comment. Ted's face said it all.

Ted cleared his throat. "You know we've got to keep Jennifer out of the loop." He was staring at his coffee cup as he spoke. "We just can't have her reporting back everything we do."

"I know."

He looked up. "You're okay with this?"

"I don't think we have much choice, Ted."

He smiled, and as if on cue, the doorbell rang.

Ted checked his watch and rose from the table. "Right on time. And John, when Kendra Banks asks, agree to keep everything confidential."

"Dammit, Ted, you said last night—"

"Hey, you want to find out what she knows or not?"

"Sure, but—"

"Good." He winked. "Let's not keep her waiting, shall we?"

I sighed. As we went to the door, I tried to recall what the penalty was for withholding information during an official investigation. Not that Ted appeared to be the least bit concerned.

Kendra Banks stood on my stoop, looking spectacular in a lavender business suit that hugged her long, willowy

frame. She carried an expensive briefcase with her initials stitched across the front. Her dazzling smile turned to ice when she saw Ted. "I thought I made it clear this was to be a private meeting, Colonel Quinn."

"Colonel Chen is also investigating the accident," I said.

"I don't bite," Ted said pleasantly.

She pursed her beautiful lips, giving him a long look. "You won't divulge what I tell you without my okay?"

"Not a word," Ted said.

I hesitated. "No."

She appraised us for a few moments. "All right." But she didn't look happy about it.

Ted led Kendra to the living room while I went to get her a cup of coffee. When I joined them, they were sitting on the sofa, talking quietly. Ted's face was all beaming attentiveness, turning on his rarely used charm to put Kendra at ease. His efforts seemed to be working. She appeared completely relaxed, all signs of her earlier anxiety gone.

I sat on the recliner and passed Kendra her mug. Jasper sauntered in, depositing himself near the entryway. As Kendra sipped, Ted said to me, "Kendra's been at Richter for almost seven years, John. She was also a cop in D.C. for a while."

My eyes popped wide. "You were a cop?"

Kendra laughed, deep and throaty. "Four years. That's what got me interested in going to law school. It's also one of the reasons I signed on with Richter."

"Richter?" I said, missing the connection.

"Absolutely," Kendra said. "Working at Richter is sort of like being a cop. The only difference is we go after crooks who wear three-piece suits."

Ted gave a little cough. "Uh, Kendra, last night you mentioned to John something about knowing the cause of the accident. . . ."

"Sure." She placed her briefcase on the coffee table and

clicked it open. Removing a thin file with a manicured hand, she slid out a photograph onto the table and gave us an expectant look.

The picture showed a man sitting at the desk. He looked younger and thinner than I remembered, but there was no doubt as to his identity.

"Joshua Thurston," Ted murmured.

Kendra's eyes shifted from Ted to me. "You mean you guys still don't get it?" She sounded disappointed.

I glanced at Ted, who was gazing at Kendra with a slight frown. "Get what?" I said.

Kendra jabbed at the photo. "Thurston *was* the reason the plane crashed."

Ted's head snapped back to the photo.

I swallowed hard. "Jesus, you mean—"

"Thurston was murdered," Kendra said.

When Kendra had finished her story, there was a long silence as Ted and I digested the information.

Two days earlier a man identifying himself as Joshua Thurston had called Kendra at the Richter Institute saying he had information to turn over. He sounded nervous and wouldn't come to her office, saying his presence would raise too many questions. Kendra was skeptical the man could be the President's brother. Still, she knew she couldn't dismiss him outright.

They met a few hours later at a small restaurant in Fairfax. Kendra had been stunned when she recognized the man sitting in a corner booth.

It was Joshua Thurston, and he really did have information he wanted to give her—information he said was devastating to the Halloran administration.

"Well?" Kendra said, tapping her foot impatiently.

I murmured, "If what you're saying is true—"

"It is," she said.

"But," Ted said, "you mentioned you don't know what Thurston was going to turn over."

"Actually, what I said was Thurston never told me any specifics on the information he had. I do know what he was going to give me."

I said, "What does that mean?"

She gave me a meaningful look. "He said he had a videotape, John."

My mind kicked into gear. "A videotape of what? Campaign financing irregularities? Maybe some kind of an illegal payment—"

"All I know is that it was something damning, involving the presidency."

"Did you actually see this tape?" Ted asked.

"No. Our initial meeting was to iron out the conditions under which he would turn over the tape to me."

"What conditions?" I asked her.

"That I would never reveal where I'd gotten the tape, including a promise not to keep any kind of paper trail or documentation with his name. He also insisted no one at Richter was to know of the existence of the tape until he authorized me to release it."

"When was he going to give it to you?" Ted asked.

"We had another meeting scheduled for last night to make the exchange."

Ted kept staring at her like something was bothering him. I had a pretty good idea what it was.

Softly, I said, "Kendra . . ."

Kendra raised her coffee mug, big eyes focusing on me over the rim.

I said, "I'm still not sure why Thurston would release information damaging to his brother's administration. Frankly, that doesn't make sense."

She gave me a tolerant smile, setting the mug down.

"You don't know much about Joshua Thurston's relationship with his brother, do you?"

"Pretty much zip," I admitted. Ted was also shaking his head.

"They're not particularly close," Kendra said.

"They aren't?" I asked. "According to the papers—"

"That's strictly PR, John," Kendra said. "Now, early on things between them were different and they were close. Thurston even ran Halloran's first few campaigns for Congress. When Halloran ran for the governorship of Virginia in 1980, something happened during the campaign and Thurston quit less than a month from the election."

"Why?" I asked.

Kendra shrugged, flipping dark strands from her eyes. "Halloran had married Alicia six months earlier. Some think Thurston had a falling-out with Alicia. Whatever the reason, Thurston felt strongly enough to have little or no contact with Halloran for years."

"Christ," Ted said. "Just because of a disagreement with Alicia."

"Who knows?" Kendra said. "Anyway, Thurston ended up getting a state job in Virginia, working with the National Guard. He was extremely bright and had a computer engineering degree. He was responsible for computerizing all the Guard's supply and inventory systems. Two years ago, he and Halloran made peace and Halloran appointed him to the Army Manpower job. A couple of sources tell me Thurston turned down a White House assignment because he didn't want to be anywhere near Alicia Halloran."

I murmured, "So Thurston still held a grudge."

"Apparently," Kendra said.

"I understand the First Lady can be pretty temperamental," I said.

"That," Kendra said with feeling, "is an understatement."

"I found her to be quite pleasant," Ted said.

Kendra looked startled, so I said, "Ted used to fly on *Air Force One*."

"So you've met her?" Kendra asked him.

Ted nodded. "A number of times. I've heard she has a wicked temper, but I've never seen it. She's also very smart. A lot of the reporters say she's the real brains behind Halloran. Her and McKenzie—"

Kendra shot forward, the words tumbling out of her mouth. "McKenzie is a disease. They both are. Halloran's problem is that he's been too trusting, given them too much influence. Halloran never should have allowed them—" She stopped abruptly and looked at me, then at Ted. Slowly, the tension left her face.

*Where did that come from?* I thought. Ted was also watching her with interest.

Kendra took a sip of coffee. She recovered with a rueful smile. "Sorry, but sometimes I . . . well . . . lose it. At Richter we uncover a lot of the crap those two pull."

"I understand," I said just because it seemed the thing to say.

Ted said to her, "You know, of course, there has to be more."

"More?"

"Behind Thurston's motive for releasing damaging evidence against his brother. No way he was doing it simply because he had a tiff with the First Lady."

Kendra thought. "If there was, he certainly didn't tell me."

I said, "I'm puzzled why Thurston scheduled a meeting with you when he had to fly out of town."

"The trip was unexpected," Kendra replied. "When Thurston phoned to cancel, he said he'd just been told about it." Her eyes hardened. "Pretty damned coincidental, huh?"

I nodded grimly. "That's why you think the crash wasn't an accident."

"Not just that," Kendra said.

"Oh?" Ted said.

"The flight. Who do you think arranged it?"

Ted blinked. "The Army—"

He stopped when Kendra shook her head.

"Jesus," I murmured.

"Yeah," Kendra said. "The White House."

Ted sat back heavily. "Thurston told you?"

She hesitated. "No, but it had to be them."

"Be easy enough to check, John," Ted said, looking to the phone on the end table.

The Office of the Air Force Vice Chief of Staff scheduled the flights flown by the Wing at Andrews. I had to call the Pentagon operator first for the number.

Major Isabelle Pilar was the distinguished-visitor support airlift scheduler. She gave me the information in three minutes. I thanked her and hung up.

When I looked at Ted and Kendra, my mouth was dry.

"The White House," I said.

**K**endra's reaction puzzled me. She kept staring at her hands, clasping and unclasping them. She looked more agitated than vindicated.

"Something wrong?" Ted asked.

Without looking up, she said, "Frankly, I wasn't convinced all this was . . . true. Even with what Thurston had said, part of me hoped that maybe I was mistaken. But now—"

"I feel the same way," I said.

"It doesn't prove anything, John," Ted said.

"True," I said. "But it's suggestive as hell." I turned to Kendra. "How could the White House have found out about Thurston?"

"I don't know. I've been tossing that around in my head. All I know is I certainly didn't tell anyone."

"Considering Thurston's apparent paranoia, it doesn't seem logical he would have mentioned it," I said.

No one said anything.

"Why are you here?" I asked Kendra.

"I'd think that would be obvious. To help you prove the crash wasn't an accident."

"Not to get the story for Richter so they can make a splash by announcing a major scandal involving the White House."

A hint of smile. "You know I'd be lying if I said no. But there is something else. . . ." She hesitated, and Ted and I gazed back, waiting.

"The videotape," Kendra said finally. "I thought it might have been in the plane's wreckage."

I didn't remember seeing any videotape when Ted and I had walked inside the fuselage. That's not something you would expect to find at a crash site, and I'm sure I would have remembered. I gave Ted a questioning look, and he shook his head no.

"Why would you think Thurston was carrying the videotape on the flight?" I asked her.

"He said he had it when he called me. I wouldn't think Thurston would leave something that important behind. He probably would have been carrying it in a briefcase. You guys didn't find one?"

"No," Ted said. "But if it was on the airplane, the recovery crew would have found it."

"That stuff's probably in the hangar by now," I said to Ted.

"Call me when you find it," Kendra said.

Ted shot me a look, telling me even he had limits on how far he bent the regs. "Look, Kendra," I said. "I want to make sure you're clear about this. Crash investigations are highly confidential. If we find a videotape, you know we can't turn it over to you."

She took a deep breath and nodded. "That's okay, John."

"It is?"

Her eyes turned cold, matching her voice. "I want who-ever was behind the plane crash punished. Now, if you don't want to work together, that's fine. I'm going to keep pursuing this. If you find the tape, just make sure it gets into the right hands. It won't be easy. These people have influence. There'll be pressure. . . ." She paused, her voice softening. "But, of course, you've already experienced that."

I nodded.

"The press conference was just the beginning. It will get worse, John. They can't afford to let the truth get out."

Her comments were scaring me a little. "Thanks for the advice."

A tight smile. "Anytime." She gathered up Thurston's photo and returned it to her briefcase. Ted took the cue, collecting the coffee mugs and heading toward the kitchen.

"So what are you going to do now?" I asked Kendra.

She sighed, clicking the case shut. "Find the videotape."

I frowned.

"Not the one from the plane, John. Thurston must have made a copy. He certainly wouldn't have given me his only one. Someone in his office might know something."

"You can get into the Pentagon?" I said, surprised.

"Sure. Almost twenty percent of Richter is retired mili-tary. We probably have more connections there than any-place in town. If that doesn't pan out, I'll try Thurston's niece. She's studying architecture over at Georgetown. He also had a live-in maid who might know something."

"You should stay out of it, Kendra. If someone really murdered Thurston and they find you snooping around . . ."

She stood, and I saw determination in her eyes. "I can't let this go, John. Other than your investigation, no one else is looking into this. Thanks for the coffee, huh?"

• • •

Ted and I stood in the doorway, watching Kendra drive away in her black Saab.

"You believe her?" I asked.

A long pause. "Let's talk on the way, John. I'll drive." I'd known Ted long enough to know what he really meant.

He didn't believe Kendra Banks.

I climbed into Ted's station wagon after dropping Jasper off at Mrs. Dickey's. Mrs. Dickey rose early, dressed nicely and still put on makeup, as if she had someplace to go, though usually she just spent the day in her apartment. Like many single elderly people, she was lonely. It pissed me off that she had two sons in the area who rarely visited. Anyway, I tried to stop by every couple of days to check on her and say hi.

After tossing a couple of spare cell-phone batteries into Ted's glove compartment, I pulled out my handkerchief and checked myself in the glare-shield mirror. I wiped off the lipstick smear on my cheek, courtesy of Mrs. Dickey.

"We'll swing by the audiovisual lab first," Ted said, easing out of the parking space. "Allison Gibson's pictures should be done by now."

"Fine." I shifted to face him. "Why don't you believe Kendra?"

"You think she was telling the truth?" He sounded surprised.

"What she said fits. If we find out the plane was sabotaged, that will confirm her story."

Ted merged into the morning traffic. "Don't forget she's Governor Banks's daughter. You know she'd love to get something on Halloran that would take him down—"

"She seemed to defend the President."

"Yeah." Ted grunted. "Which makes no sense. She can't possibly like the guy. And why didn't she tell us she was

Governor Banks's daughter? I'll tell you. We would have known she had an agenda."

"Well . . ." I sat back.

"Another thing I can't figure is why Thurston contacted her in the first place."

"She explained that," I said. "He wanted her to release the tape."

"No. I mean why her *specifically*. Thurston could just as easily have turned it over to a reporter at *The Washington Times,* or some other news organization in town. And what's with her animosity toward the First Lady? McKenzie I can understand. He's a scumbag."

I shook my head.

"You also notice she didn't have any proof for what she told us. None."

"What about the Gibson girl? You know something happened in that field last night. And how do you explain the pressure we're getting?"

For chrissakes, John. Kendra's saying the White House sabotaged the jet to kill Thurston. No way Halloran would have his own brother killed."

I watched him for a moment. "The call I made to the Eighty-ninth scheduler . . ."

He tensed. "What about it?"

"The White House put in the request for a jet on Wednesday afternoon."

Ted showed no reaction. For a moment, I thought maybe he hadn't understood.

Then he slowly shook his head. "That means they knew almost a day in advance exactly which airplane Thurston was going to fly."

I nodded. "So if they wanted to arrange something . . ." I left the statement hanging.

We slowed to a stop at a red light. Ted hunched over the

wheel, eyes straight ahead. "We better be sure about this, John," he said quietly.

"I know."

"Call the hangar. Have a search made for the tape or Thurston's briefcase. And if they find it, have them call us, no one else."

"Okay." It took less than a minute. Then I phoned the Command Post briefing room. Rita answered. She said most of the other board members had arrived. I told her we'd be there in thirty minutes.

When I hung up we were almost to the Beltway. Ted was still focused on the road, his face grim. I started to pass on to him what Rita had said, but realized he wasn't listening.

As I looked out the window, I felt a growing sense of unease at what the pictures would show.

The Andrews Air Force Base audiovisual lab was located in a square, cream-colored building on Colorado Avenue, a few blocks west of the base exchange. We pulled into a space out front. As we were getting out, we spotted two men in dark suits emerge from the audiovisual building. They came down the concrete, walking quickly. One was tall, sandy-haired, and carrying a large packet. The other was short and heavy. They glanced at us, and their eyes widened as if in recognition. The heavy guy said something and they picked up the pace.

Ted turned to me, eyebrows raised.

The men hurried by and climbed into a gray sedan. We were heading up the walkway as they drove away.

"Sons of bitches! Who the hell do those guys think they are? Jesus! Janis, you got that number yet?"

Ted and I hesitated before stepping into a large foyer with painted blue walls and a spotless white tile floor. At the far end, a jowly, red-faced chief master sergeant stood

behind the long counter, waving a phone around like a baton. He was looking impatiently at a freckle-faced female airman with frizzy red hair who was furiously flipping through what looked like a base phone book.

We approached the counter. "Something wrong, Chief Patterson?" I asked. Chief Melvin Patterson had been running the audiovisual shop since Reagan's first term and was something of an institution.

Patterson's head spun, and relief flooded his face. "Colonel Quinn. Jesus, am I glad to see you, sir." He slammed down the phone. "Yeah, something sure as hell is wrong. I was just trying to contact you or Colonel Chen. I ain't seen anything like it. Those sons of bitches think they can just waltz in here, scare my people half to death. It ain't right—"

"Slow down, Chief," Ted said.

Patterson swallowed, nodding.

"Now tell us what happened," I said.

Patterson ran a hand over his balding scalp. "About ten minutes ago, these two yahoos come barging in—"

"The two men that just left, sir," the airman explained.

Patterson's head bobbed. "Those guys make Janis here take them into the back. Then they walk around, flashing a piece of paper and badges. Order me to—"

"Badges?" Ted interrupted. "Police?"

"FBI badges."

"FBI?" Ted asked. "You're sure that's who they were?"

"Damn straight, Colonel," Patterson said. "Read it on their IDs myself."

I had a sinking feeling. "What did they want?"

Patterson gestured to Ted. "The negatives and prints. From the film you dropped off."

Ted swore.

I said, "You gave them everything?"

"Couldn't help it, sir. They had a goddamn *federal* war-

rant! Official as hell. Signed by a judge. Now, I been around a long time, sir. I don't do nothing without orders. I told them I wasn't going to give them a goddamn thing until I talked to Colonel Chen or you or General Stinson. Then one of them pulls out a phone, makes a quick call. He says a few words and hands it to me." Patterson grimaced. "A guy comes on, says he's Brigadier General Corbin, General Ware's executive officer. Jumps into my shit big time. Orders me to comply with the warrant." Patterson let out a rasping breath. "Hell, what could I do?"

"That son of a bitch," Ted muttered.

I said nothing. But I knew Ted was talking about General Ware.

"You're absolutely sure you didn't keep back anything?" Ted asked. "Not a print or a negative? Maybe one that was messed up in processing?"

Patterson thought for a moment. "No, sir. They got it all."

"Did you see the pictures?" I asked.

"I managed to sneak a peak at a couple when those FBI guys showed. But I wasn't around when Sergeant Garcia processed the roll last night. He could tell you what was on them, except he got sent out to the crash site around three this morning to help Sergeant Matthews. I told him to head on home when he was finished out there." He checked his watch. "Should be home by now." He turned to the airman. "Hey, Janis, dig up Garcia's number."

Ted took out his notebook as Janis opened a binder.

"What were in the pictures you saw?" I asked.

Patterson shrugged. "Not much. Just some artsy-fartsy shots of people dancing. They were wearing tights. You know, like ballet, except you could tell it wasn't. Looked more like that modern stuff, the way they were twisting and crouching—the kind of crap they show on PBS."

"That's it?" I asked, frowning. "No pictures of the crash site?"

"None that I saw. Garcia can tell you more."

Janis read out a phone number, and Ted copied it down.

"By the way, Chief," I said, "you get the names of those two agents?"

"Sure as hell did. Got 'em right here." He fished into his jacket pocket and produced a folded piece of paper. Opening it, he read, "Agents Holt and Morgan."

The names didn't ring any bells. As Ted copied the names into his notebook, someone to our left coughed softly.

I glanced over. A petite staff sergeant with long dark hair and blue eyes stood in a doorway behind the counter. She looked worried. "Uh, Chief, there's a problem," she said apprehensively.

"What?" Patterson asked.

She shuffled her feet. "Remember how you told me to turn everything over to those men?"

"Yeah. What's the problem, Meredith?"

"Well, I gave them everything in the packet, but I never thought to check the computer. I just turned it on, found the file—"

"The pictures?" Patterson asked. "Are you saying Garcia scanned the pictures?"

A tentative nod. "Two, but they're real dark."

"I'll be damned," Patterson said, rubbing his hands together. "Good job, Meredith." He beamed at Ted and me. "You may be in luck, sirs. C'mon back. Let's take a look."

We walked down a brightly lit corridor, past a room where two men were sitting at light tables, scanning strips of negatives. In another room across the hall, a female sergeant was hunched over what I guessed was a photo enlarger, tweaking some knobs. We came to a door that said "Darkroom." Above the door, a red sign glowed with the words "In Use."

Patterson led the way, talking nonstop. "Sergeant Matthews sent us almost sixty rolls from the site about an hour ago. Said he'll probably have another fifty or so by the time he's finished. That's over two thousand shots. We aren't set up for that kind of workload, Colonel. Hell, we only got nine people on staff. We'll need damn near three days to get all the pictures processed. Now, it'd be different if we got some of the new processing equipment. But the crap we're working with is fifteen years old. Damn Air Force. You think they'd spring—— Here we are."

Patterson turned into a smallish room with three computer-topped desks arranged in a **T** at the center. The desk to the left also contained a foot-long box-shaped apparatus I didn't recognize. A copying machine and laser printer occupied most of one wall.

As Meredith went to the desk on the left and sat down, Patterson said, "Garcia must have thought the pictures were degraded, otherwise he'd never have scanned them. He only does that to computer-enhance the pictures. Which makes me curious, since them dancing shots I saw were fine."

"So maybe the ones he scanned are photos of the crash site," Ted said. "Those shots would have been taken in moonlight and been dark as hell."

"Possibly so," Patterson replied.

"That the scanner, Chief?" I asked, pointing to the box-shaped object.

"That's it, sir. Our pride and joy. First new piece of equipment Uncle Sam let us buy in two years. Slip the negative in the slot on the side, punch a few buttons, and, presto, you got the image on the screen. Industry has had them for a while. In a few years, they'll be all over the place. Ever seen a digitally enhanced picture.

I shook my head. "I'm not really into computers."

Meredith was busily clicking on the keyboard. "Be ready in a moment," she said.

We stood behind her, peering over her shoulder. The screen showed a file with a list of names. "Chen" was highlighted, and the computer was whirring softly. To the right was a blank square roughly a quarter the size of the screen. An image suddenly appeared in the square, a blend of black and gray. In the upper right, on the edge of the frame, a time and date in white lettering: "5:56 P.M. March 3."

I tensed. The time was just minutes after the crash.

"That's the first picture," Meredith said. "Garcia must have been called out before he could enhance it. Or maybe he did enhance it and saved it to a disk. But if he did, I can't find it."

I peered at the image, trying to see something, anything.

Ted said, "You can't make out a damned thing. Except the time the picture was taken. The girl must have had one of those cameras that automatically log the time."

I frowned. "Why would she have taken pictures that wouldn't turn out?"

"This girl," Patterson said. "She know much about photography?"

"Yeah," I said. "She was studying it in school."

"Know what film speed setting she used?" Patterson asked.

"The film was sixteen hundred," Ted said.

"She use a tripod?" Patterson asked.

"I'm pretty sure she didn't," Ted replied.

"That explains why the pictures are so underexposed. Girl knew she couldn't hold the camera still enough to get a shot at that film speed. She probably set the camera for a wide-open aperture at a higher shutter speed, maybe thirty-two or sixty-four hundred, planning to push it during development."

"Push it?" I said.

"Yeah. It's a way of fooling the system. You develop the film longer to bring out detail. Since Garcia didn't know she'd taken the pictures at a higher speed, he processed the film for a thousand, big-time underexposing the shots. That's the reason the contrast is practically gone."

"So we have nothing," I said, feeling a sense of defeat.

"Hey, not so fast, Colonel." Patterson winked. "Just watch. Go ahead, Meredith."

Meredith spun the ball. The cursor moved to an icon and clicked. As the cursor shifted to a spot on the image, Pat-

terson explained, "She's going to mark the darkest spot first. Then the lightest. I've read where they're developing programs to do this stuff automatically. But this works pretty good. The computer will use those two levels as a reference to clear up the image. Pretty amazing. Here it comes . . ."

We watched the screen. A new image began to appear at the top of the square and slowly worked its way down, almost flowing. First a lighter gray, then something dark in the middle. The image continued downward. Fuzzy, but we could make out something to the right against a backdrop of darker gray. Something long and dark, almost black but not quite.

"Contrast," Patterson ordered.

Meredith did something, and the image cleared a little. The two dark objects looked vaguely familiar.

Meredith clicked again, and the picture sharpened.

"Make it full screen size."

The monitor flickered.

"Jesus," I said.

Ted hissed air through his teeth.

Meredith looked back at us, her face worried.

"Something wrong?" Patterson asked me.

Ted and I continued to stare at the screen. Even though the objects were grainy and gray, we could tell what they were. The long shape on the right was the fuselage. But I wasn't looking at that. I was focused on the object in the top left, a familiar profile, maybe thirty feet above the wreckage.

"A Blackhawk helicopter," Ted breathed.

"Yeah," I said. "Just a few minutes after the crash."

Patterson said, "So it's a helicopter—"

Ted pointed suddenly. "What's that?"

Everyone looked. He was indicating a small, dark shape beside the fuselage.

"Blow it up, Meredith," Ted said.

Meredith spun the ball, and a box formed around the object. She clicked an icon, and there it was, filling the screen. A mottled gray and black outline.

"A man," Meredith murmured.

"Yes," I said, "a man."

Thurston! He was on the ground, an arm in the air, reaching, crawling——

"Alive," Ted said.

Ten minutes later, Ted and I stepped out of the audiovisual building into the brightness of the morning sun. Off in the distance, a large jet was flying lazily around the traffic pattern.

We'd also analyzed the second picture, which had shown the helicopter touching down beside the wreckage. We'd tried to see if Meredith could enhance the numbers on the side of the helo so we could read them, but that hadn't panned out. Patterson said he'd heard about some new digital software being used by industry that might help improve the clarity, but he had no idea who might have it.

I had called Sergeant Garcia at home and woken him up. Garcia confirmed there actually had been seven shots on the roll that had been too dark to readily decipher. Things had been hectic, and he'd managed only to scan in two before he'd been sent out to the site. No, he couldn't say what was on the rest. Yes, he'd returned the negatives back to the original packet—the one now in the hands of the FBI.

*Damn.*

I had paper copies of the enhanced pictures in my jacket pocket along with a disk with the images. I told Patterson and Meredith to keep what they'd seen to themselves. I also had them delete everything from the computer.

As we walked toward the parking lot, Ted said, "Kroft has to be part of this."

I nodded.

Ted continued, "He must have sent those two Feds here after talking to you. That means he knew what was in the pictures."

I thought about that. "Kroft couldn't have sent them, at least not on his own. He doesn't have the authority. Plus there's the warrant. No way Kroft can call up a judge and make that happen."

"McKenzie, then," Ted said.

"Or higher."

After a few more steps, Ted said quietly, "It sounds like you've made up your mind the President is involved."

"You haven't?"

A pause. "We should be careful not to jump to conclusions."

I gave him a look of annoyance. "Our rescue helicopters didn't show until an hour or so after the crash. So where did that bird come from? Blackhawks are almost exclusively flown by the military. Someone with a lot of clout had to order that bird in there."

"That doesn't mean Halloran did it, John."

"Get real, Ted. Who else could—"

"Keep your shirt on, John," Ted said hastily. "I'm not disagreeing with you. But before I decide the President of the United States is involved in a murder conspiracy, I want some damn hard proof."

"Nothing but the facts, huh?" I said dryly.

Ted didn't reply.

We walked along in silence.

"Is it possible the chopper was on a training mission and saw the plane go down?" Ted asked.

"Then why didn't the crew notify somebody? Why was

it gone by the time the cops arrived?" I shook my head. "No. It didn't show up by chance."

"That means the helicopter must have been tracking the jet."

"Yeah. And it wouldn't be that difficult. Aircraft departing from Andrews fly published SIDs."

"SIDs?" Ted said, questioning the pilot lingo, which he didn't understand.

"A SID is a standard instrument departure with specific heading and altitude info. It rarely changes. All the helicopter crew would have to do is pre-position the bird on the route ahead of time. By monitoring the radios, the crew would know the Lear's approximate position. Hell, they could even be using their own onboard radar to skin-paint the Lear. When the jet went down, they would already be in the vicinity."

"But the jet was off a departure routing, making an emergency return, when it crashed."

"That shouldn't make much difference, assuming the helicopter had the jet on radar. Sure, the Blackhawk would be slower, but not much. Remember, the Lear was only flying around two-thirty before it went in."

As we approached the parking lot, Ted turned to me, his face grim. "You know, there's only one way what you're saying makes sense, John."

I nodded. "The helicopter crew had to know the jet was going to crash."

We were almost to the car. I started toward it when I realized Ted wasn't with me. I looked back and saw him on the curb, frowning deeply.

"Why did the helicopter land?" he asked suddenly.

I shook my head.

Ted closed his eyes and began talking softly in a clipped monotone. Imaging and verbalizing, like what athletes do before a competition. Not that Ted got it from sports. His

family had been Buddhists back in Hawaii, and he'd grown up using meditation to focus his mind. Anyway, that's where he picked up the technique.

I folded my arms, waiting for him to finish.

Ted was saying, "The Blackhawk crew sees the plane go down. They expect it to explode, burn. But it doesn't. They fly in, land. Why? That's risky, stupid. They could be spotted. But they have to. Why? Because . . . because they're looking for—" His eyes popped open.

I beat him to it. "The videotape."

"Had to be," Ted said. "They landed to find it. During their search, they discovered Thurston was alive—"

"So they killed him," I said.

"And the girl," Ted said, his voice thick with emotion. "They must have spotted her. Jesus. Everything fits."

I was suddenly overwhelmed with anger. "Kroft knew about the film. That means he knew about the girl, the helicopter . . . that son of a bitch."

Ted seemed to be staring through me. I expected to see rage in his eyes, but he'd gone completely calm.

He said, "We have no proof, John. None."

"I know—"

"Only theory, supposition." He hesitated. "We could even be wrong. Maybe there's another explanation."

I knew Ted couldn't believe that, and I sure didn't. "We'll just have to *get* the proof— Where're you going?"

Ted was walking away. He gave a quick wave and continued toward the audiovisual building. I was about to follow when my phone rang. It was Sergeant Anderson, the guy I talked to earlier at the hangar. His men had gone through everything that had been recovered, including Thurston's luggage.

"There's no videotape or briefcase, sir," Anderson said.

I swore.

• • •

When Ted returned a few minutes later, I was leaning against the car, smoking my first cigarette of the day. After I passed on what Sergeant Anderson had told me, Ted didn't bother to comment. He slipped a photo packet from his jacket and handed it to me.

I frowned. "What are these of?"

"Look."

I opened the packet on the hood. There were at least two dozen pictures inside. I slipped them out. Joshua Thurston's sightless eyes stared back at me.

"The pictures Sergeant Corbin took of Thurston at the crash site," Ted said.

I sorted through a half dozen or so. Pictures of Thurston, shot from various angles. "So?"

"The face," Ted said. "Take a good look, John."

I slid out a close-up of Thurston and studied it. Nothing unusual except—

"The marks on his nose?" I asked, looking up.

Ted nodded. "Dead men don't bruise."

I took a couple of puffs. "Bently said the marks were no big deal."

"Bently wasn't looking at this as a homicide. That's important. When I saw those marks last night, I also thought they might have been caused by the accident. Still, they bugged me. I'd seen that kind of bruising when I was a cop."

"Okay . . ."

"You see, John, when the crew from the Blackhawk found Thurston alive, they had a big problem. They had to kill him quick, but still make it appear accidental. That rules out guns or knives. They couldn't strangle him for the same reason—too obvious."

I stared intently at the photo again. "Jesus, they smothered him."

"And pressed too hard. Probably because they were in a hurry, or maybe Thurston struggled."

I felt a surge of adrenaline. "The autopsy. The medical examiner should be able to tell, right?"

Ted responded with a flat smile. "Hand me your phone, John."

This time I did the driving so I could drop Ted off at the hangar. He would check on the pressurization valves while I attended the briefing. He also wanted to call out to the crash site, order up another search for the briefcase or any other small piece of luggage—anything that could carry a videotape.

At the moment, Ted was on my cell phone, talking to a Dr. McNabb from the pathology department at Dover Air Force Base. From what I was overhearing, I could tell Ted was getting the runaround.

"Look, Doc," Ted said, "maybe you haven't been listening. The results could be critical to our investigation. Now, you've either performed the autopsy—" Ted clammed up, listening intently. He fumbled in his jacket for his notepad. "You gotta be kidding. Who the hell decided that? I see. Yeah. Fine. You got the number." He ended the call with a scowl. "Goddamn pencil pusher."

"The autopsy hasn't been done yet?"

"Don't know yet," Ted said, punching in another number. "Dover didn't do it."

"Why not?"

Ted held up a finger and spoke into the phone. The conversation lasted less than a minute. A third call didn't take much longer. Even though I caught only bits and pieces, I'd heard enough. I shook my head in disbelief.

"What a crock," Ted muttered as he hung up.

"So where the hell is Thurston?" I asked.

"No one knows. Or if they do, they're not saying."

I was incredulous. "Ted, you don't just lose the body of the President's brother."

Ted handed me the phone. "Apparently, there was confusion over who would handle the autopsy. Dover said they were notified last night that an Army forensics team from Rockville would handle it. But Rockville says the word they got is that the body was going to Walter Reed. And Walter Reed is playing games. Some jerk named Dr. Cooley kept parroting that he's under strict orders not to release any information concerning Thurston without the approval of the chief of pathology. A Dr. Martin."

I tapped the brakes as we came to a stop sign. "Talk to Dr. Martin, then."

"Can't. He's un-fucking-available." I could hear the frustration in his voice.

"So Thurston might be at Walter Reed?"

Ted gave me a dubious look.

"Hey, it's possible."

"He isn't there, John. Why else would McKenzie have picked up the body last night? Then there's the phone calls."

"Phone calls?"

Then I understood. "You mean McKenzie orchestrated the calls to Dover and Rockville to buy time. He wanted to

confuse people so no one would ask questions when Thurston's body didn't turn up."

"Sure."

I checked traffic and made a right. "Hell, that means McKenzie probably had Thurston's body cremated."

Ted massaged the bridge of his nose. "It's possible, but I don't think so. McKenzie knows that would raise too many eyebrows. My guess is he's taken Thurston somewhere to have a sham autopsy." He stopped rubbing, focusing on me. "This shouldn't come as any big surprise."

I was gazing outside gloomily. "It doesn't. I think what gets me is . . . is that McKenzie could pull something like this off."

"It's called power, John," Ted said quietly.

It was a little after ten when I strode into the dimness of the Command Post. The bedlam from last night had quieted, but not by much. Phones still rang continually, but at least there wasn't a constant flow of people scurrying around doing a Chicken Little routine. I passed by a bank of glowing computer screens, nodding to a few familiar faces as I went toward the back.

A security police sergeant in a crisp blue uniform sat at a desk outside of the conference room. Behind him, a sign on the door read: RESTRICTED ENTRY—CRASH INVESTIGATION BOARDROOM. The cop checked my ID against his clipboard list, then cleared me in.

Rita was standing by the conference table, talking on one of the newly installed telephones. Occasionally, she'd glance at the TV in the corner, which was playing a car commercial with the sound turned off. A slightly plump brunette major wearing thick glasses sat at one of two oversize desks against the back wall, clicking furiously on a keyboard as she peered into a computer monitor. Near two metal file cabinets along the right wall, a rail-thin lieu-

tenant colonel with gray hair sipped coffee and conversed with a tall, scholarly-looking man wearing wire-rimmed glasses and a neatly trimmed goatee.

Rita turned, waved, and kept on talking.

"John, long time no see!" the man with the goatee boomed out. He grinned broadly and strolled over, the lieutenant colonel on his heels.

"Glad you could make it, Harmon," I said.

An ex-Naval Aviator, Dr. Harmon Masters had gone on to earn an M.D. and a Ph.D. in physiology, and was now considered one of the country's foremost human factors experts. He would determine whether physiological stresses on the pilots—vertigo, spatial disorientation, maybe even alcohol or drugs—could have led to the crash. We'd worked together on a number of investigations in the past.

"Jeez, you look like shit, John," Lieutenant Colonel Tom Blaney said, his face sympathetic. "No offense."

I gave him a wry simile. "Hard to look your best when you're being skewered in the papers and have a hissy fit watched by maybe a billion people, Tom."

"Don't let the talking heads get to you, John," Harmon said. He nodded toward the TV, which now showed CNN's financial analyst at the news desk. "The press always seems to go a little nuts over these high-profile accidents."

"Bastards." Tom grunted.

"Tom, you get a chance to look over the wreckage in the hangar yet?" I asked. Tom would handle the detailed analysis of the aircraft parts to determine if they might be linked to the crash. It sounds like a bigger job than it really is. A lot of the parts would be farmed out to the specific manufacturers, who would do the actual testing. Tom's job was to keep track of everything and pass on the results to us.

Tom shook his head. "Ogden called. Said he'd brief me up after we finished the meeting." He scowled. "Heard Ted

Chen is helping out." Tom made no secret that he considered Ted an egotistical prima donna, which happened to be exactly what Ted thought of Tom.

"Relax, Tom. I'll keep him out of your hair."

I noticed Major Mattie Parker waving at me from her computer, her round face spread into a dimpled smile. Mattie would be quite attractive if she lost some weight and maybe used a little makeup. But that kind of stuff wasn't important to her.

"Hi, Mattie," I said. "You look busy."

"New software. I'll be able to input the black-box data and mesh it with the FAA's radar plots and transmission tapes to give us a 3-D picture of the plane's flight path. Pretty neat. Like an M-plot, except we won't have to mess with the wires and stuff." The M-plot was a time-phased model of the plane's flight path made with string and wires. Basically, it gave an instant picture of precisely where and when the jet was moments before a crash. The M-plot was tedious to assemble and usually ended up resembling an enormously complicated wind chime.

"You know if Colonel Ogden removed the black boxes yet?" I asked.

Mattie's curly locks bobbed. "Already on their way to the NTSB. I also talked to the FAA. They're going to send a courier over with the radar data later this afternoon."

"Good girl—"

"Got a favor to ask, sir."

"Shoot."

"The copy and fax machines still haven't arrived. Wonder if you could check with supply—"

"I'll call."

Rita hung up and came over. "John, that was Cal Brice. He won't be able to get out of Puerto Rico until tomorrow."

"If he knows what's good for him, he'll stay there," Harmon said dryly.

Cal was the guy who was supposed to be my deputy. I knew he'd been in Puerto Rico on a TDY.

"Thanks, Rita." I gestured toward the table. "Why don't we get started."

As everyone took a seat, Rita picked up a phone. Noticing my frown, she said, "I'm calling Jennifer."

"She's here?" I said, surprised.

A nod. "She and Agent Kroft were hanging around when I arrived. They left about thirty minutes ago. She wanted me to give her a shout at the hangar when you were ready."

"What were they doing here?" I said, louder than I'd intended.

Rita gave me a curious look. "Just looking around. Why?"

"Don't bother calling," I said.

Rita shrugged. "Sure, John."

I went to the security cop outside and asked to see his entry list. Kroft's name was there, and so was Jennifer's. They were logged in at 0910 and out at 0924.

"Something wrong, Colonel?" the cop asked.

I handed back the clipboard. "Everything's fine, Sergeant."

Returning to the table where everyone was seated, I began the briefing.

I provided a rough overview on the crash and a timeline the investigation was to follow. I didn't go into specifics; they all knew their jobs better than I did. I also didn't discuss the political games being played—that wasn't their problem. I certainly couldn't tell them about my growing suspicions of a high-level cover-up.

After the briefing, Mattie returned to her computer and Tom Blaney headed to the hangar. Harmon Masters left for Walter Reed to check on the toxicology tests on Rick and Judd. He would also see if he could find out anything on the status of Thurston's autopsy.

I made a call to supply to check on the fax and copier and got the usual runaround. I played the "I'm-a-colonel-and-you're-not" routine until the terrified major said we'd have the equipment first thing in the morning.

Once I passed the info on to Maggie, I took a seat at the conference table. Rita was sitting across from me, building the colored folders we would use to log the inspection results of each aircraft part. That was the drill. Everything in the jet would be analyzed. No exceptions. If the plane was sabotaged, we'd know eventually. Assuming we were given the chance.

I closed my eyes for a moment and massaged my temples. I'm not one of those deep-thinking types like Ted. When I try, I usually just get a headache. Now so many questions were dancing through my head I was getting confused.

I opened my eyes and flipped open my notebook and wrote:

## WHY WAS PLANE SABOTAGED?
Kendra says Thurston had videotape damaging to the President.

## WHAT DID THURSTON KNOW?
Videotape?
—one in plane likely destroyed
—copies?
Ask Thurston's family/co-workers/acquaintances.

## WHO ORDERED SABOTAGE?
President
McKenzie
Kroft
Combination of all of above
Others possibly involved?

## HOW DID SABOTAGE OCCUR:
Pressurization valves?
Something else

## THURSTON'S MURDER (PROOF)
Autopsy (not likely)
Witness
—Allison Gibson (likely dead)
Photos by Allison in hands of FBI

## BLACKHAWK HELICOPTER
Flown by military
All branches
Active-duty, National Guard, reserves
—CIA?

I sat back and studied the list.

Finding out what Thurston knew was going to be difficult. Some of the other stuff we could guess at, but not that. Unless the videotape turned up, we had no way of determining why Thurston was murdered.

Kendra had mentioned Thurston had a niece and a live-in maid, but the odds of their knowing anything were probably zip. Then there were the people who worked with Thurston, but Ted and I couldn't question them without eyebrows being raised and the word possibly getting back to McKenzie.

I went back over the list, putting a check mark against each item I thought was critical: the pressurization valves, which could prove sabotage; Thurston's autopsy, which was a long shot. Finally the Blackhawk helicopter. If we could find the helicopter . . .

I snapped the notebook shut and pushed back my chair to go over to Major Mattie Parker, my FAA liaison and

computer guru. I never made it, because I glanced at the TV and saw two familiar figures slowly leading an entourage across a wide stone courtyard toward a podium.

The President and the First Lady.

They wore black.

They were America's royalty, and they looked like it. Even though he was approaching sixty, President Roland Halloran looked years younger. His perfectly blow-dried hair was black and thick, his skin was tanned and smooth, and he had a reassuringly sensitive face the cameras and voters loved. At forty-two, blond and blue-eyed Alicia Halloran was still strikingly attractive. Her features were too rounded to be considered beautiful, but she was slender and graceful, with a healthy, California-beach-girl quality. For some reason, she'd always rerminded me of Doris Day.

In the background, a large gray building came into view. To the right an American flag was visible fluttering on a flagpole, a detail of rigid Marines standing nearby. The American embassy in Russia, I concluded.

President Halloran and the First Lady strolled up to the podium, hand in hand, the entourage fanning in a semicir-

cle behind. I recognized the secretary of state and the American ambassador to Russia, but that was about it.

Halloran paused at the podium, somber-faced, adjusting his notes as he gazed across the small, almost intimate, crowd of dignitaries and reporters. Alicia Halloran whispered something into his ear. The camera lingered on her.

What Kendra had said about the First Lady's influence over Halloran was well known, though I'd never heard her characterized as corrupting. Rather, the First Lady was commonly regarded as a paragon of virtue, a bright and beautiful woman completely dedicated to supporting her husband. Much of Halloran's political success could be directly attributed to his wife's popularity. The public practically worshiped her, thanks to her tireless support for an endless number of family- and child-oriented programs. The fact that she was a looker didn't hurt.

Maybe her public persona was nothing but a carefully packaged PR campaign, but I didn't think so. She seemed like a genuinely good person, which is why Kendra's animosity toward her was so puzzling.

Alicia Halloran gave her husband a brave smile. Halloran faced the audience, took a deep breath, and began speaking.

I had started toward the TV to turn up the volume when Halloran's voice blared out.

Rita came over, the remote in her hand. She was frowning. "What is this, some kind of impromptu memorial service?"

"Looks like it."

In a solemn voice, Halloran was saying, ". . . be a brief statement to thank the American people for their support in such a trying time for our family. Not many of you knew my brother, Joshua Thurston, but you should have. Joshua was a good, decent man and a loyal American who died in

the service of his country. He was also a wonderful, caring human being. I remember when we were growing up . . ."

"Looks like this will be a long one," Rita murmured, parking herself on the edge of the conference table.

I nodded, joining her. Halloran was a gifted, though notoriously long-winded, orator. He went on for ten minutes, eulogizing his brother by recounting humorous anecdotes from their Virginia childhood and their early days in politics. He portrayed Thurston as a loving, loyal confidant, even magnanimously crediting his brother for much of his own early political success. The longer Halloran spoke, the more his emotions surfaced. His voice wavered and cracked, and I could clearly see the anguish on his face. In midsentence, Halloran suddenly stepped back from the mike. The camera closed and Halloran's face filled the screen. He was blinking rapidly, eyes misting.

"Jeez, you think the Prez is gonna lose it?" Major Mattie Parker asked from her desk. She sounded hopeful.

I didn't reply. I was staring at Halloran's grieving face, certain he couldn't be faking. I began thinking maybe Ted was right; Halloran couldn't be behind Thurston's death. Yet with everything that had happened—

"He does that a lot, you know," Mattie said. "Cries. Remember Hurricane Andrew. When he was talking to that little girl who lost her family. They kept replaying it on TV. The President was really bawling during that one."

Halloran did have a reputation for being open with his emotions. He came off as human and caring, which rang up votes. When he began speaking again, his wife's arm was on his shoulder.

His voice shaking with emotion, Halloran said, I thought I could get through this, but . . ." He paused, swallowing, tears rolling down his cheeks.

"Yep, he lost it," Mattie said almost happily. She returned to her computer.

The President gave a brief wave and slowly made his way back across the courtyard, arm in arm with the First Lady. The camera pulled back, showing the grief-stricken President being comforted by his wife. A tender moment, and I couldn't help but wonder if this had been just a well-orchestrated photo op. That picture would be plastered on the front pages across the country, which meant Halloran's approval rating was about to rocket out of sight.

The scene changed to the CNN studio. A solemn-faced Marsha Blaine sat at the anchor desk and announced quietly, "I think I can say that all of America shares the President's grief—"

Rita hit the mute button. "You've got to admit he's good. He practically had me in tears."

I was surprised by her sarcastic tone. Rita'd always been a diehard Halloran fan. "You mean you didn't swallow that?"

She sighed and returned to her stack of folders. "The act is getting old, John. At first I thought it was refreshing for Halloran to be so sensitive. But that . . ." She nodded at the TV "That was a little much."

"You don't think he was sincere?" I said.

"No. I think he's sincere, all right." She made a face. I just don't think we should see him blubbering all over the place. I mean he's the President, for chrissakes."

I nodded. I wanted to convince myself Halloran hadn't just been putting on a show, but I couldn't.

I pushed away from the desk. "Mattie, I need a favor. . . ."

"Sure, Colonel," Mattie replied, looking up at me over her glasses. "I can call up Rich Majesky over at Washington Approach and see if they tracked a Blackhawk in the area. He's a shift supervisor. He should be able to dig up the info pretty quick."

"If that doesn't turn up anything, try all the military bases within a couple hundred miles. See if they had any birds up this way"

Her curly locks bobbed as she made notations in a notepad.

"One more thing," I said. "You know anything about computer imaging enhancement software programs? You know, to clear up pictures."

"Sure. Some of that stuff is becoming commercially available, but it's still pretty expensive."

"I'm talking state-of-the-art software." I explained what I needed.

When I finished, Mattie was sucking thoughtfully on the end of her pen. Her face brightened. "Yeah. Over at the Defense Intelligence Agency. The intel targeting guys. They have all sorts of software to enhance satellite shots. Amazing stuff. When I was working AWACS during the Gulf War, some DIA types came over and gave us an intel briefing. They showed us shots taken during a sandstorm in Iraq. Couldn't see much at first, but then the briefers showed the same pictures after they'd computer-enhanced them. Bingo, I saw Scud missiles, people. Pretty neat."

"Set something up for today. The sooner the better."

She jotted on the pad. "Anything else?"

"That's it, Mattie. Thanks." As I turned to leave, a phone behind me rang.

I was almost out the door when Rita called. She held out a phone. "Darcey Mobley," she said.

I frowned, then remembered. Darcey had been Rita's slightly scatterbrained predecessor in the public affairs office. A knockout with a spectacular figure, she had been very popular with the male reporters who covered the President. One of them had pulled some strings and gotten her a job at a major paper.

I took the phone and heard the loud sounds of traffic, like Darcey was standing near a busy road.

"Hello, Darcey."

As she began talking in that little-girl falsetto of hers, a car horn blared, almost drowning her out. Still I understood her.

"Jeez, John, I think you're in trouble," Darcey said.

I pressed the phone to my ear, listening to the sounds of traffic.

"Something wrong, John?" Rita asked.

"What're you talking about, Darcey?" I said into the phone.

There was a pause, then Darcey began talking rapidly. "I work the police beat, John. Minor stuff, muggings, DWIs, an occasional robbery. Normally I wouldn't know about this, but Tanya Kingman is a good friend. She's a secretary. We do dinner occasionally, see a movie . . ."

Rita spun. I heard a click as she picked up.

". . . So anyway, Tanya comes up to me about a half hour ago and asks me about you. Tanya knows I worked out there. I ask her why the interest. She says her boss is going to release a column tomorrow that's going to nail you. She says it's real bad. I figured you should know. But

I didn't want to take a chance calling from the office, so I waited to get to a pay phone. I'm real sorry, John."

My stomach churned. I knew the answer, but I asked anyway. "Darcey, who do you work for?"

"The *Post.* I thought you knew—"

"And your friend's boss . . ."

"Mr. Walling."

I swallowed, saying nothing. Rita was watching me, her face pained.

Darcey said, "John, you there?"

"You know what's in the article?" I asked.

"Some. Walling found out you and Rick were good friends. He's bringing that up, saying that's proof you can't be objective. Tanya says he really works you over. What's this all about, John? What does he have against you?"

"I don't know, Darcey. But thanks."

A pause. "Sure, John. Take care, huh."

When I hung up, my hand was trembling. Rita was looking at me, a sad expression on her face. Mattie was simultaneously talking into a phone and pecking on her keyboard, oblivious.

"John, how bad can it be?" Rita said. "It would be just innuendo, suspicion—"

"That's enough."

"Christ, I'm sorry, John."

"Sir!" Mattie shouted, the phone to her ear. "Major Lynn Sanders from DIA says she can probably help. She'll be free around 1530 hours today. That okay?"

I blinked. "Uh, sure. Fine."

Mattie returned to the phone.

Rita touched my arm. "Anything I can do—"

"There isn't." I went over to Mattie to get Major Sanders's phone number, then I left.

• • •

The anger I felt from Darcey's call gave way to an odd sense of relief. That I was going to be canned had been inevitable; the only question was when, and now I knew. Along with that knowledge came a sense of freedom I was damn well going to make the most of.

Sure, I was about to break about half a dozen Air Force regulations, and Ted would probably be bugged because I didn't talk to him first, but I didn't give a damn about that either.

As I walked to the parking lot, I took out Kendra's card and made the call.

Office sounds. Then a bubbly voice said, "Richter Institute. Legal."

I identified myself to Miss Bubbles and asked for Kendra. I was getting into the car when Kendra came on. "My, my, you're full of surprises, John. I wasn't expecting another call for a couple of days. Does this mean you found the tape?"

Ignoring the question, I started the car. "Who in Richter knows about the tape?"

"I told you. No one but me—"

"C'mon, Kendra. A story this big?" I put the car in gear and headed down Command Drive.

"That," Kendra said, "is precisely why I haven't told anyone. The story is too big. There would be leaks."

I thought it over. "Okay, I just had to be certain." I hesitated. "We can work together, but I want one last shot to run whatever we find up my chain of command."

"You must be kidding, John. You can't be that naive. Jesus."

"That's the deal." After a moment, I went on. "Remember, you said you don't care how the truth gets out, only that it does."

"If your way doesn't work—"

"It's all yours," I said.

"You didn't find the tape, huh?"

"How did you know?"

"You wouldn't be calling if you had." An audible sigh. "Okay. I'll try to find a lead on the tape or any copies. You figure out what caused the crash. We share everything. Agreed?"

"Absolutely."

"Look, there's something about me you should probably know."

"You're Governor Ken Banks's daughter."

"You knew?"

"Ted figured it out."

"And that's not . . . a problem?"

"Not unless you've suddenly become a Halloran fan."

A sarcastic laugh. "Not likely. Anything else you need, John?"

"Actually, there is. . . ." I told her about Holt and Morgan.

When I finished, Kendra said, "Odds are they're part of the cadre Halloran installed into the FBI when he took over. Most were state cops who worked for Halloran when he was governor. The regular FBI types can't stand them."

"Did you know these guys when your father was governor?"

"No. They were probably assigned to the detail later. After my father . . ." She fell silent for a moment, then asked, "Why did Morgan and Holt want the photos, anyway?"

I explained briefly and told her we were working on an ID of the chopper. Ahead, the flight line was coming up. "Look, I've got to run. Call me if you come up with anything."

"Sure, John. Just remember, that goes both ways."

Then she was gone.

I slipped the phone into my jacket and took a right toward the hangar.

• • •

Hangar number six was the nearest of the twin hangars located on the south end of the Andrews Air Force Base flight line. My watch read ten minutes after eleven when I parked next to a line of cars in the makeshift parking lot maybe fifty yards away. A red-roped security perimeter spanned the hangar entrance in a giant half-circle.

I walked quickly across the bright concrete toward the entry point, manned by a security policeman. Inside the hangar, I could see the fuselage, one of the wings, and a few smaller pieces from the plane. Once everything was recovered, a scaled-down grid of the crash site would be marked out on the floor. The pieces would then be laid out precisely in their original relative positions, so the wreckage pattern could be studied to determine if it gave any indication as to the cause of the accident. In this case, with the wreckage generally intact, the pattern wasn't going to tell us much.

Most of the thirty or so people milling around inside were Air Force personnel. My eyes settled on the three civilians standing by the fuselage, and I felt my temper rise.

Kroft with Jennifer. I couldn't make out the face of the man they were talking to, since his back was to me. I spotted Ogden and Tom Blaney over to the right, near a set of metal doors leading to the maintenance offices.

But no Ted.

I approached the security cop. He ran the drill, checking my name against a list.

Jennifer was pointing toward the back of the fuselage. Kroft walked over to take a look. The second man turned, following. I saw the beard—

I stared, dumbfounded.

*Him? Here?* I was outraged.

"Go on in, sir," the cop said. He started to salute, but I was already walking away.

As I entered the hangar, I heard rapid footsteps to my right. "John—" A hand touched my shoulder.

Ogden, shaking his head. Tom Blaney stood by his side.

"What the fuck is Walling doing here, Nate?" I snapped.

"He's authorized to be here."

I felt like I'd been slapped.

"General Ware approved it . . . ," Ogden said.

I shrugged his arm loose. "Fuck—"

". . . supposedly as a PR move, to show we've got nothing to hide."

"Well, if it isn't Colonel Quinn," a snide voice called out.

I looked over and saw Walling staring at me, his hands on his hips, his hairy face opened into an arrogant grin. He strolled toward me, Jennifer on his heels. Kroft remained by the plane, watching.

"Easy, John," Ogden said into my ear.

The hangar, which had hummed with voices, went quiet. People were focused on me, faces tense. Most of them were obviously aware of last night's scene.

"Prick," someone muttered.

As Walling sauntered up, the plastic grin never left his face. He removed one of those tiny cassette recorders from his jacket and held it out. I wanted to shove it up his ass.

"How about a response to the charges your investigation is biased in favor of the pilots, Colonel?" Walling asked.

I gave him a hard look. "No comment—"

"Some people are saying the Air Force is worried about the political fallout if the pilots are found negligent. Care to comment on that?"

"No."

Behind Walling, Jennifer shifted her feet, looking decidedly uncomfortable.

"Come, come, surely you can say something in your defense," Walling said. "These allegations are serious, Colonel. The American people have a right to know."

"No comment."

"Many people think you'll be removed from the investigation soon."

I gazed at him evenly. "You, for instance."

Walling's face became a mask. "What about the statement by Senator Rivard that he intends to call for a congressional investigation?"

That one shook me. Rivard ran the Senate's Armed Forces Committee. I tried to sound calm. "I've got nothing to say."

Walling's eyes bored into me. A disdainful smile came to his lips. I braced myself expecting him to bring up my relationship with Rick.

Instead, Walling clicked off the recorder. "Have a helluva nice day, Colonel." He casually strolled out of the hangar.

Jennifer was staring at me. Was there something in her eyes? Shame? She turned and followed Walling.

A hand patted me on the back. "Man, what's with that son of a bitch?" Ogden asked.

"Maybe he had a domineering mother," I said dryly.

Ogden managed a smile.

A few maintenance troops gave me nods of support. Behind me, Tom Blaney suddenly clapped his hands loudly. "Okay, back to work, people. Show's over—"

I gave Ogden a sympathetic look. "You look beat, Nate."

"You noticed, huh? Gonna grab a few hours of shuteye, then head back out to the site. Probably be finished out there in a couple of days." He grinned. "Then the rest of the bullshit is up to you."

"You're all heart."

"I told Tom Blaney to work on removing those valves. We tried to jack up the fuselage earlier, gain access to the hellhole panel. No go. Damn thing is too structurally unsound. We're going to have to brace it first with beams. Might not get those valves until later this afternoon. That okay?"

"Have him do it as soon as he can. What the hell was Walling doing here, anyway?"

A shrug. "Getting a tour of our setup, checking out how we handle an investigation, that sort of thing. Dr. Johnson and Kroft showed him around. I listened in for a bit, but Dr. Johnson and Kroft seemed to be answering all his questions about the crash."

I frowned. "Kroft was answering questions?"

Ogden suppressed a yawn. "Surprised me a little, too. But the man knows his stuff. Must have done some flying. Interesting fella, Kroft."

As Ogden spoke, I looked past him toward the parking area. Jennifer and Walling were having an animated dis-

cussion. I saw her spin away angrily and walk back toward the entry point. Walling stared after her for a moment, then hurried over to a dark blue sedan. Kroft stood by the fuselage and watched them, his square face troubled.

"Yeah, Kroft's a real interesting fella," I murmured.

"Here, John." I glanced down to see Ogden holding out a small envelope.

"Rick's wedding band," he said softly.

I peered inside the envelope, then slipped it into my jacket pocket. "You seen Ted?"

Ogden pointed toward the metal doors at the back.

I'd taken a half-dozen steps when a voice said, "Colonel Quinn—"

I recognized the deep baritone before I turned.

Kroft came to a stop a few feet away. "I should apologize for Mr. Walling, Colonel. I hope you understand I had nothing to do with him being here."

I glowered but kept quiet.

"You're wrong about me, Colonel," Kroft continued. *Christ. What's with this guy?* "I'm busy, Kroft."

Kroft held out a hand. "The photos of the Gibson girl."

"You must be kidding."

"Colonel, may I rermind you—"

"No," I snapped. "Let me remind you. Check with your boys, Morgan and Holt. They've already got the goddamn photos."

Kroft looked at me, stunned. "You don't have them?"

"Give it up, Kroft. You know I don't. Now get the—"

But Kroft was already rapidly walking away. I frowned, confused. His reaction didn't make sense. He had to be the one who'd told Holt and Morgan about the film. Unless—

I swore softly.

Someone else knew.

The big metal door at the far end of the hangar read OP-
ERATIONAL MAINTENANCE SQUADRON SHIFT SUPERVISOR.

I pushed through into a cluttered office that smelled of
stale cigarette smoke. A fat sergeant with a mat of stringy
hair sat at a battered desk, munching on chips and reading
a biker magazine. The sergeant casually glanced up, then
slapped the magazine shut and struggled to his feet.

I waved him to remain seated, reading his name off his
oil-stained fatigues. "I'm looking for Colonel Chen, Rick-
etts."

Ricketts gestured nervously with a grimy hand.
"Down . . . down the hall. Second door on the right, sir."

I went to the door and heard Ted's voice: ". . . that's
right. The entire site. I don't give a damn, Carl. I want to
know the second you find anything, you got that?"

I poked my head in as Ted slammed down the phone. He
was sitting at a desk that looked even more dilapidated

than the one outside. Two nervous-looking buck sergeants sat before him in straight-backed wooden chairs.

"Come in, John," Ted said, eyeing me. "Guess you noticed Walling poking around."

"I noticed."

Ted waved a hand. "Say hi to Sergeants Timmons and Glover. Timmons was the crew chief on the bird that crashed. Glover here works for passenger services."

I gave the two sergeants a nod. Their eyes never left the eagles on my shoulders.

Ted looked at them and said, "They both remember Thurston having a briefcase, right, guys?"

Emphatic head bobs from the men. Before I could get too excited, Ted added, "But we haven't located the briefcase, John."

Ted abruptly leaned toward the men, his eyes hard. "Don't mention the briefcase to anyone else, you got me?" he said menacingly.

"No, sir," Timmons barked. Glover shook his head vigorously.

"I hear you've been talking, I'll have your asses tossed in the slammer so fast it'll make your heads spin."

Timmons licked his lips. Glover's mouth opened, then snapped shut.

Ted flicked his head toward the door. "Beat it."

The two men practically ran out.

I took a seat. "Playing a little rough, aren't you?"

Ted grinned. "Figure they'd keep quiet that way. Don't want the word to get out we know a briefcase was on the plane."

I glanced at the phone. "What was that about?"

"Lieutenant Colonel Carl Kandel is handling recovery ops at the site now. He was giving me some bullshit that he didn't have the manpower to run another complete sweep of the site." Ted winked. "But I talked him into it."

"It'll be a waste of time. The briefcase is missing because it contained the videotape."

"The guys in the chopper wouldn't have had much time to search. We could get lucky."

I rubbed my face. "Anyway, we're running out of time." I told him about Darcey's call.

Ted tented his fingers on the desk, speaking slowly. "Well, it's not like we weren't expecting this. It's pretty clear their plan was to destroy your credibility so they could have someone else put in charge." He gave me a long look, and I knew he was talking about Jennifer. After a moment, he added quietly, "You thought about what I said last night?"

"Yeah."

"And . . ."

I reached into my pocket and removed the envelope. I slipped out the ring and slid it over to him.

Ted's face softened. "Rick's?"

I nodded.

"You know, there's no guarantee we'll even succeed. Probably won't."

I shrugged. "I would have made a lousy general anyway."

Ted smiled, returning the ring. "Okay."

I related Kroft's surprise over the photos being appropriated by Morgan and Holt, and my suspicions about Jennifer. Then I told him about the meeting at DIA and my talk with Kendra.

"Good. I was about to suggest calling her."

His comment surprised me. "I thought you didn't trust her."

He leaned back, folding his hands behind his head. "I don't, John. But time is the critical element now, and we need all the help we can get. The way I see it—" He broke

off, looking past me. "You got something for me, Sergeant Durrel?"

I turned as a female staff sergeant walked in, holding a small cardboard box.

"Yes, sir," Sergeant Durrell said, coming over. "Airman Bishop found this wedged under a seat leg in the cabin. It's Mr. Thurston's."

She set the box on the desk, and Ted and I peered inside. We saw a leather binder with a small gold plaque engraved with Thurston's name.

"Thank you, Sergeant Durrell," Ted said without looking up.

As Durrell left, Ted removed the day planner. He opened the cover and quickly began flipping pages. I drew my chair around to see.

Ted stopped, and I read the date: Wednesday, March 2, the day before Joshua Thurston died.

The writing was neat and precise. Thurston had three morning appointments, all with military officers. In the afternoon, there was only a single entry, at four P.M.

*Meeting with K.B. at Flannaghan's.*

Ted flipped a page to Thursday, the day of the crash. Another appointment with K.B. for 7 P.M.

"Looks like Kendra was telling the truth," I said.

"So it seems," Ted said.

I frowned at something in his voice. "You don't sound convinced."

Ted shrugged. He flipped back to Tuesday. "Interesting," he murmured.

I nodded. A number of what seemed to be routine appointments during the day, but what had caught Ted's interest was the entry at eight that evening.

A meeting with President Halloran.

Ted turned to Monday. "Another meeting with Halloran at seven." He flipped to Sunday. "Again. At eight."

He began turning the pages faster, going back two months, but there were no other appointments with Halloran. He leaned back, his face thoughtful. "Thurston had no meetings with his brother for two months, then had three in three days. Now, the question is were those meetings tied to his death?"

I didn't reply. I was rereading Thurston's appointments over the past week to see if we'd missed anything. After a few moments, Ted joined me.

We were on the Tuesday. I was about to turn the page when Ted pointed to an entry written in the margin.

*Call Lieutenant Colonel Mike Keele.* Below was a phone number.

"So Thurston called some light bird," I said.

"Maybe nothing, but I know Mike. He's one of the OSI's top investigators."

The Office of Special Investigations, located on Bolling AFB just southeast of D.C., was the Air Force's criminal investigation arm.

I tried to sound calm. "This guy Mike have a particular specialty?"

"Homicides," Ted said, and reached for the phone.

"Mike should be in later this afternoon," Ted said, hanging up. He yawned, rubbing his eyes.

"You don't seem surprised Thurston might have been checking into a homicide," I said dryly.

A tight smile. "I'm not. I knew there had to be something extremely serious behind Thurston's murder."

I paused, waiting for him to state the obvious. When he didn't, I said, "You know, if Thurston discovered Halloran was involved in a murder—"

Ted looked at me like I was crazy. "Don't be silly, John. Halloran never killed anyone."

My eyes popped wide. "You can't be serious. Have you forgotten what Kendra said? Thurston was going to turn over evidence that would bring Halloran down."

"I don't care what she said. The facts don't point to Halloran."

I couldn't believe what I was hearing. "How the hell can you be so certain?" I snapped.

Ted sighed, giving me a look of impatience. "Four points, John. One, we don't have any evidence linking Halloran to the cover-up of a murder. Two, Thurston was his half brother, and I still don't believe he'd have him killed. Three, Thurston's meetings with Halloran last week suggest to me he was working with Halloran, not against him." He paused, eyeing me. "And four, Halloran's in fucking Russia."

The last statement threw me. "What does being in Russia—"

"Tell me, John," Ted interrupted, "if you were going to run a murder conspiracy, would you do it from eight thousand miles away?"

"Of course not, but—"

"Neither would Halloran. Neither would anyone. That would be stupid as hell and—"

From the hallway came the sound of a distraught voice. "John! Where are you? John!"

"Speak of the devil," Ted muttered.

When Jennifer walked in, she wasn't crying but she was definitely on the verge. Her face was pale and her lips quivered. She held out her phone in a shaky hand.

In the years we'd been married, I'd never seen Jennifer this upset. One of her particular talents had always been her ability to control her emotions.

I stood and guided her to a chair. Ted hopped up and came around.

"What's wrong, Jennifer?" I asked.

She looked at her cell phone. "Jimmy Ray just called. The sheriff's office just received word."

"The Gibson girl?" Ted asked.

"What did he say?" I asked.

She looked to me, blinking rapidly. "They . . . they found her body floating in the Potomac."

I felt sick. "When?"

Jennifer's face became blank. "He . . . he didn't say."

Ted went to his desk and snared a phone. "What's Jimmy Ray's goddamn number?"

Jennifer passed it on, and Ted spoke for less than two minutes. Hanging up, he faced us, shaking his head grimly. "Some guy fishing with his kid found her floating off Maryland Point about two hours ago. She's been taken to the Baltimore City Morgue."

"Cause of death?" I asked.

Ted shook his head. "You got my keys?"

"You going out there?"

"I want to know how she died, John," he said quietly.

"They won't have performed an autopsy yet."

"Like we've got time to wait."

Jennifer was frowning at Ted. Color had returned to her cheeks, and she seemed to have already recovered from the shock of hearing the news.

I tossed Ted his car keys. "You drive."

"I'm coming," Jennifer said.

Ted gave me a slight head shake.

"No, Jennifer," I said, gently placing my hand on her arm. "You should stay. You've had a shock . . ."

Jennifer rose, shrugging my hand away. "Don't be so damned patronizing, John. I want to know what happened

to that poor girl. Now, either I come with you or I'll drive out myself." She placed her hands on her hips. "Well?"

I knew the look.

I made two calls before I finally reached the coroner on duty.

Dr. Harvey Vinjaya spoke in a clipped British accent. In the background I heard classical music, and I wondered if that made cutting into bodies easier to take. Dr. Vinjaya sounded puzzled when I identified myself.

"From the Air Force? You want to look at a body we have?"

"Miss Allison Gibson. I understand she's been sent there."

"Miss Gibson? No—" He cupped the phone. Muffled voices. He came back on, sounding irritated. "Wait a moment." The phone banged as he set it down.

I drummed the table, listening to Beethoven's "Ode to joy" as Ted and Jennifer watched.

Finally, Vinjaya picked up. "I apologize, Colonel. A slight mix-up. She is here. just arrived for processing. Now, what is your interest?"

"I'm a military accident investigator."

"Aircraft accidents?"

"Yes."

"Ah . . ." Vinjaya made a clicking sound with his tongue.

"Doctor, I wonder if—"

Vinjaya interrupted, an undercurrent of excitement in his voice. "What is the nature of the accident you're presently investigating?"

"I'm really not at liberty to talk about specifics."

"Perhaps the one in the papers. The one involving President Halloran's brother?"

"Doctor, please . . ."

"I understand. Not over the phone. But you think this girl's body is connected to a crash you're investigating? Might her body have come from the same plane?"

"There's a possibility, yes," That wasn't exactly true, of course. But her death was related.

The doctor's tongue clicked again. "Fascinating. That might explain it. Yes, yes, by all means come. I think you'll find it quite interesting."

I dug out my notepad. "Your address . . ."

The drive north on I-295 to Baltimore took almost forty minutes. I rode in front with Ted, while Jennifer sat silently in the back. Her reaction convinced me she wouldn't knowingly be involved in a murder conspiracy, but I couldn't shake the damning implication that she was involved with McKenzie.

Something else also concerned me—the way Ted kept looking in the rearview mirror. A couple times he speeded up, going well above the speed limit, only to slow down a few miles later. After the second time, he gave a grunt of satisfaction.

The morgue was located in the University of Maryland Medical Center, near the city center. We drove through an automatic gate into the loading area, parking two spots over from a black hearse. Two bored-looking attendants were loading a coffin into the back. A local sports-talk show blared out from the radio in the cab.

We passed through steel doors into a large room of gleaming white tile. From somewhere inside we heard the faint sounds of classical music. Ahead and to our right were two identical sets of metal slab doors. A young Hispanic man in green surgical scrubs sat behind a Plexiglas window to our left.

As we walked over, the window opened and the antiseptic smell of formaldehyde wafted out. "Help you?" the man asked. He had a swarthy complexion and short curly hair. His name tag said "Jorge Ortega."

"Dr. Vinjaya, Jorge." Then I explained.

Jorge looked down at something out of sight. "Oh, sure. You're here for the Gibson girl." He shook his head, grimacing. "That's a bad one. Been here two years, and haven't seen many bodies busted up like that. Let me buzz Dr. V. He's pretty excited about this one." The window closed.

Jennifer stepped off to the side, hugging herself. I watched her for a moment.

A door across from us opened and a lean, handsome man of East Asian descent stepped out. He squinted at me through blackrimmed glasses. "Colonel Quinn, I'm Dr. Vinjaya."

We shook, and I introduced Jennifer and Ted, then thanked him for seeing us.

He clicked his tongue. "Not at all, Colonel. As soon as you told me you were investigating a plane crash, I knew this had to be related. Frankly, that's the only explanation, considering the tremendous trauma to the body. The cooler is this way. . . ." Vinjaya smiled graciously at Jennifer and led us to the second set of doors. As we pushed our way inside, we were greeted by a pungent, sweetly rotten odor.

The room was big and square and very cold, with at least two dozen long metal tables that gleamed under the harshness of the recessed fluorescent lights. I counted

seven body bags—five white, two black—on the tables. Music came from speakers mounted at opposite corners in the ceiling. I figured some psychologist had probably done a study that concluded classical music improved morale for people who worked with corpses.

When Jennifer made a faint, gagging noise, Vinjaya gave her a sympathetic smile. "The smell takes some getting used to, I'm afraid."

Jennifer nodded. She pointed. "The body bags. Why the different colors?"

"Black is used for bodies that have been breached or traumatized. Accidents or burn victims or ones that have already begun to decay. Those require special handling. Are you sure you're all right?"

"Fine." Jennifer smiled weakly.

Vinjaya led us to a table near the back upon which lay a black body bag. As we gathered around, he said, "We haven't performed the autopsy, but that will probably be just a formality. Cause of death will undoubtably be related to the impact trauma."

When Vinjaya reached for the bag, Jennifer tensed; Ted's face remained blank. Vinjaya pulled the zipper, adjusted the opening, then stepped back.

Jennifer sucked in a sharp breath. I felt the bile rise in my throat. Ted continued to stare, expressionless.

Allison Gibson may have been pretty once, but not now. She lay faceup, nude, her bloated body a mass of purplish bruising. Below her breasts, three jagged pieces of rib poked through the skin. Her crushed, misshapen face was what got to me, particularly the eyes, which were now grisly empty sockets.

"Her eyes," I murmured. "What happened?"

"She must have struck the water facedown," Vinjaya said. "The force of the impact drove her eyes back into her head. She also suffered a number of obvious fractures.

Pelvis, vertebrae, ribs . . . That's why I think this might be related to your—"

Jennifer stepped back suddenly and turned away. Vinjaya watched her, concerned.

I was focused on Ted. His blank expression never changed. I had the feeling he'd known all along what had happened to her.

"I think that's enough," I said.

"Of course," Vinjaya said.

As he zipped up the bag, Jenmifer said, "Doctor, you were saying this might be related to . . ."

"Yes, yes. To your investigation. She fell a great distance before striking the water. I suppose she could have jumped from one of the bridges over the river, but that's highly unlikely. They simply aren't high enough to generate the velocity for this kind of damage."

Jennifer stared at him in disbelief. "You're saying she fell from an airplane, Doctor?"

"The only explanation. From a plane or a helicopter."

"But not ours," I said quickly.

"Oh?"

I shook my head. "The accident we're looking into is completely unrelated. No one fell from the plane we're investigating. That would be impossible. It never broke up in the air."

Now Vinjaya looked confused. "Then why did you come here?"

"Military regulations, Doc," Ted said, flashing an apologetic smile. "The Air Force is sticklers for everything. They have us check out all the leads. You know how it is."

Jennifer's eyes darted between Ted and me. "Hey, what are you guys trying to—"

"Dr. Vinjaya!"

We turned. Jorge Ortega stood by the doors, motioning. "Doctor!"

Behind him were two men in suits, one tall and gangly, the other heavy, with a crew cut.

"Shit," Ted muttered as Vinjaya hurried over.

"John, who are they?" Jennifer asked.

I gave her a dark look. "You don't know?"

"Should I?"

"You're sure, huh?"

"What's that supposed to mean?" she snapped.

Her anger seemed genuine. Anyway, Jennifer couldn't have tipped them off, since she was with us the whole time.

So maybe we had been followed.

I recognized Agents Holt and Morgan from the audiovisual lab, though I didn't know who was who. They stood over in a corner with Vinjaya. The tall man did all the talking. Vinjaya nodded his head almost continually and became increasingly agitated. Twice he looked our way and glowered.

"Who are those guys?" Jennifer asked me again.

"We'd better go," Ted said.

"Dammit, John—"

"Shut up, Jennifer," I grunted, and she blinked in shock.

Ted started for the exit.

"Wait," I said to him. "I want to know what the hell they're doing here."

Vinjaya seemed very angry now. He shot us a final glare, hurrying from the room.

The two men conferred briefly and walked toward us.

The tall agent smiled at me and held out his FBI ID with a shiny badge that I ignored. In a twangy drawl, he said, "I'm Agent Randy Morgan. This is Agent Pete Holt—"

"Get to the point, Morgan," I said curtly. "What do you want?"

Morgan's smile faded into a tight line. "We want you to leave, Colonel. Now."

"You've got no authority—"

Holt cut me off, an edge to his voice. "You're interfering with a federal investigation." He, too, had a southern accent, but not as pronounced.

"What the hell do you mean, a federal investigation?" Ted demanded.

"The kidnapping of Miss Allison Gibson," Morgan said.

"Aw, Christ . . ." Ted shook his head.

Jennifer looked a little dazed. "A kidnapping? You think she was kidnapped?"

"Bullshit," Ted grunted.

Morgan's face turned hard. "Colonel Quinn, I'll ask you once more. If you don't leave immediately—"

"You'll what?" I snarled. "Call your fucking handlers and tell them I was uncooperative? Or maybe throw cuffs on us and drag us to jail? Go to hell!"

Morgan turned bright red. He started to say something, but I brushed past him, heading for the door.

I was still shaking with anger as I climbed into the car. I massaged my temples, trying to calm down.

Ted started the engine and glanced over with obvious approval. "Nice going, John. I didn't know you had that in you."

I didn't reply. Ted grinned, pulling out of the parking space. Once we passed through the gate, he made a left into traffic.

From the backseat, Jennifer said, "So why did you think I knew those men?"

Ted watched her in the rearview mirror as I turned around. Jennifer stared back, arms folded, face tight.

"You really didn't?" I asked.

"How many times do I have to say it. Jesus. Why would you think I knew them?"

"They're involved in the investigation. We thought you'd probably run across them." The explanation sounded lame, but it was the best I could do.

Jennifer gave me an icy look. "I'm supposed to believe that? What about what happened back there with the Gibson girl? You guys didn't act very surprised when you saw her. And what was that song and dance with Dr. Vinjaya, telling him her death was completely unrelated to our investigation? You obviously don't believe that, or you would never have come here."

Ted was hunched over the wheel, eyes fixed straight ahead, a subtle way of saying he was staying out of it.

"I don't know what you're talking about, Jennifer," I said stiffly, facing front.

"Don't insult my intelligence by lying, John. You never were a very good liar anyway."

That bothered me. During our marriage, I'd never lied to her. Now she was just being mean.

"What about the film we found?" Jennifer asked. "Did you get it developed, or is that some damn secret too? I thought we'd reached an understanding last night. But now . . . Jesus, you guys make me sick, with your goddamn games—"

I spun, angry now. "You want to talk about secrets, fine. How about telling us why McKenzie brought you into this thing? And here's another one. Remember your prima donna act at the press conference, *my* press conference. What was that all about? Oh, I forgot. You won't talk about *that*."

I saw shock in her eyes. She took a ragged breath, fighting to hold her anger in check. "You son of a bitch—"

"Am I, Jennifer? Why? Because I don't want you reporting on every goddamn thing we do? Tell you what, you want to know about the film, ask McKenzie. You obviously told him about it. While you're at it, ask him what he knows about that dead girl back there."

That threw her. The anger on her face was replaced by uncertainty. "What do you mean?"

"You really don't know, huh?" I said sarcastically. "Those men back there confiscated the film. Makes me damn curious what they don't want us to see."

"You're lying, John."

"Yeah? Well, maybe. But do yourself a favor. Ask McKenzie."

"I didn't tell him about the film."

"No? Well, you sure told someone."

Jennifer started to respond, then caught herself. I saw doubt in her eyes. She looked away.

I turned around, expecting her to fire back a response. Jennifer always had to get in the last word. But she didn't make a peep all the way back to Andrews.

When we pulled into the parking area near the hangar, Jennifer hopped out before the car rolled to a complete stop. She hurried to a red Mercedes and climbed in. Jennifer would have a Mercedes, I thought. Tires squealed as she roared off down the street.

"You think I was a little rough?" I asked Ted as Jennifer's car disappeared around a corner.

Ted killed the engine. "It needed to be said."

"How deep you think she is into this thing?"

"Hard to say. I'm almost certain she doesn't know anything about the girl's death."

"Because of her reaction in the morgue?"

Ted nodded. "Her shock was real, but she evidently mentioned the film to someone."

"She made it pretty clear she didn't tell McKenzie. And Kroft is out, since he didn't know about it."

Another nod. "Which leaves us with two questions. Who did she tell? And why, if she wasn't trying to cover up the girl's death?"

"Could be she just happened to mention it, not understanding the significance."

"Maybe." He reached for the door handle. "You coming?"

I shook my head. "Think I'll run by the Command Post."

As he handed me the keys, I asked, "You think those FBI guys followed us?"

Ted thought, then shook his head. "I think they were going over there to run a little damage control. Their job is to keep the details of the girl's death quiet."

I nodded. "So how'd you figure out how the girl died?"

Ted shrugged. "Nothing magical, John. I tried to put myself in the place of the helicopter crew. They have a witness they can't leave at the crash site. The logical solution would be to take her with them to dispose of later. So when Jennifer said she'd been found in the river . . ." He didn't bother to finish.

I closed my eyes for a moment, picturing the girl's terror as they forced her out of the helicopter. I felt something close to hate.

"You have a handgun?" Ted asked quietly.

I glanced over, startled.

"McKenzie's going to know we're onto him. You have a pistol or not?"

I shook my head. I'd never been into guns. Sure, I fired one each year for my annual qualification. But I wasn't like Ted, who had a small arsenal from his police days.

"No matter. I'll let you use one of mine." He opened the door and climbed out.

As I slid into the driver's seat, I felt fear for the first time.

Driving to the Command Post, I saw the signs for base housing and remembered the ring in my pocket. For a moment, I was tempted to continue past the turn; I didn't want

to see Rick's wife Janet now, see her grief and devastation. What would I say to her?

I flipped on the blinker, hoping something would come to mind.

Lieutenant Colonel Rick French's house was a modest three-bedroom at the end of a quiet cul-de-sac on the western end of the base. As I drove up, I saw Rick's bass boat in the driveway, the cover still on. I tried to recall how many times we'd gone fishing. Three. No, four. The last time had been almost a year before. He'd called a number of times since, but I'd always been too busy. Doing what, I didn't recall. It couldn't have been anything important.

As I parked along the curb, I was mildly surprised no other cars were there. Flying squadrons were close-knit units, and I figured people would be stopping by constantly to comfort Janet. The house was silent and dark as I walked to the door. No one answered the bell, and I felt a sense of relief.

I was about to leave when a woman called out from the next yard. She said Janet and the girls had gone to Janet's parents' house in Springfield and she wasn't sure when they were coming back. We spoke for a few minutes about what a tragedy Rick's death was, and how it was going to be so hard on Janet and the girls. The woman started to tear up, saying how life wasn't fair. Taking a good man, like Rick.

When I returned to the car, I sat for a long time. Finally, I drove to the Command Post.

"**C**'mon, Rich, what do you mean you can't send over the packet," Major Mattie Parker was saying into the phone. She pushed back from her desk, shaking her head. "We need the information. You guys can't—" Mattie fell silent when she spotted me standing in the conference-room doorway.

Rita was sitting at the second desk, also on a phone. She called out, "We got problems with the FAA, John."

"What?" I asked, coming over.

"Hang on, Rich," Maggie said. She cupped her phone. Rita did too, which confirmed she'd been listening in on the call.

"The FAA says they can't release the flight data packet to us," Rita said.

"*What?* Why?"

Mattie gave me a look of annoyance. "I'm talking to Rich Majesty. He's giving me some story about how the tapes were requested by Mort Conklin's office—"

I said, "The FAA administrator?"

"Right. Anyway, the tapes are gone."

I snared a phone from the table, punching the extension that was lit up.

Maggie said, "Rich, we've got Colonel Quinn on the line—"

"Rich, Colonel Quinn. What the hell is going on?"

An apologetic voice said, "Look, I'm sorry, Colonel. Hell, I'm not sure I've got a handle on everything myself. I just came on shift. All I can tell you is word came down ordering us to box up the original radar and voice tapes, including the dupes we made for you, and send them over to Mr. Conklin's office. At least that's what Marv said."

"Who is Marv?" I asked.

"Marv Brinker. The shift supervisor before me."

"Did the order come from Mr. Conklin?"

"The man himself. Marv spoke to him."

"Did someone from Mr. Conklin's office pick them up?"

"Uh-uh. Marv delivered them personally."

"I see."

"Look, you should be able to call over there and get the dupes without any problems."

*Like hell,* I thought. Ted was right. They had power.

Rich said tentatively, "Colonel?"

"I'm still here, Rich. Who was the controller?"

"The controller—"

"The radar controller manning the scope when the Lear crashed. Is he around?"

"Uh, that'd be Gloria Peters. She's off shift now. She works swings—"

"You have a number?"

"I'm not supposed to release that information—"

"Don't give me that bureaucratic crap, Rich."

A pause. "Hang on a sec." I dug out my notepad and a

pen. Rita was watching me, a frown on her face, and Mattie was gnawing on her lower lip.

A moment later, Rich came back and read off a number. "Hey, you didn't get it from me."

"Thanks, Rich," I said. "One more thing. Were you watching the scope when the plane went down?"

"Uh-uh. Came over after Gloria told me she lost the jet. I initiated the emergency net."

"Did you see any other aircraft in the vicinity?"

"Sure. That's a busy corridor for airline traffic."

"I mean helicopters."

"A helo?" he said, surprised. "No. Not at first. Saw the Air Force rescue birds when they came in, but that was later. 'Course, that doesn't mean much. Like I said, I wasn't really watching the scope."

"Did Gloria mention a helo in the area?"

"Not that I recall. But things got pretty hectic."

"Do me a favor and ask around. See if anyone noticed a chopper in the area."

A pause. "Why the interest in a chopper, Colonel? You think the crew saw something?"

"Just running down leads. Call Mattie if you come up with anything, Rich. Thanks again for the help."

"Sure. But if anyone asks, we never had this conversation." He hung up.

Rita started to say something, but I waved her off and punched in Gloria Peters's number.

Gloria Peters answered on the third ring. Her speech sounded slightly slurred and disjointed, like I'd woken her up.

I identified myself and asked if I could stop by. She said that was no problem; she'd been expecting someone to call about the crash. Rita copied down her address as I repeated it—a house less than twenty minutes north of the base near a state park. I told her I'd be there around two.

After I hung up, Mattie came over carrying an electronic organizer. "Sir, you want me to call Mr. Conklin, see if we can get the tapes?"

I nodded even though I knew it was a waste of time.

As Maggie phoned, Rita said, "What is it, John? Why would Mr. Conklin want the originals and the dupes?"

I shook my head. "I don't know."

"And the helicopter . . ."

"That's probably nothing. I heard one might have been in the area."

Her eyes searched my face like she was trying to determine if I was telling the truth. She must have decided I wasn't, because she asked, "What's really going on, John?"

I shook my head. "You don't want to know."

"C'mon, John—"

"Please, Rita," I said sharply. "No questions, huh?"

A hurt look crossed her face, and I immediately regretted my tone. Softly, I said, "I'm sorry, but I really can't get into this."

A barely perceptible nod.

We looked to Mattie, who was replacing the receiver, her face bewildered. "I don't get it."

"What?" I asked.

"Mr. Conklin's deputy said he doesn't know anything about the tapes. Said we must be mistaken."

Surprise, surprise. I started for the door.

"John," Rita called out. "Take care, huh?"

I looked back with what I hoped was a reassuring smile. "I will."

Walking toward the car, I noticed a maroon sedan parked maybe five spaces over. Two men in suits were visible in front. No surprises there.

As I drove away, the sedan followed. I needed a couple minutes to figure out how to handle the situation.

I called Ted first and gave him a heads-up. Then I phoned the Security Police and spoke to Chief Master Sergeant Haney.

"Sure, no problem, Colonel," Haney said after I told him what I wanted.

Ted was standing in the hangar parking area when I pulled up. I hopped out and tossed him the keys.

"That them?" Ted said, his eyes focusing past me.

I glanced to the maroon car parked across the street in the education center parking lot. "Yeah. Not very subtle, are they?"

"They want to be seen, John. They want you to be intimidated. In a way, this is good news."

I shot him a look of disbelief. "*Good* news? You crazy?"

"It is, John. They wouldn't risk something so obvious unless they were worried." He winked. "We must be getting close. Did you get everything set with Chief Haney?"

I nodded.

"Fine. Let's ditch these guys and see if Gloria Peters can tell us anything about the helicopter."

The Pearl Harbor Gate on the east side of the base was usually closed, open only in the mornings and evenings. As we approached, Ted nodded in satisfaction when he saw the gate was open, manned by a trio of security policemen. We'd been driving the speed limit of thirty-five. About two hundred yards away, Ted suddenly gunned the accelerator, trying to catch the driver of the sedan napping.

We flew through the gate with maybe a forty-yard lead. Ted immediately jammed on the brakes to keep from blowing through the intersection about a hundred yards beyond. Looking back, we saw the sedan fishtailing wildly as the

driver locked the tires to avoid slamming into the gate, which was closing. The sedan's driver pounded the steering wheel in frustration. One of the security policemen, a burly chief master sergeant, waved to us.

I waved back as Ted pulled out into traffic.

Gloria Peters lived a few miles south of Highway 214, about halfway between Washington, D.C., and Bowie, Maryland. Once we turned off the Beltway, the area became surprisingly rural. We followed a winding, two-lane blacktop road to a secluded ranch house surrounded by heavy woods. Ted and I parked in the driveway, then followed a stone pathway that cut across a neatly trimmed lawn toward the front door.

"Just a minute," we heard a muffled voice call after I rang the front bell. Moments later the door opened, revealing a short, heavyset woman with medium-length dark hair, holding a can of Diet Coke. She looked to be in her thirties and was dressed casually in a pair of faded jeans and a bulky University of Maryland sweatshirt.

"Miss Peters?" I said.

She smiled, showing little gaps in her upper teeth. "Come in, Colonel Quinn. And please, it's Gloria."

After I introduced Ted, Gloria Peters ushered us into a small, carpeted sitting room with a large picture window bracketed by pale blue drapes. The furnishings were modest but comfortable, and everything was neat and tidy. Ted and I sat on a floral sofa that faced the window, giving us a view of the lawn and the trees.

"May I get you something to drink?" Gloria asked, holding up the can.

Ted shook his head.

"No," I said. "This shouldn't take long."

She sat in an overstuffed chair to our right, her face be-

coming serious. "What exactly would you like to know, Colonel?"

"Briefly, we'd like an account of what you saw on your radar screen leading up to the time of the crash." I paused. "To include any aircraft in the vicinity of the Learjet."

"And their exact locations to the Lear at the time it went in," Ted said. "Or as near as you can remember."

Gloria responded with a slightly bewildered look. "Can't you get that from the radar tapes?"

"We'd still like to hear your account," Ted said.

Gloria shrugged, taking a sip from the can. She checked her watch, then gave an apologetic smile. "Do you mind if we wait just a few minutes? I'd rather not go through all this twice."

I frowned. "Twice?"

A head bob. To me she said, "After I spoke with you, Colonel, I received another call from a man in the FBI who said he had a few questions. I thought it would be easier if we all got together—"

"Jesus," I said. "You *told* him about our meeting?"

She shifted uneasily in her chair and set down the Coke. "Uh . . . sure. Look, I didn't think it would be a problem, and—"

"The agent's name?" Ted demanded.

Gloria swallowed, clearly flustered now. She nervously ran a hand over her hair, then opened her mouth to respond.

I was looking right at her when I heard the sound of cracking glass. An instant later, I saw Gloria's head snap violently to the side. I saw blood and tissue spray from a hole above her temple. I saw her pitch over and shudder once, then become still. I heard Ted's voice shouting at me.

But I couldn't move.

I continued to stare in horror at Gloria's inert frame. Her head was resting crookedly on an armrest. Blood ran down the side of her face, staining the fabric.

"Get the fuck down, John!" Ted shouted.

I felt his hand on my back, but I was already moving, throwing myself to the floor. A moment later, we heard another brittle cracking sound and something hard thumped into the sofa back where I'd been sitting.

I lay flat, my heart pounding. My eyes went to the window. Two starred holes about halfway up.

"The drapes," Ted said. "Can you get to the drapes?"

Ted was prone to my right, blocked in by me and Gloria Peters. "I think so." I rose up slightly.

Another crack and something whizzed inches from my head. I dropped.

"Crawl!" Ted ordered.

I did, flat on my belly, the carpet scratching my face. I

managed to reach the drapes without any more shots being fired.

Once I drew them closed, Ted was on his feet, going toward the front door. I heard him click the lock before he disappeared to the back of the house.

I looked to Gloria Peters, feeling mesmerized and sickened. She stared with unseeing eyes. The bullet had entered from the right, tearing out a two-inch-diameter hole behind her left eye as it exited. Blood continued to drip from the grisly wound.

"Doors are secure," Ted said when he reappeared. He went to the side of the window, peering through the drapes.

"See anything?" I asked.

"No. The shooter must be in the trees."

"I didn't hear a gunshot."

"He was using a silenced rifle. Fairly large caliber, judging by the holes in the window."

I went to the other side of the window and peeked out. Deep shadows fell across the lawn from the sunlight filtering through the trees. The scene looked quiet and peaceful. A minute passed. Then two. Nothing moved.

A drop of perspiration slid down my forehead. I wiped it away. "How long do we wait?"

"Patience, John."

I looked outside again.

Another three minutes passed before Ted said, I think we're okay, John. Shooter's probably left by now, He's not going to risk hanging around with the element of surprise gone." He looked to Gloria Peters and grimaced. "Besides, he got the one he wanted."

"He tried to kill *us*, Ted," I said.

"Sure, because we were targets of opportunity. But he came here to kill Gloria Peters. Without the radar tapes, she was the only one who could tell us about the chopper."

He frowned, noticing me removing my phone. "What are you doing?"

"Calling the cops." I punched in the number.

"Don't."

"Why not?" I asked. The phone began to ring.

"Hang up," Ted ordered, coming over.

"Sheriff's department," a voice said.

"Dammit, hang up," Ted said.

I stared into his determined eyes and ended the call. "Why the hell don't you want me to call the cops?" I demanded.

"We'll call later, after we've gone."

"You fucking nuts? We can't just leave."

"No? What are you going to tell the police?"

I blinked. "What do you mean?"

"Think about it, John. Without proof, there's no way the cops will believe Gloria Peters was murdered by a government killer with ties to the White House. If we toss in the part about how her death is part of a conspiracy to cover up the killing of the President's brother, the cops will think we're completely crazy. And you can bet the minute we mention the White House, the first thing they'll do is call in the Feds."

I understood what Ted was saying, but—

"Look, John. You really want to call, call." He paused, eyes boring into me. "Just remember, we're running out of time to finish this thing. Once the cops get hold of us, we'll be tied up answering questions for days. That means McKenzie wins."

I was torn. I knew I was out of my league and should listen to Ted. But the idea of leaving . . .

"Trust me," Ted said quietly.

I slowly pocketed the phone. "I hope to hell you know what you're doing," I murmured.

"I do." With a final glance toward Gloria Peters, he

headed for the door. Unlocking it, he said, "We'll both go in the passenger side. Keep low and move quick."

I gave him a dark look. "I thought you said the shooter had left."

Ted shrugged. "Ready?"

I took a deep breath and nodded.

Ted threw open the door. . . .

Once we drove past the trees surrounding the house, we sat up. Even though there'd been no more gunshots, my pulse was racing and I was panting like I'd just sprinted a hundred yards. My mind kept seeing Gloria Peters, lying there . . .

"You going to be okay, John?"

When I glanced over, I was amazed. Unlike me, Ted appeared completely at ease, no hint of tension on his face.

"Christ, weren't you scared back there?"

A shrug. "Sure. But one of the first things a cop learns is to control fear. If he can't . . ." He smiled sympathetically. "Anyway, I've been in these situations before. You haven't."

"I guess." I tried to compare my reaction now to what I'd felt flying over Iraq. I couldn't remember being afraid then. In war you're prepared to accept risk and are trained to handle it. But in this situation I was out of my element—a novice against professionals.

My hand still shook a little as I knocked a cigarette from the pack. I smoked in silence until Ted said, "You can call the cops, John. Tell them there's been a shooting but nothing else."

After I made the report, I disconnected when the dispatcher asked for my name. No sooner had I slipped the phone into my jacket than Harmon Masters called from Walter Reed. He sounded upset.

"We have a big-time problem, John," Harmon said.

I thought Harmon had to be referring to something he'd learned concerning the autopsy. "What did you find out, Harmon?" I asked. Ted glanced over at the mention of Harmon's name.

"Bastards!" Harmon spat. "You're not going to believe this crap, John. There's no excuse. It's incompetence. Jesus, I'm pissed!"

"What the hell are you talking about, Harmon?" I asked.

"The toxicology report. I just got through reading the goddamn thing."

I tensed. "What about it?"

Harmon took a deep breath. "It says that Lieutenant Colonel Rick French had a blood-alcohol level of point zero one four."

My mouth fell open.

"What is it?" Ted asked.

"That's impossible," I said into the phone. "Rick would never drink before a flight."

Ted's eyes widened in understanding. "Aw, Christ."

I said to Harmon, "Someone there at the pathology lab must have made a mistake—"

"They didn't make a mistake, John."

"They must have."

"No," Harmon said. "I should have explained. I'm not talking about Walter Reed's findings. Their tests were fine. Both pilots were clean. No alcohol."

He lost me. "Then who—"

"The FBI," Harmon said. "I'm looking at the FBI report, John."

"Oh, for the love of—" I swore, visualizing tomorrow's headlines: "AIR FORCE PILOT DRUNK." The press would have a field day and Rick French would be judged guilty by acclamation.

"I'm sitting here with Dr. Paul Marbury, John," Harmon said. "He's the chief of the Walter Reed pathology lab and

personally supervised the testing. He had the techs run two separate batteries of tests on two different tissue samples from each pilot. All tests were negative. Can't understand how the FBI lab came up with a different result. They must have mislabeled a sample or somehow contaminated it."

"Why was the FBI doing the testing, anyway?" I asked. "That's not normal procedure."

"You'll have to talk to General Morrissey, the hospital commander. He's the one who had Marbury send over the samples to the FBI." Harmon paused, then in a suggestive tone added, "I think it was basically a political decision. With all the crap in the papers about how pilot error might be involved, someone up the chain of command probably thought it'd be a good idea to have a third party outside of the military do a separate analysis. Now, as I see it—" He stopped when a voice in the background said something. "Sure, no problem," Harmon answered. Then, to me: "Dr. Marbury is picking up, John."

"Colonel Quinn?" a husky voice said.

"I'm here, Dr. Marbury," I said. "What's on your mind?"

"Frankly," Marbury said, "I think you may be overreacting to the FBI results. I'll call the FBI, send them a new sample. I'm sure a retest will come up negative."

"Fine, Doc," I said sarcastically. "You do that."

"Just tell those bozos they better not blow it again," Harmon said. "Or else we could be in real trouble."

"Why?" Marbury asked. "Am I missing something? My tests proved the pilots were clean."

"Doesn't matter, Doc," I said. "Like Harmon says, no one is going to believe a test done by the miltary exonerating our own pilots if a separate FBI test says one of the pilots was under the influence."

"Believe me," Marbury said reassuringly, "the FBI won't make the same mistake twice."

A couple of caustic responses popped into my head, but I managed to stay quiet.

"I'll call the FBI immediately, Colonel," Marbury said. "We'll get this thing straightened out."

I sighed. "Sure, Doc."

There was a click as he hung up. I said to Harmon, "You check into the autopsy?"

"Yeah. Popped into the autopsy room as soon as I came here. Ran into a nurse I know. We bullshitted for a couple of minutes, nice and friendly. Then I mentioned I wanted to check out the paperwork on the Thurston autopsy, and she clams right up. Says she can't help me. I turn on the charm, tell her I'm working with you. It still took me almost ten minutes before she finally told me that Thurston never arrived at Walter Reed."

"So no autopsy was performed—"

"No, John. An autopsy *was* done. It just wasn't done here. She said the body was flown to Bethesda Naval."

I felt a faint spark of hope. "Then we should be able to get a copy of the results."

"Not so fast, John. The doctor who did the autopsy was some handpicked civilian. The White House had insisted that no military physicians be involved. No telling when or if those results are going to come down."

"I see."

"I'll keep asking around. If I find out anything, I'll call. I gotta tell you, this stinks." He hung up with a bang.

I briefed Ted. I must have sounded discouraged, because he said, "We've still got the photos. DIA might be able to ID the chopper."

"And if they can't?" I said.

The only response was the hum of the tires over the road.

We were on I-495 westbound when Tom Blaney finally called to report he'd completed a checkout of the Learjet's

pressurization valves. I had him repeat the results twice to be sure I heard him right, then thanked him and slipped the phone back into my jacket.

Ted glanced at me anxiously.

"Nothing," I said, making no attempt to hide my disappointment. "The goddamn valves checked out completely normal."

Ted shot me a look of disbelief. "Impossible. Tom's mistaken."

"He ran each valve on the test stand twice. Both operated perfectly."

Ted slowly shook his head. He looked completely baffled. "Everything we saw. The evidence of overheating. Dammit, it has to be the valves, John."

I said nothing. It was pointless to argue.

Ted's mouth opened, hovered there for a moment, then snapped shut. His expression smoothed into a hard mask, which I understood. He was trying to comprehend the unthinkable.

He'd been wrong.

I settled back and tried to relax but couldn't. I still felt tense and nervous, and found myself continually looking at the cars behind. We were still on the Beltway, heading toward D.C., and I was surprised when Ted put on the turn signal. Then I saw the exit for Oxen Hill and I understood what he had in mind.

**T**he Tin Palace.

That's what a Pentagon intel buddy calls the six-story, futuristic, aluminum-sided Defense Intelligence Agency building on Bolling Air Force Base. Considering the military's conservative nature, most people find the design a surprise. The rumor mill has it that the purpose is functional rather than aesthetic. Metal walls are supposed to be tougher for listening devices to penetrate. Of course, the real truth could simply be that some influential congressman had a lot of stock in Alcoa Aluminum. Anyway, the building was definitely an eye-catcher.

We were fifteen minutes early when we parked near the front of the cavernous parking lot. Ted had placed the two handguns we picked up at his place in a box lying on the floorboard of the backseat, since we'd never make it past DIA security carrying them. As Ted climbed from the car, his somber expression told me he was still trying

to understand Tom Blaney's report on the pressurization valves.

We followed the concrete walkway past a granite pedestal inscribed with a quote from President Reagan: *Let us never forget that good intelligence saves American lives and protects our freedom.* TV cameras mounted near the glass doors tracked us as we entered a green-carpeted lobby with thirty-foot-high ceilings. On the wall to our right was another inscription: *Committed to Excellence in Performance.*

A pretty generic motto, but I guess you can't come out and say something like DIA—Committed to Being the Best Military Spy Organization in the World.

As the Military's equivalent of the CIA, the Defense Intelligence Agency served as a clearinghouse for intel gathered by the various services. Satellite photography was one of DIA's specialties, which is why Major Mattie Parker had suggested coming here. If there was any place in the military that could enhance degraded photos, this was it.

An overweight DOD cop with two extra chins sat at the security checkpoint, which was complete with a metal detector and a baggage scanner. I had started toward him when I felt a hand on my shoulder.

When I turned, Ted was smiling, tugging on his mustache. "I was right. It is the valves."

"How?" I asked dubiously.

Ted took me by the arm, leading me off to the side. "Tom Blaney checked out the valves but not the power source to them."

I gave him a blank look.

Ted sighed. "Remember what I said last night. Once power is removed, the valves automatically spring-load open."

"Yeah . . ." Then the light came on. "Shit. So if someone

screwed with the power, somehow interrupted electrics to the valves—"

"They'd go full open, turning the cabin into a sauna. And it wouldn't be hard to do. Just rig up something on the wires leading to the valves. It could be anything. A small aneroid with a switch to short out the wiring. Maybe a solenoid of some kind, the type that can be activated electrically."

I was getting excited. "Sure. That would explain why the valves are functioning normally. And if something is rigged to the wiring, we should be able to find it."

"Even Blaney couldn't miss it," Ted said dryly. "Got your phone handy? I'll have him check it out."

"It's in the car. I wasn't sure if I could bring in—"

But Ted had about-faced and was rapidly walking toward the door.

"Help you, Colonel?" a gravelly voice behind me called out.

I nodded, and went over to the cop, who checked my ID, had me sign a log, then told me to wait while he called a Major Lynn Sanders to escort.

As I took a seat in the lounge area a few yards away, I saw Ted standing by the car, animatedly talking into the phone. When I looked back a few minutes later, Ted was punching in another number. Probably to Lieutenant Colonel Mike Keele, the OSI homicide investigator whose number was in Thurston's planner. The OSI Headquarters was here on Bolling, and Ted had called on the way, checking to see if Mike had returned to his office.

"Major Sanders says it'll be a few minutes, Colonel," the guard called out.

I waved and got comfortable, but only until Ted reappeared through the glass doors, an anxious look on his face.

Ted took a seat next to me and leaned close. He spoke

fast, keeping his voice low. "Finally got hold of Mike Keele. We were right. Thurston *was* interested in a murder. Thurston contacted Mike to request the file of an old unsolved homicide case from the Richmond Police. Thurston never explained why he wanted the file. Mike turned it over to Thurston a couple days ago."

"Who was the file on?"

"A young woman murdered almost ten years ago." Ted paused. "Melissa George. You know her, John. Remember the reason Kendra Banks's father lost the governor's race . . ."

When the answer popped into my head, I felt like I'd been slapped. "I'll be damned. Melissa George was the woman who accused Governor Banks of the affair."

"Yeah," Ted said, rising. "And it gets better. Mike made a copy of the file. He said I can swing by his office and take a look."

"Take my phone," I said. "I'll call when I'm through here."

As Ted left, my head was spinning. Why would someone from the White House kill Melissa George?

Then I recalled the rumors that the Banks scandal had been a setup, engineered by someone in Halloran's camp.

If that was true—

There was a sharp cough, and I looked up to see a female major smiling at me expectantly. She was tiny, not more than five feet, with dark curly hair, an intelligent face, and thin wire-framed glasses. It seemed as if all intel types wore glasses. Too many years sitting at light tables pouring over satellite photos, I decided.

As I walked over to Major Lynn Sanders, I removed the photo envelope from my jacket.

"Hmm," she said as we crossed the lobby toward the spiral staircase that led to the second floor. She was studying

the first computer-enhanced picture of the helo. I passed her the second. She gave it a couple of seconds and looked up. "That it, sir?"

I nodded, trying hard to read her face, but she wasn't giving anything away.

We reached the stairs, and Major Sanders went over the pictures one more time. She shrugged, handing them back to me. "Not much to work with, I'm afraid. For what you're asking, the software we use to enhance the satellite images won't be much good on those. There simply isn't enough detail, sir."

"Then you can't help me?" I asked her.

She gave me a bright simile. "Oh, I didn't say that, sir. We might. We just won't be able to use the standard photo-enhancing software. But we've got other imaging software that might help. C'mon up."

We trudged up the stairs and made a left down a corridor lined by offices. "Actually," Major Sanders said, "it's getting so most of the imagery we deal with in intelligence isn't photographic."

"It isn't?" I asked, surprised.

"It makes sense when you think about it, sir," Sanders said. "Film-based pictures are too restrictive. They need to be taken in daylight or in clear weather. So the military made it a priority years ago to develop other imagery systems that could operate at night or in cloudy conditions. After all, what good is a surveillance system if the bad guys only have to wait until dark or a storm to avoid being seen?"

"What are you talking about specifically? Infrared cameras?"

"That's one, sir. Another is ASARS, which stands for advanced synthetic aperture radar system. Essentially, ASARS is to conventional radar what a laser is to light—much more coherent and focused. There are others sys-

tems, but they're Top Secret." She paused, her voice taking on a slight air of superiority. "Strictly need to know, and I can't discuss those. You understand."

"Sure. No problem." I held back a smile. Intel officers loved to point out they had access to information you didn't.

"Anyway," Sanders continued, "using these alternative systems is a trade-off, since you sacrifice clarity and detail. And that can be a real problem. Sure, we can tell if something is a missile. But sometimes it's hard to tell the exact type or specifics about the warhead. The technology is improving, and we're getting better. Bernie is the man you want to see."

"Bernie?"

"Chief Master Sergeant Bernard Ferguson. He's our resident ASARS imagery specialist."

I was curious why she was taking me to a radar expert, and asked her about that.

Sanders explained, "The images from ASARS cameras, since they are radar based, have always been the most difficult to decipher clearly. The military has spent big bucks developing software programs to improve picture quality. It's amazing what they can do now. Bernie's office is just around the corner."

We turned right toward the back of the building. The offices were gone now, replaced with doors that said things like "Imagery Analysis Lab" and "Photo Interpretation Center."

Major Sanders knocked on a door with a plaque that read: ASARS PROCESSING. When there was no response, she led me into a stark white room packed with high-tech equipment: a control console that looked like it could launch the shuttle, a wall of TV screens and an oversize videotape player, a large mainframe computer that hummed softly, shelves crammed with oversize plastic videotape containers.

"Bernie," Sanders called out. "Bernie, you in?"

A lean, graying black chief master sergeant emerged from a small door at the back, carrying a soft drink. He wore gold-rimmed glasses, reinforcing my theory about intel types. Breaking into a grin, he said, "Hi, Major."

Sanders introduced me and explained what I wanted. I handed Chief Ferguson the packet, and he studied the pictures.

"I don't know, sir," Ferguson said thoughtfully. "I can clean up the helicopter, get a lot more detail. But you want the tail number or the unit logo, huh? Frankly, the software isn't designed to enhance that kind of thing. Hang on." He set the pictures down and went over to the console. He punched a few buttons and pointed us to a monitor on the wall. The monitor flickered, and a green image appeared. The image resembled an old-style radar return, except it was more focused and not as spokey. The dark green outline near the bottom vaguely resembled a ship.

"See that?" Ferguson said. "That's a Russian cruiser. Now you can't tell a whole lot other than it's a vessel of some kind. Now watch." He punched another button. Behind us, the mainframe computer hummed louder. The monitor went blank for an instant, then a second image reappeared.

"Impressive," I murmured. The transformation was amazing. Sure, everything still looked green. But now you could clearly see the ship, the superstructure, even make out the crewmen on deck.

"Have you tried picking up things like logos or emblems?" I asked.

"That would be impossible, sir," Sanders said. "A radar return wouldn't pick those up."

"I was talking about photos," I said patiently.

Sanders gave Ferguson a questioning look.

"Actually, no," Ferguson said. "But, hey, I can give it a

shot. We just got this software in and haven't had much time to experiment. Won't take long to find out."

Sanders checked her watch. "Bernie, call me when you're done and I'll escort Colonel Quinn out." To me she added, "I've got a few things in the office to attend to, sir."

As she left, Ferguson waved to a chair toward the end of the console, which contained a couple of built-in keyboards and had a phone bank on each end. "Take me a minute to get set up, sir."

I drew out the chair, which held a couple of magazines. A copy of *Time* was on top. I felt a sense of revulsion as I gazed at the man on the cover.

"Sorry, sir," Ferguson said. He looked a little embarrassed as he picked up the magazines and deposited them on the end of the console. "Sometimes it gets a little slow in here."

"I understand," I said, easing into the chair.

Ferguson moved quickly. He took the photos and fed them into a scanner the size of a copying machine. Then he sat at the console, punching buttons and tweaking dials, occasionally giving grunts of satisfaction. He went over to the mainframe and did something to the back, then returned and punched more buttons.

Finally, he swiveled his chair around. "I'm ready, sir."

One of the monitors came to life.

The picture of the crash site with the Blackhawk hovering in the air appeared, blurry and unfocused. Ferguson clicked, and the image zoomed in on the helicopter. More clicks as he zeroed in on the nose of the chopper.

"A serial number should also be on the tail," I said.

"Lighting is slightly better here," Ferguson said. He grinned. "Keep your fingers crossed. Here goes."

He punched an illuminated button and sat back. The screen went blank. A second passed. Then two.

"Now," Ferguson murmured.

As the picture appeared, I leaned forward. I wasn't sure if I was imagining it, but just below the nose I thought I saw faint markings.

"I'll be damned," Ferguson said. "We got it."

I frowned. "You gotta be kidding, Chief. You can make out the number?"

"Of course not, sir. But we can see *something*. I was

afraid the camera hadn't picked up any differentiation. But it has. Trust me. We're there. Now all I have to do is reset the values . . ." He rapidly typed into a keyboard.

I gave him a dubious look, trying not to get excited. But if he really thought—

"Here comes the picture," Ferguson said.

I counted to two, and there it was. "Son of a bitch," I said.

"We got lucky," he said. "The photo had just enough light."

I stared at the numbers, my heart racing. Still faint, but you could definitely tell what they were. "Can you print that, Chief?" I managed.

"No problem." He typed in a command, then hopped up, heading toward the back. Somewhere a printer whirred.

A few moments later, he reappeared and handed me the copy. "This all you need, sir?"

"That's all, Chief. Mind if I make some calls?"

He gestured to the phone on the counter. "Knock yourself out, sir." He winked. "And next time, bring me something difficult, huh?"

I grinned, my hand reaching for the receiver.

First I called Ted, who said he'd be at least another twenty minutes. Next, I spoke with Lieutenant Colonel Todd Hartley, the Blackhawk PEM at the Pentagon and an occasional racquetball partner at the Pentagon's athletic club. PEM stood for program element monitor, which was a fancy title for the guru who oversaw the various funding and operational requirements for a specific weapons system. Todd took less than a minute to trace the tail number in his computer.

"It belongs to the Twenty-first Aviation Company," Todd said.

"An Army outfit?" I said.

"Yeah. Army National Guard."

My hand tightened on the phone. "Guard? Where?"

In the background, someone shouted for Todd. "Just a minute," Todd hollered back. I heard the sound of a keyboard clicking.

I said, "Todd . . ."

"Gimme a sec, John. I'm looking up the unit. Yeah. Here it is. Richmond-Bird Airfield."

Another shout.

"Uh, John, I've got to catch my car pool. So if you've got nothing else."

I stood there, the phone pressed to my ear, my body tingling. I'd been bothered all along that a military unit would be involved. By definition, they were apolitical and tough to influence. But Guard units were different. They were filled with political appointees and controlled by the governor. And Richmond meant Virginia—

"Yo, John."

"I'm here, Todd. That's it. Thanks."

My next call was to the only guy I knew in the National Guard Bureau with the connections to get what I wanted quickly. As the exec to the Guard two-star, Lieutenant Colonel Henry Colby would either have the information at his fingertips or know whom to ask.

Three minutes later, Henry promised to fax out the 21st Company personnel roster to Andrews before he went home. Ideally, I would have liked the unit's actual flight schedule or the aircraft's maintenance log, which could have given me the names of the pilots. But those records were kept at the unit, and there was no way to request them without raising suspicions. But eventually we would find out. The reason I wanted the personnel roster was to make a quick check for any likely candidates.

Like Kroft.

As I cradled the phone, Ferguson said, "I buzzed Major Sanders, sir. She should be down shortly."

"Thanks."

He disappeared into the room at the back, and I began tapping the counter, troubled by the implication dancing through my head. My eyes fell on the magazines Ferguson had placed on the console. The copy of *Time* with McKenzie's grinning face was still on top. In big letters across the bottom: "Will the King-maker make his own White House run?" I picked up the magazine and began to read.

A few minutes later Major Sanders arrived, and I called out to Ferguson. When he appeared, I held up the magazine.

"You mind if I take this?"

He seemed surprised. "Uh, no, sir. I'm done."

"Thanks again," I said.

Major Sanders deposited me in the unsecured area of the lobby, and I returned to the lounge and plopped down. It was quitting time, and a stream of people strode past, heading toward the exit. Through the windows I could see a line of cars snaking down the long drive toward the commute home. The sun was still bright, but off in the distance thick clouds were visible.

Not that I was paying all that much attention. I was thinking of the connection between a murdered girl tied to a campaign and a helicopter from a unit manned by appointees of a governor.

And I wondered what Ted would say about Halloran now.

I crossed my legs and opened the copy of *Time*. More pictures of McKenzie, most with him at the White House. *Jesus, if that son of a bitch ever became president . . .*

I'd barely started reading when the security cop called

out to me. "Your friend just pulled up." He pointed to the window. Ted was parked out front, motioning.

"Thanks," I said, closing the magazine. I rose and joined the exodus heading for the door.

As we drove away, Ted said, "You ID the chopper?"

"Yeah." After I told him, Ted was silent, his face unhappy.

I cleared my throat. "You know, as governor Halloran would have appointed a lot of the Guard's leadership."

Ted nodded vaguely.

"They would have owed him. He would have a lot of influence."

"I know."

"So if Halloran wanted to arrange for a helicopter . . ."

"Yeah, yeah. You made your point, John." He sounded annoyed.

I shook my head, confused by Ted's reluctance to admit Halloran's involvement now. Ted, of all people, had to realize—

I frowned. We'd passed through the Bolling gate, but instead of going toward Andrews, Ted had turned north, toward D.C. I asked him why.

"To see Kendra," Ted answered. "She called, said she had something important for us."

"She say what?"

A head shake. "Here." Ted produced a manila folder from the backseat.

"The file on Melissa George?" I asked.

A nod. "Mike wouldn't release the entire file. I made copies of some of the more interesting stuff. Look it over and we'll talk."

I flipped open the cover.

Xeroxed press clippings of Melissa George's murder from the *Richmond Tribune,* which covered a period of roughly three months. I read the first couple of clippings in

detail, then scanned the subsequent articles, which rehashed much of the earlier info. The fact that Melissa George was the woman who brought down Governor Banks was mentioned but not sensationalized. That made sense. The story was old news, and the paper probably didn't want to be accused of rekindling the scandal.

I learned from the accounts that Melissa George had been murdered in her Richmond home on a summer evening almost twelve years earlier. The cause of death was listed as extreme physical trauma. Robbery had been thought to be the motive, because her place had been ransacked and jewelry and money taken. The police had no witnesses, no leads, and no suspects. The last article I read quoted an unnamed police source as saying the prospects of solving the case were dim.

Prophetic, I thought dryly.

Next I came to a Xeroxed color picture of a young woman with long dark hair, wearing a white evening gown. Even though the image was grainy, you could tell the woman was very attractive with a drop-dead figure. A sash ran down from her shoulders across the gown, with the words "Miss Richmond, 1980."

"A local beauty queen," I murmured. That hadn't been in the press clippings.

"Yeah. Melissa George was one very attractive girl."

"Shame," I said, and turned the page—

I stiffened. Another photo, a close-up. Even though I knew Melissa George had died from physical trauma, I wasn't prepared for this. The face that peered back was virtually unrecognizable. The nose was flattened and appeared broken, the lips split, the eyes blackened, the cheeks bruised and swollen, and there was a lot of caked blood.

"Jesus," I said, "someone sure did a number on her."

"Actually, she didn't die from the beating," Ted said.

"Oh—"

"She was stabbed. Once. In the heart."

"Stabbed? The press reports said the cause of death was trauma. And the pictures make it pretty clear—"

"I know. Cops do that all the time. Withholding key information only the killer would know. Strange, though . . ." He trailed off, his face thoughtful.

"What's strange?"

"Hmm. Oh, that someone beats her almost to death and then decides to stab her."

"Maybe the killer just wanted to be certain she was dead."

He shrugged. "Anyway, the stabbing is mentioned in the police report." He eyed me, brows knitted suggestively. "There's another item I think you'll find interesting, John."

I read on.

The narrative of the police report was almost a dozen typed pages and contained numerous references to appendixes, most of which Ted didn't bother to copy. I read through it quickly, and nothing jumped out. The main points I'd already gleaned from the news accounts. I was about to ask Ted to explain when I noticed a name typed at the bottom of the last page.

The detective in charge of the investigation.

"Son of a bitch," I murmured. "Randall A. Morgan."

"Yeah. Our tall FBI friend."

I sat back and stared at Ted.

"Something the matter?" he asked.

"What the hell is wrong with you?"

"What are you talking about?"

I held up the file. "For chrissakes, Ted, you know as well as I do that if the bullshit about Melissa George being paid

off to lie about the affair was true, that means Halloran would've had a helluva motive to have her killed."

"I agree."

My eyes widened. "You do?"

"Sure. I agree he had a motive." A pause. "But that doesn't mean he had her killed."

"No? How about the chopper? Halloran's the only one with the clout to pull it off. As governor, he could easily have arranged for this goon Morgan to hush up the murder."

Silence. Then, dismissively: "Look, we went through all this. I already explained why I don't think Halloran—"

"That's not good enough."

His jaw tightened, but when he responded his voice was quiet, almost resigned. "Okay, John, but you're probably not going to buy it."

"Try me."

"I've met Halloran a couple times. Frankly, I like the guy, and when I—" He held up his hand he saw I was about to respond. "Let me finish, John."

I closed my mouth, giving him a dark look.

"When I was on *Air Force One*," Ted said, "I used to talk to the reporters. They had a nickname for Halloran. You know what it was?"

I shook my head.

"Boy Scout One. Don't laugh. It's true. Want to know why? When Halloran decided to run, the reporters did the usual digging into his past for dirt and came up with zip. Hell, Halloran never even had so much as a parking ticket. Guy's a fucking straight arrow, and everyone knows it."

"People change—"

"Not that much."

"What about the goons he brought into the FBI? They worked for him when he was governor."

"He didn't pick them, John. Governors and presidents don't worry about that nit-noy shit. As a rule, they also don't get involved on appointments to Guard units. Their staff handles that stuff."

"McKenzie?"

"My guess. Hell, it's no secret McKenzie's installed handpicked people throughout the administration. That's how come he can pull this thing off."

I tried to think of a comeback but couldn't. McKenzie's power was an accepted fact. "So you're convinced McKenzie is acting without Halloran's knowledge."

Ted nodded.

"If that's true, McKenzie must somehow be behind the killing of Melissa George."

"Yeah. But that brings us back to McKenzie's motive. Why would he have killed her?"

"Maybe he was involved in the scandal, and to shut her up—"

I stopped, frowning.

"What is it, John?"

But I was thinking hard, trying to remember. I plucked the copy of *Time* from the dash where I'd tossed it and began flipping pages.

Ted gave me a questioning look.

"The dates," I said. "If I'm right, McKenzie couldn't have been involved in the scandal with Melissa George. . . . Here it is."

The page contained a brief synopsis of McKenzie's career, separate from the main article. I scanned down. "I was right. McKenzie didn't join Halloran's staff until 1982, which was two years after Halloran had been elected governor. He couldn't have orchestrated the scandal."

"Maybe McKenzie was tied to him before that unofficially. What did he do before he joined Halloran?"

I read lower. I swallowed hard when I saw the name. "Jesus," I murmured.

"What?"

When I told Ted, he looked equally stunned.

We both now knew McKenzie had no apparent reason to have been involved in the scandal or to kill Melissa George.

Because before Halloran, McKenzie had worked for another Virginia governor—the honorable Kenneth Banks.

A car horn blared behind us, but Ted showed no reaction as he tried to understand. Finally, at a red light, he turned and gave a sigh of frustration. "I still don't buy it. McKenzie has to have a role in either the murder or the scandal. If not, why the cover-up?"

I didn't answer. Ted wasn't really looking for a response.

"Well," Ted said, "maybe Kendra can shed some light on McKenzie's role."

"Kendra?"

Ted nodded. The light was green, and we were rolling again. "Obviously, she's been withholding information from us. For instance, she has to have known all along McKenzie's up to his eyeballs in all this, yet she conveniently omitted the fact that he worked for her father. She also lied to us about why Thurston contacted her."

I didn't follow Ted's last comment at all and asked him to explain.

"Because," Ted said, "we know Thurston was looking into the death of Melissa George. Like us, he probably figured her death was somehow tied to the scandal of Governor Banks. It would be logical for Thurston to contact Kendra to see if she knew anything."

"So the story about Thurston wanting to go public—"

"Another lie. No way Thurston would have wanted to destroy his brother."

"And what Kendra said about the videotape . . ."

A pause. "I'm not sure. That part may be true. Probably is. Someone took Thurston's briefcase for a reason." Ted slowed the car, putting on the turn signal. We were in the northwest part of the city, and traffic was heavy. Ted nosed his way onto Connecticut Avenue.

I glanced at McKenzie's face on the *Time* cover, recalling Kendra's comments this morning. How she seemed to despise McKenzie, a man who'd worked for her father.

The question was why—

Ted pointed. "I think the building we want is on the right."

The address Kendra Banks gave Ted was an upscale coffeehouse next to an Indian restaurant a few blocks north of Dupont Circle, on the corner of Connecticut and Q Street. Every available parking spot along the street was taken. An easel sign in front of the coffeehouse said parking out back. Ted took a right at the light and made a quick left down an alley that ran behind the redbrick building. The small lot was full, but Ted managed to squeeze into a spot next to a Dumpster.

As I opened the car door, Ted said, "Wait, John," and reached to the box in the back. He produced a small snub-nosed revolver in a nylon ankle holster with a Velcro clasp. "You never know," Ted said quietly.

I hesitated. "Okay."

I watched him strap his on first before I figured out how to wear mine.

If you're not used to wearing a weapon, the feeling is uncomfortable. You're continually aware of the weight of the gun and you think everyone can tell you're carrying. As I

walked across the alley toward a wooden door that read "D.C. Bean Company," the pistol against my right ankle felt the size of a bowling ball.

"Try not to walk so stiffly, John," Ted said. "Shorten your stride a little."

I did. I still felt awkward.

"Better," Ted said.

Before we went in, Ted touched my arm. "You mind letting me handle Kendra?"

I told him I didn't. I appreciated his asking. We both knew that since the killing of Gloria Peters, he was calling the shots. I opened the door, and we stepped into the smell of coffee and the buzz of conversation.

We continued down a darkly paneled hallway, entering a large open room of soft lighting, polished wooden floors, and forestgreen walls. There were maybe twenty tables on the main floor, with another dozen stools along an oak and brass coffee bar. Behind the bar were huge glass cannisters filled with coffee beans with tropical-sounding names like Coca Cobana Zest and Jamaican Jolt.

I did a quick scan. The place was half full, an eclectic mixture of suited business types and jeans-and-T-shirt college kids. Two waitresses were working the place, shuttling orders to the two guys at the bar.

Toward the front, a silhouetted hand appeared against the sunlight streaming in through a plate-glass window.

The hand waved. "Colonel Quinn."

Beside Kendra sat a woman with stylishly cut close-cropped black hair.

"Who's that?" I murmured to Ted.

Ted shrugged.

"Glad you could make it, gentlemen," Kendra said as we approached the table.

"Hi, Kendra," I said. Kendra wore the same lavender

suit from this morning and looked as striking as ever. My eyes went to the other woman.

"Oops, my manners," Kendra said.

The woman wore a timid smile, and you could see sadness in her eyes. Ted and I smiled back politely as Kendra made the introduction.

John, Ted, I'd like you to meet Miss Carolyn Thurston, Joshua Thurston's niece."

Ted and I managed to keep our surprise in check as we sat down. Carolyn Thurston was in her mid-twenties, trim and petite, with large expressive eyes and sharply defined features that gave her a slightly sophisticated look. She wore a tailored jade-green pantsuit with jade earrings. She wasn't a beauty, but the package was appealing.

The waitress, a blond girl with a spiked haircut, took our orders. Ted ordered a regular coffee and I asked for a latte. Kendra and Carolyn had mugs that appeared untouched.

When the waitress left, Kendra said to Carolyn: "Go on. Tell them what you told me."

Carolyn Thurston focused on me. Her voice cracked a little as she spoke. "Is it true what Miss Banks said? You . . . you think my uncle was murdered?"

Ted shot Kendra a look of annoyance.

"Hey," Kendra said. "She wanted the truth, Ted. What did you expect me to say?"

"Yes, Carolyn," I said quietly.

Carolyn bit her lip. "I had a feeling something . . . something was wrong."

"Why?" I asked gently.

"Tell them about the men," Kendra said.

"Men?" Ted said.

Carolyn nodded vaguely, extending a finger toward the window. "See that white brick house on the corner across

the street? The big one with the iron fence. That's my uncle's place."

The house Carolyn indicated was an enormous three-story catty-corner to us. Not exactly a mansion, but close. Here in the heart of D.C., the house would go for a couple mil easily. I recognized Kendra's Saab, sitting out front.

"Nice place," I murmured.

Before Carolyn could respond, Kendra explained, "Thurston's deceased wife had the money. Thurston lived off a trust that gave him a million or so a year."

"This morning," Carolyn continued, "my uncle's maid Maria called me in hysterics. She said men were there searching my uncle's house. When I arrived, there must have been twenty people going through everything. His papers . . . files . . . I couldn't believe it."

"Who were they?" Ted asked.

"Some kind of police. They had badges—"

"FBI?" Ted said.

"I . . . I didn't really notice."

"Did they say why they were searching?" he asked.

A nod. "Papers. They . . . they said he had classified papers from work. Military information that was secret."

I frowned at the tone in her voice. "But you don't believe that."

Carolyn hesitated, then shook her head. "If that was true, why did they search Maria's room? Or the guest room? They even went through the garage. It . . . it didn't make any sense. My uncle wouldn't have kept papers there," She picked up her coffee and sipped. Her hand shook.

"Now, Carolyn," Kendra said softly, "tell them the rest."

Carolyn seemed puzzled.

Kendra prompted, "The tape . . ."

I tensed.

"You *know* about the videotape, Carolyn?" Ted said.

A tentative nod.

"She saw what was on it," Kendra said, her voice containing a hint of excitement.

Ted and I edged closer to the table.

Carolyn swallowed nervously. "Actually, I . . . I only got a brief look. The night before my uncle died, I—"

"Who's got the latte?" the waitress interrupted cheerfully.

After the waitress left, Carolyn continued, "Two nights ago, I was at my uncle's for dinner. We ate together at least twice a week. After dinner, he retired to his study. I stayed, talking to Maria for a few minutes. On my way out, I went to his study to tell him goodnight. That's when . . ." She swallowed hard. "He . . . he jumped to his feet when I walked in and became very angry. I . . . I'd never seen him quite like that. So upset." Her eyes misted. "He . . . he told me to never to barge in like that."

I was confused. "What does this have to do with a videotape?"

Carolyn dabbed her eyes with a napkin. "He'd never acted that way before. That's why I knew I must have interrupted something he . . . he didn't want me to see."

I understood then. "Are you saying your uncle was looking at a videotape when you walked in?"

"Yes."

"How do you know he wasn't just watching a television show?" I asked.

"He clicked the remote and the TV went blank. You know, like it does. With a tape."

"You saw something on the screen?" Ted said.

Carolyn's eyes went to Kendra.

"It's okay," Kendra said.

"Yes," Carolyn said to Ted. "I saw the screen for maybe a couple of seconds."

I said, "And . . ."

Carolyn took a deep breath. "I saw a woman. Lying down in a room. The woman looked like . . . like she was hurt pretty bad."

"Hurt?" I said. "How?"

She hesitated. Then, in a voice that was almost a whisper: "Because her face was covered with blood."

I sat there, my heart pounding. A look at Ted's face confirmed he was thinking the same thing.

Melissa George.

Around us soft conversation continued and a man two tables away roared with laughter. From the bar we heard the tinkle of coffee mugs and the hiss of the espresso machine.

Finally, Carolyn said, "My uncle was a good man. He wouldn't have been involved in . . . a woman's death."

"We know," Ted said. He gave her a sympathetic smile.

"Can you tell us anything about the woman in the tape?" I asked. "Maybe the color of her hair . . ."

She gave me a blank look and shook her head.

I glanced to Ted to see if he had any questions. He calmly sipped his coffee, eyes on Kendra.

Carolyn said quietly, "This has been very trying. If there's nothing else . . ." She started to rise.

"Tell them your uncle's opinion of the First Lady," Kendra said.

Carolyn eased back down. "He . . . disliked her."

"Why?" Ted asked.

"It had something to do with his brother's campaign."

"He told you that," Ted said.

"No. That was common knowledge in the family. We all knew he and the First Lady had a . . . disagreement."

"Did you know about what?" Ted asked.

A head shake.

Ted eased back in his chair. "Thank you, Carolyn. You've been very helpful."

Carolyn rose slowly. "Please, if you find out anything . . ."

"We'll let you know," I said.

As she left I looked to Ted, who was again focused on Kendra. I folded my arms, waiting for him to begin.

"Well?" Kendra said. Her beautiful face was tight with anticipation, and I could see excitement in her eyes.

Ted quietly sipped his coffee. "Why didn't you tell us she would be here?"

"I wanted to surprise you guys." She smiled, looking pleased.

"How did you get her to confide in you?"

A shrug. "I drove by Thurston's house to see if I could interview the maid, Maria. I must have arrived shortly after the men left, because both Carolyn and Maria were very upset. No wonder. You should see the inside of the house. Christ, what a mess. Anyway, once I told Carolyn about my suspicions over her uncle's death, she opened right up. She was nervous the men might return, so we came here. So, c'mon. What do you guys *think?*"

Ted folded his hands on the table. "What do *you* think?"

Kendra's eyes flashed in irritation. "Hey, what is this? You guys don't seem too concerned that we have a dead girl who might be tied to someone in the White House."

"Do you know who the girl is?" Ted asked.

"No. Should I?" She sounded completely candid.

Ted gazed at her, shaking his head. "Kendra . . . Kendra . . ."

"What's that supposed to mean?" Kendra said. She was getting angry.

"We know, Kendra," Ted said quietly.

At first, nothing. Then the first crack in her armor appeared. You really had to look to see it. A slight tightening around the perfect jawline and a hint of concern in the eyes.

"Know what?" Kendra said. She tried to sound casual, but she didn't quite pull it off.

Ted didn't reply. He just kept looking at her.

Kendra's eyes flickered to me. She was blinking more frequently. She started to say something but didn't.

I stared calmly into that perfect face.

Seconds passed. Kendra looked to her hands and shifted in her chair.

"Why did Thurston really contact you?" Ted asked suddenly.

Her head snapped around. "I told you—"

"We know Melissa George is the girl in the video and that Thurston was looking into her death," Ted said.

That did it. Kendra visibly started. Her eyes fell to her coffee cup. "How—"

"Doesn't matter. We know."

She exhaled slowly. When she looked up, her face was calm. "I was going to tell you eventually."

"Do it now," Ted said.

A nod.

"I'm going to ask questions, and I want the truth," Ted said.

Another nod.

"I want to know what Thurston told you about the videotape."

"Yes—"

"I want to know about your relationship with McKenzie."

"Okay," Kendra said.

"Good. Let's get started. . . ."

Ted went through his questions rapid fire, and I had to concentrate hard to keep up. Ted was obviously doing it intentionally, to keep Kendra off balance. Like a cop grilling a suspect.

"Thurston contacted you because he was looking into the death of Melissa George, correct?"

"Yes."

"Did he tell you why he was investigating her death?"

"Because of the tape. He said it showed Melissa George being murdered, but . . . but it didn't show the murderer."

Ted seemed surprised. "That's confusing. How can that be?"

"He said the tape was altered."

"Altered how?"

"I don't know. I never saw the tape. All Thurston told me was the tape had been altered to incriminate the wrong person."

"Incriminate who?"

"I don't know."

"How did Thurston obtain the tape?"

"He didn't say."

"Did Thurston know how the tape was made?"

"He didn't say."

Ted took a different approach. "When you told us he was going to turn over the tape to you, was that a lie?"

"No. Thurston knew the accusations by Melissa George against my father were a fabrication and that someone in the Halloran campaign had been responsible. He thought I should be the one to release the story."

"But that would mean he would destroy his brother."

Kendra's cool evaporated. "No. You don't understand. This investigation was Halloran's idea. President Halloran asked Thurston to find out the truth."

"Even if the outcome damaged Halloran politically?"

"Yes. Thurston said President Halloran was committed to exposing the entire story."

"Did Thurston tell you if he suspected anyone of the murder?"

"No."

"You're certain?"

Kendra paused. "No, he never mentioned it."

"McKenzie maybe—"

"I said he never mentioned it." She sounded defiant.

"Tell me about McKenzie. Was he close to your father?"

"He . . . he was my father's chief of staff."

"So they were close. You knew McKenzie well?"

"Yes. Fairly well."

"Why didn't you tell us about your father's relationship to McKenzie?"

"I . . . I don't know. I guess maybe I thought . . . I guess I was afraid you might suspect I imight be involved with him. You know, part of what he was doing."

"Why do you dislike McKenzie so much?"

"He's scum."

"That doesn't answer the question."

"Lots of reasons. He's evil, ruthless—"

"Was it something he did to your father?"

Kendra, startled: "No—"

"Now, Kendra, come on. The truth. . . ."

"I told you no."

Ted leaned forward. "Tell me, do you have any idea why McKenzie might have killed Melissa George?"

Kendra was clearly agitated now. I don't know—"

"No idea at all?"

Kendra shook her head emphatically. "I . . . I need to use the rest room."

Ted hesitated, "Okay." And as he sat back, I thought I saw a smile.

Ted and I watched Kendra walk quickly down the hallway toward the rest rooms at the back.

"So what do you think, John?" Ted asked.

I hesitated. "She confirmed that everything is tied to Melissa George's murder. She also seemed to be telling the truth about Halloran asking Thurston to investigate."

Ted nodded.

"And about the videotape being altered."

Another nod.

"But when you began questioning her about McKenzie, she seemed evasive as hell."

"Yeah. Clearly, she didn't want to go there. Anything else?"

I slowly ran a hand over my face. "I'm not sure how to take her statement that Halloran was willing to go public with the tape. And that bit about the tape framing someone for the murder seems like a stretch."

"She had no reason to lie about those points, John."

I frowned. "I thought you said earlier she had to be lying about Thurston wanting to go public."

I did. But Thurston would release the information with Halloran's approval."

"You honestly believe Halloran would reveal something that could damage himself politically?"

Ted responded with a tight smile. "I told you Halloran's a straight arrow."

"Yeah, but . . ." I shook my head. I didn't see any politician committing political suicide. Especially a president.

Ted sipped his coffee and gazed out the window. "Anyway, Kendra obviously believed it."

"You going to push the angle with McKenzie when she gets back?"

Ted's brow furrowed slightly, eyes focusing on something outside. "I don't think that's going to be possible, John."

"Oh—"

Ted pointed out the window.

A number of pedestrians were strolling down the sidewalk. A moment later, I spotted the tall woman in the lavender suit, hurrying across the intersection. I swore.

But when I glanced to Ted, he seemed unconcerned.

My jaw tightened. "You *knew* she wasn't coming back."

Ted set his cup down. "Actually, I was surprised she answered as many questions as she did."

I was watching Kendra again. She was getting into her Saab in front of Thurston's house. As she drove off, I glared at Ted. "Christ, you just let her walk out of here."

"How was I supposed to stop her, John?" He flashed a reassuring smile. "Besides, it doesn't really matter anyway. Kendra answered the most important question. She confirmed McKenzie murdered Melissa George."

"Come off it, Ted. You never even asked her if McKenzie was the killer."

"Oh, but I did. I just didn't use those words."

My mind went back.

Ted said, "Remember her reaction when I asked if she knew *why* McKenzie would kill Melissa George?"

"Sure. That's when she became really agitated. That's when she asked to leave."

"Exactly," Ted said. "She felt trapped. She knew if she lied, I would know. So she did the only thing she could. She walked out before I could pursue the subject. But her actions essentially told us she thinks McKenzie is the killer. Or is at least involved."

I sat back slowly. "If that's true, why wouldn't she tell us? Why would she protect McKenzie?"

Ted drummed the table. "That I can't figure out. The only logical answer is she must be protecting someone else."

"Like who? She certainly wouldn't cover for Halloran—"

I froze.

"Something the matter, John?"

But I was thinking I had to be wrong. Still, if Kendra was protecting someone . . .

I glanced at Ted, running a hand over the back of my neck. "Hell, you're going to think I'm a little nuts." Then I explained.

He beamed at me afterward. "That's it, John. That's the only explanation. Kendra has to be protecting her father."

"Even though he's dead."

"But," Ted said, "his reputation isn't."

I thought. "And if McKenzie fucked him over . . ."

"Explains Kendra's hate." Ted grinned, motioning for the check. He sounded upbeat. "Things are definitely coming together. We'd better get back to the hangar. Tom Blaney should have something for us by now."

As we emerged out the back door into the hazy sunlight, we saw a soft-drink truck parked in the middle of the alley, blocking our car. A stocky man in sweat-stained coveralls was loading cases onto a dolly.

"Hey, buddy!" Ted yelled. He pointed to his car.

The man glanced over. "Be just a minute."

Ted fired off a dirty look, but the man was grabbing another case.

"It all seems so complicated," I said, still trying to understand.

"Yeah . . ." Ted was scowling, tapping his foot impatiently as if trying to get the man to hurry.

I said, "So McKenzie killed Melissa George and framed someone for the murder using a videotape. Odds are his motive was somehow linked to her scandal with Governor Banks." I paused. "And somehow Halloran got wind of the murder and, through Thurston, was checking into it with

the intent to have the whole thing made public. That about how you see it?"

"Something like that," Ted said, his eyes on the man, who was now wheeling the dolly toward the Indian restaurant door.

I sighed. "Still leaves a helluva lot of unanswered questions. Like how did Thurston get the tape in the first place? And who did McKenzie frame? And what was McKenzie's link to the scandal involving Melissa George?" I rubbed my face. "Christ, what a mess.

"The truth has a way of coming out if you know where to look."

"Do you know?" I asked.

Ted thought. "The key is finding the tape."

I snorted.

"Actually," Ted said, "we know who has the tape."

It took me a second. "McKenzie?"

Ted nodded.

"Hell, the tape might as well be on the moon."

"But it isn't," Ted said.

To me, our next step was getting clearer by the minute. I gave a little cough. "I think we've done all we can on our own, Ted."

Silence.

I took a deep breath. "We should notify General Cramer."

Again no response. The man emerged through the door, wheeling the empty dolly.

I said, "Ted . . ."

"I heard you, John. Briefing Cramer will be a mistake."

"Ted, we need help."

"Not Cramer."

"Then who?"

A pause. "I don't know. It's . . . difficult to know who to trust."

"You can't think Cramer would sit on this."

"General Ware is."

I didn't have an answer.

The man latched the dolly onto the truck, slammed a panel closed, and walked to the cab. As he drove away, we headed for the car.

"You mind driving?" Ted asked.

"Uh, no."

He handed me the keys. "I'd like to use your phone."

"Sure." I passed it over.

Once we were on the road, Ted retrieved the copy of *Time* from the backseat. He read the McKenzie article carefully, occasionally making notations in his notepad. When he finished, he made a phone call to Andrews Public Affairs, requesting bios on McKenzie and Governor Banks. Because of all the VIPs that accompanied the President on *Air Force One,* the Andrews P.A. office had a monster database of bios—sports figures, politicians, entertainers, the works.

Ending the call, Ted said, "We need to swing by and pick them up on the way to the hangar."

"Okay." I kept glancing at him, waiting for an explanation. Finally, I asked, "What are you looking for?"

A diffident shrug. "I'm curious about the timeline."

"What timeline?"

Instead of replying, Ted made another call, this time to Chief Haney at the security police squadron. Something about logbooks. Hanging up, Ted immediately folded his arms and closed his eyes.

But I knew he wasn't tired.

He was annoyed with me.

It was a little after five P.M. by the time we fought our way through rush hour and arrived back on Andrews. I stopped at the Wing Public Affairs office, waiting in the car while

Ted went inside. He returned a few minutes later with a brown folder.

"You get what you wanted?" I asked.

A barely perceptible nod. He gazed silently out the window.

I sighed and started the car. I understood Ted's concerns, but I thought he was letting his animosity toward Cramer cloud his judgment. While I wasn't sure if I trusted Cramer either, the guy had gone to bat for me after the press conference the night before. And the fact of the matter was we couldn't handle this situation ourselves. Regardless of what Ted thought.

Before I gave Cramer a call, I still wanted to check out one last item, and I drove to the hangar.

The sun hung low over the sky like a bright orange ball as Ted and I strolled over the ramp toward the security entry point in front of the hangar. Dark clouds were visible on the horizon, and the air was turning chilly. I tried to remember if the forecast called for rain.

"John," Ted said cryptically. "You're walking like you've got a pole up your ass again."

I gave him a look of annoyance, then pivoted, returning to the car. I tossed the gun into the glove compartment. Rambo I'm not. Besides, no one was going to take a shot at me here.

Strolling back, I saw Ted inside the hangar, deep in conversation with Tom Blaney and a chief master sergeant. They were clustered in a circle, peering intently at something in Blaney's hand. Ted suddenly glanced over and motioned.

My pulse quickened, and I broke into a jog. Behind me, I heard the sound of cars approaching.

A lot of cars.

Looking back, I immediately understood the implica-

tion. Darcey's phone call had led me to believe I wouldn't be relieved until morning.

I was wrong.

A gleaming black limo with a fluttering four-star flag led five unmarked sedans across the tarmac toward the entry point. Trailing was Jennifer's red Mercedes. The convoy rolled to a stop in front of a suddenly very nervous looking security cop. Car doors immediately popped open and at least a dozen somber-faced men in suits swarmed out.

I shook my head in disgust when I saw McKenzie and General Ware emerge from the limo. My eyes went to the Mercedes. The glare on the windshield made it difficult to see clearly. I could make out two people in the front seats, heads bobbing and turning like they were arguing. The driver's door flew open, and Jennifer stepped out. She walked away quickly, clearly agitated. Moments later, General Cramer emerged and stared after her grimly.

*Cramer and Jennifer?*

By now the men in suits were rushing past the stunned cop toward the hangar, barking out orders for everyone to cease and desist what they were doing. They swirled around inside and began herding the maintenance troops over to one end. I couldn't believe what I was seeing. This was an official military investigation. The whole thing was completely outrageous.

That's when I noticed another car slowly approach. It parked well back of the others. A tall man climbed out and leaned against the hood, folding his massive arms, watching.

Kroft made no move to come forward.

I looked for Ted, but he wasn't standing with Tom Blaney or the chief master sergeant anymore. Finally, I spotted him striding rapidly toward the fuselage, which was now sitting waist high on steel beams. Ted crouched

below the open hellhole panel. He reached inside, and I saw a flicker of white in his hand—

"Colonel Quinn!"

I recognized the angry voice even before I turned.

Cramer was standing with McKenzie and Ware. Jennifer was maybe ten yards back. Cramer gazed toward me coldly and said something to Ware.

Ware motioned majestically.

As I went over, my eyes never left Cramer.

Ted had been right about the son of a bitch after all.

General Ware glared at me without speaking, the waning sunlight glittering off the eight stars on his shoulders. Cramer stood beside him, eyes fixed on me in a malevolent stare. McKenzie remained off to the side in his thousand-dollar suit, smiling smugly.

For an instant, I wished I'd brought the gun. I wished I could have shot him, right then and there, and ended this.

I looked past McKenzie to Jennifer. The change in her appearance over the past few hours surprised me. Her face was drawn and there were bags under her eyes. She seemed older somehow, and tired. She blinked often, and her upper lip trembled. She wasn't enjoying this.

"You're in a great deal of trouble, Colonel," Ware finally said, his voice filled with contempt.

I gazed back, my face blank.

"Frankly," Ware spat, "your handling of the investigation has been sloppy. I've had reports that you've been biased, letting your friendship with one of the pilots cloud your judgment. Your actions have led to a public relations nightmare and embarrassed the military. *Are you listening to me, Colonel?*"

I was, but my eyes were again on Jennifer, who was looking even more miserable. I slowly returned my gaze to Ware and gave him my best "fuck you" look.

Ware reddened, tiny veins pulsing over his temples. "My God, you're an insubordinate bastard, Quinn! Consider yourself relieved of your duties!" He paused, nostrils flared, seeming to dare me to respond.

I said nothing.

When Ware spoke again, his voice was icy. "Colonel Quinn, I also wish to inform you that I am considering court-martialing you. Contrary to my direct order, you deliberately chose to ignore the most obvious cause of the accident, which, as the evidence now indicates, can be attributed to gross misconduct by the pilot, Lieutenant Colonel French—"

"That's a lie, General," I said.

Ware looked at me in shock. "Why, you arrogant son of a—"

I stepped forward, cutting Ware off. "Save it, General. You won't dare court-martial me. You can't afford to have me reveal what I know at a trial. For instance, how would you explain your order, which was clearly illegal. Sure, I know about your evidence. But it's fabricated, and I'm betting it couldn't stand up to close scrutiny." I shook my head in disgust. "Tell me, sir. When did you decide your integrity was for sale?"

Ware's face shook with rage, but my eyes were on Cramer. When I made the last statement, I'd been looking directly at him.

Before Ware could respond, Cramer exploded, "You're way out of line, Quinn. Get the hell out of here or I'll have your ass hauled in for insubordination! Now!"

I didn't move. I was enjoying this.

"Goddammit, Quinn—"

I turned and walked away. I felt oddly calm, almost relieved. I took maybe twenty paces before I risked looking back.

Ware, Cramer, and McKenzie were huddled close, con-

ferring. I was startled to see McKenzie reach up and pat Cramer's back. The gesture was familiar. Too familiar. Like a coach encouraging a player going into the game.

A nagging suspicion began to grow.

As Cramer escorted Ware and McKenzie to the limo, the suspicion evolved into a certainty.

I'd assumed Cramer had only recently decided to sell out.

Wrong again.

As the commotion continued in the hangar, I went over to the edge of the security perimeter, watching Ted by the fuselage. He was engaged in a heated argument with the lanky agent. The agent's back was to me, but I recognized him anyway. Morgan.

Morgan suddenly grabbed Ted by the arm. Ted slapped the hand away and stormed out of the hangar. Morgan shouted for Ted to stop. Ted kept walking. Morgan started after Ted, then pulled up, throwing out his hands in exasperation.

I turned at the sound of approaching footsteps. Jennifer stood before me, her eyes soft and sad. "I'm so very sorry, John."

I nodded warily.

"Christ, you were right . . . about everything." She sounded bitter.

I wanted to believe her, but . . . "What do you want, Jennifer?"

"I . . . I want to help you find the truth."

"A little late, aren't you? I've just been canned. You're the one in charge now. If you want the truth—"

I stopped when Jennifer shook her head.

"I'm not in charge, John."

My eyebrows shot up. "You aren't?"

"No. I've been removed from the investigation too. I thought they told you."

My mind kicked into gear, trying to figure it. If not Jennifer . . . ? And then I knew, even before Jennifer said it.

"General Cramer's in charge," Jennifer said.

I felt a surge of anger as the pieces fell into place. I asked, "Who is going to replace you from the NTSB?"

"No one. The investigation is going to revert completely back to the military."

I nodded. Of course that's the way it had to be handled now.

"What about the rest of my team?" I asked. "Cramer going to replace everyone with his own people?"

"That's what I understand." Her eyes flickered past me. "Look, I'd better go." She sounded suddenly nervous.

I followed her gaze. The black limo containing McKenzie and Ware was moving away, but Jennifer wasn't looking at the car. She was focused on Cramer, who was watching us.

"How do you know him?" I asked.

Jennifer started to respond, then stopped. She shifted uneasily, and I saw something in her eyes. Not fear exactly, but—

"I'll call, John," Jennifer said quickly. She pivoted, hurrying toward her car.

As I watched her leave, I realized I'd made another mistake. It never had been McKenzie and Jennifer. The question now was what was Jennifer's link to Cramer? Was he the one she'd mentioned the Gibson girl's pictures to?

Jennifer was almost to her car when her head turned sharply, looking at Kroft coming toward her. They spoke briefly. Jennifer seemed to do most of the talking, occasionally pointing in the direction of the hangar. I had the impression she was explaining what was going on. Once

again, Kroft seemed out of the information loop. An outsider.

Moments later, Kroft stepped away, and Jennifer climbed into her car and drove off.

When I looked to Cramer, he was strolling toward the hangar. Out of the corner of my eye, I noticed Ted approaching. I expected to see him enraged.

Instead, he was smiling and there was a slight spring to his walk.

"What the hell have you got to be happy about?" I asked as he strolled up.

"All this," Ted said, gesturing toward the hangar where the agents were funneling the maintenance personnel toward the entry point. "The bastards did all this to stop us, but they're too goddamned late." He sounded amused.

"Late?" I grinned. "Hell, you *did* find something."

The smile again. "Not here, John."

We headed across the ramp toward the parking area.

As we walked, my eyes fell on Kroft, returning to his car. Only now he had a phone to his ear. I pointed him out to Ted, mentioning my curiosity over his lack of participation.

Ted shrugged thoughtfully. "It's puzzling."

I gave him a sideways glance. "You get the word Cramer's in charge, not Jennifer?"

"I heard." Then he turned and gave me a long look.

"Yeah, yeah. I was wrong. So shoot me. It's pretty clear the son of a bitch has been working with McKenzie from the beginning. I also think Cramer set me up to take the fall."

"I agree."

"The why is not to hard to figure. He and McKenzie knew the only way to get the Air Force brass to agree to a finding of fault against the pilots was to crank up the po-

litical pressure. To do that, they needed a patsy to attack in the press. That's why Cramer had a colonel instead of a general running the investigation. Easier to go after. And with all the mud that's been slung at me and the investigation, and with the results of the toxicology tests, no one from the Air Force will bat an eye when Cramer announces the pilots fucked up. Smart bastards."

We reached the edge of the parking area and angled toward the car.

I said, "You know Jennifer's connection is to Cramer, not McKenzie."

Ted stopped so suddenly, I went by him a couple of steps.

"You're certain?" he asked.

"Pretty sure." I quickly recounted my discussion with Jennifer, including my concerns that Jennifer had told Cramer about the Gibson girl's pictures.

Ted's jaw muscles flexed. We began walking again, only more slowly. "That means Cramer's in this deep."

"Very."

"And Jennifer actually seemed afraid of him?"

I nodded.

"You believe her when she said she wanted to help?"

"I'm not positive, but . . . I think so."

"Did she say when she'd call?"

"No."

"You have her number?"

I shook my head.

Ted's face became worried. "We need to contact her soon, John. If McKenzie or Cramer realizes she is willing to cooperate with us . . ." He didn't bother to finish, but the implication was clear.

Something knotted in the pit of my stomach.

"Rita might have Jennifer's office number," I said. "She contacted her last night."

Ted nodded. We'd arrived at the car, and I started to swing around—

"Here," Ted said.

Ted was holding out an envelope. I knew it had to contain whatever Blaney had found in the jet. At first, I couldn't feel anything inside. Then, at the bottom, something thin, hard . . .

"Get in before you open it, John," Ted said.

As we drove away, I was opening the flap of the envelope when I heard Ted say, "What the fuck does he want?"

To our left, I saw Kroft jogging toward us. I expected Ted to pull over, but he came down hard on the gas.

"You're not going to stop?" I asked, surprised.

"Why?" Ted said.

I couldn't think of a reason. When I looked back, Kroft was watching us, shaking his head.

I returned to the envelope. Moments later, I peered inside, feeling mildly disappointed.

A single piece of wire.

Ted began to explain.

When Ted finished talking, I was still rolling the wire between my fingers, studying it. The wire was maybe six inches long, sheathed in red rubber. One end was clipped

neatly, while the other appeared torn, the rubber blackened slightly like it had been scorched.

"This is one of the electrical leads to the valves, huh?" I said.

Ted nodded. "Notice the blackened end, the way it's ripped. I'm betting there was a small explosive charge attached that was set off either through a pressure switch or remotely by radio. When the charge was activated, it blew the wire, removing the power to the valve. Bingo. The valve opened and hot air got dumped into the cabin."

"Then there should be two of these," I said.

"I'm certain. Tom had only found that one when we arrived."

I scratched an ear. "Maybe I'm missing something here. Shouldn't Tom have been able to spot the actual device? I mean, a pressure switch would have been tough to miss."

Ted shook his head. "That's the beauty of the design. The device was almost certainly made of some kind of composite that would easily disintegrate. The explosive itself was probably very small, maybe the size of a large firecracker. When it went off, it blew the wire and destroyed the device. Look—" He reached into his shirt pocket and handed over a folded white handkerchief.

"Open it carefully."

I did.

Against the white fabric I could make out faint bits of a cream-colored residue, like grains of sand but slightly bigger.

Ted said, "I ran the handkerchief over the interior of the fuselage, near where Tom found the wire."

"That's what you were doing when you got into it with Morgan."

Ted nodded. "Bastard demanded to know why I was poking around the hellhole panel. Even threatened to

search me." He flashed a tight smile. "I told him I wasn't into being groped by big ugly white guys."

I grinned at the image.

Ted said, "You know, we're damned lucky the plane didn't explode into a fireball on impact, which is obviously what they had counted on. The fire would have burned the residue from the device, and the impact and explosion would have made it difficult, if not impossible, to tell just how the wires were torn apart. It was a helluva plan. Almost perfect."

"Except the jet didn't burn." I looked at the handkerchief. "Now we have proof. Once we have these particles analyzed, we'll be able to show the presence of the explosive and the composite—"

"It won't mean much by itself, John," Ted interrupted. "By tonight, the interior of the plane will be cleaned of any traces of that stuff. Any further testing will turn up nothing. Without additional verification, we run the risk of our charges being dismissed as meritless. People will accuse us of manufacturing the evidence."

I slowly folded the handkerchief. "Primarily because of me."

Ted hesitated, then nodded.

It wasn't fair, but it was reality. Who was going to take me seriously? I'd been fired and my integrity maligned. McKenzie's contacts in the press would exploit the hell out of those points.

I reminded Ted that we still had the photos showing the helicopter at the crash site.

"So what?" Ted said. "They prove the chopper was there, but we can't prove the crew actually killed Thurston. Hell, because of the way McKenzie handled the autopsy, we can't even prove Thurston was murdered. No. We need something irrefutable tying McKenzie to all this. We need something giving him a motive to kill Thurston."

"Meaning the tape."

"Meaning the tape."

"How do we get it from McKenzie?"

Ted sighed. "I don't know, John."

I passed him the envelope and handkerchief. "This is frustrating."

"I know."

"Christ, they have all the bases covered. It's hard not to be discouraged."

"Don't be."

For some reason his comment irritated me. Without the tape, Ted knew there wasn't the slightest chance we'd ever—

I swore.

We were approaching the Wing Headquarters, which housed the Command Post. Three sedans were parked in front against the curb. I was staring at a man leaning against the hood of one of the cars, smoking a cigarette.

It was Holt, Morgan's fat sidekick.

"No mystery why they're here," Ted murmured.

Holt eyed us with disdain as we drove around the circular drive and pulled into a spot maybe twenty feet away. He remained against the car, puffing and watching.

As I reached for the door, Ted said, "I should be by in fifteen, twenty minutes to pick you up, John."

"Huh? You're not coming in?"

"No. I want to check on a few things with the security cops."

"The logbooks?" I said, remembering the earlier phone call.

"Yeah. I had Chief Haney pull the logs from the flight line patrols. Figured one of the cops might have noticed someone unusual near the Lear the night before the crash. Worth a shot, anyway."

"Fine." As I got out, I thought Ted was wasting his time. Flight line patrols normally didn't log people on the ramp. Logistically, that would have been impossible. Hundreds came and went on the flight line, and all the cops did was check their access badges.

No, for the cops to actually log a name, it would have to be somebody important, somebody like—

I was in midstride when it dawned on me what Ted had in mind. I stumbled, almost fell. Holt's face sprouted into a grin. He began to laugh.

Not that I gave a damn.

I was thinking of the name Ted would find, the name of someone the cops would have noticed and written down.

Walking up the steps toward the entrance, I began to tremble, Holt's laughter ringing in my ears.

Once inside the Command Post gloom, I immediately headed toward the briefing room. When I arrived, I saw what I expected. Of course McKenzie would send his boys here. McKenzie would want all records confiscated to make sure we had nothing that would even suggest the crash hadn't been caused by pilot error.

Through the open briefing-room door, I could see a number of men inside, rummaging around. Rita was arguing with one. She looked extremely agitated. Instead of the security cop, a young Fed in a neatly pressed suit stood guard.

The Fed smiled thinly at me. "The room is off-limits, Colonel Quinn."

I was tempted to ask him if he'd once been a Richmond cop. Instead, I told him to get Major Sollars.

The agent shrugged, then leaned his head inside the door and shouted for Rita. She materialized a few moments later.

"What the hell is this, John? These guys just burst in,

saying they were authorized to requisition everything. And I got a call from General Cramer saying the team was disbanded."

I took her elbow and guided her back a few steps. "All true. General Cramer's taking over with his own team."

Rita's face fell. "Aw, Christ, I'm sorry, John."

"Yeah, well . . . Where's Mattie?"

"Gone. Back to her BOQ—"

"Does Harmon know?"

A head shake. "But I called, left a message at his hotel."

"Fine. You got Jennifer's number?"

"Sure. Her office number is in my briefcase."

"Jot it down for me and get your things."

She hesitated, then disappeared back into the room.

The agent gave Rita's backside an appreciative look. I guess they weren't all robots after all.

Rita appeared a minute later, carrying a large black handbag and a briefcase. She handed me a folded piece of paper, and we went down the hall.

"Jesus, John," she said softly. "Why were you fired? Did Cramer find out about Walling's article?"

I don't know. Maybe."

She gave me a look as if she was trying to understand. "There's a lot more to it, isn't there?"

I hesitated, then nodded.

"But you won't tell me?"

"Can't."

"That bad?"

"Worse."

She exhaled slowly. "So what now?"

"Nothing. We're through." I made a motion like I was washing my hands.

She studied me thoughtfully. "You really finished with this?"

"Absolutely."

"Uh-huh. Why do I think you're lying, John?"

I didn't even try to answer. We were almost to the exit. "Go home, Rita. Have a nice dinner and get some rest. Give the girls a hug for me, huh?"

She knew I was trying to get rid of her. She also knew I had my reasons for keeping her out of it. She gave a reluctant nod. "Be careful, John. And if there's anything I can do . . ."

"Go home," I said.

She gazed back, then squeezed my hand and walked out. Watching her go, all I could think of was her comment this morning.

*Visibility kills, John.*

"Hello, you've reached the number of Dr. Jennifer Johnson. I'm not in at the moment . . ."

I drummed impatiently on the desk I was sitting at in the Command Post admin office. I left a message at the beep, then fumbled in my notebook for the number of Chad Owen, Ogden's NTSB buddy. A woman answered. Chad wasn't in. I asked if she could dig up Jennifer's home number.

"I'm sorry, sir. It's against NTSB policy to release—"

I hung up on her and swiveled around to face the cute redheaded airman clicking away on a keyboard at an adjacent desk.

"Airman Collins, you got phone books around here?"

Airman Collins looked up from her computer, pointing to a metal cabinet toward the back. "In there, sir. Second shelf."

I went over and found five telephone books. One from D.C., and two each from Maryland and Virginia. A minute later, I knew I was wasting my time. The first listing had five Jennifer C. Johnsons and a half-dozen J. Johnsons.

I swore silently and checked my watch. Twenty minutes

had passed since Ted dropped me off. I snatched a folder off the desk, thanked Collins, and hustled out.

In addition to calling Jennifer, the folder was the second reason I'd come to the admin office. Inside was the fax listing the personnel assigned to the 21st Aviation Company out of Richmond Bird. There were forty-two pilots and twenty-six flight engineers in the unit.

I'd recognized a name.

Fifteen minutes later, I was standing just inside the glass doors of the lobby, watching the sunset. I'd tried Jennifer's office number twice more and had gotten her machine. With each call, I felt increasingly helpless and frustrated. No matter what Jennifer had done, I couldn't forget she'd been my wife.

For some reason, I also thought of Cole Rison, the image of his broken body lying on the sand.

I'd failed him too.

I was about to turn away and have a seat when Ted rolled up. As I came down the steps, I noticed the night air had turned cold, and I pulled my jacket closed. The Feds had left after securing the briefing room and removing boxes of files. I was a little surprised one car hadn't remained behind to keep an eye on Ted and me. McKenzie had to know we weren't about to drop the investigation.

As I folded myself into the passenger seat, Ted said, "Sorry I'm late."

"No problem. You check the logs?"

Ted slowly cruised around the circular drive. "There was only one name."

"Cramer's?"

A nod. "You figured it out too, huh?"

I shrugged. "We know he's part of it. And whoever sabotaged the jet had to be someone in the military."

"Still," Ted said, "I wanted to be sure. Just because Cramer was here the night before Thurston's flight didn't mean he could rig the jet. That would take someone familiar with a Lear."

"Okay . . ."

"That's why I was late. I went by Public Affairs again. Had them pull Cramer's bio."

"And?"

"Cramer was a Lear pilot for a couple of years. Right out here, as a matter of fact. Same unit as Rick French."

I felt myself getting angry again. I gazed into the night until the feeling went away. We were turning toward the main gate. "Christ, why would the son of a bitch get involved in something like this? Guy had the connections, the ability to make it to the top on his own. Doesn't figure."

"Who knows? Everyone knows the guy's on a power trip. Or maybe he felt pressure to keep up with his legacy. Being a fucking Cramer and all. Anyway, it's pretty clear McKenzie's been greasing the skids for Cramer for a while."

Which meant Ted had found something else in Cramer's bio. I looked at him, watching the oncoming headlights dance off his face.

"Six years ago," Ted said, "Cramer was assigned to the White House. Know where he worked, John? Office of the

White House Chief of Staff. Cramer was a lieutenant colonel at the time, and now he's got two stars. And he'll probably pick up his third on the next promotion board. Seems pretty fucking clear they— What's bugging you?"

I was staring back, my head slowly going back and forth. I hadn't really been following what Ted had been saying. Not since Ted had mentioned Cramer had been at the White House.

"Jennifer," I said.

"Jennifer?" Ted repeated.

"She was a White House Fellow. Five bucks says she was there the same time as Cramer."

"Shit," Ted murmured.

I nodded.

"You ever get hold of her?"

"No." I explained.

Ted swore.

I said, "You know, I always wondered what Cramer had against me."

"What do you mean?"

"Maybe this is a stretch," I said, running a hand over my head. "But I'm thinking Jennifer is a beautiful woman and Cramer's a good-looking guy. A real ladies' man. They were both military pilots, which meant they would have a lot in common. Be natural if they got together."

"A relationship. You think they had a relationship?"

"Why not? And ever since I've been working for Cramer, the guy's acted like he's been pissed at me. And he seemed to know a helluva lot about my background." I shrugged. "Maybe me being Jennifer's ex was the reason. That might even have something to do with his selection of me to head the investigation."

"To what? Ruin your career?"

Ted's tone told me he wasn't buying it. I wasn't sure if I was, either. Still, nothing else made sense. "Forget it, Ted."

"Jealous, then? He was somehow jealous."

I sighed. "I don't know." To change the subject, I held up the folder on my lap. "I received the personnel roster for the Twentyfirst."

"And . . ."

"Holt is one of the pilots."

"Anyone else?"

"No."

"Doesn't matter. We'll identify the rest of the crew eventually."

"At least that clears Kroft."

"For the flight only."

"You still think he's involved?"

"He was there with McKenzie the night they took the body, John. He had to know that was part of the cover-up. He also has to be aware of all the rest of it. And remember his phone call to you this morning . . ."

"I know, but—"

"There's another point I haven't mentioned. When I stopped by to check the logbooks, someone had already been by to get Haney to turn them over. Haney finally did, but he stalled and made copies first because he knew I wanted them." He gave me a meaningful look.

"Kroft?"

"In person."

We drove, wrapped up in our thoughts.

"You doing okay, John?" Ted asked, concern in his voice.

"Uh, sure." Then I understood. "You mean now that my career is over?"

"Yeah."

"Actually, I hadn't really thought about it."

"You will, John," Ted said quietly. "I still think about what could have been. You know, if I'd played the game and learned to keep my mouth shut." He shrugged.

"You have regrets?"

A long pause. "Not really."

I smiled at him in the dark.

We were following a line of cars heading out the main gate, the usual Friday-night crowd heading out to dinner or to party. I removed my phone and punched the redial. I listened for a moment and hung up.

"Jennifer?" Ted said.

I nodded, pocketing the phone. "So what now?"

"Nothing. Relax. Have dinner. Figure out our next step."

"That's it?"

"Unless you can think of anything else."

I couldn't.

"Anyway, Tiki's expecting us. Besides, you look like you could use a drink." He glanced at the clock on the dash. "The news should be coming up. Should have something on Gloria Peters's murder."

I pushed the button. A Temptations tune blared out. I switched to one of the local talk stations. After a car commercial, the six-o'clock newscast came on. When it ended, I turned the radio off. Ted glanced at me and shook his head. I expected him to say I told you so, but he didn't.

My removal from the investigation had been the lead story. There were also reports on three other murders, including a driveby shooting that had killed a five-year-old girl. Then came Gloria Peters. Her death was being investigated as a home-invasion robbery. The police had named a local gang member as a possible suspect.

I turned, studying the traffic behind.

"They're out there, John," Ted said quietly. "They're just being careful this time."

I removed the gun from the glove compartment and put it on my lap.

• • •

My condo was a straight two-block shot down from Ted's place. As we approached my building, I spotted at least half a dozen press vans along the street. A cluster of reporters were camped out by my door. A female correspondent with a mane of blond hair was standing about twenty yards away from the group, talking into a camera, her face visible under the harsh brightness of a spotlight. She was a talking head for one of the local stations, but I couldn't remember which one.

As we rolled by, my phone rang.

A tentative voice: "John?"

Relief gushed through me. "Jennifer, where are you?"

"I'm at National Airport." She paused. "With my son. . . ."

The bright neon sign glowing the words "Happy Hawaiian Lounge" seemed oddly out of place above the modest two-story brick building wedged in between a dance studio and a flower shop. I was still talking with Jennifer when Ted pulled into a spot along the street. Waiting for me to finish, he collected the various folders, Thurston's planner, and the copy of *Time*.

As I spoke with Jennifer, I could hear the apprehension in her voice. She told me the boy's name was Mark and he was six. Jennifer was sending him to her parents in Seattle. To get him away, protect him.

And she also mentioned something else, even though I didn't ask. She knew I'd wonder because of Mark's age. He wasn't mine.

After I hung up, I briefed Ted about the call. Then I slipped the pistol into my ankle holster and we got out.

Approaching the entrance to Ted's bar, we heard soft

rock music wafting out. The door opened and an attractive couple in their thirties emerged. The guy weaved and seemed to be hanging on to the woman, who was looking more than a little annoyed.

"Hey, Ted," the guy said, blinking in recognition. "How ya been?" His voice was thick, the words slurred.

"Fine, Rich. Hi, Mandy. You driving, Mandy?"

She glared at Rich. "I'm trying to, but—"

"Hey, I can drive," Rich said. He let go of Mandy's arm, and the swaying increased. "See, I'm fine, Ted. Great."

"Give Mandy the car keys, Rich," Ted said.

"Aw, hell, Ted—"

"The keys," Ted said a little more firmly.

Rich gazed back unsteadily. He finally shrugged, fished around in his pocket, then handed over a set of keys to Mandy.

Mandy gave Ted an appreciative srmile.

"Here, John," Ted said, handing me the folders under his arm. "C'mon, Rich. I'll walk you to the car."

As they left, I opened the door and went inside.

The interior of the bar was cozy and warm. The lighting was subdued and the walls were a deep blue, accented with a wood trim that matched the floor. A dozen tables occupied the main floor, with a long bar running along the right wall. To my left, Elton John was singing "Candle in the Wind" from a vintage sixties jukebox. There was nothing remotely Asian about the decor because Ted, after buying the place, spent what was left renovating the apartment upstairs into something Tiki would live in. He kept telling me he was eventually going to redecorate, but I knew he wouldn't. Not as long as business remained good.

Except for one table with three clean-cut men who barely looked old enough to drink, the crowd was late thirties to fifties, mostly aging yuppies stopping off for a drink on their commute home. Often people from the base would

pop over, but tonight I spotted only one other uniform and I didn't recognize the guy.

A number of faces were looking at me with more than a passing interest, which reminded me of the play I was getting on the television newscasts. I tried not to feel self-conscious.

Two waitresses were working the tables. One, a blonde with a chubby face, passed by with a tray of drinks. She flashed a dimpled smile. "Hi, John."

"Hi, Marla." I spotted Tiki standing behind the bar next to a handsome dark-complected man in his early twenties. She noticed me and gave a wave, her pretty round face spreading into a welcoming grin. Barely five feet, stockily built, with long shimmering dark hair, Tiki looked like she could have stepped right out of Michener's *Tales of the South Pacific*. The young man was their second-oldest son, Matthew, a grad student at the University of Maryland.

"You look beat, John," Tiki said when I came over. She was already pouring me a glass of Scotch. "Where's my better half?"

I set the pile on the bar. "Baby-sitting some guy named Rich. He'll be back in a minute." I looked to Matthew. "Your mom's got you working, huh?"

Matthew winked. "She's never heard of child labor laws."

Tiki slapped Matthew lightly on the shoulder. "Remember, I gave you life."

"Like you'll ever let me forget."

"Careful, Matthew," Tiki said.

Matthew grinned, hastily retreating to the other end of the bar.

Tiki shook her head at him, but there was affection in her eyes. She slid the drink over to me.

When I reached for it, Tiki took my hand in hers. "Ted told me," she said quietly. "You going to be okay?"

I gamely nodded.

"Food is upstairs. In the oven. I had Carlos throw together a couple of Reubens." Carlos was the cook/busboy/janitor. His culinary expertise began and ended with sandwiches and chicken wings.

"Thanks." I took a large swallow of Scotch, enjoying the warmth. "My ex-wife will be dropping by. Send her up."

Tiki was now pouring a glass of bourbon. "I saw her on TV. She's pretty."

"Yeah . . ." Tiki kept looking at me as if expecting more. I was relieved to see Ted appear.

"Hi, honey." He waved to Matthew, then leaned over the bar and kissed Tiki's cheek. "Where's that Magic Marker board you got for Tessie's birthday?" Tessie was their oldest grandchild.

"Why?" Tiki asked suspiciously.

"Just need to borrow it." He picked up the bourbon and took a sip.

"It's in the hall closet. I just wrapped it—"

"Fine. C'mon, John."

"Ted—"

"I'll rewrap it, honey. Promise." He smiled at her sweetly.

"Hmm. This I have to see."

Ted tried to look hurt.

Tiki fought back a smile, waving us away. "Go on. Just give me a hand later, huh? Matthew wants to go to a party tonight with his friends." She gestured to the table of young men I'd noticed earlier.

Ted grinned, motioning me to pick up the stuff we'd collected off the bar. We headed for an unmarked door in the back corner. Ted walked quickly, as if in a hurry.

I followed him through the door into a small hallway leading to a wooden staircase. I asked, "Why do you want a kid's marker board?"

"Figured it would be easier. Make sure the door's locked, John."

"Easier for what?" I asked, trying to check the knob without spilling my drink.

When I turned around, Ted was already going up the stairs two at a time.

Ted and Tiki's spacious three-bedroom apartment was a stark contrast to the bar. Here everything was light and airy with a distinct Southwest feel. The furniture was blond and rustic, and the polished wood floors were covered with colorful throw rugs made from Native American blankets. Pictures of their kids and grandkids were everywhere. Ted had done much of the renovating work himself. I helped some, but wasn't much good at that kind of thing. Even though Ted couldn't stand the decor, he'd never told Tiki. She loved it, and that was all that mattered.

When we entered, Ted immediately crossed the living room, flipping off two lamps. He went to one of the windows overlooking the street and put a hand on the drapes.

"What are you doing?" I asked.

He looked back to me in the entryway. "Kill the lights, John."

I hesitated, then deposited the stuff under my arm on a small decorative table a few feet away. I turned and flipped the wall switches by the door.

The room went black. A sliver of light appeared as Ted drew back the drapes. I walked toward it.

As I came up behind Ted, he stepped aside. He was holding the drapes back about an inch. He gestured with his hand holding his drink. "Take a look, John. Dark blue Sable about a half block up the street."

I leaned forward. The street was well lit. I understood a moment later. "Two people inside."

"Yeah. Saw them drive up when I was walking back. Guy and a gal. Noticed they stayed in the car."

I stood in the dark as Ted walked back across the room. I winced when the lights came on. "I should call Jennifer, tell her not to come."

Ted shrugged, angling toward the hallway leading to the bedrooms. "McKenzie's bound to find out sooner or later. Besides, she's safer here. You mind grabbing the sandwiches and bringing them to the study?"

"Sure."

As I went to the kitchen, I saw Ted remove a package from the hallway closet.

Ted called his third bedroom a study, but that was charitable. Other than a desk and small bookshelf, the rest of the space was taken by a bunk bed his grandkids used when visiting and Tiki's sewing table. On the walls, instead of mementos of Ted's military career, there were more family pictures and a bulletin board tacked with crayon drawings addressed to Grandpa.

When I walked in carrying two trays, Ted had the marker board propped up on the edge of his desk. On the floor out front was a wad of pink wrapping paper with little teddy bears saying "Happy Birthday." Ted was drawing a line in blue Magic Marker across the middle of the board. He stopped, consulted the contents of a folder, then began making evenly spaced slash marks in the line.

I came around, set a tray on his desk, then went over to the only other chair in the room, the one Tiki used for sewing. By now I'd figured out what Ted was up to.

I drank more Scotch, listening to the faint sounds from the jukebox emanating through the floor. Then I picked up my sandwich. I was hungry and I wasn't going to wait for Ted to finish the timeline.

• • •

Fifteen minutes later, I'd finished eating and was feeling a slight buzz when Ted finally tossed the marker to the desk. While he'd worked, Ted had taken maybe three bites from his sandwich and barely touched his drink.

Ted angled the board to me and kicked back in his chair. "Well, what does the timeline tell us, John?" He was using his professorial tone.

I looked to the board.

Below the slash marks, he'd neatly written the following:

—May 4, 1975, McKenzie joins Governor Banks staff.
—Oct. 3, 1980, Melissa George accuses Governor Banks of affair.
—Oct. 5, 1980, Thurston resigns from campaign staff.
—Nov. 4, 1980, Halloran wins election for governor of Virginia.
—June 5, 1982, Melissa George is murdered.
—June 8, 1982, McKenzie becomes Halloran's chief of staff.
—Dec. 3, 1982, ex-Governor Banks commits suicide.
—Nov. 1, 1988, Halloran is elected President.
—Nov. 3, 1992, Halloran is reelected.
—Feb. 27, 1994, Thurston and Halloran meet.
—Feb. 28, 1994, Thurston and Halloran meet.
—March 1, 1994, Thurston and Halloran meet.
—March 3, 1994, Thurston dies.

I studied the timeline for almost five minutes, regretting how dull and slow the Scotch had made me. Ted watched me, nibbling on his sandwich.

"Two dates in particular jump out," I said finally. "The first is the day Thurston resigned from the Halloran campaign. October fifth. Two days after Melissa George accused Governor Banks of the affair. That suggests his

departure was linked to that revelation. It also indicates someone in the Halloran camp was behind the scandal."

Ted gave a nod of approval. He pushed his plate away and picked up his drink. "Why do you think that?"

"I can only come up with two reasons Thurston would have resigned. One, because he himself was involved in the scandal and Halloran found out and made him quit, or, two, because Thurston discovered someone in the Halloran camp was behind the scandal so he got pissed and resigned."

"Which conclusion seems more logical?"

I hesitated. "I'm leaning toward Thurston not being involved in the scandal. Everything we know about the guy indicates he was pretty honest. Plus Kendra said it was Thurston's decision to quit, not Halloran's. But hell, I'm not sure. I guess he could have been part of it."

Ted was silent. He kept looking at me. I had the feeling I was missing something important.

Finally, Ted said, "And the second date you noticed . . ."

"The day McKenzie joined Halloran's campaign staff. June eighth. Three days after Melissa George's murder. Again, that indicates there's a link between the two events. But the connection is tougher to figure. The only thing I can come up with is, well, kind of crazy."

"Go on."

"What bugged me was why Halloran would hire McKenzie in the first place. A guy who worked for his rival—"

"That's not unusual, John. McKenzie was a talented political analyst."

"Maybe. But the timing, only three days after Melissa George's death, makes the situation suspicious as hell. Particularly if you tie that in with what Kendra said about the tape." I gave him a meaningful look.

"You're referring to her comment that the tape was altered to frame someone," Ted said.

"Exactly. If that's true, and the tape showed someone in Halloran's camp committing the murder—"

"Blackmail," Ted said. "You're suggesting McKenzie blackmailed someone on Halloran's staff to get himself hired. Pretty damn good, John. That's the same conclusion I reached." He looked pleased.

I slowly folded my hands across my chest. "There's more."

"Okay . . ."

"You know this implicates Halloran," I said quietly. "He would have been the one to sign up McKenzie. So if anyone was being blackmailed, it had to be Halloran."

"Not necessarily, John."

"Get real, Ted. McKenzie became Halloran's chief of staff. Who else had the clout to hire the son of a bitch for a job that important?"

Ted sighed deeply, shaking his head. The teacher disappointed in the pupil.

"What?" I said, feeling a trace of annoyance.

"You're forgetting someone." He paused. "Someone who was almost certainly involved with the scandal and possessed the clout to have McKenzie brought into the campaign."

I was completely lost. I was about to ask Ted what the hell he was talking about when he suddenly rose from the desk.

From the hallway outside, I heard the faint sounds of knocking.

As we went to the front door, the answer popped into my head like a jolt.

I shook my head in astonishment. *Son of a bitch*—

"Hello, Jennifer," Ted said, opening the door.

Jennifer wore beige slacks and a green sweater that matched her eyes. She was quiet as Ted led her into the living room. I joined her on the sofa, which was covered with brightly colored stripes that reminded me of an American Indian sand painting. Ted sat across from us in a leather recliner.

Jennifer shifted in her seat, fidgeting with her hands. She stared at the floor, then at the walls, and back to the floor again.

I asked, "You get Mark on the plane okay?"

She nodded slowly, gazing at me. "This is . . . difficult, John."

I know." I felt for her. Jennifer had always been proud, independent. Now her protective shell was gone. She was again the Jennifer back in pilot training, the one who needed help.

"Christ, John, I'm so very sorry," she said, her voice cracking slightly. "You have to believe that."

"I do."

"Want to tell us how you became involved in all this?" Ted asked gently.

Jennifer nodded.

"Was it McKenzie who contacted you?" Ted asked.

She shook her head. She focused on Ted, avoiding me.

I knew what was coming.

"It was Max," she said.

She meant General Maxwell Cramer.

In a quiet, halting voice, Jennifer explained.

I'd been wrong about when Jennifer and Cramer first met. True, they'd been at the White House together. But they'd known each other before, when Jennifer had transferred to Cramer's unit during our divorce. They dated, and Jennifer became pregnant. Neither one wanted to get married, and Jennifer toyed with the idea of having an abortion. In the end, she couldn't.

So she did the single-mother thing. With money from her family, she was still able to pursue her career and earn her Ph.D. She and Cramer remained in contact because of Mark. At the White House, they resumed their relationship and Jennifer found herself falling in love with Cramer. She wanted to get married. Cramer resisted; he enjoyed the single life. Six months ago, Cramer finally agreed to having her and Mark move in.

Cramer had used his contact with McKenzie to get Jennifer the NTSB job. Cramer also had approached her about working the crash, saying it would be good for her career.

"Of course, I agreed," Jennifer said bitterly. "But I didn't know about the cover-up, all the rest of it."

"If you didn't," Ted said, "why did you go along with the theory about pilot error in the press conference?"

"Because I honestly believed they could have been responsible." She gave me a long look. "And because I thought you were trying to hide that fact. Protect your friend."

"You were aware of my friendship with Rick French last night?" I asked, surprised.

"Max told me. I know why he did now. He . . . he was trying to influence me. Make me suspicious of you. He also told me other things. . . ."

"Go on," I said.

"He told me your orders were to make sure the Air Force wasn't going to be charged with negligence. He said that's why they chose you, because of the Medal of Honor. You were a war hero. No one would question you."

*Like hell,* I thought.

She smiled sadly. "I guess I let my personal feelings get in the way. I still harbored some resentment. Silly. After all these years. Anyway, I made it easy for him to sway me."

The realization that Jennifer believed I might actually be corrupt stung. Then it occurred to me that I'd done the same thing. I had believed the worst of her, and I felt a little ashamed.

Ted cleared his throat. To Jennifer he said, "So you were never going to take over the investigation?"

"No . . ." She seemed on the verge of saying something else. Instead she sagged back, fidgeting again.

Finally, she looked at me, and I saw anguish in her eyes. "How . . . how deeply is Max a part of this?"

I didn't want to be the one to tell her. I glanced to Ted to pass the ball.

"You're certain you want to know?" he asked her softly.

"Yes."

"It's . . . bad."

"Please . . ."

Ted took a deep breath. "All right."

After he told her, Jennifer slumped back against the sofa, head bowed, the picture of dejection. She obviously cared a great deal for Cramer. For some reason, the realization made me uncomfortable.

"Jennifer," Ted said.

She slowly focused on him.

"Do you know anything about a tape?" Ted asked.

"Tape?" she asked dully.

"A videotape," I said. "We're looking for one Thurston had with him on the plane."

Jennifer was shaking her head when I saw a flicker in her eyes. She went completely still.

"Yes?" I said.

"I do remember seeing a videotape, John."

Five minutes later, Ted rose and began pacing. He managed to look both anxious and pensive, reflecting the significance of Jennifer's revelation.

I said to Jennifer, "You can't be certain the tape is still there?"

"No," Jennifer said.

"We still have to check, John," Ted said, continuing to pace. To Jennifer he said, "What time was that meeting between Cramer and McKenzie tonight at the White House?"

"Seven-thirty. I was supposed to attend, but . . ." She shook her head.

"No idea how long it will last?" Ted asked.

"Not really. Maybe an hour."

"If you don't show, will they wonder why?"

"Probably."

Ted checked his watch. "To be safe, we've got to be on the road in the next thirty minutes."

"What about our friends outside?" I asked.

Ted pivoted, facing me. "There's a way. We'll have to use two cars."

"You mean split up because they can't follow both of us."

"No. We can all still go together. Matthew and his friends can help."

I frowned. Jennifer was puzzled too.

Ted quickly ran through his plan.

"Christ," I said afterward. "That's almost too easy."

Ted's face became troubled. "Except that I've got to break the news to Tiki that I won't be around to help her out tonight. She's not going to be happy." He gave a deep sigh. "Back in a minute."

"Funny," Jennifer murmured as he left. "He almost looked frightened."

I smiled. "I think he is."

When Ted, Jennifer, and I entered the bar ten minutes later, I could understand Ted's trepidation over telling Tiki he was leaving. The crowd had grown by about a third, and Tiki looked swamped as she tried to keep up with the drink orders. We continued to the entrance, where Matthew was waiting with his friends. Ted called out to Tiki as we went by. She glowered at him, but managed to smile at Jennifer and me.

Jennifer and I went to one of the windows, while Ted chatted with Matthew. Matthew and his group left a moment later, going to a battered ragtop Jeep sitting out front. I peered down the street and spotted the Sable parked against the curb between a Corvette and a minivan.

"Still there," I murmured to Jennifer.

Jennifer nodded. She gazed at me, her eyes shiny. "When I think about all those people who died. And to think I told Max about the Gibson girl—"

I put a finger to her lips. "Don't, Jennifer. It wasn't your fault."

She nodded dumbly, and I could see the guilt in her eyes.

I took her hand and held it.

A few moments later, we saw the Jeep drive away. Ted opened the front door, and Jennifer and I followed him into the night.

Walking to Ted's car, we made a conscious effort not to look in the direction of the Sable. Jennifer got in back and I took the passenger seat. Ted sat behind the wheel, eyes on the rearview mirror, while Jennifer and I gazed out the rear window. The Jeep appeared moments later, coming slowly down the street. We couldn't see the Sable because of the line of cars blocking our view. Ted started the engine and shifted to drive.

The Jeep rolled to a stop. The high beams flickered.

Ted immediately pulled out and the Sable came into view. The Jeep was abeam it, boxing it in. A horn blared, then the Sable's doors flew open and a man and a woman jumped out. They began waving, gesturing angrily at the Jeep. The man ran around the front of the Jeep and began knocking on the driver's window. Matthew and his friends piled out. Behind them, other cars began to back up. More horns. By now the woman and man were staring after us. The man pulled a phone from his jacket—

We turned a corner.

I smiled at Ted and eased back in the seat.

Now everything depended on whether we could find the tape.

When Jennifer had awakened around three A.M. the night before, Cramer wasn't in bed. She'd gone to look for him and found him in his den, hooking two VCRs together.

Upon seeing Jennifer, Cramer became agitated and angry, ordering her to go back to bed.

But she'd thought it odd he would record something so late. She recalled seeing a videotape on his desk. She remembered because the tape was lying next to a briefcase. A dirty briefcase, one that looked twisted and bent, as if thrown to the ground with great force.

"About a mile farther, Ted," Jennifer directed. "The road leading to the house will be after a sharp bend."

We'd turned off Indian Head Highway about ten miles south of Piscataway National Park, and were now winding past large estates built along the Potomac River. We cruised past a thick wall of trees and came to the bend. Ted turned left down a black-topped road. After a few hundred yards, we stopped at an iron gate. Sweeping gilded letters spelled CRAMER across the grillwork. And centered below was a fancy emblem resembling a coat of arms.

"This place used to belong to Max's grandfather," Jennifer said, opening her door. She went over to a keypad on the gatepost and punched in a code. The gate whirred open.

Gaslights lined the driveway as we drove past a sprawling lawn to a large Colonial house fronted by tall columns and a wrap-around porch. Beyond the house, we could see the blackness of the Potomac River and a stone walkway

curving toward a dock, where the silhouette of a boat bobbed gently.

As we climbed out of the car, the night was cold and quiet, the air heavy with mist.

"Big place," Ted murmured, looking around.

"Almost fifty acres," Jennifer said. "It's worth a fortune."

Ted and I followed her up the steps to the front door.

We entered a tiled foyer with a glittering chandelier. Before us rose a mahogany staircase, hallways running down either side. A formal sitting room was off to our right, a dining room next to it.

"This way," Jennifer said, pointing to the hallway on the left.

She led us over deep red carpeting to the rear of the house, stopping at a set of wooden doors. She tried the knob and frowned.

"Funny. It's locked."

My eyebrows inched up. "And it normally isn't?"

"Never."

"You know where there's a key?" Ted asked her.

Jennifer shook her head.

Ted studied the door, then looked to me. "Opens inward, and the lock isn't too strong."

"Step back, Jennifer," I said.

Her eyes widened when she realized what we had in mind. "He'll know."

"I'm sure he will," I said.

Ted gave me an expectant look.

"My back," I said apologetically.

Ted sighed. It took him four kicks to pop the doors open.

We walked into a darkly paneled room filled with books. My eyes immediately went to the far wall where two large paintings of somber-faced men in full military regalia

peered down onto a massive teak desk. Both men wore four stars, and the resemblance was unmistakable.

I was overwhelmed with disgust.

Cramer's legacy.

I peered around the room. A smaller desk with a computer and a printer occupied a corner next to a couple of wooden file cabinets. Then came a long table with detailed models of military aircraft that Cramer had probably flown. One was a Lear. Above was a wall filled with photos of Cramer, a number showing him in front of the White House. I spotted two of him with McKenzie, arms around each other.

Jennifer quickly stepped around me to a cabinet. She opened it, revealing a television, two VCRs on shelves below. She powered up the VCRs and punched the eject buttons.

Nothing happened.

Ted said, "Tape's got to be here. Why else would he lock the door?"

"You take the desk," I said. "I'll check out the file cabinets."

Three minutes later, I slid the last drawer closed. I looked to Ted, who was staring at a bottom desk drawer.

"Locked?" I asked.

"Yeah. Jennifer, where does Cramer keep his tools?"

Ted twisted sharply on the prybar. The sound of splintering wood and the drawer popped open.

Jennifer and I were standing over Ted, peering down as he reached inside. I saw some brown manila folders and stapled sheets of paper. Ted's head shifted forward, blocking my view. He rummaged around a bit, then tensed. He slowly drew his arm back.

"Here," he said, and handed me a plastic videotape container.

The weight told me it contained a tape, but I popped it open anyway. "Only one?" I said.

"Yeah," Ted said, rising. "My guess is Cramer probably turned over the original to McKenzie after he made a copy."

"So he could use it for a little blackmailing of his own?" I asked.

"Possibly."

"So that's it," Jennifer said bitterly. "That's what all the killing was over."

I nodded.

"Why? What's on it?"

I went to the TV to find out.

Jennifer and Ted were sitting on the edge of Cramer's desk when I stepped back and pointed the remote at the VCR.

The TV screen fluttered and the interior of a house appeared. A living room. The shot was taken from above and was slightly grainy, the color washed out. Going clockwise, I saw window drapes, sofa, a couple of chairs, a wooden coffee table, then a wall.

A woman walked into the room. She moved fluidly, languidly. She was tall, slender, with long dark hair, almost black. Her back was to us. She wore skintight jeans and a yellow sweater. She slowly turned, facing the direction she'd come from.

Melissa George was even more stunning than I remembered from the photo. Not a classic beauty on par with Kendra, but she possessed a seductive quality. Her lips were full, almost pouty, and her large breasts strained against the sweater. She was the type of girl men fantasized about.

Her mouth moved like she was speaking to someone, but there was no sound, which I found curious. I mentioned that point to Ted.

"Notice the slight glare," Ted said, after a moment. "That's reflection off of glass. From the angle, I'm guessing the camera's rigged from outside a window, looking down into the room."

I nodded. The girl was looking directly into the camera lens. She laughed, twisting her body in a seductive pose.

"She knows the camera's there," Ted said, stating the obvious.

"Yeah," I said. "Wonder who's with her."

"Who is she?" Jennifer asked.

"Melissa George," I said. Jennifer gave me a blank look. "I'll explain later."

On the screen, Melissa George had stopped posing. She said something and checked her watch. She shrugged, went over to the sofa, and sat. She began to tap her foot. She kept looking to her left, at a person or persons out of view.

"She seems to be waiting for something," Jennifer murmured.

"Or someone," Ted said.

The tapping stopped. Melissa looked into the camera again. She smiled coyly. Leaning back, she licked her lips provocatively. Very seductively, she lowered a hand to her crotch and placed the other on a breast. Closing her eyes, she stroked herself with feigned passion.

"Jesus," Jennifer said.

"Not exactly a wallflower, is she?" Ted added.

I didn't reply. My eyes were glued to the screen. Melissa was squirming. Her hands moved faster. She slid lower, going almost flat. Her lips began to move rhythmically. Suddenly her eyes opened and she sat up. She threw back her head and began to laugh. She wagged her finger. Naughty, naughty.

I swallowed to find my voice. "At least we know whoever's with her has got to be a guy."

"What's going on now?" Jennifer asked. Melissa's head had turned, as if she heard something. She quickly rose, smoothing her clothes. She brushed back her hair. She was talking again. She nodded and knelt down, reaching under the couch.

"Huh? What was that all about?" I said.

No one answered.

A moment later, Melissa stood, walked quickly to her right, and disappeared from view.

We stared at the empty room.

Melissa reentered thirty seconds later, stopping near the middle of the room. Then someone else appeared, and I stared in surprise. Even though Ted's comments had prepared me for this possibility, I'd still expected to see McKenzie, maybe even Halloran.

Instead, I was looking at a woman wearing a long coat, a wide-brimmed hat, and a scarf around her neck. Her back was to us, and we couldn't see her face.

Melissa extended her hand to a chair, inviting the woman to sit. The woman shook her head. She removed her hat, and blond hair spilled out. As she placed the hat on the chair, her head bobbed slightly, as if she was speaking. Melissa responded, and they appeared to converse for a few seconds. As they spoke, Melissa's face grew increasingly cold. Occasionally, we caught a brief glimpse of the woman's profile, but not enough to tell who she was. Suddenly, the woman grabbed Melissa's arm, and Melissa's lips twisted into a snarl. She jerked her arm away and tried to move back. The woman followed, gesturing wildly, angrily—

"What the hell brought this on?" Ted asked.

Melissa's face was livid now. She seemed to be shouting. Ted must have been right about the camera being behind a window because we finally began to pick up faint, muffled words. As the two women raged at each other, I

noticed Melissa was drifting to her left, causing the other woman to turn. Melissa's movements seemed awkward. Then I realized she was trying to position the woman for the camera.

The blond woman pivoted, following Melissa. She was still waving her arms, appearing furious, almost out of control. Slowly her face came into view. A profile, and then—

We saw the woman clearly, her face knotted with rage. But she was one of the most famous people in the world, and we easily recognized her.

It was Alicia Halloran.

Jennifer gasped. Ted remained silent, as did I.

I ran a hand over my face. The clues had been there all along, but I hadn't been paying attention. Not until the discussion with Ted. That's when I remembered the comment of Thurston's niece Carolyn: *My uncle had a falling-out with the First Lady.*

And Kendra: *The First Lady's a disease.*

And Carolyn again: *My uncle disliked her . . . something to do with the campaign.*

And Ted: *There's someone else with clout who was almost certainly involved with the scandal.*

Then there was the timeline, which showed Thurston had quit Halloran's campaign two days after the scandal broke.

And my own conclusion that Thurston quit the campaign because he found out someone from Halloran's camp was behind the scandal.

I shook my head. I still had a difficult time believing that Alicia Halloran was the one who engineered the scandal.

I took a deep breath and braced myself for what was to come.

On the TV, Melissa George's face was tight with anger

as she took in the First Lady's tirade. Finally, her lip curled disdainfully and she shot back a response. The First Lady went still, looking stunned.

Melissa began to laugh meanly. She waved a hand dismissively.

Alicia Halloran stared back, her face becoming a mask. She started to reach for her hat—

And then it happened.

Melissa was stepping back, still laughing, when Alicia Halloran lashed out with her hand. She caught Melissa squarely on the side of the head. The force of the blow coupled with Melissa's own momentum caused Melissa to topple backward. She twisted, throwing her arms out to break her fall. Her head struck the corner of the coffee table. She crumpled on the carpet, her body limp.

Alicia Halloran stared down at Melissa in shock.

From our angle we had a clear view of Melissa's face. Above her left eye, we could see a deep gash. Blood ran down the side of her head onto the carpet.

Alicia knelt down beside Melissa. She reached out, tentatively touching Melissa's face. She instantly recoiled. She looked around furtively, wiping her hand on her coat. She sprang to her feet, eyes searching the room, and quickly walked to a phone on an end table.

She stopped.

She looked again to Melissa, who was bleeding heavily, and picked up the phone. She stared at the receiver for a moment and then slowly hung up.

She gazed at Melissa a third time.

Then she retrieved her hat from the chair and donned it, pulling the brim low over her face.

And a moment later she was gone, and the screen went blank.

For a moment, no one spoke.

"My God," Jennifer said. "She killed that woman."

"No, she didn't," Ted said quietly. He was gazing at me as he said it.

I nodded my agreement. I punched the rewind button and faced Jennifer.

"The First Lady was framed," I said.

But Jennifer wasn't looking at me, and neither was Ted. Their eyes were focused behind me, toward the door.

"I'll take the tape, John," a voice said.

**G**eneral Cramer stood in the doorway holding a shotgun with an ornately carved handle. He seemed completely at ease. "You should have quit while you were ahead, John."

My hands balled into fists. I stared into the barrel pointed at my chest. "You murdering son of a bitch."

He shrugged. "Hello, Ted."

"Fuck you, sir," Ted said pleasantly.

"Always the smart-ass, eh, Ted." His eyes went to Jennifer. "I gotta tell you, Jen, I'm real disappointed in you."

Jennifer was staring at him in horror. "For God's sake, Max. Why? All those people—"

"McKenzie's got a shot at being President, Jen," Cramer answered simply, as if that explained it all.

Jennifer seemed confused. Then her shoulders slumped in understanding.

"For chrissakes, Jen," Cramer said. "Don't give me that sanctimonious look. You knew from the beginning the

crash was suspect as hell. Yet you were more than willing to play along." He flashed a tight smile. "Like it or not, baby, you're not a helluva lot different than me." He paused. "Where's Mark? Mrs. O'Brien's?"

Jennifer shook her head. She stared at the floor. She seemed dazed. "I . . . sent him to my parents'."

Cramer nodded. Softly, he said, "You know it doesn't have to be like this, Jen."

Jennifer swallowed, looking up. "What do you mean?"

"You give me your word to keep your mouth shut, I'll talk to McKenzie. Maybe we can work something out."

Her eyes widened in disbelief. "You can't be serious."

A look of regret crossed Cramer's face. "Don't be a fool, Jen."

Jennifer's mouth slowly opened, then closed. Her eyes went to me, then Ted. Finally, in a strangled voice, she said, "Go to hell."

Cramer sighed. The barrel moved. "C'mon."

Before we left, he made me get him the tape.

Cramer guided us to the formal sitting room near the front door. Ted and I sat in chairs facing the large picture window, while Jennifer took the couch to our left. Cramer went over and drew the drapes, leaving a gap of maybe a foot. He sat in a chair beside the opening, keeping the barrel of the shotgun on Ted and me while he took out a cell phone and made a call. He mentioned our names, then hung up.

He smiled thinly at me. "You know I never liked you, John."

I nodded vaguely.

"Any idea why?"

I hesitated and shook my head.

"Her." He looked to Jennifer. "She used to talk about you all the time when we first got together. Compare me to

you all the fucking time. That pissed me off— Hey, don't look so shocked, Jen. You know you did."

Jennifer glared at him, saying nothing. She glanced at me and looked away.

Cramer said gloomily, "Anyway, I knew she still had a thing for you. Figured she'd get over it after a while. Then you get the medal and it started all over again." He shook his head. "And she fucking didn't understand why I wasn't big on getting married. Hey, what the fuck are you doing, Ted?"

Cramer swung the barrel toward Ted. His finger tightened on the trigger.

Ted was leaning over, scratching his calf. He froze, then slowly sat back. "Nothing. An itch."

"Well, don't do it again. You just sit there and don't fucking move."

Ted did. So did I. For about forty minutes. Until we heard the sound of a buzzer.

Cramer glanced out the window through the gap in the drapes. "Open the gate, Jennifer."

Jennifer went over to a control box by the front door and pushed a button. A few moments later, we heard the sound of a car coming up the drive.

In spite of the chill in the room, I began to sweat.

We saw the headlights flicker across the window. We heard the car doors slam. We heard footsteps cross the porch.

Cramer rose, motioning us to stand. He glanced at Jennifer, shook his head sadly, and looked to the door. As I got to my feet, I saw it open.

The blur of movement to my left startled me.

I started to turn and saw Cramer's eyes widened in shock. He pivoted, bringing the shotgun around.

A shot erupted next to me, and I flinched, my ear ringing. Cramer's head snapped back, a bloody hole where his

right eye had been. He swayed drunkenly and began to topple—

Jennifer screamed.

"The door!" Ted yelled.

I looked. Holt was standing in the doorway, Morgan just behind. Holt reached inside his jacket—

I lunged toward Jennifer. "Get down!" I shoved her hard to the floor.

Two shots, rapid-fire. I spun around and saw Holt buck violently, two red stains on his chest.

I dropped, going for my gun. Ted ran past me. More gunshots from outside. Something shattered nearby. Ted swore, throwing himself to the floor.

By the time I had my gun out, I saw Ted crouching by the door. Holt was lying at his feet, staring up with vacant eyes.

I heard the sound of a car starting. Tires squealed.

Ted sprinted outside, and I followed. Ted was on the front porch. He fired after the sedan tearing down the drive. I aimed, tried to track it—

"What the hell?" Ted said.

I blinked, confused. I lowered my gun.

The gate was open, but at least three cars had suddenly pulled up, blocking the exit. Figures sprang out. The sedan continued to bear down on them. Flashes erupted as they began shooting.

The sedan careened wildly, then spun sharply right. The angle was too great for the speed and the car flipped, landing on its roof. We heard a screech of tortured metal as it slid along the asphalt in a shower of sparks and slammed against the right gatepost.

We heard shouts as the figures ran over to the sedan. A few moments later, a handful detached and returned to one of the cars blocking the exit.

The headlights came on and the car slowly came up the drive.

I said, "Let's get back inside. Maybe we can hold them off until I can call the police."

"That won't be necessary, John," Ted said, putting his gun away. "I think we're all right. They obviously aren't working for McKenzie."

"Who are they, then?"

Ted thought for a moment. "It seems there's only one choice. My guess is your hunch was right after all."

"Right about what?"

But Ted was drifting behind me, his face preoccupied. I focused on the car, which was rolling to a stop well behind Ted's. The doors flew open. Four people sprang out, crouching behind the doors. They had guns pointed at us.

"Drop the gun, Colonel!" a voice barked.

"Goddamn you, Ted," I snarled. I glared back to him.

The porch was empty.

"Now!" the voice yelled. "Drop the gun now!"

I hesitated and tossed it aside.

"Lie down!"

I did.

Two of the four ran toward me. One was a woman, and I recognized her. She'd been outside of Ted's place earlier.

I tensed, expecting the sound of a gunshot.

An hour later, Jennifer was shivering next to me in the backseat of Ted's car. I'd started the car and had the heater going, but that didn't seem to help. I'd tried to talk to her, comfort her, but she was unresponsive. Instead, we watched in silence as the scene unfolded around us.

Two men in hospital whites were wheeling a gurney with Cramer's body toward an unmarked ambulance. A second ambulance had departed minutes earlier with the bodies of Holt and Morgan. Occasionally, we'd catch glimpses of people through the windows searching the house. By the gate, a large wrecker was winching up one side of Morgan's car to turn it right side up so it could be hauled off. No medical examiner had appeared to look at the bodies before they'd been taken away, and there'd been no police. I mentioned that point to Ted, but he only shrugged.

My eyes went to the front steps, where Ted was talking

with the woman who had leapt from the car earlier. She seemed to be running the show. We'd been kept completely in the dark as to why she and her people were here. All we knew was they had badges that said "Secret Service."

Ted had made that deterrmination earlier, figuring they must be working with Kroft.

The woman was shaking her head at Ted. She stopped, her face puzzled. Ted said something, and the woman nodded hesitantly. She pivoted and walked quickly to a car as Ted watched her with a tiny smile. She leaned into the car and retrieved a phone, then began punching in numbers.

Ted yawned and made his way toward me.

The woman was talking now, but hung up after a brief conversation, looking around anxiously. She spied a couple of male agents over by the porch and hurried over in their direction.

I rolled down the window as Ted approached the car. "She still won't tell me why they're here, but I think it's pretty clear they came to arrest Cramer," he said.

"That explains why Kroft wanted the logs. He must have been looking into this thing the whole time."

The woman was talking with the agents. She pointed to us. "What's that all about?" I asked.

Ted stroked his mustache. "Figured I'd stir things up a bit."

One of the agents, a compact man with dark hair, broke away and came toward us.

"It appears to be working," I said. "What did you say?"

Ted smiled at me. "I told her to tell Kroft we have the tape."

That's why Ted had gone back into the house. To retrieve the tape. "They'll find it eventually," I said.

"But they don't know that, John."

"Gentlemen," the agent said. "I'll need you to come with me."

I walked with Jennifer toward a corner of the driveway in front of the house. I stopped, giving her a soft smile. Gently, I brushed hair from her eyes.

"Ted and I have to leave," I said. "The agents said they'll take you to a hotel in a few minutes. They want you to get some things."

Jennifer exhaled slowly, hugging herself. "So it's over?"

"Not quite."

"McKenzie?"

"Yeah." I'd explained earlier about him and our suspicions that he'd really killed Melissa George. She'd asked what his motive was and I had to tell her we didn't know.

She looked to a car where Ted and the agent were waiting. "Where are you going?" she asked.

"Don't know. They won't say."

She gazed out into night. "After this is finished, John, I . . . I'd like to get together. To try to explain things better."

"That's not necessary."

We stood in silence. A drop of rain touched my cheek. I looked up at the dark silhouettes of clouds rolling across the sky.

Jennifer said, "Maybe I should hate him. But it's . . . hard. When I first met Max, he was different. Sweet in his own way. Supportive. He . . . he helped me a lot, after you and I split. Sure, I knew he was always ambitious, felt the pressure from his family. To prove himself. But he still would never have done something like this. I . . . I think working with McKenzie changed him, corrupted him . . . pushed him over the edge."

The car horn honked.

"Look," I said softly. "I've got to go. Call my home. Leave a message on my machine where you're staying."

She appeared not to hear.

I touched her cheek. "Jennifer . . ."

"I'll call, John."

I felt more drops. "You'd better get inside."

She kept staring into the dark. "You go."

I hesitated, then left.

As we drove away, it began raining heavily. Jennifer never moved.

Ted rode up front with the agent, who told us his name was Bryant but nothing else. The rain was beginning to taper off a little as Bryant turned off Massachusetts Avenue onto a quiet street lined with large brownstones, not far from Embassy Row. He pulled over to the curb, parking behind a dark sedan.

"I'll wait here," Bryant said. He pointed at the car in front. I squinted through the window wipers and made out two heads.

Ted gave Bryant a look of annoyance. "Don't you guys get tired of this James Bond bullshit?"

Bryant's face remained blank.

Ted and I got out. As we approached the car, the passenger's door opened and a man emerged. "Get in the back, gentlemen," he said, then continued over to our car.

We got in.

The driver shifted to face me. "Busy night, Colonel," he said dryly.

"Hello, Kroft."

Kroft shook his head at us. "I wish you'd stayed out of this." He sounded irritated.

"Did you really expect us to?" I asked.

Kroft ignored the comment. "So you have the tape?"

I nodded.

"Where is it?"

I looked to Ted.

"We'd like a few questions answered first," Ted said.

"I don't have time to play games, Colonel," Kroft snapped.

Ted gazed back calmly.

Kroft's jaw hardened. "I want that goddamn tape."

Ted said, "Just a few questions . . ."

"Sorry."

Ted shrugged. "Let's go, John."

I reached for the door—

"Wait." Kroft was looking at us. "Dammit, this is a classified operation—"

"Don't give me that crap," Ted said wearily. "We already know most of it anyway."

Kroft blinked warily. "Such as . . ."

Ted leaned forward, eyes boring into Kroft. "We already know the plane was sabotaged by General Cramer under orders by McKenzie to kill Thurston. We know Halloran was having Thurston look into Melissa George's death. We know McKenzie had Thurston killed to keep him quiet about his investigation and to stop him from releasing the tape. We know about the First Lady and Melissa George." He paused. "And we know a helluva lot more."

Kroft looked stunned. "Jesus."

Ted tried not to smile and failed.

"You got proof for any of this?" Kroft asked.

Ted hesitated. "Some."

"You know how the airplane was sabotaged?"

Ted nodded.

Kroft looked suddenly uncomfortable. "I'll have to clear this."

Ted stretched back, spreading his arms across the seat. "We got time."

Slipping a phone from his jacket, Kroft punched in a number. It seemed to take a long time before he got a connection.

"Agent Kroft for the President," he said.

Then he opened his door and stepped out into the rain.

**F**ive minutes later, Kroft got back in the car. His hair was damp, and beads of water ran down his face. He ran a big hand over his forehead, wiping the moisture on the car seat. He focused on Ted. "You will turn over the tape?"

"You've got my word," Ted said.

"In addition, we need the specifics on how the plane went down."

"Fine."

"The President also wants your assurance you won't pass on any information until you've met with him."

Ted hesitated. "That depends on three points."

Kroft tensed. "Oh?"

"First, we have to be satisfied on the extent of the President's involvement. He better not be dirty."

Kroft visibly relaxed. "He isn't. And the second point . . ."

"McKenzie. We want the son of a bitch."

"No problem," Kroft said with a curious smile.

"We also want the Lear pilots to be officially cleared of any responsibility," Ted said.

"Way ahead of you," Kroft said. "We were going to take care of that."

"Fine. We've got a deal." Ted looked to me for confirmation, and I nodded.

"Let's begin with Thurston," Ted said, shifting to get comfortable. "How did he get the tape?"

"From President Halloran," Kroft said. "And Halloran got it from McKenzie. Halloran was about to fire McKenzie about a week ago because of the fallout from the campaign financing investigation."

"So McKenzie was the one who took illegal funds," Ted said. He was looking at me when he spoke, as if to make a point.

"Apparently," Kroft said. "Not that anything will ever be proven. McKenzie's covered up his tracks too well. Anyway, McKenzie gave Halloran a copy of the tape, threatened to go public with it if he was fired."

"Wait," I said. "You're saying Halloran never knew about the tape before last week?"

Kroft nodded. "The First Lady never told him. McKenzie's been using the tape to blackmail the First Lady for years. He got the First Lady to sponsor him and push him with Halloran. That's how McKenzie gained so much influence."

"No money?" I asked.

Kroft snorted. "McKenzie's not interested in money. His motivation was strictly power. He was counting on the First Lady to help him in his own run at the presidency. President Halloran confronted the First Lady, who told him everything. That's also when the President learned of the First Lady's role in the scandal with Governor Banks."

I said, "So she was the one who paid Melissa George to lie about Banks?"

"Not true," Kroft said.

I frowned. "You mean the First Lady didn't pay—"

"No," Kroft interrupted. "You were right about that, Colonel." Seeing my confusion, he added, "Maybe I'm not making myself clear. The First Lady did pay Melissa George something like fifty thousand dollars. But only to come forward, not to lie."

I caught on a second later, but Ted beat me to it.

"Son of a bitch," Ted said. "So Banks did have an affair. No wonder he didn't fight very hard to clear his name. He couldn't. The damn thing was true."

I closed my eyes, picturing Melissa George in the video. I felt for Banks. A man had to be made of stone to resist a woman like her.

"I'm curious," I said, opening my eyes. "Why did the First Lady continue to allow herself to be blackmailed? She had to know someone else killed Melissa George."

Kroft thought. "A couple of reasons. First, she couldn't prove she didn't commit the murder, and second, she knew if the tape became public, everyone would know her role in the scandal."

"Why did the President have his brother digging into the Melissa George case and not you or someone in law enforcement?" I asked.

Kroft shrugged. "My guess is he wanted someone he knew he could absolutely trust. The story was too volatile."

"He obviously confided in you," Ted said.

"Sure," Kroft said. "But only after he'd learned of his brother's death. Even then, he didn't tell me anything other than to look into the crash and determine if it really was an accident. He also wanted me to keep an eye on McKenzie." He paused. "Once I told him I thought McKenzie was

engaged in a cover-up, he finally revealed the rest and authorized me to run an investigation." Kroft glanced at me. "That's when I called you, Colonel. This morning."

"Your friendly little warning," I said dryly.

Kroft managed something approaching a smile. "Obviously, I wasn't very effective."

I asked, "Any idea how McKenzie even knew Thurston was looking into Melissa George's death?"

Before Kroft could answer, Ted said, "McKenzie probably found out about the meetings at the White House between Thurston and Halloran and put two and two together. Then there was Thurston's request for Melissa George's murder file. One of Morgan's buddies in the department could easily have tipped him off that the file had been requested."

Kroft was nodding his agreement. "We also found listening devices in Thurston's office, home, and car."

"Those were your men searching Thurston's house today," I said, surprised.

"Yeah," Kroft said. "We were trying to find the tape."

"A bug would explain how McKenzie knew Thurston had a tape on the airplane," Ted said.

"You seen the tape?" I asked Kroft.

Kroft shook his head. "But the President gave me a brief description. Why?"

I rubbed the back of my neck. "I'm trying to figure out why the First Lady met with Melissa that night."

"Money," Kroft said. "The President said the First Lady told him Melissa had demanded a quarter of a million dollars or she was going to go public with the fact that she'd been paid."

"Greedy thing," I murmured.

"What set the First Lady off?" Ted asked.

"The President didn't say." Kroft hesitated. "But the First Lady is known for her temper." He shrugged.

"What about the President authorizing Thurston to go public with the tape?" Ted asked. "We understand Thurston was going to turn it over to Kendra Banks."

Kroft's brow knitted. "Governor Banks's daughter. Sorry. I don't know anything about her and Thurston. Now, one of my men checking into Melissa George's murder interviewed her to see if she had anything helpful. She didn't. And she didn't mention Thurston."

"Oh?" Ted said. "When did he talk to her?"

"Early this evening. Caught her at her office. Why?"

Ted didn't reply. He was lost in thought.

Kroft gave him a look of annoyance. "I can tell you two the President has expressed to me he intends to release the information." His eyes went to me, then Ted. "That's why he wants to talk to you. He would like to be the one to go public."

Ted's face turned somber. He gazed outside and gave a slow head shake.

I understood. Before, when I thought Halloran was part of all this, I wanted his head. But now, with all we'd learned, it seemed somehow . . . unfair. Once everything got out, the backlash would be swift. Halloran would be crucified by his political enemies, and impeachment was a definite possibility.

We sat listening to rain drum on the roof.

Finally, I asked Kroft, "Why were your people following us?"

"That's pretty obvious, John," Ted said, his eyes going to Kroft. "He knew McKenzie would send people after us."

"I was going to tell you on the flight line, but you drove away," Kroft said.

I scowled at Ted, but he was looking at Kroft.

"And your people at Cramer's place," Ted said to him. "You sent them out to arrest him?"

"Actually, we had one team watching his house and another tailing him. The plan was to arrest Cramer quietly in his home once we got the go-ahead from the President. My people went into a panic when you guys suddenly showed. It really turned into a mess when Cramer arrived and they saw him holding that gun on you. Agent Cryer finally made the call to—"

I said, "Agent Cryer?"

He flashed a wry smile. "The female agent you pissed off when you gave her the slip. Once you were spotted, she and her partner drove out to Cramer's. She made the decision to go in once Holt and Morgan drove up." Kroft slowly shook his head. "I gotta tell you, she told me odds were you'd all be dead either way. But she figured it was worth a shot."

"Reassuring," I murmured.

Kroft's phone rang. "Excuse me."

He spoke for less than thirty seconds and hung up. He gave us a tight smile. "Looks like we can take care of the second point you guys wanted."

"McKenzie?" Ted said.

"Yeah. We got the go-ahead. The President just landed at Andrews. He wanted to be around when all hell broke loose.

"C'mon." He grabbed a walkie-talkie off the front seat and stepped out.

I gave Ted a puzzled look. He smiled knowingly. "You didn't realize why Kroft was sitting here, huh."

I shook my head.

"Kroft's been keeping McKenzie under surveillance." He pointed to the brownstones across the street. "Ten bucks says McKenzie lives in one of those homes."

McKenzie's brownstone was a large and elegant three-story at the corner, with a dime-size lawn and an awning overlooking a railed landing. The rain was down to a drizzle as Kroft, Ted, and I stopped on the sidewalk out front. Bryant and the other agent continued around the corner.

Kroft checked his watch. "We'll give them a minute to get in position out back."

An elderly man in a raincoat walking a poodle crossed the street toward us. He stared at us for a moment and looked at the walkie-talkie in Kroft's hand. He hurried down the sidewalk.

Watching him, Kroft said, "Shouldn't take us more than a couple minutes to bag McKenzie. His housekeeper works until five, so the only problem is what to do with the girl."

"What girl?" I asked.

"Dunno. She walked up about thirty minutes ago, and McKenzie let her in."

"Girlfiend?" I said.

Kroft shrugged. "Don't know. All I can tell you is she's black."

It took me a second to make the connection. I spun around to Kroft. Ted swore.

Kroft looked at us, startled. "What's wrong?"

"The girl," Ted said. "What did she look like?"

"It was too dark to get a good look—"

"Tall," Ted said. "About six feet."

"Yeah. About that. Now, what's the big deal—"

He stopped when he saw Ted bolt across the walk toward the front steps. "Dammit, Colonel." He jogged after him, and I followed.

Ted was ringing the front bell. Kroft grabbed Ted's arm and held it. "What the hell are you doing?" he demanded.

"The girl might be Kendra Banks," I said.

"Aw, Christ," Kroft said, letting go of Ted's arm.

Ted rang the bell continuously for almost a minute while Kroft tried the lock and banged on the door.

There was no response.

Kroft stared at the door. He swore softly. "Too big to kick open."

I went down the steps to a window covered with a metal grille. Through a sliver in the drapes I saw dark green carpeting and the edge of a picture frame on a wall. Nothing moved.

Ted and Kroft looked at me, and I shook my head. Kroft spoke into his walkie-talkie, then he and Ted made their way down the steps.

We went around back.

The alley behind the house glistened dark and wet in the light of a nearby streetlamp. We stepped around a large

puddle toward Bryant and the other agent standing at the back door, which was punctuated by four small windows. We saw no lights inside.

"We can bust out one of the windows and probably reach the knob," Bryant said to Kroft.

"McKenzie might have set the alarm," the other agent said.

Kroft responded by removing his gun from his waist holster, flipping it around and rapping hard on a pane with the butt. There was a cracking sound. A second rap and the glass shattered.

We waited, but there was only silence. Kroft knocked glass free around the edges and reached inside the pane. We heard a click. The other agents took out their guns, following Kroft through the door. Ted and I brought up the rear.

Kroft flipped on a light switch, illuminating a laundry room. We filed through a swinging door into a large, immaculate kitchen with granite countertops and copper pots hanging from a ceiling-mounted rack. Another door was open in the corner, and we heard footsteps going down. Kroft and Bryant went out into a hallway. Ted and I trailed as they peered into each room, ending up at the staircase by the front door. Kroft went up slowly, Bryant on his heels. I was about to follow when I saw Ted pick up something off the floor.

"What's that?" I murmured.

Ted grimly held up a single feather. The edges looked wet and tacky, and were stained a dark pink, almost red. I knew it was blood.

Ted placed the feather on the edge of the floor and pointed to faint red marks on the carpeted steps.

When we reached the landing on the second floor, we saw more red marks leading toward a room to our right.

The door was open, and a moment later we heard Kroft say, "Aw, Christ."

Ted hurried forward, and I followed.

We entered a brightly lit office complete with two computers, a large copy machine, and rows of file cabinets. We saw Kroft and Bryant standing by a desk, looking down at something on the blue-tiled floor. Ted blocked my view, and I stepped aside to see.

I swallowed hard, gripped by both revulsion and relief.

McKenzie lay on his back, his face locked in agony, a grisly hole in the middle of his forehead. A balled-up white cloth protruded from his mouth. A sock, I realized. His elbows and knees were bloody and shattered, bits of bone visible though his clothes. Covering him were hundreds of small feathers.

"Check upstairs," Kroft ordered Bryant. "The girl might still be here. Then call this in code two."

Bryant bolted out.

"Code two?" I said.

"Don't ask, Colonel," Kroft said.

"Was anyone watching the alley earlier?" Ted asked.

Kroft shook his head.

"She's gone," Ted said. "We saw a feather downstairs. Probably stuck to her shoe when she left."

"I saw it," Kroft said. He stared at McKenzie. "Five shots. Four in each of his joints to make him suffer, and the last to finish him off. And we were sitting out front and never heard a thing."

"Because of this," Ted said, stepping around the pool of blood surrounding McKenzie. He reached behind the desk and picked up a battered pillow, which had blackened circles maybe an inch in diameter in the fabric. In the middle of the circles were small bullet holes, with matching ones on the opposite side.

Kroft nodded. "Smart girl."

"She was a cop," I said.

Kroft gave me a surprised look.

Ted was staring at the pillow. He tossed it aside, shaking his head. He looked confused. "I don't understand," he murmured.

I didn't either. Why would Kendra kill McKenzie? Her beef was with the First Lady for paying Melissa George to come forward. Sure, maybe McKenzie screwed over her father sometime before, but this went way beyond that. This was hate.

Ted was still, vacant eyes staring at a wall.

"What's with him?" Kroft asked after watching him for a few moments.

I was about to answer when Ted abruptly slapped his forehead. He sounded angry. "God*dammit*. I'm so fucking stupid. *Jesus*. I should have seen it sooner. That has to be it." He looked to Kroft and demanded, "How soon can you get Kendra's home address?"

Kroft blinked, caught off guard. "Uh, couple minutes."

"Get it," Ted ordered. "We have to hurry. Odds are we might even be too late."

Kroft hesitated, then pulled out his phone and made the call. He cupped it moments later. "They're pulling it up."

"Good." Ted growled. He was shifting from one foot to the other, his face tight with anxiety. I'd never seen him like this.

"What are we going to be too late for?" I asked.

"The tape. Kendra is going to destroy the tape. She has to destroy the fucking tape." He saw Kroft, and I didn't understand and said, "That's why she came here. Killed McKenzie like this. It was to make him talk. Tell her where the tape was." As he spoke, his eyes were darting around the room.

"But why would she kill McKenzie for the tape?" I asked. "It showed the First Lady—"

"Not that one, John. Remember what Kendra told us. The one we saw had been altered to frame the First Lady." Ted spied something. He quickly went around the desk to the copy machine and knelt down.

I followed and saw him peer inside a small steel safe, its door open. He reached in and felt around, then slowly rose, still looking down at the safe. "That's it. That's where McKenzie kept the tape." He rubbed his face. "Dammit, I should have known."

I said, "You're talking about the original tape, right? The one that shows McKenzie actually killing Melissa George?"

He looked at me. "You're wrong about that, John. That's what I thought, too."

I frowned.

"Remember the police report, John. What caused Melissa's death? That's the key. She was beaten *and* stabbed. That always bothered me. Why both? The first event was brutal, an act of rage. The second was calm, one stroke of the knife."

I didn't see his point and was getting frustrated. Then the answer hit me. "My God," I murmured.

"Two different people," Kroft said.

Ted nodded.

"And McKenzie was one?" Kroft asked.

"Yeah," Ted said, eyeing him. "And the second person was the reason Kendra had to get the tape."

I knew whom he was talking about now. But Kroft was completely bewildered until I told him.

The Majestic Apartments was a glass-and-chrome high-rise north of Sheridan Circle in the northwest part of the city. We pulled out front fifteen minutes after leaving Thurston's. On the way, Kroft had called to have the building superintendent meet us.

Mr. James Vega was a large black man with a cheerful face. He was waiting in the lobby wearing a robe. Kroft showed him his ID and Vega handed him the key. We took the elevator to the penthouse on the twelfth floor.

Kroft listened at the door, then carefully inserted the key in the lock.

A fish tank bubbled in the entryway as we passed into a tastefully furnished living area. Kendra was seated at a chair maybe fifteen feet away, her back to us, staring intently at a big-screen television in a gleaming black cabinet. To her right, flames crackled in a fireplace, a neat stack of logs out front.

We moved toward her, the carpet quieting our footsteps. We could see the TV screen, and the image was chilling.

Finally, Ted said, "Hello, Kendra."

Kendra whirled around in shock. We saw tears in her eyes. She leapt up, making a strangling noise. She sprang toward the television, pawing at the VCR below.

Kroft lunged toward her, grabbing her arms as she popped out a tape.

"You bastard!" Kendra snarled, kicking wildly. "You fucking bastard! Let me go!"

Kroft held her in his big hands easily.

"It's over, Kendra," Ted said. He sounded sad.

Kendra kept flailing, swearing. She still had the tape in her hand. She dropped it to the floor, tried to step on it. Kroft yanked her away, and she made a guttural sound.

"It's no use, Kendra," Ted said sharply.

Kendra spun around, tears rolling down her cheeks. Her eyes went to Ted. She choked, "You son of a bitch. You fucking son of a bitch."

"I know," Ted said.

"He deserved to die. The bastard." Kendra arched her back as if to make one last try to escape, then went completely limp, her legs seeming to buckle.

Ted picked up the tape. "Are you finished?" he asked her quietly.

She was breathing hard, almost panting. She focused on him with dead eyes. "Don't do this. Please. I'm begging you. My father couldn't help it. That bitch. It was her fault. She made him . . ." She looked away and began to cry. "That bitch . . . that bitch . . ."

"Take her to the chair," Ted said to Kroft.

Kroft almost had to carry her over. He sat her down, eyeing her warily before releasing his grip. He remained next to her. Kendra wrapped her arms around her shoul-

ders, slowly rocking back and forth, blankly staring at the floor. She never looked up.

Not even when Ted played the tape.

Ted rewound the tape to the point where the First Lady left the room. We saw a handsome black man with graying hair enter and kneel over Melissa. We saw him caress her tenderly, bathing her face with a towel. We saw Melissa regain consciousness, and the two of them moved over to the couch. We saw them talk, then begin to argue. We saw the black man's face turn to fury. We saw him leap upon her, hitting her uncontrollably. We saw Melissa cower, screaming as the fists rained upon her. We saw the blood and the gore.

It seemed to go on forever, well after Melissa passed out. I had to keep looking away.

The last thing I saw before the screen went blank was Governor Banks staring down at Melissa in horror, as if suddenly aware of what he'd done.

There'd been no appearance by McKenzie. But McKenzie would have been careful about that.

Ted popped the tape out and went to Kendra. He spoke to her quietly for a few moments. She didn't react at first. Finally, her head snapped up and she shot him a look of disbelief.

Ted nodded reassuringly.

"Okay," Kendra whispered.

"She's willing to talk," Ted told Kroft and me.

Kendra sat in the chair, staring dully into space. Her voice was low and surprisingly calm. She spoke slowly, with long pauses. "He couldn't resist her. He tried . . . but you saw her. She loved . . . loved toying with men . . . tempting them. After their affair, he . . . he told me he tried to break it off. She became furious. I guess no man had ever turned

her down. Rejected her. Anyway, that's when she contacted Thurston, said she'd go public if he paid her. Thurston said no, but somehow Alicia Halloran found out about the offer, agreed to pay. When the scandal broke, it . . . it almost killed my father. And it wasn't just the shame. He knew . . . he knew he'd let his race down. He couldn't handle it. My mother couldn't either. She tried, but . . . she left him and my father began to drink . . . try and kill himself with the bottle. I tried to help . . . tried to get him to stop. . . . Anyway, Melissa called him a couple years later. Out of the blue. Told him she was sorry and maybe could make it up to him. She had this idea . . . this plan. My father agreed. He was desperate and . . . he never could resist her. So they decided to lure the First Lady . . . get her to admit she'd paid Melissa. Get it on videotape and go public. I don't know what my father was thinking . . . hoping for sympathy maybe, show the world he was set up. Maybe he wanted revenge against Alicia. Destroy her reputation, too. They got everything ready, and Alicia Halloran showed . . ." Kendra swallowed hard, finally looking at us. "The rest you know. You saw what happened."

We were quiet for a few moments. Even though I knew what she'd done to McKenzie, I felt sympathy. I couldn't help thinking she was another victim.

Ted asked softly, "What made your father angry?"

Kendra took a deep breath. "Melissa was greedy. She knew having Alicia Halloran slapping her on tape was worth a fortune. She told my father she'd changed her mind, wanted to sell the tape to Alicia Halloran." Kendra paused, her voice becoming tight. "When she told him that, he . . . felt betrayed. Something snapped and . . ." She couldn't finish.

"When it was over, your father must have called McKenzie?" Ted said.

Kendra nodded, her tone bitter. "They'd been close. He thought he could trust the son of a bitch."

"McKenzie came over and told your father he'd handle things?"

Another nod. "My . . . my father wanted to call the hospital, but McKenzie said he'd take care of everything. McKenzie convinced my father he couldn't be seen at the house."

"So your father left?"

"Yes."

"And later found out Melissa was dead. Stabbed."

"Yes."

"And he also learned McKenzie kept the tape and was working for Halloran."

She seemed to take a long time to answer. "But that betrayal wasn't even the worst of it. It was what McKenzie did afterward. In a way, I'm . . . I'm partly to blame. I'm the one who convinced my father to tell the truth."

Ted was nodding sympathetically, as if he understood. "Your father must have told McKenzie what he had in mind."

"Yes. I couldn't believe it when I found out. But my father wanted McKenzie to know he was finished." She shook her head. "That was a mistake," she said quietly.

Kroft was looking at me, brows knitted, indicating he wasn't following the conversation either.

He gave a little cough. When Kendra and Ted glanced over, he asked, "What are you talking about?"

"Governor Banks never committed suicide," Ted said.

Kroft's stunned face mirrored mine. "My God," he said slowly. You mean . . ."

"McKenzie had him killed so he couldn't talk," Ted said.

Kendra's head bobbed in agreement. "I couldn't prove it, but . . ." Her eyes misted, and she wiped at them.

"Man," Kroft said. "That guy was a piece of work. Hell, he deserved what he got."

No one spoke for a moment.

I asked, "Kendra, was Thurston really going to turn over the tape to you?"

A flat smile. "No. He contacted me to see what I knew about Melissa George's murder. He also asked me about the videotape, trying to find out if I knew who made it. I told him I wouldn't answer any questions until I saw the tape."

"That was what your second meeting was for, the night Thurston died. He was going to show it to you."

She nodded.

Ted gave me a questioning look to see if I had anything else. I shook my head. I could have asked Kendra why she'd lied to us about Thurston, but the answer to that was obvious now.

Ted gave Kendra an odd smile. "Where are the other tapes you took from McKenzie?"

She hesitated.

"I'll need them both," Ted said.

Kendra rose and went over to a drawer next to the television. Ted followed. She removed a videotape, which Ted placed in the VCR. He played it for a moment, then popped it out, looking expectantly at Kendra.

"The other tape is in there," she said, pointing to cabinet doors below the VCR. "It's still in the recorder."

When Ted opened the doors, I expected to see a second video recorder. Instead I saw a compact stereo system. Ted ejected a cassette tape from the tape deck, stared at it, and nodded.

"Damn," I murmured, slowly catching on. "That's what we saw Melissa George doing when she knelt down under the couch. She was keying a cassette player."

Ted nodded. "They had to have the First Lady admit to

paying Melissa. Since the video camera was rigged outside the house, it would have been tricky to run a mike cord into the room without the First Lady noticing. The simplest solution was to record the conversation with a hidden cassette player." He held out the cassette to Kendra. "You listened to this?"

She swallowed. "Some."

He slipped the tape into his jacket. "Now the gun," he said softly.

"My purse." Kendra gestured to a black handbag on an end table by the chair.

Kroft picked up the bag, found the gun, and slipped it into his pocket.

"Just one more question, Kendra," Ted said, looking to the fireplace. "Why didn't you burn the tapes as soon as you arrived?"

A slightly mystified look crossed her face. "I . . . I'm not sure. I guess I wanted to know for certain . . . see for myself. That it was all true."

He held up the one from the drawer. "But you were going to keep this one."

She didn't reply. Then a slight nod.

Ted gave her that same odd smile. He handed her both videotapes and then the cassette. "Go ahead."

"Thank you," she said softly.

"Hey," Kroft said. "What the hell are you doing?"

Ted gave him a hard look. "Let's finish this here."

"Colonel, you know I can't—"

"It's better this way," Ted interrupted.

Kendra was walking across the room now. I understood what she was going to do, so when Kroft started to go after her, I grabbed his arm.

"Let her go, Kroft," I said.

Kroft took a deep breath, uncertainty in his eyes.

"It's better for the President," I said.

His eyes flickered. He nodded slowly. "Okay."

We watched as Kendra dropped the tapes into the fire.

The elevator opened and we stepped inside. Kroft pushed the button for the lobby and asked, "Why did Kendra Banks want to keep the second videotape?"

"To release it," Ted said. "Kendra wanted to publicize it to humiliate the First Lady. That's why she came to John and me. She was hoping to somehow talk us into turning it over."

"Same reason she made up the story about Thurston going public," I added. "She wanted to sway us to hand her the tape."

Kroft asked, "What about why she killed McKenzie tonight?"

Ted seemed puzzled. "To get the tapes—"

"No. I mean why tonight in particular," he said. "She could have killed him anytime over the years and took the tapes. What caused her to act tonight?"

A tiny smile as Ted gazed at Kroft. "You did."

*"What?"*

Then the elevator doors opened and we saw Mr. Vega waiting for us in the lobby. He spied us and hurried over.

After Kroft returned the key and we were walking toward the exit, Kroft demanded, "So how the hell am I responsible?"

"Actually," Ted said, "it was the agent who interviewed her. He must have said something that made her realize you were after McKenzie. Or maybe she figured if you were investigating Melissa George's murder you might somehow learn McKenzie was involved. Whatever the reason, she knew if McKenzie felt threatened, he would release the original tape, showing the beating. She couldn't allow that."

"Well," Kroft said, "wish I could say I was sorry."

We went through the automatic doors and turned toward the car sitting against the curb. The rain had stopped, and we could see the moon peeking through a thinning layer of clouds.

"By the way," Kroft said. "Where's the evidence you have?"

"My place," Ted said. "You can drop us off and I'll turn it over."

"That where the other tape is?"

We reached the car. Ted walked over to the passenger door, looking at Kroft over the roof. "First, I'd like my car and my guns returned."

Absolutely. I'll have someone deliver them tonight."

"I'd like that taken care of now."

Kroft gave him a look of exasperation. He quickly made a call. "On the way. Now, how about the tape?"

When Ted told him, Kroft broke into a big grin. "Winnie the Pooh, huh."

"In Cramer's son's room," Ted said. "It's on the second shelf above the TV."

Kroft laughed, slapping the side of the car. He really thought it was funny. "Get in, you son of a bitch."

It was almost two in the morning, and Ted and I were in his office, nursing drinks. Tiki had gone to bed a few minutes earlier, and most of the lights in the apartment were off. Kroft had also left after spending the last two hours going over everything in detail with us so he could brief the President.

I rubbed my eyes and glanced at Ted sitting at his desk. "So what do you think the President is going to do?" I asked.

Ted thought it over. "I don't think he has much choice."

"He's going to keep this all quiet?"

Ted nodded. "He knows it's the only decision. If the scandal is made public, the political fallout will devastate the country."

I shook my head. I still didn't see how all this could be hushed up. Explaining away McKenzie and Cramer's deaths would be difficult enough, not to mention the

Blackhawk crew if they were arrested and brought to trial. I mentioned my concerns to Ted.

"There are ways, John," he said vaguely.

"How?"

Ted shrugged.

"What about Ware?" I asked. "What's going to happen to him?"

Ted swirled his drink, staring at it. "Maybe nothing."

My eyes widened in disbelief. "You can't be serious."

He sighed. "John, you have to realize Halloran couldn't afford to go after him. Not now."

"So the son of a bitch walks. What about McKenzie's goons in the FBI? They get off too?"

"Possibly."

I swore.

"You're losing focus, John. Halloran has to keep the best interests of the country in mind. McKenzie and Cramer were the important ones. Ware was a pawn, and so were the others."

I shook my head. "It doesn't seem fair."

"It isn't. But that's life. Besides, we made a similar decision tonight."

I stared back for a moment, then nodded. We had let Kendra go after allowing her to destroy the tapes.

He gave me a half-smile. "The best thing you can do is to put all this behind you. Get on with your life. Now, have you decided if you want to stay in the Air Force?"

I slowly let out a breath. "No."

"Consider staying in, John," he said. "The military needs good people, and everyone isn't like Cramer or Ware."

The statement sounded odd coming from him. If anyone should be down on the military, it was Ted. "I know, but . . ."

"Think about it."

I forced a smile. "Sure."

He raised his glass. "We did well, John. For us, it's over."

I drank.

As I got up to leave a few minutes later, Ted was spreading a sheet of pink wrapping paper with little blue teddy bears on his desk. He began telling me about the birthday party he and Tiki had planned for Tessie, their granddaughter. I could hear the excitement in his voice. I was amazed at his change of demeanor. He seemed to have completely forgotten what we'd just gone through. When I left, he was carefully wrapping the Magic Marker board, humming to himself contentedly.

Downstairs, Carlos, the cook, was mopping the floor. He had the jukebox on with the volume turned down. Ironic, I thought, when I realized it was the same Gordon Lightfoot song I'd been listening to just before I got the call about the crash.

Carlos let me out, and I walked home.

There were no reporters outside my building. When I walked into my condo, I was struck by the quiet and I didn't like it. I'd always enjoyed living alone, but now I wanted someone to be here. I went around flipping on lights. I turned on the stereo to a softrock station, then went over to my answering machine. Maybe twenty messages from reporters and another from my mother, which made me feel a little guilty. There was nothing from Jennifer.

I made a drink and picked up the phone. It was almost ten on the West Coast, and my parents were reading in bed. My mother answered, and it was good to hear her voice. She asked if I was eating right and if I'd quit smoking, and I lied on both counts. After promising her I would call Colleen Simpson, the girl she'd been trying to set me up

with, my father came on. We made small talk until he finally told me he had to make a decision next week on whether to sell the lumber mill. I told him I didn't know if I wanted to take over. I could tell he was hurt, but I didn't know what else to say.

I went out on the patio and sat by the gas grill I never seemed to use. I smoked a cigarette, looking up at the stars. Maybe I was looking for divine intervention or a voice to guide me.

The phone rang as I was coming back inside. I heard the sadness in Jennifer's voice. She said she almost didn't call but she thought I should know she was leaving tomorrow afternoon to fly to Seattle. She said she still wanted to get together to talk things through but now was too soon. She had to get away, let some time pass first. She asked me to forgive her, and I said I would. After that there was an awkward silence where neither one of us could think of anything to say. Finally, Jennifer told me goodbye after promising to call again.

As I cradled the phone, I knew she never would.

I felt no disappointment, only a quiet acceptance. We were too different and always would be. At least seeing her had brought a sense of closure. I'd always wondered *what if,* and now I knew.

Even though I was exhausted and feeling the Scotch, I knew sleep wouldn't come. So I made a fresh drink and went back outside. I stayed for an hour and never heard the voice I was looking for, but it didn't really matter.

I think I'd known all along what I was going to do.

## Saturday

I awoke around ten to find more press camped outside my door. I'd turned off my phone ringer before going to bed, and there were a dozen or more new messages on my answering machine. Two from Kroft and one from Rick French's neighbor, telling me Rick's wife, Janet, was back at home. I called Kroft first.

"Where have you been, Colonel?" Kroft asked. "I've been trying to get ahold of you all morning."

I yawned. "Rough night. Just rolled out of bed."

"Hell, wish I could sleep in. You seen the article in the *Post?*"

"Uh-uh. My copy's on my doorstep along with about a zillion reporters."

Kroft laughed and asked if I had a fax machine so he could send me the article. After I passed on the number, he told me what was in it.

"Jesus," I murmured. "That should make the President's decision easier."

"Should," Kroft said vaguely. "By the way, Halloran just announced he's relieving General Ware."

I didn't say anything.

"Hey, I thought this would be good news."

"It's not enough. He'll still be retiring as a four-star."

"Yeah, well . . ." He fell silent.

I sighed. Ted had called it. Halloran was allowing Ware to quietly step aside in exchange for keeping his mouth shut. McKenzie's squad of FBI goons would probably get the same treatment.

I rubbed my eyes. I was still feeling tired. "Anything else?"

"You won't be meeting with the President today. He wants to let things play out first. He and the First Lady will see you and Colonel Chen later in the week to personally thank you. I'll let you know."

"Fine." I expected him to hang up.

"Oh, and you might want to catch the evening news, Colonel." The connection went dead.

I frowned, listening to the dial tone. I went into the kitchen and made a pot of coffee. By the time I got up to my study, the fax of the *Post* article was waiting.

The headline read: TWO VIRGINIA GUARDSMEN DIE IN CAR ACCIDENT.

The article said the driver had apparently lost control on a rural road near Richmond and driven off a steep embankment. The time of the accident was thought to be late Thursday night or early Friday morning. There had been no witnesses. The dead were identified as Captain Steven Warren, a pilot, and Sergeant Wayman Tulley, a flight engineer. Fatigue was thought to be a possible factor, since the two had flown earlier that evening.

Had Holt killed them to keep them from talking, as

Kroft had concluded? Or had there really been an accident? Not that I cared about why the men were dead, only that they were.

I slowly crumpled the article, thinking of Allison Gibson. Then I thought of Rick French and Judd Wilson, and Thurston, whose death started all this. And Gloria Peters. And Governor Banks. And greedy and beautiful Melissa George.

I sat in my office for a long time until I didn't want to think anymore. Finally, I went downstairs and made two calls. The first was to Janet French to tell her I'd like to stop by, and the second was to Ted to ask for a ride.

I snuck out the back twenty minutes later and Ted picked me up around the corner. We arrived at Janet French's house around one. There were a number of other vehicles there, friends from the squadron.

Janet and her daughters cried when I brought out the ring. The scene was wrenching. I told Janet the plane had malfunctioned and Rick had done everything he could. Ted and I left an hour later.

On the way home, I asked Ted if I'd done the right thing, keeping the truth from Janet. For once, he didn't have an answer.

When he dropped me off on the corner, he said something surprising.

"I'm going to miss you, John."

I watched him drive away, wondering how he knew.

The reporters were still outside when I got home, so I kept the curtains drawn and stayed away from the windows. I knew I should eat, so I made a sandwich, though I ended up throwing most of it away. I tried to take a nap, but felt restless and gave up after about thirty minutes. I lay in bed, surfing through the channels on the TV, hoping to find something to hold my interest. Finally, I saw one of those

late-breaking news bulletins on CNN and understood what Kroft was trying to tell me earlier.

The commentator said the White House chief of staff and presidential hopeful Riley McKenzie and Major General Maxwell Cramer had been found shot to death at Cramer's Maryland estate. Preliminary reports indicated General Cramer had killed Mr. McKenzie, then turned the gun on himself. The commentator said an unknown source involved in the investigation had confirmed that while the two had been close friends in the past, General Cramer and Mr. McKenzie had been seen arguing heatedly at a White House meeting over the cause of the airplane crash that took the life of President Halloran's brother, Joshua Thurston. According to the source, General Cramer deeply resented McKenzie's interference in the investigation and authorities were speculating they'd had another argument that escalated tragically out of control. A White House spokesman confirmed that Mr. McKenzie had driven out to General Cramer's home to discuss the matter. . . .

I clicked off the TV and stared at the blank screen. Even though everything was finished now, I felt unsettled. I wondered if we were doing the right thing. Would keeping the truth from the American people make it easier for another McKenzie to come along?

In my heart, I knew I really didn't want to know the answer.

Normally, getting a waiver to separate early from the Air Force was a tricky thing, but in my case, I didn't think it would be a problem. I was a pilot who couldn't fly. Besides, the President of the United States owed me a favor.

I picked up the phone to tell my father I was coming home.